CATCH YOUR DEATH

CATCH YOUR DEATH

Louise Voss and
Mark Edwards

**WINDSOR
PARAGON**

First published 2012
by Harper,
an imprint of HarperCollins*Publishers*
This Large Print edition published 2012
by AudioGO Ltd
by arrangement with
HarperCollins*Publishers*

Hardcover   ISBN: 978 1 445 84790 0
Softcover   ISBN: 978 1 445 84791 7

British Library Cataloguing in Publication Data available

Printed and bound in Great Britain by
MPG Books Group Limited

For the kids: Gracie, Ellie, Poppy and Archie.

Prologue

Sixteen Years Ago

The world was on fire.

Or maybe she wasn't in the world any more. Maybe this was Hell. The heat, the taste of sulphur on her tongue, the sickness, the torment. Screams rang through the air, relentless, monotonous, a one-pitch yell of despair. She opened her eyes and saw a figure stooping over her; a hovering devil, with flaming red hair. She tried to shout but all that came out was a rasping noise, and the devil's face was close, the brimstone smell of its breath in her nostrils.

'Kate. Kate, get up. Come on.'

She stared, blinked. Slowly, a face came into focus. Not a devil, but Sarah, her red-headed room-mate.

Sarah pushed aside the thin sheet that covered Kate's body and took her by the hands, pulling her up. Kate's pyjamas were damp and cold, but her skin was desert-hot. Her fever was nearing 105 degrees. Sarah was in a similar state, but she'd been lying on top of her sheets, too ill to sleep.

Kate's bare feet touched the floor. It hurt. Everything hurt. Her body was a bruise, tender to the touch.

'Come on.'

Kate could still hear the screaming, and put her hands to her ears to block it out. She'd only ever felt this ill once before, as a child. She had the vaguest memory of a nurse with black skin and kind eyes sponging her down with cold, cold water which dripped down her narrow heaving chest, and soaked the waistband of her pyjama trousers. She'd cried, weakly, at the ordeal. Cried for her mother, even though her mother was already gone.

She wished the nurse was here now, to cool her with water, to put out the fire that raged across her skin.

Her eyes fixed on the curtains. At some time during the night, as she drifted in and out of feverish dreams, she had seen little men with malevolent eyes swinging on those curtains. Sarah opened the door and, holding each other up, they stepped into the corridor. Kate had a vague idea that she was supposed to be angry with Sarah but she couldn't remember why.

At the same time that Kate and Sarah left their room, another couple of young women emerged from the next room. Denise and Fiona, the Glaswegian girls they weren't allowed to be in contact with, but had communicated with, talking and giggling like boarding school girls through the walls, figuring out ingenious ways to pass notes out of the windows, attached to the end of a cane Sarah had found in the Centre's gardens.

'Is it real?' Fiona asked. Her voice was thick, her nose bunged up. Kate thought she was speaking a foreign language. Or maybe the language of Satan. What if these were all devils, taking her to be tortured, dragging her into Hell? She panicked and tried to pull away.

Denise caught her and she nearly fell, but the Scottish girl managed to stop her from crashing to the floor.

'It can't be a drill,' Fiona said, answering her own question.

2

'Let's just get out of here,' said Denise, leading the way.

She gripped Sarah by one hand and Kate, who kept pulling back, looking around her with wild eyes, by the other. Where was everyone else? Were they the last people left in the building?

'We're going to die,' Kate said. 'We're going to die.'

Denise shushed her. 'No. We're not. The exit's just around this corner. Come on, Kate. We're nearly there.'

They turned the corner and came face to face with a wall of thick smoke.

'Oh God!'

Kate emitted a small yelp of fear and struggled, but Denise held tight. 'Calm down.'

They were all sweating now, as the corridors filled with heat, and the smoke pricked their eyes, bringing forth the tears. Four young women in their pyjamas; holding on to one another, paralysed by the most primitive fear of all.

'We'll have to go back,' Denise said.

They turned round and ran—even the sickly Kate and Sarah, with Denise and Fiona holding their hands. They heard a crack and a crash in the distance and suddenly smoke was filling the whole corridor, rushing up behind them, chasing and overtaking them. It caught them and, like drowning swimmers, they panicked and gulped in lungfuls of the stuff, acrid and bitter and lethal. Coughs racked their bodies.

Sarah fell to her knees. Fiona stopped and tried to pull her back up. Denise let go of Kate so she could help, and as they struggled to get Sarah to her feet, Kate peered ahead. They were engulfed

3

now, the smoke filling the whole corridor, and her eyes streamed as she tried to make sense of what she could see.

There were figures coming at them through the smoke. The devils. Come to claim her. The screaming continued.

One of the devils grabbed hold of her. She tried to fight but the devil was too strong. It lifted her and carried her deeper into the smoke. She kicked weakly. Each of her friends had been taken hold of too. She decided not to fight any more. She just wished she'd had a chance to say goodbye to Stephen.

Stephen's face was the last thing she pictured as she slipped into the welcoming darkness.

*   *   *

When she came round she was lying on the grass outside. She lifted her head and saw that Sarah was lying nearby. Sarah lifted her arm and waved weakly. Kate tried to speak to her, but a moment later she passed out again.

*   *   *

The next time she awoke, she found herself in the eye of a storm of chaos. Doctors and researchers ran around with their white coats flapping. A man in a red uniform, a fireman, stood nearby, drinking from a white cup. She could hear the seesawing wail of a police siren mixed with the piercing, steady scream of an alarm.

She rolled onto her side and coughed hard, spitting out black phlegm.

'Kate!' Denise appeared. 'Are you alright?' Her

blonde hair was grey with soot, her cheeks and forehead smeared with it.

Kate sat up. Her chest hurt. Her head hurt. But she was alive. 'What happened?'

'Don't you remember?'

She concentrated. 'I remember . . . devils. A scene from Hell. I thought I was dead.'

'I thought we were going to die too. The Centre was on fire. It looks like the whole building we were in has been burned out.'

For the first time, Kate looked properly at the scene before her. In the darkness, clouds of smoke still rose from the long thin building that she'd called home for the last week. Fire engines stood close by, the uniformed men lined up with hoses, sending ribbons of water into the fire to fight its rival element.

'We were lucky,' Denise said.

'Was anyone killed?'

'I don't know.'

'What about Fiona?'

'Fiona's just over there. I don't know where Sarah is though. They brought her out with us but I haven't seen her since.'

'She was here a minute ago. When I came round I saw her. She waved at me. Then I passed out again.'

'Maybe they've already taken her to hospital . . .' She trailed off. 'There were other girls in there, though. I haven't seen them bring anyone else out, but it's too chaotic to know what's going on.'

Kate pushed herself to her feet, her head spinning, her eyes blurring. She was so sick. What the hell had they given her yesterday? This was no common cold.

5

'I'm going to check on Fiona and see if I can find Sarah,' Denise said, touching Kate's hand then disappearing into the chaos.

As Kate tried to steady herself, to stop the world rotating around her, a man in a white jacket came up to her. Kate squinted at him. He was tall and thin; kind of creepy. He reached towards her, uninvited, and laid a hand on her brow, making her flinch away. She knew she had a reason to be afraid of him, but in her delirium she couldn't remember what it was.

'Kate. You shouldn't still be out here . . . you're too unwell.'

She ignored him. 'Do you know Stephen? Stephen Wilson? Have you seen him?'

He shook his head. 'Come on—you really should rest. You've inhaled a lot of smoke. And you have a fever.' He looked around as if searching for someone to help. He muttered something under his breath. Something about somebody interfering?

She didn't hear any more because his words were drowned by her own coughing fit. Her throat felt like a raw wound.

The creepy man helped her sit down. He looked around again then said, 'Stay here, okay? Just stay here.'

Another coughing jag filled her eyes with tears, and when it passed, he'd gone.

*   *   *

She needed to find Stephen. He'd told her he was staying late tonight. She'd been planning to meet him. He said he might have something to tell her. She stood up again, concentrating all of her

6

remaining energy into staying upright, and headed towards the building and the firefighters.

'Stephen,' she tried to call, but her voice was too weak. She was dizzy and nauseous. She wanted to lie down, to sleep. But she desperately needed to find him—just see him and make sure he was okay before she could rest. There was no reason, really, to think he could have come to harm. His office was in a separate wing of the Centre. But still, she wanted to be sure. She loved him.

In the distance, she could see figures close to the building, the darkness and smoke reducing them to silhouettes. Two firemen were carrying out a stretcher with a motionless form on it; a form of approximately Stephen's height and build. One arm flopped over the edge of the stretcher and, as they grew closer, Kate saw the familiar bulk of the chunky wristwatch Stephen always wore. It was blackened, like the arm to which it was attached, but she was certain she recognised it.

It *was* Stephen. She tried to run, but her own legs were too weak, her lungs too clogged. Her bare feet slipped on the grass and she lurched forward. When she got to her feet, the scientist—the same man who'd touched her forehead—blocked her way.

'You have to rest,' he insisted.

'But Stephen,' she said, reaching out towards the building, and suddenly there was movement all around her, an ambulance speeding past, firefighters running towards the Centre, and the scientist grabbing her arm and producing a needle which he stuck into her. A quick jab, and an even shorter struggle before haziness enveloped her. Once again, she passed out.

The last thing she saw was the scientist frowning

down at her, while behind him paramedics crouched on the grass beside Stephen, and one of them shook his head.

She never knew if she actually did scream, or had just imagined it.

1

Present Day

The woman lying on the bunk appeared to be dead, until she sneezed; the violent motion making her skinny body spasm. She opened bloodshot eyes and lifted an arm, trying to pull a tissue from the box on the bedside cabinet. But as she reached out, her body spasmed again and she knocked the box to the floor. Too weak to pick it up, she lay still, until a further series of sneezes rocked her body like gunshots.

There were two men watching the girl. One was in his early forties but appeared younger because of the lack of lines on his face. His skin was tanned from a recent holiday in Bangkok, and at first glance he was unusually handsome, like a model in a commercial for razors or fast cars. But anyone gazing at his face for more than a few seconds would notice something strange. He still looked like a model, but a model in a magazine or on a billboard, frozen in time, unanimated. Worst of all were his eyes, which were small and lifeless like a shark's. Secretly—because no-one dared criticise him to his face—he had been described as a robot.

His name was John Sampson.

The other man, whose name was Gaunt—nobody had ever heard him use his first name—was taller and paler, with skin that spoke of months and years spent in artificially-lit places like this. He was so thin he appeared to be wasting away. When he was locked in the laboratory, he often forgot to eat. Food

9

wasn't important. Nor was sleep. There was too much to do; too many exciting things to be discovered and tested. Nodding towards the woman on the bunk, he said, 'She arrived last night. We picked her up at Heathrow and brought her straight here.'

Sampson said, 'What is she? Chinese? Thai?'

She reminded him of a girl he'd met in Bangkok. He wondered idly if that girl's family were still looking for her or if they'd given up by now. If they even cared.

'Vietnamese, actually. Her name's Lien. Twenty-three years old, resident of Hanoi. Doesn't speak a single word of English—oh, except "please". "Please, please, please." She said that quite a few times, before she lost the ability to speak. I wonder what promises they made to her at the other end? A new life in England: a good job, a flat, a washing machine and a colour TV . . .?'

Sampson peered at Lien through the one-way glass.

'What is it? Bird flu?' he asked.

Gaunt, who wore a doctor's white coat and spoke with an upper-middle-class English accent, took off his glasses and sucked on them. Finally, he said, 'No. This is something new.' He smiled. 'It's very impressive, actually. I have to hand it to our friends in Asia these days. Sars. Avian Flu. Both very impressive. But this one's even better.'

'It's fatal?'

The doctor laughed. 'Oh yes. Infinitely more so than Avian Flu.'

John Sampson looked at Lien again. She had tried, while they were talking, to pick up the glass of water that sat beside the tissue box, but she had knocked that over too. Water dribbled down the side of the

10

cabinet and pooled on the floor.

'I'd like to talk to her.'

'I'm afraid that's not possible. She's extremely contagious. She'd just have to breathe in your direction and you'd catch it.'

'Shame.' Sampson would have liked to find out how the girl was feeling.

'Want to see exactly how contagious this is?'

Gaunt gestured for Sampson to follow him. They walked a little way down the harsh, bright corridor, beneath fluorescent strip lights that flickered occasionally, and stopped in front of another small room with one-way glass. A second woman, this one Caucasian, with bleached hair and dirty roots, sat on the edge of the bed. She looked miserable and confused. Not as far gone as Lien, but she had a red nose, pink eyes, and she held a box of tissues in her lap.

Sampson waited for the doctor to explain.

'She's a prostitute. Serbian; she was brought here last night. She was clean—no viruses, no problems, remarkably healthy for a woman of her profession. How old do you think she is? About twenty-six?'

Sampson nodded slowly. The girl was beautiful. He pictured himself holding her, sitting with her as she died. She would explain what her pain and suffering and fear felt like. He would stroke her dirty hair as she breathed her last breath.

Gaunt said, 'We put her in a room with Lien for twenty seconds. They didn't touch or even speak to one another. She started showing symptoms eight hours later. But she herself isn't contagious yet. You can talk to her if you want.'

Sampson raised his eyebrows.

The doctor drummed his fingers on the glass and

11

the girl looked up. A gold chain, bearing a locket, hung around her neck. Beneath the sickness, she looked angry and defiant. Her mouth moved but they couldn't hear what she was saying. Maybe she was pleading. Or spitting words of fury. Whatever, her words were as futile as her hopes.

'This is the most remarkable thing about this virus,' the doctor said, ignoring the girl. 'It has a safe period. For fifteen hours, the carrier isn't contagious, even though they start to exhibit symptoms. My Asian contact told me they wanted to develop a virus that would be safe to work with for short periods. With this strain, the carrier can be safely transported to a far off place, just like Lien here. Could be useful in war. Like a time bomb. And it suits our aims perfectly.'

Sampson nodded, not taking his eyes off the young prostitute. 'So the people who were on the plane with Lien will be fine.'

Gaunt continued talking. Something about how close they were to completing their plans. Sampson tuned him out and continued to watch the girl sniffling on the bunk. He was waiting for the doctor to shut up and open the door, so he could talk to her and find out the answers to his questions. After that, when she became contagious and he had to leave her, he would find out what job the doctor had planned for him.

Who would he want killed this time?

2

Present Day

England was just as she remembered it. Grey,
oppressive skies, even in summer, people rushing
from place to place, avoiding one another's eyes,
locked into their own personal spaces. The music
they used to isolate themselves came from an iPod
these days rather than a Walkman, and the litter
on the streets carried different brand names, but
apart from that, it was like stepping into a time
warp. Even the teenagers wore the same clothes
she'd worn twenty years ago. Punk and goth were
fashionable again. Bleak fashions for a bleak city.

It was so good to be back.

Kate Maddox felt an urgent tug at her arm and
looked down into a pair of wide blue eyes—eyes
like her own, Vernon had always said. 'His mother's
eyes and his father's nose.' She hoped that was all
Jack had inherited from his dad. Other attributes
mother and son shared were dark brown hair; Kate's
long and wavy, falling over her shoulders; and Jack's
cropped close, but in exactly the same shade of
chestnut; freckles across the bridge of the nose which
were only really visible in summer, and an infectious,
easy laugh. Like Kate, Jack would probably be tall
and slim when he grew up. She was secretly pleased
that he would one day, hopefully, tower over the
short-legged, bull-necked Vernon.

'Mum, Mum, look—there's that robot I was telling
you about.'

Jack was pointing towards a shop

13

window—Hamleys, she realised, the giant toy shop that she had once dragged her own parents around—and a white toy robot lumbering around in the window. She only had the vaguest recollection of Jack telling her about this robot, but it was clear that it had been occupying his thoughts recently. It was amazing how, in the midst of upheaval, he could still fixate on such things. Actually, it was reassuring. Although she hadn't yet explained to the six-year-old exactly how different things were going to be from now on. She'd been putting it off.

'Can we have a look? Please?'

'Okay.'

She allowed herself to be led over to the window where Jack pressed his palm against the glass and watched the white and silver robot as it performed a number of tricks. 'It's so cool,' he breathed.

'Hmm.'

He gazed up at her. 'I'd be really happy if I had one.'

She smiled at his disingenuous turn of phrase, then caught herself and frowned. 'I think it's probably too expensive.'

Jack squinted at the price tag. 'It's eighty pounds. How much is that in dollars?'

'Too much.'

She sensed him deflate and felt a blow of guilt, then annoyance at her own guilt. £80 *was* too much for a toy, although she and Vernon had both bought Jack a lot of expensive gifts recently. Guilt gifts. Competitive gifts. Most of those toys were still in Boston, in Jack's cluttered bedroom with the Red Sox bedspread and posters covering every inch of the walls.

The robot's eyes flashed red and Jack squealed

14

with laughter. 'Cool. I can't wait to tell Tyler about this.'

Tyler was Jack's best friend. Hearing his name brought back that feeling of guilt with a vengeance. Was she a bad mother? What would Jack say and do when she told him? She looked at the robot and at Jack's rapt expression as he watched it; and then she decided to infringe the first rule of parenthood: never back down once you've already said no.

'I guess you have been a good boy recently.'

*   *   *

Thirty minutes later they were in McDonald's in Leicester Square—another treat for Jack, who wasn't normally allowed to go into such unhealthy and additive-laden places. Every other kid in the place was gazing enviously at Jack's white robot.

Jack cradled it on his lap while he ate his veggie burger with one hand, Kate trying to be relaxed at the sight of the ketchup threatening to drip at any moment. The bloody robot was nearly as big as her son and now they were going to have to lug it round with them. What had she been thinking? She'd let her guilt get the better of her.

'I'm going to call him Billy,' Jack announced solemnly. 'Billy, this is my mum.'

The robot bleeped on cue.

'Pleased to meet you, Billy,' Kate said, forking a piece of tomato.

'Mum, where does the Queen live?'

'Nearby, in Buckingham Palace.'

'Billy and I would like to visit her.'

'I'm sure she'd be fascinated to meet Billy, but I don't think the Queen allows visitors.'

Jack thought about this. 'Is it because I'm American?'

'You're half British.'

'Which half?'

'The best half.'

'Daddy said that most British people are stuck up and have dirty teeth, like that man over there.'

The man Jack was referring to, who did indeed have teeth that looked like they'd fall out in shock if a toothbrush ever went near them, looked angrily over, and Kate shrunk down in her plastic seat.

'Jack, shush.' Most British people were stuck up? That was the most hypocritical thing Vernon had ever come out with—he was the bloody snob in the family. He was the one who refused to fly economy because of the *hoi polloi*. He was the one who didn't have a single acquaintance without an Ivy League education.

'Are my teeth American?'

'Yes.'

'What about Billy's?'

'I don't think he's got teeth. But if he did, they'd be made in China like the rest of him.'

'Mum, what do robots eat?'

She grabbed one of his french fries and held it up. 'Microchips?'

They both giggled, and the man with the mossy teeth gave them an equally dirty look.

'Come on, we ought to get going. I'm tired and I need a bath.'

'Are we going back to the hotel?'

'Yup.'

'Mum.'

'Yes?'

'I don't have to have a bath, do I?'

'It depends how good you are between now and bedtime.'

They left the restaurant and joined the throng outside. With Kate holding her son's hand, they edged their way through a crowd gathered around a juggler.

As they reached the kerb, she stuck her arm in the air as she spotted a taxi with its orange light on, but another man, a businessman with a phone stapled to his ear grabbed it first. The cab crawled away—traffic didn't speed in this part of London, where gridlock had become something else for tourists to write home about—and she cursed under her breath. She looked around for another cab.

And saw a ghost.

3

'Stephen!'

Life is full of moments like this—snap decisions, taken unconsciously, and when people ask, later, 'Why did you do that?' the only honest reply is, 'I don't know.' The sole explanation she could think of was that, in that moment, she was flung back in time to a night when she thought she'd died and gone to Hell. When she'd walked in despair through the grounds of the Cold Research Unit and searched for her lover.

And if she'd seen him then, she would have called out his name, like she did now.

But he didn't react.

The man on the other side of the road didn't flinch or alter his expression. He just stood there, drinking from a Starbucks cup, staring into the middle-distance and frowning. He wore a grey pinstriped jacket and faded blue jeans. His hair needed a cut and flopped over the rim of his glasses. Staring at him, she recognised the same traces of age she'd noticed in the mirror: the crow's feet, the lines at the side of the mouth that held a history of smiles, the lines on the forehead that mapped a legacy of sadness. When the wind ruffled his hair she noticed that it was receding, just a little. But it was definitely him. Even though it couldn't have been.

Kate felt as if she'd just been punched in the solar plexus; as breathless as the night the Centre caught fire. The people and the traffic around her blurred. Only Stephen stayed in focus. He began to walk away, dropping his coffee cup into a rubbish bin, and moving off quickly.

'Mum, are we looking for a taxi?'

'Yes. I . . . come on.'

'Where are we going?'

She didn't answer. She escorted Jack across the road and followed the man who looked so like Stephen, but who couldn't be Stephen, because he had been killed in the fire that night. He made his way up a quieter street towards Shaftesbury Avenue.

'Mum, why are you walking so quickly?'

'I'm in a hurry.'

Jack whined. 'But I'm tired. My legs hurt.'

She should have stopped then, stuck to her original plan—a taxi back to the hotel, a hot bath, let Jack watch the kids' channel on the hotel TV. This was insane. Stephen was dead. He'd been dead for sixteen years. This was just a guy who looked like him, a doppelgänger. Isn't everyone supposed to have a double somewhere? Or maybe she was just

18

imagining the likeness, fulfilling a fantasy that Stephen was still alive. She hadn't seen him for sixteen years, so how could she say this man looked just like him?

But he did. She had carried Stephen's face locked in her memory for a decade and a half. Whatever else she'd forgotten, she had never forgotten *him*. This guy did look exactly like him, and that was weird and worth investigating.

She felt compelled to follow him, despite her son's complaints.

He turned the corner onto Shaftesbury Avenue. The faces of famous Hollywood actors gazed down at her from theatre billboards; Jack made some comment about 'Chitty Chitty Bang Bang'. The ghost, or lookalike, or whatever he was, turned right. Luckily, the crowds slowed him down so he didn't get too far ahead even though she was having to drag along her son, plus his robot. He turned another corner, then another, and they found themselves on a quieter street lined with Chinese restaurants and shops flogging cheap bags and *faux*-silk.

'Mum, Billy's tired too,' Jack said, waving his robot in the air, and just as she was about to respond, the man stopped and turned around.

He looked straight at her. 'Why are you following me?' he asked.

*   *   *

Kate felt like an idiot. This was an act of madness, the kind of thing Vernon accused her of. *You need help. Some pills. You should see someone. Let me call Doctor Mackenzie.* And she'd cry, get angry, protest—*I'm sane. There's nothing wrong with me. I don't want any drugs. I don't need them.* It was the way he looked at her. It made her believe she *was* losing her mind.

God only knew what Vernon would have said about this.

The ghost/lookalike took a few wary steps towards her. He gazed curiously at her, then down at Jack and back at her.

'Stephen?' she said, holding her breath.

He shook his head. 'You've made a mistake.'

He didn't seem angry. At least that was something. He wasn't going to shout at her. But even though he said she'd made a mistake and, of course, she knew he couldn't really be Stephen, he didn't only look like her long lost boyfriend—he sounded the same too. His voice was identical: well-spoken English, a soft voice, intelligent. Sexy.

She realised that Jack was looking up at her with wide eyes, scared of the strange man. She put her hand on Jack's head and smiled. The man must have seen the boy's fear too. He winked at him.

'I'm really sorry,' Kate said, in a rush. 'I've made a stupid mistake. You look exactly like someone I used to know, this guy I used to be close to, and I had to try and find out if you . . . it's stupid because . . .'

'He's dead.'

She stopped her babble and stared at him.

'I assume you're talking about Stephen Wilson?'

She nodded dumbly.

The man smiled with one corner of his mouth. 'He was my brother.'

4

Ania, the hotel babysitter, was well-used to neurotic parents who felt pinned between anxiety and eagerness—the eagerness to get out and see the city, not spend their vacation tied down by the kids. But this woman, with her little boy, seemed more worried than average. Her voice trembled as she spoke and she dropped her handbag on her way to the door. Her purse, her keycard and tissues all tumbled onto the carpet and she bent quickly to scoop them up. Highly-strung. Or up to something. She had that air about her. She was doing something that made her ill at ease; something secret.

If she had to bet on it, Ania would wager that it involved a man.

The boy, on the other hand, was relaxed, leaning back in his chair clutching a toy robot to his chest, his free hand expertly handling the remote control, flicking from cartoon to pop video to wildlife programme. He giggled at the sight of meerkats playing on screen. Perhaps he didn't realise that his mother was about to go out. Or perhaps he was secure enough in her love to know that she'd be coming back—it was the ones who were insecure who usually freaked out the most.

Ania finally managed to get the nervous woman out into the corridor. The boy had an American accent but the mother was English. It was intriguing. Where was the father? Not that Ania was really all that interested. As long as she got paid, who cared? She liked the boy, though. He seemed like a nice kid.

The woman said, 'Here's my mobile number, and the name and number of the restaurant, just in case. I'm Kate, by the way. And you've already met Jack.'

'Okay.'

'Bye Jack, sweetie,' she called. 'See you later.'

'Bye.' He didn't look up. The meerkats were more interesting. Ania was relieved—no tantrums to deal with. Good. She felt a sudden tickle in her nose, and sneezed.

Kate turned back. 'Have you got a cold?'

She shook her head. 'Maybe I am getting one.'

'Hmm. Well, it depends if your body has encountered this virus before. If so, your antibodies will fight off the cold and it'll go away.'

Ania nodded, not knowing what to say. She was pleased when the anxious mother finally left.

*   *   *

Kate emerged from the tube station and checked her watch. As so often happened, she had rushed out in a hurry and arrived early. Vernon was always going on about her obsessive need to be punctual and reliable. In the early days, he found it endearing; a positive character trait. Later, it became another sign of her uptightness.

She walked up Charing Cross Road and stopped outside a bookshop full of medical and scientific books. She recognised some of them. There was a famous book called *The Plague on the Horizon*, which contained several quotes from Kate. She had a signed copy back in Boston. The author had interviewed Kate because of her involvement in the investigation of the West Nile Virus, a potentially lethal illness that had first been seen in the US, in

New York, in 1999. WNV, as virologists called it, caused muscle weakness and confusion in some people, and could lead to meningitis, paralysis and death in others. It was a particularly interesting virus (and when Kate said this to non-scientists they would raise their eyebrows, wondering how anyone could find such a horrible thing so interesting) because of the way it was transmitted. Mosquitoes became infected after feeding on virus-carrying birds, such as crows. One of those mosquitoes could then infect a human. Kate's team were trying to develop a vaccine for WNV. So far, they had not been successful.

Kate caught sight of her reflection in the dark glass. Her face was pale, her eyes wide. She hadn't been able to decide whether or not to wear make-up. This certainly wasn't a date, but sometimes make-up made her feel more confident, less exposed to the world, so she'd put on a slick of lip-gloss, a touch of mascara. Still, she wasn't looking her best. A large part of her wanted to be locked up safely behind the door of her hotel room with the TV on and Jack beside her. She hoped he'd be okay. That babysitter had seemed capable enough, but—she let her imagination reach out—what if she was a child-killer, a front for an international child-slave racket, or just plain irresponsible?

She castigated herself. Don't be ridiculous, Kate. Relax. It's a reputable chain hotel, the woman had references.

She pushed her hair behind her ears and stood up straight. All you're doing, she reminded herself, is meeting the brother of an old boyfriend.

His name was Paul.

'We were twins,' he had said, a second after they'd

23

met in the street and he had told her he was Stephen's brother. Stephen had never mentioned he had a twin, which seemed very odd in retrospect. Maybe he did tell her, but she'd forgotten. So much of that summer was obscured behind thick fog. When she tried to remember those days, it was like trying to read a road sign without her contact lenses in. No matter how hard she strained, she couldn't make out the details through the haze and, in the end, the effort became painful and she gave up.

When she played back that meeting with Paul in her mind, it made her cringe. She had felt so awkward, standing there with Jack, having to talk loudly over the roar of the London traffic. Paul seemed uneasy too. She couldn't blame him—being confronted by a woman who is staring at you like you're a phantom would do that to anyone.

'How did you know Stephen?' he had asked.

Kate had been aware of Jack looking up at her. Part of her wanted to turn and run. But she was hypnotised by the face of this stranger who looked so much like the man she'd loved long ago. Alongside unease, his face showed kindness, just as Stephen's had. She had the sudden urge to launch herself at him, wrap her arms around him and kiss him. For years she had dreamt of a moment like this—of bumping into Stephen and him telling her, 'It was all a mistake. Reports of my demise were exaggerated.' And they'd embrace, and the years would disappear.

Except this wasn't Stephen.

'We were friends,' she said.

'At university?'

She almost told a second lie, but said, 'No. I met him at the Cold Research Unit in Salisbury.'

'Oh.'

She said, 'I was there.'

He spoke softly. 'There . . . when he . . .?'

'Yes.'

Jack had spoken up then. 'Mummy, what are you talking about? Billy's bored. And he needs to pee.'

Jack's words broke the tension and the adults laughed.

Kate said, 'Look, I'm really sorry. I don't normally follow strangers through the streets.'

Paul smiled. 'It's okay. It's understandable.'

'Maybe. But I'd better go and get Billy and his master back to the hotel.'

'Hotel? You don't live in London?'

'We live in Boston,' said Jack.

'Really?'

Kate went to turn away, but hesitated. She didn't want to say goodbye, but lingering there was pointless.

Paul said, 'Wait,' even though she hadn't yet moved. 'Would you like to meet for dinner?'

'I . . .'

'It would be nice to talk to someone who knew my brother. Our parents won't talk about him because it's too upsetting. I never see any of our old friends these days. Sometimes it feels like he never existed.' He smiled wryly. 'Except I see him every time I look in the mirror.'

Kate didn't know what to say.

'So, dinner? You can bring Jack and—Billy, is it?—if you like.'

Before she could change her mind, she blurted, 'Where? What time?'

He pointed up the street at a restaurant. 'Do you like Chinese? We could meet there at seven.'

'Alright.' She turned away, then realised she hadn't

25

told him her own name.

'I'm Kate,' she said.

Something happened when she said that; it was as if the name meant something to him but he wasn't sure what. The moment passed and he smiled. 'Okay, I'll see you later.'

*   *   *

She killed twenty minutes walking slowly through Soho towards the Chinese restaurant. It was a warm, overcast evening, and the streets were rammed with people in T-shirts standing outside pubs. She hadn't smoked for years, but she had a craving for cigarettes. And cider. She thought she knew why, too: she was going to meet a man she didn't know for dinner, something she hadn't done for a long, long time. It threw her back in time, made her feel like a teenager. She wouldn't smoke or drink cider, or go to bed with this man, but she wouldn't be enormously surprised with herself if she did. She'd done enough out-of-character things recently.

She paused outside the restaurant, inhaled the smell of cooking rice and sweet and sour sauce and MSG. She watched a trio of chickens rotating on a spit in a window opposite and had to look away. She hadn't eaten meat, either, for years. Another thing that irritated Vernon—living with a goddamn vegetarian.

'You enjoyed the taste of meat when we met,' he said, the underlying innuendo making her shudder. She had to stop thinking about him. But how could she? When he found out what she'd done, as he would very soon . . . She didn't want to think

26

about it.

She didn't have to. Paul arrived at that moment, appearing out of nowhere and grinning nervously at her.

'I left Jack with a babysitter at the hotel,' she said. 'I hope he's OK. I just thought it would be easier to talk without interruption.'

'Sure,' he said, easily.

She'd been worried that he might think she was planning to come on to him, farming her son out to a stranger, being a bad mother—but he didn't seem at all fazed. 'I'm starving,' he added.

'Me too,' she said, although she wasn't.

He led the way into the hot, noisy restaurant, waves of chatter rising and falling against a backdrop of the clatter of plates at a service hatch. A waiter showed them to a table, chucked a pair of menus down on the table and zoomed away again.

Seeing how taken aback Kate was, Paul said, 'They're famously rude in here. It's part of the appeal.'

They exchanged pleasantries about the warm weather and Chinese food for a few minutes, ordered drinks and studied their menus.

The waiter reappeared. 'Yes?' he demanded, looking as though he wished he was anywhere else but here.

Paul gave the waiter a few numbers from the menu, and Kate did the same.

'You're vegetarian?' he asked. When she nodded, he asked, 'Do you eat fish?'

'No, I'm vegetarian.' She immediately regretted her snappiness. 'Sorry, it's just that everyone always says that—it's like an automatic response. Proper veggies don't eat fish.'

27

'I'll remember that.' He pretended to make a note on an invisible notepad. 'Fish have feelings too.'

He was charming. Just like Stephen—or rather, how Stephen would be if he'd had sixteen more years to practise. She had to keep reminding herself, though, that this wasn't Stephen. She had to remember that she had only met this man this afternoon. Her fantasies were not coming true. On the way over, she kept asking herself why she was doing this, what her motives were. There were, in the end, two things.

One, she had never been able to talk to anyone else about Stephen. Now, like his brother, she relished the chance to talk to somebody about him, somebody who knew him intimately. Perhaps that way, after all these years, she could achieve some kind of—and she hated the word but couldn't think of a better one—closure.

Two, she was glad of the distraction. She had only been able to think about one thing since arriving in London, and her brain needed a break from the worry. What better way to stop fretting about the future than to concentrate on the past?

'So,' Paul asked. 'What brings you to London? Visiting relatives?'

It was far too complicated to explain, even if she'd wanted to. 'No. Well, not really. Jack and I are just about to move over here.' She played with her chopsticks, unsure of how much to tell him. 'I'm looking for a place at the moment. Actually, I'm kind of shocked by the price of property in London.'

'Where do you live at the moment? Oh yes, Boston, wasn't it?'

'Yes.'

'Nice.' He waited for her to give more details but

28

she wasn't forthcoming. 'And what do you do in Boston?'

'I work at Harvard.'

'Doing . . .?'

Kate laid her chopsticks on the table. 'I'm a professor in the department of immunology and infectious diseases. I specialise in the study and treatment of viruses.'

She watched Paul closely to see his reaction. Telling people what she did usually had two effects. Weak men, the kind who were intimidated by clever women, would try to outsmart or belittle her. Other people would inch away, like people she talked to on the extremely rare occasions she went to parties, as if they might catch something from her.

Paul didn't appear to be at all intimidated or frightened. 'Cool. So is that how you knew Stephen? You worked with him at the Cold Research Unit?'

'No, I was a volunteer there. I'd only just graduated. And after that, I went to Harvard and, apart from the odd visit, never came back.'

'Until now?'

'Until now,' she echoed, thinking how strange it was that you could summarise a life so quickly and painlessly, missing out all the important facts. Of how she went to Harvard, still in a state of shock, only weeks after Stephen's death. The years she spent in the graduate research programme. Meeting and marrying Vernon Maddox—a man who could not have been more different to Stephen—and having Jack. The glorious day she became Professor Kate Maddox. Work, and Jack, had both continued to be fulfilling and enjoyable, but the rot had well and truly started to set in with Vernon by then. His fuse had grown shorter and shorter over the years,

29

seemingly in inverse proportions to his nasal hair. What Kate had initially thought was passionate and forthright about him soon became perceived as merely hectoring and unpleasant.

She didn't tell Paul all this, though.

'And what do you do?' she asked.

'You might not believe this, but I chase viruses too.'

'Really?'

'Yes—but a different kind to you. Computer viruses. Or I should say, the scum who create them and send them out across the internet.'

'You're a cop?'

'No. Not really. I work for an internet security firm. It's a very exciting business.'

She smiled. 'Sounds a bit geeky to me.'

'Er, says the professor of—what was it?— immunology and infectious diseases?'

'Touché.'

Paul laughed. 'Actually, a lot of people think it's a geeky job, and I do spend a lot of time staring at computer screens. But so must you.'

'You're right. Too much time.'

'Except now you're moving to London. Are you moving to a university over here? Kissing the Ivy League goodbye?'

He asked a lot of questions. Stephen had been curious like that too, interested in others.

Their food arrived, the waiter plonking it down on the table, shoving their glasses out of the way then stomping off. Kate was too busy trying to decide how honest to be to feel aggrieved by the waiter's rudeness. Should she tell Paul that she had no idea about what she was going to do professionally; furthermore, that she didn't care right now?

She said, 'I'm considering my options at the moment.'

'I see.'

They emptied their beer bottles and Paul put his hand up to order more. Kate licked her lips. She hardly drank at all these days and the beer tasted good: sweet and mood-changing. Tongue-loosening.

'Tell me about Stephen,' she said. 'What was he like as a kid?'

Paul dipped a spring roll in sweet chilli sauce, and took a bite. 'He was the leader, at first. He was born second—five minutes after me—and after that he spent his, I mean our, childhoods making up for it. He was the first to say "Daddy", the first to walk across the living room instead of bum-shuffling, the first to climb the tree at the end of our garden. He was the first to get a girlfriend. Melissa, that was her name. She lived just down the road. A ponytail and freckles. We had a camp, which was really just a space between some bushes, and he took her in there and snogged her. I was so jealous.'

He laughed, rather awkwardly. 'I suppose I was jealous of him in a lot of ways. We were competitive, always wanting to get the best marks at school or win at football. For once, I was better at that than him—he was hopeless—but he was better academically. Being good at football won me more points at school, but getting good grades went down better with my parents.'

'Go on,' Kate said softly. She felt as though she could listen to him talking about Stephen all night.

'I don't know what to tell you next. There's so much.' He was thoughtful for a moment. 'There was a period when we were in our early teens when we didn't want to be twins any more. We wanted to be

31

individuals. I took the lead in this—Stephen really was an academic, always buried in a book, or carrying out experiments with this chemistry kit he had, which he upgraded every year. By the time he was a teenager it seemed to take over his whole bedroom. We called it his Gaseous Empire.'

He smiled at the memory, then continued. 'Stephen lived in a dream world—a world of the mind—so he barely noticed when I went out of my way to look as different from him as I could. I cut my hair really short, got into hip-hop.' He grinned again. 'Break-dancing was big around that time.'

'I remember it well.'

'Stephen wouldn't, if he was here. He didn't know anything about what was going on in the street. I used to take the piss out of him for it. So did my friends. They all thought he was the world's biggest nerd, and couldn't believe he was my brother. I used to bring my mates round when my parents were out and we, my little gang, would rip the piss out of Stephen, call him the Prof, all this stupid stuff. We were gits.'

Kate didn't say anything. My poor baby, she thought, and for a second she felt angry with Paul. Neither of them had eaten anything for several minutes. Paul was staring into the middle distance; into the past.

'There was this kid that I used to hang around with called Terry. I didn't really like him but he decided he wanted to join our group because he liked the same kind of music as we did. And everyone else was terrified of him. He was a little psycho, the kind of boy who tortured frogs for a laugh and terrorised the younger kids with demands for money. The kind of person I'd do anything to avoid these days.

'He waged war against Stephen. Every day, in the playground, or on the way home, he'd be there, taunting him. It was never physical, but Stephen was the kind of kid who despised confrontation. Terry would go up to him and say something like, "I heard you called me a wanker," and Stephen's voice would break as he denied it. Stephen clearly did think Terry was a wanker, but he would never have dared say it, even to me.'

Kate wanted to reach into the past and hug Stephen. And slap this Terry. A vision rose up of herself stepping in, defending her boyfriend.

But she understood what it felt like to be bullied. She'd allowed it to happen to her for a long time. It was only recently that she'd had the courage to stand up for herself.

She said, 'Didn't you do anything?'

Paul pushed his noodles around his plate with a chopstick. 'No. I mean, I'd say, kind of weakly, "Come on Terry, leave him alone," but that was about it. I was scared of Terry too—he was so unpredictable—and I suppose there was a part of me that was glad. Glad that it wasn't me. That I was the cool brother. It's awful, isn't it?'

Kate didn't respond. She wondered what kind of teenager Jack would grow into. A cruel one? Or a soft one like Stephen? She prayed neither.

Paul said, 'Then one day, Stephen totally surprised me. Terry was doing the old "You called me a wanker" routine, and "Do you want a fight?" and Stephen put down his school bag—I can picture him dropping it—and said, "OK, then." And he stepped forward and punched Terry right in the mouth. Knocked him over.'

'Bloody hell.'

'That's what I thought. I felt like cheering. And Stephen coolly picked up his bag, stepped over Terry—who was too shocked to move—and walked off. I'd like to say Terry learned the error of his ways, but the next day he started bullying someone else, someone younger and more timid, but he never bothered Stephen again.'

Paul sighed. 'I still felt ashamed that I hadn't done anything to help. Eventually we became friends again. We had to be, really, we were brothers. Sometimes, usually at four in the morning, I wake up and start thinking about it. I wish there was some way I could make it up to Stephen. I'd ask for forgiveness, if he was here now.'

Finally there was an awkward pause in the conversation and she could see him struggling to say something.

'Are you OK?' she asked.

Instead of speaking he reached into his pocket and took out a folded sheet of paper. He didn't show it to her, just held it, gazing into space. Kate could almost hear his thoughts ticking away. Stephen used to do this too.

He said, 'As soon as you told me your name was Kate, it rang a bell.'

'Stephen told you about me?'

'Yes. In a manner of speaking. It wasn't something I'd thought about for a long time, but yes, I recognised your name straight away. I went home to check, to make sure I wasn't imagining things, or mis-remembering, and there it was, in black biro.'

'I don't understand.'

Paul tapped the piece of paper. 'A few days before he . . . before the fire, he wrote to me. He mentioned

34

your name.'

'And you've kept the letter all this time?'

'I've kept every souvenir of Stephen I could. But this letter—I would have kept it anyway.'

'Why?'

He handed it to her. 'Read it and you'll understand.'

She hesitated before taking the piece of paper from him, and as it touched her fingertips she felt a thrill, a shiver, as if the ghost she thought she'd seen earlier had touched her.

5

She couldn't hear the clatter and murmur of the other diners any more. There was a wall of silence around her and Paul. The words on the page were all she was aware of. She recognised Stephen's handwriting. Before seeing it again she would never have been able to describe it, but as soon as it was there before her she knew those looping Ls, that tight, messy scrawl. A doctor's handwriting. They'd joked about it more than once.

The letter covered two sides of A4. She read through the first section quickly. Stephen started with a few unremarkable statements and observations—the weather, the cricket, hope you were able to watch it, etc—and then the tone of the letter changed suddenly. The writing got more uneven, even more messy. It looked like it was written in a rush. There were mis-spellings, crossings out. So unlike the Stephen she knew.

Stuck in his flat one day, when he was at work, she had unearthed an old notebook from the back of his bookcase. In the notebook were poems, a couple of fragments from stories that he'd started writing, observations about places he'd been. It was beautifully written, with immaculate spelling and grammar. She never told him she'd found the notebook in case he was embarrassed. He might, she feared, even be angry that she'd been snooping around. Then there were the notes he wrote her; cards that went with little gifts he'd bring home to her. He was careful and always accurate. This letter, with its mistakes and heavy pencil marks must have been written when drunk. Or under extreme stress.

Towards the end of the letter, the following passage screamed out at her:

I met a girl, her name's Kate. We've had to keep our relationship secret from the people here, but I don't think we're the only ones with secrets . . .

Kate was unable to read the next segment, two lines had been crossed out with thick black pen, obscuring all but the tips of a few tall letters and the tails of some others. She picked it up a little further on.

I hope you meet her some day. If you do, and I'm not there, tell her I loved her. Tell her she was right. And tell her to forgive me.

'Are you okay?' Paul asked, touching her wrist.

She snatched her hand away as if his fingers were red hot then looked up, dazzled, briefly unable to speak. *Am I okay? No.*

She stared at the letter again, reading it over like someone who's just received a letter telling them

36

that sorry, the blood test result was positive, you failed the exam, you didn't get the job you so badly wanted, I don't love you anymore. '"Tell her she was right."' She read the sentence aloud. 'Right about what?'

Paul raised an eyebrow. 'I was hoping you'd be able to tell me that.'

'And what does he want me to forgive him for?'

'You don't know?'

She screwed her face up, tapped her temples with the flat of her hand, perhaps hoping to knock the memories loose. Here was that thick fog again, descending over her mind, obscuring the past.

Paul said, 'You know something? I've kept this letter for years. I must have read it a hundred times. And every time, I asked myself what Stephen was talking about. What were the secrets? Who was this girl Kate and what was she right about? After Stephen died I became obsessed with finding out what he was talking about. I mean, it was obvious to me that he wasn't feeling himself when he wrote this letter. He was normally so calm and rational. Not unemotional, but with his head screwed on, you know what I mean?'

Kate did know.

'What had this Kate person done to make him like this, and what had he done to her, that she had to forgive? I asked Mum and Dad if they knew anything about you, but they said they'd hardly heard from Stephen in the months before he died. I spoke to the couple of close friends he had, but they didn't know anything either. You were a mystery woman. Nobody had a clue who you were. This letter was the only proof that you existed. I puzzled over it for ages and then I made myself forget about it—I had

37

to, in order to be able to get on with my life. But I always hoped that one day I might find this Kate, and that she'd be able to tell me what she was right about.'

Kate's voice trembled. 'I don't know. I don't remember.'

'Can't you try? Think back?'

'You don't understand.'

She explained to him about how patchy her memory was. 'It's so frustrating. I can remember some stuff incredibly clearly, but then there are these holes. I hardly remember anything about my second stay at the Centre, which was when it burned down.'

'You stayed there twice?'

'Yes. It's . . . well, maybe I'll explain why another time. This letter was written during my second stay. So whatever I was right about, it's something that must have happened then.'

'Could it just be something to do with your relationship? Maybe he's saying you were right about, I don't know, that you could make it work, while he was doubtful. Something like that?'

'No. It can't be. What about this stuff about secrets?' She was quiet for a few seconds, though the bubble around them remained, sealing out the chatter of the other diners. 'You're going to think I'm crazy, but although I can't remember the details, I do know that there was something, something we couldn't agree on. Something to do with the CRU itself, or Stephen's job. I can almost see it. Almost taste it. But it's like . . .' She paused.

'What?'

She looked into his eyes. 'I'm scared. Scared of whatever this truth is. I feel like the heroine in a horror movie, standing outside the door of the big creepy house, grasping the handle, knowing that when I pull open the door I'll finally see what the monster looks like. But I don't want to see.'

Paul leaned forward. 'In the films, the girl always goes into the creepy house.'

'I know. But my brain won't let me.'

'Why not? It just seems so odd that you can't remember. Sixteen years isn't all that long ago.'

She sipped her beer, wondering if he disbelieved her. Her heart was still pounding in her ears, but the initial shock had faded a little and the cool scientist inside her had stepped forward. Here was a problem. How was she going to solve it?

She shook her head and sighed. 'I'm really jetlagged. I'll be able to think about it more clearly tomorrow—not that I think I'll have remembered anything else, but perhaps I can figure out *why* I can't remember. Do you mind if we leave now?'

'Where are you staying?' he asked.

She told him the name of her hotel.

'That's on my way. Let's take a taxi and I'll drop you off there.'

The next few minutes—the walk to find a cab, the taxi ride—passed in a blur. When the taxi pulled up outside the hotel, Kate said, 'I'm really sorry that I can't answer your questions about the letter.'

'Hmm.' He appeared to have fallen into a slightly bad mood.

'It's not something I can control—I wish I *could* remember.'

He didn't reply.

Kate pushed open the car door and climbed out, then walked quickly into the hotel, head down, through the revolving doors and towards the lift. She didn't have the energy to talk about the holes in her memory again, to justify herself to this guy she'd just met. She felt emotionally drained. She didn't want to have to think about anything else until tomorrow. All she wanted was to see Jack, to give him a cuddle before going to bed.

*　　　*　　　*

The taxi pulled away and headed around the hotel's circular forecourt, back towards the main road. Paul sat back in his seat, trying to process everything.

He couldn't believe that she had forgotten almost everything from that summer. God, it was frustrating. But then a stab of guilt hit him and he regretted the way he'd acted at the end of their encounter. He wouldn't be surprised if she didn't want to talk to him anymore. And that would be terrible—not only because it meant that this link to his brother was lost, but also because . . . well, he liked her.

'Stop the car, I need to get out.'

The driver glared back at him. 'You what?'

Paul thrust a ten pound note at him. 'Sorry. Changed my mind.'

He needed to talk to Kate again, to apologise. And maybe he could help her recover her memories, find out what it was that had happened that summer. This fire—the official story was that it was an unfortunate accident, but what if that was a smokescreen? Bad choice of words, he thought to himself, grimacing. It had always seemed like a weird coincidence that Stephen had written this strange, emotional letter a few days before he died. Before, he had never had any way of going about finding out the truth. But now he'd found Kate, there was surely a chance. He would go after the truth, for his brother's sake. To make amends for all the times he'd wronged him in the past. He cringed at the corny sentiment—but it was true.

*　　*　　*

The lift doors pinged open and Kate made her way towards her room. She glanced at her watch. Nine o'clock—Jack should be asleep by now. The babysitter would probably be watching TV and would be surprised to see Kate back so early. She might raise a questioning eyebrow, wonder what had gone wrong. Maybe this overprotective parent couldn't bear to be away from her child for more than a couple of hours.

Kate took her keycard out of her wallet and swiped it in the lock. She pushed the door open.

The room was empty.

The babysitter, and Jack, were gone.

6

John Sampson glanced at the LED clock on the dashboard. 22:02. He'd been parked outside the McDonald-Taylor Research Institute, on the outskirts of Oxford, for hours now. This part of Oxford was industrial and grey—out of sight of the dreaming spires, but still connected to the university. Here, research was carried out in anonymous, flat buildings. Tourists didn't wander round this part of town gaping with awe, buying postcards and photographing one another in front of places they'd looked up in their guidebooks and found their way to. Nobody looked twice at these buildings except for a few animal rights protestors. And it was those protestors who were responsible for making Sampson wait.

They were hanging around by the fence. A couple of middle-aged women; a younger woman, quite attractive in a sallow vegan way; and a bloke with a beard. Sampson had driven by earlier that day and seen the same group, plus a half-dozen others. Now only the hardcore remained. They carried placards that said STOP THE CRUELTY. Some featured grim pictures of monkeys with the word TORTURED above them. Sampson wondered what they'd think if they saw the things he'd seen a few days ago: the sick women imprisoned in tiny rooms; their blank despairing faces, shivering and whimpering. Would the protestors be as upset at the sight of cruelty to people? The question genuinely interested him. He wondered idly if these bleeding hearts would be able to teach him how to feel.

He took a long drag of his cigarette then crushed it to death in the car's pull-out ashtray. He didn't have time to think about that shit right now. He had a job to do. And the fucking protestors were stopping him from doing it.

How long were they going to be? Beyond them, a single light was burning in the window of the institute. Only one car remained parked in the staff car park.

The car belonged to Dr David Twigger, a scientist specialising in the study of viruses in animals. The protestors were outside because of the macaque monkeys and rats he used in his experiments. He argued that although he wished there was an alternative, using the animals was essential. He

42

pointed out that the research carried out here was on diseases that affected animals not humans. They were trying to *save* animals, stop the viruses that affected pets, farm animals and wild creatures. The protestors argued that this was all very well, but why should some animals suffer so that others might be saved in the future? They also stated their belief that the only reason so much effort was put into studying these diseases was because scientists were worried they may spread to humans. Avian, or bird, Flu was a prime example.

It was a moral maze—Sampson was glad he had no morals—and in actual fact the institute did not attract much in the way of protests, unlike Huntingdon Life Sciences and other controversial places where the scientists and staff were threatened daily. The protests here were low-key and mild-mannered, carried out by a small bunch of locals.

Ignoring the protesters, Dr Twigger worked until after dark, dedicated to his research. All the other staff had gone home and now it was just Dr Twigger and a couple of security guards. The building was surrounded by CCTV cameras and barbed wire, but because this lab concentrated on animal diseases and didn't store viruses that could harm humans and because of the low-level protests, security was not too tight, especially compared to some of the research facilities Sampson was familiar with. The protestors waited outside so they could scream abuse at Twigger as he drove home, possibly pelting his car with eggs for good measure, but no-one had ever physically attacked him or the building.

Tonight it looked as if Twigger wasn't going to come out. Not until the early hours anyway. Sampson watched the little group of protestors gather in a huddle, debating what to do next. From their body language it looked like the younger woman wanted to stay, but the others, especially Beardy, wanted to go home to their beds and the sleep of the righteous.

The majority won the argument and they shuffled away, taking their placards with them.

Sampson watched them go. At the corner of the street, they parted, the three older members of the group heading one way while the young woman went the other. For a moment he considered following her. He could grab her and lock her in the boot of his car until later. See if she *could* teach him something.

But he didn't have time. Twigger might come out while he was away, meaning Sampson would have to come back tomorrow. That wasn't going to happen. He wanted to get this over with tonight.

He watched the sallow vegan woman walk away. She was probably a student at the university. She would never know what a lucky escape she'd just had.

He opened the glove compartment, grabbed a balaclava and pulled it over his head. On the front of the balaclava were three letters: ALF. Everyone would think the protestors had suddenly decided to step up their efforts. Next, he put on a pair of black leather gloves, then opened the car door, got out and walked towards the fence.

On the way, he spotted some leaflets that the protestors had dropped. He picked one up and studied it. A cat stared out at him—the most miserable cat he'd ever seen—and the text below detailed the experiments that had been carried out on this cat and many others like it. 'Tortured in the name of science.' Sampson shook his head. These people didn't know the true meaning of torture. He could have taught the vegan girl if he'd had time, but now it was too late. The leaflet would come in handy, though. He folded it and stuck it in his back pocket.

Climbing the fence was easy for him. At the top he used a pair of wire cutters to snip through the barbed wire, then dropped gently onto the grass on the other side. He was thirty yards from the building. He took a deep breath. He needed to work quickly; this was what he was good at.

A camera swivelled towards him as he broke into a jog towards the building. He knew the camera would record the letters on the balaclava. He knew the security guards—probably ex-police or ex-army, dulled by too many nights sat staring at screens on which nothing ever happened—would panic and come out to meet him before calling for back-up. And even if they did call for back-up, Sampson would be in and out before they arrived.

He was right. The outside lights came on and the door was flung open. Two guards came running out, one with a crewcut, the other with short blond hair. The crewcut came towards him first, shouting 'Stop' as he ran. But in the harsh light Sampson saw confusion on the guard's face. He didn't understand why the guy in the balaclava was still running towards him in a straight line. Charging him. As Crewcut stopped and raised his gun, Sampson, without stopping, unsheathed the knife he had just pulled out of his pocket, releasing it expertly, it spun in the air before landing deep in the guard's throat.

Crewcut dropped to the grass. A few steps behind, the blond guard saw his colleague fall, and stumbled to a halt. He raised his gun and fired, but Sampson had anticipated this and veered to the left, the bullet cracking past him. Before the guard could fire another shot, Sampson was upon him.

He grabbed the guard's arm at the elbow and wrist and, raising his thigh, pushed his forearm swiftly down and snapped it. The guard choked on his own scream. Sampson took hold of the sides of the man's head and, with a single twisting motion, broke his neck.

He stepped over the body and ran into the building through the door the inept security guards had left open, looked left and right to get his bearings, and ran towards the laboratory where Dr Twigger's light burned bright.

Sampson kicked open the lab door and found Dr Twigger waiting for him. The scientist stood at the far end of the laboratory, holding a metal bar. Sampson imagined the doctor probably kept this bar with him for security. What a waste of time. Behind him stood a row of six cages, each containing a macaque monkey. The brown-furred monkeys stared at him implacably from behind the bars. Between Sampson and the doctor was a bench bearing lab equipment: high-powered microscopes, a computer, test tubes, a jumble of flasks and dishes and the other paraphernalia of lab life. A pair of rubber gloves lay inside-out on the bench, as if they'd just been hurriedly removed.

Dr Twigger was a thin man in his late forties with hair that needed cutting. He looked like a frightened man who was desperate not to show that fear.

'Get out,' he said shakily, holding up the bar.

Sampson walked up to him and punched him in the face before the doctor could swing the metal bar, which he wrenched from Twigger's grip. He threw it across the lab, the loud clanging making the monkeys jump and screech. They leapt about their cages, baring their teeth. Sampson glanced at them.

Twigger pulled himself upright. Blood trickled from his left nostril. He wiped it on the sleeve of his white coat.

'If you're planning to free these animals you're making a big mistake. They're sick and will attack humans. A monkey in that condition can do a lot of damage.'

Sampson ignored him. He walked over to the computer and pressed a key on the keyboard, keeping one eye on the doctor. He examined the figures on the screen, then crouched down and unplugged the hard drive.

'Where are the backups?' he said.

'Backups? There aren't any.'

Sampson put the hard drive down on the bench and walked towards Twigger, who took a step back towards the cages. The monkeys leapt forward in their cages, hissing.

'Where are the backups?' he repeated.

'There aren't any . . .'

Sampson grabbed the doctor and turned him round, clutching the back of his neck. With his free hand he opened the door of the closest cage and pushed the doctor's head inside. Dr Twigger knew not to cry out. Sampson felt him tremble.

The monkey sat on the floor of the cage, eyeing the doctor's scalp and baring its sharp teeth.

Sampson said, 'So they can do a lot of damage?'

The doctor spoke in a whisper. 'Yes. Please.'

'I can't hear you.'

'*Please.*'

47

He pushed Twigger's head in further, glad of the leather gloves. The other monkeys were clinging to the bars of their cages, watching, waiting. If monkeys could make plans, dream of revenge, then surely they'd dreamt of getting revenge on this man who caged them and made them sick.

'Where are the backups?' he repeated.

Twigger's voice had risen an octave. 'In the safe.'

'Where's the safe?'

'In . . .' Without warning, the monkey jumped across the cage, screaming. Twigger screamed too, but at the last moment Sampson pulled him clear and slammed the door in the monkey's face. It struck the bars and landed on the floor of the cage, screeching.

'The location of the safe and the combination,' Sampson said in his usual quiet monotone.

Twigger had pissed himself; Sampson could smell it. Twigger looked nervously over his shoulder at the monkey, who was now prowling around his cage, shaking his head.

Sampson was beginning to lose his patience. He took hold of the doctor again and moved to push him back towards the cage.

Twigger yelled, 'No. The safe is next door. Combination 6471.'

'Thank you. And the AG-769 virus?'

'What?'

'AG-769. Where is it stored?'

The doctor was clearly confused. 'Why do you want that?'

'Just tell me where it is.'

But the doctor had already given it away. His eyes had flicked towards the left.

'Thank you,' Sampson said.

He pushed the doctor to the ground and knelt on his chest. He squeezed Twigger's nose between forefinger and thumb and clamped a hand over his mouth. The doctor's eyes were wide, pleading. The monkeys gazed down from their cage. Eventually, Dr Twigger stopped trying to struggle. Sampson had hoped he might feel something at the moment of the doctor's death—not sympathy or sadness, necessarily, words he'd looked up in the dictionary and tried to understand—but something.

As always, he felt nothing.

Aware that he'd wasted precious seconds getting the combination out of the doctor—next time, he'd just go for the testicles; that always worked quickly— he opened the freezer and removed the vials containing the AG-769 virus and stored them in a padded wallet which he kept in his inside pocket. Back in the car he would transfer them to a portable freezer. He picked up the computer hard drive and realised he'd almost forgotten something. He took the animal rights leaflet with the picture of the cat out of his back pocket and left it lying on the dead doctor's chest.

In the office, he opened the safe and removed the backup disks that contained the crucial data.

He exited the building and walked through the darkness towards his car.

As he got in, one of his two mobile phones rang. It was his second phone. Only one person had this number. Was Gaunt checking up on him to make sure he'd done what he'd said he would? The arsehole. He'd never let him down before.

'I'm done,' he snapped as he answered the call.

The voice on the other end was calm. 'Excellent. I knew you would. But that's not what I'm calling about.'

'No?'

'No. I've got another urgent job for you. We've just had a tip-off about an old . . . patient who's just returned to the UK.'

'Right.'

'Her name's Kate Maddox.'

7

Cold panic flooded Kate's insides as she entered the hotel room. This couldn't be real.

'Jack? *Jack!*' She cried out his name. Where was he? She started to repeat his name in her mind over and over as she stood in the centre of the room, turning in a slow circle, her hand on her brow. In a kind of trance, she opened the bathroom door, looked inside. Stupidly—or, at least, she would think it was stupid when she looked back later—she checked the closet and behind the sofa, as if he might be hiding there, waiting to spring out and yell, 'Boo!' She felt suspended in time, waiting for reality to kick back in, for this strange, slow-motion sickness to pass.

A second later, she sprang back to life.

She flung the door open and pelted down the corridor towards the lift, her coat billowing behind her. She thumped the button, jabbed it, jabbed it again, stamped her foot and muttered, 'Come on, come on, fucking come *on,*' as she waited for the red numbers above the lift door to change. The numbers descended—9, 8, 7—with sadistic, agonising slowness. She was about to give up and take the

50

stairs when the lift arrived. The doors pinged open and revealed a middle-aged woman in a fur coat. The woman didn't appear to be in much of a hurry.

Kate reached into the lift, took the woman by the elbow and pulled her firmly but gently into the hallway, stepping past her and pressing the close button, the woman's mouth frozen in a circle of surprise as the doors slid shut.

If she thought jumping up and down would have made the lift descend faster, Kate would have done it. Scenarios from dark films and newspaper headlines played out in her imagination. Jack, in the hands of a paedophile. Jack, floating face down in the freezing Thames. But these images passed quickly. Terrifying as they were, these things were not her number one fear. She hadn't woken every night for the last week dreading strangers. Her fear wore a familiar face; utterly familiar. The face which had been on the pillow beside her most mornings for the past decade, since she had promised to love, honour and obey him forever, in a little church in a Boston chapel.

People broke promises all the time. The thought passed fleetingly through a deep seam in her brain, and was gone again, pressed out by the panic of Jack's disappearance.

Could Vernon really have found them so quickly? Could he really have figured out what she was planning and come looking for her? She didn't have time to consider the answer. The lift doors sprang open and she dashed out—straight into a Japanese businessman who was waiting with his luggage by the lift. Arms windmilling, he toppled backwards and Kate stumbled, losing a shoe, but she was soon on her feet and running towards the desk. The receptionists stared at her. Everyone in the lobby

51

stared at her. She didn't give a damn.

She slapped her palms on the desk. 'Call the police.'

'Madam, what's the matter?' The chief receptionist, with hair tied back in an efficient ponytail, spoke softly.

'My son. Have you seen my son?'

'What does he look like?' The receptionist seemed like she was used to dealing with hysterical guests and spoke to Kate as if she were reporting a dry-cleaning disaster. Kate wanted to reach across the desk and shake her. Her maternal instincts had taken complete control. Nobody, nothing else mattered.

The receptionist said, 'Can you describe . . .?'

Kate didn't allow her to finish. 'He was with one of your babysitters in the hotel room and now he's gone. They've gone.' Her voice trembled on the last word as she tried to stop herself from crying. She needed to be strong. And these idiots didn't get it. Another wave of panic crashed through her, nearly knocking her off her feet.

The receptionists exchanged worried looks. One of them said, 'I'll get the manager.'

The main receptionist said, 'What's your room number, madam?'

Kate shook her head. '502. My son has been kidnapped. For god's sake—just call the police!' She raised her voice with her last sentence, her words wobbling on the last few words.

The receptionist touched her forearm. 'Madam, how old is your son? What does he look like? We might have seen him.'

She took a deep breath, tried to calm herself. 'He's six. He's got light brown hair and he was wearing a

. . .' She paused. What had he been wearing? She pictured him sitting on the bed watching TV, already in his pyjamas. She'd made him get ready for bed after his bath because she hadn't liked the idea of the babysitter undressing him. And now, right now, what was the babysitter doing to him? Betraying him. Betraying both of them. How much had Vernon paid her to do it? Kate fumed inwardly. *Where was he?*

'He's wearing orange *Finding Nemo* pyjamas, with a big clown fish on the front, you know, from the movie . . .'

The receptionist nodded over Kate's shoulder. 'Like that boy over there?'

Kate swung round.

A small figure in orange pyjamas with an open denim jacket over the top of them was tumbling gleefully out of the lift, still clutching Billy the robot. He turned immediately back and pressed the button on the elevator's side panel as if to summon it, although it was already standing there open, with the babysitter waiting indulgently inside. He was laughing at something the babysitter was saying.

'Jack!'

Kate ran across the lobby. The moment she reached him she scooped him up and hugged him so tight he shouted, 'Ow!'

'Oh thank god . . .' She turned to the babysitter. 'What the hell were you doing? You stupid . . .'

'Mum, Ania let me go up and down in the elevator. It was brilliant. We went right up to the roof and got out and went in the roof garden and I saw all of London.'

Still squeezing him, Kate said, 'How many times have I told you not to go off with strangers?'

Jack wriggled. 'Ania's not a stranger. She's my friend. Can I get down?'

Kate put him down and turned back to the babysitter, who put her palms up.

'Hey, I'm sorry—he would not settle so I tell him we can go in the lift as special treat, if he go to sleep straight after. We had a deal.'

Kate narrowed her eyes. 'Get out of my sight.'

'I would never have taken him out of the hotel. This is not fair. I did not expect you back so soon. But if that's the way you feel, I am sorry.' Ania shrugged and stalked off towards the desk and the gawping receptionists.

Kate knew that in a while she'd feel hot with embarrassment. She would regret shouting at the babysitter, though she thought it was totally out of order to leave the hotel room with Jack for anything less than a fire alarm (she still shuddered at the mere thought of a fire alarm).

She'd feel pretty bad about dragging the woman with the fur coat out of the lift, too, and for knocking over that businessman. If she'd come out of the room two minutes later, Jack would probably have been in the lift already, instead of the fur-clad woman, and all this embarrassment could have been avoided. She'd have to apologise. Right now, though, she just felt relief. Her greatest fear hadn't come true. Not yet anyway.

She crouched down and stroked Jack's hair, thinking, *from now on, I'm not going to let you out of my sight.*

'So you had fun?' she said, forcing a smile.

'Yeah, it was awesome.' Spotting something behind her, he said, 'Hey Mum, look. It's that man.'

'What?'

54

'That man we met today.'

Kate turned her head and found Paul looking back at her from his position by the door.

*   *   *

Paul had walked into the hotel just as Kate emerged from the lift and collided with the unfortunate businessman. He watched with astonishment as Kate bowled past this guy, sprinted over to the reception desk and started gesticulating. He couldn't hear what she was saying, and could only see the back of her head. What the hell was wrong with her?

Seeing her knock people over and shout abuse at the hotel staff, he wondered whether she deserved the apology he'd planned to give her.

He almost walked straight out again.

But as he turned to go, he saw the kid, Jack, coming through the doors of the same elevator, just minutes later, with some other woman, and then Kate had turned around and the look on her face—the sheer relief—told him the whole story of what was going on here. She wasn't crazy. She was a mother. Paul didn't have kids of his own, but he remembered times when he was small and he'd wandered off, obliviously walking around the supermarket or garden centre while his parents searched for him frantically. He remembered their joy and anger when they found him—or sometimes him and Stephen, the two of them having disappeared together.

So instead of leaving, he hung around, waiting for Kate to notice him. He still wasn't sure about her. He didn't know anything about her. And although he understood how panicked she must have felt

55

when she came back to the hotel and found her son missing, he still thought she'd over-reacted a little.

Later, when he found out the whole truth, he would understand exactly why Kate had behaved as she did.

8

'Do you want to grab a coffee?' Paul nodded towards the hotel's lounge area.

Kate hesitated. 'I don't know. It's way past Jack's bedtime.'

But Jack was far too hyped up to want to go to bed now. Ania's strategy sucked, thought Kate. She herself wasn't tired anymore either. Her body was still flushed with adrenaline. Add that to the fact that they had only been in the UK for a few days and their body clocks were out of kilter, so it wasn't surprising that they felt wide awake.

'I really want to talk to you about what you said earlier,' Paul said.

Jack piped up: 'Mum, I want a hot chocolate.'

She sighed. 'Okay. But then it really is bedtime, no more messing around.'

'Do you like hot chocolate?' Jack asked Paul intently, as if something mightily important depended on the answer.

'It's one of my favourite things in the world—particularly when it comes with squirty cream, and those little marshmallows on top,' replied Paul, and Jack nodded his approval.

'Can I have marshmallows and squirty cream on mine tonight?' he asked Kate, who rolled her eyes but nodded.

Jack and Paul smiled at each other, and something about this little exchange squeezed Kate's heart. This was scarily close to an old fantasy of hers: of Stephen being the father of her child. Like the family she'd so often dreamt about. But then she shook the fantasy away. It was ridiculous. Reality check, Kate. Stephen's dead. Paul is his brother but he's a stranger. And Jack's father is an arsehole called Vernon.

She needed a coffee badly.

They sat on soft, cracked-leather sofas, Kate and Jack on one side, Paul on the other. Kate sipped her coffee. Paul was agitated, clearly wrestling with a series of questions, unsure of what to ask first. Kate could see that she and Paul were both alike in a lot of ways—used to dealing with computers, data, facts. The scientist and the computer geek—or rather, expert; Paul was too cool to be a classic computer geek, not to mention too good-looking. Put them in the lab or in front of a PC and they were like dolphins in water. Ask them to deal with awkward questions and they floundered and flapped.

She looked at Jack, who was trying to appear grown up as he blew on his hot chocolate.

'Nice?' Paul asked him, and he shrugged.

'No marshmallows,' he said gloomily, but he hadn't kicked up a fuss about it, as Kate had feared he might.

She was a good mother. She was sure of that, despite what Vernon said and what Ania the babysitter, and probably all the hotel staff, thought. They probably thought she was an over-protective psycho.

All of a sudden Jack started to waver, and swayed

57

on the sofa. Kate had to take his mug from him, and moments later he closed his eyes and leaned back, falling asleep.

'He's a sweet kid,' Paul said.

'I know. He's especially lovely when he's like this.'

'You don't mean that.'

She raised an eyebrow. 'You clearly don't have any children.'

'No. No nephews or nieces either.'

Kate stroked her sleeping son's hair. It was so soft, his scalp warm beneath her palm. She shuddered, remembering how terrified she'd been at the thought of losing him. She took a big gulp of coffee.

'Will you tell me about you and Stephen now?' asked Paul. 'Tell me what you remember. Like, how did you meet him? Can you remember that?'

Kate stared into her cup. 'I do. I remember meeting him, and I remember losing him. It's a lot of the stuff in between that's lost.'

'I'm sorry if I seemed irritable earlier, but I have to admit I don't get it. It doesn't sound possible that you could forget so much.'

'But it is!'

'Sorry . . .'

'No, it's okay. I know it makes me sound stupid. How could I have forgotten the most important summer of my life? It's amnesia, but I don't know what caused it.'

'Have you ever been to see anyone about it, to get help?'

She shook her head. 'For years, I haven't wanted to remember. It's too painful.'

'So you've repressed it?'

'I don't know. Maybe.' She sighed. 'I've been too busy with my work, with bringing up my son. Until

I came back to England and saw you, I'd done a pretty good job of forgetting there was even something I was supposed to remember. And now you come here, show me a letter—a literal blast from the past—and ask me to tell you everything. Do you know what it's like? It's like when you try to remember the details of a book you read years ago. You remember that you read it. You can still recall a few scenes and the general gist of what it was about, but the rest of it, the details, the ending— it's all gone, or at least buried so deep that you can't get to it.'

Kate rubbed at the little scar just by her hairline, putting her fingers under the long side fringe that she had grown to conceal it. Vernon had given her that injury—in one of his monumental rages he had thrown a hardback library book at her retreating back. She had turned round at just the wrong moment, and the book's sharp, plastic-covered corner had cut her forehead. It had got her three stitches and a very penitent husband—at least for a week or two.

Paul spoke softly. 'Kate, it's okay. I'm sorry. After my initial attempts to find out what the letter was all about, I forced myself to put it from my mind too—until today. You're the only person who can help me find out.'

'I know.' She finished her drink.

'Just tell me what you do remember.'

'Okay.' She touched the rim of her coffee cup. 'We're going to need more of these though.'

Kate checked that Jack was still fast asleep, and began.

'It was sixteen years ago. I sat my finals in May, and then—well, I didn't know what to do for the

59

summer. I remember being out with my friends, still wearing my gown, sitting down on the banks of the river drinking cheap wine. All the other students on my course were delighted to have finished. There was a lot of talk about the future, about jobs and travelling, but I knew I wanted to carry on studying. Virology was my passion, even then. I know it sounds like a weird thing to be passionate about, but there is a reason. I'm digressing though. The important thing is that after my exams, I wanted a rest. Somewhere to recharge my batteries.

'I remember going back to my Great Aunt's—I suppose I should explain that my parents had both died when I was little, of a rare virus called Watoto. It probably doesn't take a psychologist to work out why I ended up studying in that particular field . . .'

'I'm sorry . . .'

'My Aunt Lil brought me up, and after my finals I went back to her house in Bath. I remember sitting down one evening after dinner and telling her that I wished I could go away on holiday, but I didn't have any money, and she said, "Leonard is always looking for volunteers. Why not go and stay there?"'

'Who was Leonard?'

'Leonard Bainbridge was an old friend of the family. He was the top man at the CRU. Maybe Stephen told you about him?'

Paul shook his head. 'He told me very little about his work.'

'The CRU was the Cold Research Unit, a research centre that was set up by the government after the war. Its remit was to find a cure for the common cold, with the main aim of reducing the economic costs of the virus—caused by absence from work, mostly. It was based just outside Salisbury, on the

60

grounds of a former military hospital.'

'I remember Stephen going to live in Salisbury. But I thought he was working at that other microbiological research place—Porton Down. That's in Salisbury too, isn't it?'

'It's in the area, a few miles out of town on the other side. But the CRU was a completely separate establishment. I did some research and found out that it was true that the Unit was always looking for volunteers. They used to advertise in the local paper, promoting a stay at the Unit as a kind of quirky holiday for people who wanted to do their bit for Britain, like Butlin's with less singing and more sniffing.'

Paul grinned and Kate went on. 'So, they asked people to go and stay there for ten days to help them with their research. It was free, of course. They'd put you up, feed you, and the worst that could happen would be that you might be given a cold. Not even flu—just an ordinary cold.'

She smiled ruefully. 'I'd had plenty of colds—and worse—before. I could deal with it. It seemed the perfect solution—a place for me to relax and, because of my interest in viruses and health, I thought I might also be able to do some good by volunteering, and maybe even learn something. Aunt Lil reassured me that the countryside around Salisbury was a really nice place to go for a quiet holiday. You weren't allowed to talk to other people, apart from the staff, or your room-mate. But that was fine with me; after four years of university, I felt quite happy to not talk to anyone much for a while.'

Paul sipped his coffee and waited for a moment while Kate gathered her thoughts.

'I didn't really know Leonard that well, although I'd met him a few times at my parents' house when I was a little girl, and always liked him. But Aunt Lil phoned him at the Unit and said I wanted to go along as a volunteer. I was listening to her side of the call. It sounded like he was trying to put her off the idea, but she pressed him and he finally gave in. I went at the very beginning of June. It was a beautiful summer that year. Record-breaking heat.'

Jack murmured something in his sleep. He had Billy the robot cradled against his stomach—hardly the most cuddly of toys. Kate wondered how long it would be before Jack grew bored of the robot and moved onto the next must-have toy. Or perhaps he'd return his attention to the grubby teddy that went in and out of favour.

'So anyway,' she said, 'I packed my suitcase and took the train to Salisbury.'

'Which is where you met Stephen?'

'Yes. Whatever memories have deserted me, that one remains: the day I met your brother. And fell in love.'

9

Sixteen Years Ago

Kate Carling felt remarkably carefree, considering that she had just lugged a bag of textbooks on the train from Bath. Textbooks she suspected that, diligent as she was, she probably wouldn't get around to reading. She'd just finished her finals, and this trip was supposed to be a break from study.

But old habits die hard, and she'd be starting her post-graduate virology studies in October—there was no harm in bringing the books, just in case she was bored, was there? Her shirt was sticking to her back when she finally arrived at her destination late in the afternoon, and both her shoulders ached from carrying the heavy backpack of books—but she was happy in the knowledge that she didn't actually *have* to do any study; not unless she wanted to.

A friendly middle-aged man in a rusty old white minibus had picked her up from Salisbury train station and driven her through the centre of town, pointing out the soaring grey spire of the ancient Cathedral to their right—as if she could have missed it! Gradually the houses thinned out, and the spire became a tapering narrow spear behind them, until all of a sudden it seemed as if they were back in the countryside.

'Here we go,' said the man cheerfully, as he pulled up in front of a series of unprepossessing grey and green Nissan huts. 'Home sweet home! Let me give you a hand with your things. Lordy, what've you got in there? Bricks?'

'Textbooks. In case I get bored of reading trashy paperbacks and painting my toenails.'

The man laughed. He had a shiny bald pate and big yellow teeth, but nonetheless there was something very endearing about him. 'Well, you might need them. No late nights down the pub here. Let me show you to your quarters, madam. One of the doctors will be along in a bit to get you checked in and sorted out. I'm Geoffrey, by the way. Caretaker, gardener, chauffeur and general dogsbody. You'll see me and my colleague, Mr Sampson, wandering around looking like we don't know what we're doing. We're the ones without the white coats . . . Here we are now, room seventeen. It's not the Ritz, but you should be comfortable here.'

'It's fine. Thanks very much.'

Kate was pleased to see that her room was in the end hut, with a view over rolling hills dotted with meadow flowers. As soon as Geoffrey had gone she flung open the window, fanning her hot face with the folder of useful information that had been left on the desk for her. The air smelled of grass and warm earth. Two white butterflies flitted across her line of vision, and swallows were swooping high above her. She sighed with pleasure. OK, so maybe it would mar her enjoyment if she did catch a cold— but it was worth the risk. All her meals cooked for her, long solitary walks, and lots of sleep, unhindered by all-night, Pro-Plus-fuelled study binges? She was going to feel like a new woman by the end of the two weeks.

She turned back and surveyed the room: basic, whitewashed walls, twin beds, two desks, a small TV, transistor radio, bedside cabinets, and a door leading to a tiny bathroom. She hoped her room-mate would be nice. Someone awful would definitely put a damper on things, even more so than a streaming cold. Maybe she'd be lucky and get the room to herself. She unzipped her suitcase, pulled out a fresh t-shirt, removed her washbag and retrieved Buster, her childhood teddy.

Propping Buster up on the pillow of the bed nearest the window, she stripped off her sweaty shirt and flung it into a corner. Then she went into the bathroom, filled the basin with tepid water, and washed her face, neck and armpits with a flannel.

64

She towelled herself off, and was just walking back into the bedroom in her bra when, to her shock, the door opened and an extremely tall and attractive man in a white coat walked in, carrying a medical case and a clipboard.

Kate squealed and covered her breasts with her arms. He didn't look much older than her, which made it even more embarrassing. 'Don't you people knock? Is this what I've got to expect—no privacy at all for the next two weeks?'

'I'm really sorry,' said the man, blushing to the roots of his hair in a very un-doctorly manner. 'I did knock, actually. You mustn't have heard me.'

'Excuse me a moment,' she said, trying to sound dignified as she grabbed her clean t-shirt and retreated back into the bathroom.

When she re-emerged, the man had put his bag on one of the desks. He'd obviously regained his composure too, because he was now grinning at her, in a distinctly cheeky way.

'Let's start again, shall we? I'm Dr Wilson. I just need to take a few details from you, and a blood sample, if that's OK.'

'Kate Carling—although I'm guessing you know that already,' said Kate, unable to prevent herself grinning back at him. He just had one of those faces which made her want to smile: a lovely curved mouth, great big brown eyes, and the sort of floppy hair which she had adored in Robbie Williams in her teenage years. She became aware that they were staring at each other, holding the gaze for longer than was strictly necessary.

Dr Wilson cleared his throat, and took a ballpoint pen out of the breast pocket of his lab coat. Kate was pleased to notice that he didn't have a whole row of pens, like most of her fellow biochemists at Oxford had. She glanced down at his feet, and was even more relieved to see trendy Adidas trainers, rather than the green towelling socks and open-toed sandals which she was beginning to fear might be the actual uniform for the profession.

'Now, if we could just go through this basic health questionnaire . . . Do sit down.' He pointed towards the edge of the bed, as he turned the chair at the desk around to face her. 'Have you ever had any of the following: Mumps? Measles? Influenza? Chicken pox? Pneumonia?'

'No, no, yes, yes, no,' said Kate obediently, looking at Dr Wilson's slim hands as he ticked boxes. The list went on and on, until Kate found herself tuning out and answering automatically, whilst unable to take her eyes off him.

'Any other illnesses so far not mentioned?'

Kate tuned back in. 'Oh. Yes. When I was twelve, I had the Watoto Virus.'

Dr Wilson sat up. 'Really? Good grief. That's rare. I've never met anybody else who's had that. You were lucky to survive.'

'I know. Apparently it was touch and go for a while. We were living in Africa at the time. My parents both died from it. My sister was the only one who didn't contract it.'

'It's an extremely nasty one, isn't it?'

Kate managed not to allow her voice to betray the pain she felt whenever she talked about the virus. 'Yes—the name comes from the Swahili word for children because the first victims were at a school near the River Nile in Kenya.

'We were in Tanzania. There had been a few outbreaks close to the Nile over the last fifty years:

66

Tanzania, Uganda, Egypt, and Rwanda, I think. My parents had taken me and my sister out of school for a year while they were working in a village for an international aid organisation. We just happened to be there when an epidemic broke out. It killed dozens of people in the village. It was really bad timing.'

Stephen had stopped writing notes. He jiggled his biro between his teeth and regarded her with sympathy and something akin to awe.

'I've read about it. It's like Ebola, only with airborne transmission?'

Kate shuddered, recalling the symptoms she'd watched her parents suffer, writhing on their camp beds in the hut, right up to the point of haemorrhage.

'Flu-like to start with, fever, coughing, sneezing— then the bloody vomiting and diarrhoea. Luckily for me, the aid agency airlifted my sister and me across the border to a hospital in Nairobi. Miranda was quarantined and never contracted it, and I managed to survive after a good few weeks on a drip. It's got an eighty per cent fatality rate, so we were both incredibly lucky.'

Stephen exhaled loudly. 'You're an optimist, aren't you? I would say that you were incredibly *un*lucky to have got it in the first place.'

'Wrong time, wrong place, I suppose. Lucky that I didn't actually watch them die . . .' Her voice cracked and tailed off, and she looked away, embarrassed.

'I'm really sorry about your parents,' he said.

'Thanks, Doctor,' she replied awkwardly.

'Please, call me Stephen.'

'Really?' Kate was genuinely surprised. That seemed very informal. Perhaps . . . Oh no, don't be silly, she told herself. He couldn't possibly fancy her this immediately, could he? She didn't believe in love at first sight . . . but he was definitely having a very strange effect on her.

Dr Wilson—*Stephen*, thought Kate, trying out his name in her head and liking the way it felt—cleared his throat. 'Well—yes—Stephen's fine . . . although perhaps not when there are other people around . . . One more question, by the way, I forgot to ask earlier: marital status?'

He met her eyes again, slowly, and Kate's heart started hammering so hard that she was glad she was already sitting on the edge of the bed. She couldn't help glancing behind her at its crisp white pillowcase and hospital waffle-weave blanket, and then blushed, in case he realised she was imagining them rolling around on it.

'Single,' she said firmly. 'Definitely . . . single.'

* * *

They chatted a little more about Kate's illness, and Stephen visibly relaxed, becoming more animated and lively. He was gorgeous, Kate thought. Did he talk to all the young, attractive-ish women like this, or was it just her?

Somehow she knew it was just her.

'Right, let's get your blood sample, so we can analyse it this afternoon.'

He tied a length of black rubber tubing above her left elbow, gently holding her forearm and peering at the veins that sprang up thick and red. At his touch Kate's skin broke out in goosepimples.

'Now, this'll just be a little prick—uh, I mean, a small scratch.' Kate swallowed hard and looked over his shoulder, in order to stop a smirk escaping. His hands were shaking very slightly, but nonetheless Kate barely felt a thing as he slid the needle into her vein. They both watched in silence as the syringe filled with viscous dark blood.

'All done,' he said, expertly removing the needle, sealing the tube and labelling it, then sticking a tiny round plaster on the soft skin inside Kate's elbow. 'Since you aren't yet in quarantine, you can go to the dining room for your supper at six. I think most of the others here are already quarantined, so you might be on your own. If you could read the instructions in that folder, that'll explain the rules about contact with the other patients, and what you are and aren't allowed to do if and when we give you a cold.'

'If?'

'Yes—we don't give a cold to everyone who comes here; you might be part of a control group. Oh, your room-mate should be along this afternoon too. You've got a lady called . . .' He consulted his clipboard, '. . . Mrs Harrington. Georgina Harrington. She's in her fifties so don't go having any wild parties and keeping her up all night, will you?'

Any disappointment that Kate might have felt about having a room-mate so much older than her was instantly diminished by the way he was smiling.

'No wild parties?' she queried, straight-faced. 'But what on earth will I do to stop myself getting bored while I'm here?' He slowly reached out and touched the back of her hand with his forefinger.

'I can promise you won't get bored. At least not on my shifts, anyway.'

After he'd gone, Kate lay back on her bed replaying the entire meeting in her mind, a huge smile spread over her face. She couldn't believe what he'd said to her—nor what she'd said to him. It wasn't at all like her to be so forward and flirty. There was just something about Stephen Wilson and his blond floppy hair and the way he looked at her with those big brown eyes . . .

She changed her mind about going for a walk, and retreated into the bathroom again, this time to pluck her bikini line and shave her legs. She hadn't expected she'd need to do this—but she now had the distinct feeling it might be necessary. Pity she'd have to share with this Georgina woman. Although maybe Stephen had his own room where they could . . .

. . . No, stop it, Kate told herself. He's the doctor! Probably nothing's going to happen.

But somehow she knew that it would. 'No, I don't think I am going to be at all bored,' she said out loud.

10

The effort of telling the story had taken its toll on her. Kate tried to bite down on her yawn but it escaped, and then Paul yawned too, and they looked at each other and laughed.

'I think I need my bed,' she said.

'Me too.'

As they stood up Paul turned to put his jacket on,

and when he turned back he caught her eye. Something passed between them. Or was she imagining it? The tiredness that made her body feel strange, the state of the high emotion she was in, the mention of bed, and the undeniable fact that this man looked almost exactly like Stephen—it was a dangerous mix. She averted her eyes and concentrated on lifting Jack—god, he was getting heavy—hoping she hadn't flushed pink the way she knew she did, and, if she had, hoping Paul hadn't noticed.

When she looked more closely at him, she could tell they hadn't been absolutely identical. She was sure that Paul was slightly taller and bulkier, and he had a tiny chip at the side of his front tooth ... although what did their similarities or differences matter anyway? The point was, he wasn't Stephen. It would feel like a betrayal to get involved with his brother—wouldn't it? Not that Paul would be interested in her, she felt sure. He would undoubtedly see it as a betrayal too. He could be married himself, for all she knew. Although he hadn't mentioned it, and he wasn't wearing a ring ... She wanted to slap herself. *Kate, what the hell are you thinking? This is the last thing you need now.*

'Let's meet here tomorrow morning,' Paul said. 'Nine o'clock?'

'Make it nine-thirty.'

'Okay.'

He hovered. What was he doing? She had this awful feeling he was trying to decide whether to kiss her goodnight.

'Night, Paul,' she said.

'Okay. Night.'

She watched him walk across the lobby. At the

revolving doors he looked back at her and nodded. A little shiver went through her.

*　　　*　　　*

After putting Jack to bed—he hadn't stirred all the way from the lounge to the room; again, she had paranoid thoughts about being a bad mother because he hadn't cleaned his teeth or washed his face—Kate lay down and tried to join him in sleep. But her brain was too active and her heart refused to slow down. She got up, fetched herself a glass of water and went out onto the balcony. Her room had a view of the river, the lights of the South Bank shimmering orange and lemon on the water. Voices floated up to her: a man shouting, a woman laughing. A plane drifted in the space between clouds.

Her life was in a mess. Her marriage was over, she had no home or job, and probably no friends any more. The only people she had were Aunt Lil, who barely recognised her, and her sister Miranda and her family.

When she'd boarded the plane in Boston she'd experienced the intoxicating thrill of new-found freedom, a euphoria that had made her want to stand up in her seat and scream with joy. But like a prisoner who busts out of jail after years inside, the euphoria didn't last long. The outside world was a scary place.

But even though a primitive part of her—the part that longed for safety and comfort—wanted to flee back to the States, she knew she had done the right thing. She would get through this period.

If Vernon doesn't find you, an internal voice

72

whispered.

No, he wouldn't find her. And if he did, what could he do?

He'll say you've kidnapped your own son. He's always threatened that he'd hunt you down if you ever tried to take him away. He'll take Jack back. You'll lose him.

No! That couldn't happen. She had brought Jack to England for his own good. It was the right thing to do. And she was English—the law would protect her here, wouldn't it? They wouldn't let Vernon take her son away from her, would they?

Kate thought back to how powerful her initial attraction to Vernon had been, and how unbelievable it seemed to her now that she could ever have felt that way about him.

He had never been a particularly good-looking man, but he was possessed of that magical aphrodisiacal quality, charisma—and he'd had it in spades. The first time she saw him, he'd been giving a talk at a literary festival in Boston, on Gertrude Stein's life and work. Kate had gone along on a whim, feeling that she needed to exercise the non-scientific synapses of her brain before they withered and died completely. Gertrude Stein and Alice B. Toklas had always fascinated her. She'd turned up at the library where the free talk was taking place, and sat down in the middle of a long curved row at the front. Vernon had strode out before his meagre audience with the demeanour of a man taking the stage at Madison Square Gardens, rather than giving a lecture to half a dozen people in a library. What a prat, Kate had thought—until he began to speak. He was so passionate, so smart and articulate, and he knew his subject so well, that

73

by the end of the talk, all the women present had fallen for him. He knew it, too—he made lingering eye-contact with each one, and when he asked, 'Any questions?' there was a glint in his eye that made every woman there want to cry, 'Will you go on a date with me?'

But it was Kate he'd chosen that day, breaking away from the two breathless sophomores who were quizzing him afterwards, and introducing himself to her by the 'Just Returned' shelves.

'I love your accent,' he'd said. 'Can I buy you dinner?'

The months that followed had felt to Kate like skydiving—a constant teetering on the edge of new experiences, a rush of adrenaline and the thrill of the new. Vernon introduced her to a world of culture she'd never experienced (or been able to afford) before: the ballet, the opera, art-house movies, poetry cafes. He gave her a reading list as long as her arm, horrified that she'd never read the Beat Poets, and declaimed extracts of *On The Road* to her as they lay in his double bed, his arm hooked casually around her neck, a joint in his free hand.

However, despite her infatuation, there were elements of his personality with which she was less than enamoured right from the beginning: the way he frequently mocked his colleagues and students, mercilessly picking on their weaknesses. Kate laughed at first, because he was funny in his cruelty, but after a while she tried to change the subject when he would gossip and slander. They had occasional bust-ups, great screaming painful rows in which he called her boring and straight and she walked out and said they were finished. But he always came after her, wooing her back into his life

74

and bed with his words, tender again. It was unlike any other relationship she'd ever had, and the volatility of it excited her.

Things started to go downhill too soon, though, when Vernon failed to be appointed for the professorship he'd thought was in the bag. They'd been married a year by then, Jack was a new baby, and money was tight. It didn't help that they were living in a tiny one-bed apartment on campus. Unfortunately, the timing roughly coincided with Kate being awarded her own PhD, and Vernon could barely bring himself to congratulate her. On the day of her graduation ceremony he made an excuse about having a migraine, and she later discovered he'd been seen in a bar with one of the prettier of his freshman students.

She was distracted from her unwelcome memories by the sight of a mosquito flitting about near the window. She immediately thought of her work instead—the many long hours staring into an electron microscope, studying the West Nile Virus and others like it. Viruses are so tiny that they can only be seen with a modern electron microscope. So tiny that hundreds of thousands would fit on the size of a pin. Kate and her fellow researchers spent their lives absorbed in this miniature world.

If only all her problems were as small—not huge like all this stuff with Stephen and Paul. She hadn't come back to England to chase ghosts. Honestly, she hadn't even thought about Stephen or the Cold Unit on the way back here—it had been the last thing on her mind. As she'd told Paul, she hadn't thought about it for years.

But now she'd met Paul and read the letter, and a wound she'd thought long-healed had been torn open again. Feelings she thought were dead had proven themselves well and truly alive—and kicking.

Tonight, after Paul left, she had toyed with the idea of checking out at dawn and moving to another hotel. She didn't need this complication. She had to find a school for Jack, a new job for herself. She had to get settled as soon as she could, for Jack's sake, and so that Vernon wouldn't be able to accuse her of being some kind of irresponsible vagrant.

But would she be able to move on with her life without finding out the answers to all of these questions? She decided that she would spend another day, maybe two, with Paul, trying to figure out what had really happened. She owed Stephen that much. After that, even if they hadn't unearthed the truth, she would have to put it aside and try to settle down.

What Kate didn't know was that within forty-eight hours she would be on the run for her life; and that settling down wouldn't be an option.

11

Paul was waiting in the reception area when Kate emerged from the lift the next morning, Jack close by her side. He stood up to meet her, looking as tired as she felt, but also relieved. Perhaps he'd been worried that she might have done a disappearing act. She decided against telling him how close she'd been to doing just that. She also wouldn't tell him how relieved *she* felt, because getting dressed she'd wondered if he would actually be there. What if he'd had a change of heart? She could imagine him sitting at home, laughing to himself, thinking how crazy he was to get involved with this looney tunes chick with the dodgy memory.

Even though he looked tired, he also looked as if he'd made a bit of an effort before coming out. His hair had been washed and was fashionably spiked, though it had gone a little flat on one side, and he seemed to be wearing aftershave. Maybe a touch too much. 'What is it?' he said, looking alarmed. 'Have I got something on my face?'

Kate realised she had been staring rather intently at Paul so she laughed and shook her head.

'I've brought my laptop so we can . . .' He stopped himself, realising he'd forgotten something. 'Morning Jack,' he said.

'Hello. Um.' He looked to his mum for help.

Paul laughed. 'Don't worry, mate, I couldn't remember names when I was your age either.'

Jack looked puzzled. 'My name's Jack, not mate. You smell funny.'

'Jack!' Kate exclaimed. 'Sorry about that. You don't smell funny. You smell . . . nice.'

Paul's face twisted with awkwardness as he struggled to find a response. He was saved by Jack saying, 'Mummy, what are we having for breakfast? I'm hungry.'

'How about going to Starbucks?' Paul asked. He added, 'They have wi-fi there.'

'They might have wi-fi, but I'm not sure if you can get a very healthy breakfast there,' Kate said. But now Jack wanted to go to Starbucks. She gave in. McDonald's yesterday, now this. When this was over she was going to feed Jack nothing but organic fruit and vegetables for a month.

Paul said, 'I called my parents last night. I just wanted to double check that they hadn't received

77

any letters from Stephen before he died, just in case he wrote to them too. They hadn't, and then I felt bad for ringing and stirring things up, making them think about him.'

Kate touched his arm. 'I imagine they think about him every day anyway.'

'Yeah. I guess you're right.'

'They say you never get over the loss of a child.' She had to raise her voice slightly to be heard over the din of milk being frothed in big stainless steel jugs.

Paul frowned. 'I just wish that sometimes they'd realise that even though they lost one child, they still have another.'

Kate waited for him to continue, but at that moment they reached the head of the queue, and the barista took their order. She looked at his profile as he paid for them all, and felt that familiar tightness in her throat. *Don't* cry, she fiercely told herself.

They found a table at the back of the coffee shop and sat down. Kate was remonstrating with Jack—'No, you can't have a cake for breakfast, Jack'—even though the pressure in her throat and behind her eyes had increased so much that she could barely speak. She had to get up again immediately.

'I just need to go to the loo. Jack, be a good boy.'

In the toilet, Kate put her face in her hands and let the tears come. After a few moments she blew her nose and wiped her eyes, laughing at herself as she looked at the creature in the mirror with the mascara streaks. She quickly washed her face in the sink. She doubted Paul would notice the sudden absence of mascara, unless he was an unusually observant man. What if he knew she'd been crying and asked why? What would she tell him? She wasn't

78

even sure she knew.

She fixed a smile in place and came out of the bathroom—but when she looked in their direction, the table was empty, and her heart jumped into her throat.

'Hey, Mummy!'

They had just moved to a different table, Jack and Paul with Billy the robot perched on the chair between them. She crossed the room on rubber legs. Paul had his laptop open. He said, 'Jack wanted to sit by the window. Are you okay? You look pale.'

'I'm fine.' She quickly composed herself, glancing at the newspaper that lay between them, finding herself hooked by the headline. The lead story was about a 'controversial' scientist who'd been found murdered in his lab. Animal rights extremists were being blamed, although they denied involvement. There was a heartbreaking picture of the doctor with his family. The story sent a shiver through Kate's bones, and she folded the paper and dropped it onto an empty chair. 'So what are you doing?' she asked Paul.

He swivelled the laptop so she could see the screen, then brought up Google and typed 'cold research unit Salisbury'. He scanned through the list of results. 'These are sites telling the history of the Unit. Maybe there's something on there that could help us.'

'Let's have a look,' Kate said, skim-reading the page. There was a black and white photo of part of the Unit, taken from a distance. The blocky, utilitarian buildings and the green spaces beyond. A chill made the hairs on her arms stand on end. She read *The Unit burned down without having found a cure for the common cold*. All those years of research with no success. Had it all been a waste of time? The possibility made her feel intensely sad, especially for Leonard and Stephen.

'This just gives the official history of the place, and a very abridged version at that,' she said.

He went back to the search engine page and clicked on a few other results. There was very little information available.

'The internet isn't going to be much help to us,' he sighed. 'Which is a shame. I get so used to finding everything I want on Google.'

Kate drummed her fingers on the table. Next to her, Jack was happily drawing a picture of Billy standing on an alien planet, firing a laser beam at a many-tentacled alien. She could sense Paul's growing frustration and wished so badly that she could help him.

'Who else would know what Stephen might have been talking about? Is there anyone else that you might have talked to about it? Friends? Family?'

'Apart from my sister Miranda, Aunt Lil's my only family, and she wouldn't be able to help even if I'd told her everything. She's got dementia. She barely recognises me now.'

She thought back to her frustrating visit to the nursing home two days before. It had been one of the most depressing experiences of her life. The lively, caring woman who'd looked after her and Miranda all those years after her parents died, was completely gone, replaced by a paper-skinned complaining creature with a body and mind that didn't work properly any more.

'Oh, that's terrible, I'm so sorry. It happened to my gran. It's so awful to lose someone like that, when they're still alive. It's like you can't even grieve for them.'

Tears filled Kate's eyes again. 'Yes, that's exactly how I feel. And she didn't even know who Jack was—she kept calling him Ernest, who was her little brother.'

Paul was looking at her with such sympathy that she had to look away. 'So, no, we wouldn't get anywhere with Lil, and I know that I didn't talk to Miranda about any of it. We aren't that close, and anyway she was away at Uni in Edinburgh at the time.'

'You've told me about when you first went to the Unit. Tell me what happened on your second visit, after the fire? What do you remember?'

She glanced at Jack. He was still engrossed in his drawing.

'I remember the night of the fire itself.' She told Paul about the rush from the building, passing out and waking up outside. And then seeing Stephen's body being carried out. After that, she said, she must have passed out, although she had this strange, vague recollection of a doctor, a guy in a white coat—or that might have been mixed up with her next memory: waking up in hospital.

'I asked them how long I'd been in hospital, and they told me three weeks. I couldn't believe it. Three weeks—lost. Apparently, I had woken up a few times, but I couldn't remember it at all. That was one of the first things they asked me: what do you remember?

'At first, I couldn't remember anything. I had no idea what had happened to me. They told me amnesia was common among people who've suffered a trauma, without telling me what the trauma actually was. I heard the doctors and nurses whispering about me. They told me I needed to rest and get strong before I could leave. So I let them look after me.'

She stared through the window at the London street. A couple walked by, hand-in-hand. A homeless man begged for change across the road. Red buses and black cabs. After sixteen years in Boston it all seemed so strange.

'It took me a couple of days to remember the fire and Stephen. I think I started screaming when I remembered. All the nurses came running and, well, I guess I was sedated. When I woke up again there was this man who came and sat by my bed and talked to me about how I felt. I assumed he was a therapist. He told me I had missed the funeral. He kept asking me what else I could remember. I told him that I could remember going into the Unit, and then the fire. That was it. You know, thinking about it now, I got the impression he seemed relieved when I told him that.'

Paul was shaking his head. Now he was the one who looked as if he was going to cry.

'Are you OK?' Kate asked.

'Sorry. You just reminded me of the funeral—it was so horrible, knowing that Stephen was in that coffin, so badly burned that my folks couldn't even identify him. It had to be done by his dental records . . .'

Kate bit her lip. When would she stop feeling so over-emotional?

'Go on,' said Paul. 'I'm fine now.'

They smiled watery smiles at each other.

'I stayed in the hospital for another three weeks after that. It seems like a dream now. White walls, white sheets, people in white coats like angels coming to see me and talk to me in quiet voices. They brought me books and puzzles to do. No TV or radio. Great food. But I don't remember what, if anything, was physically wrong with me. I wasn't in plaster, or in pain. I can't imagine why I needed to stay there for so long.'

'So it wasn't a normal NHS hospital?'

'No. They said it was a private clinic. Actually, no one told me very much at all. Whenever I asked questions I'd be told that I needn't worry, that I was in safe hands. And the thing was, I was so tired that I didn't have the energy to ask too many questions. There were other patients there. I would see them sometimes if I got up to go for a walk around, although I was always escorted and never got the chance to talk to anybody else. I heard a woman crying in the night a few times. Perhaps the other patients heard me crying in the night. Though most of the time I felt alright.'

'Did they have you on drugs?'

'I was given a ton of pills every day. I was told they would help me get better quicker, and help my memory come back.'

'And what about your aunt? Did she visit you?'

'I asked to see her and they said it was difficult. Apparently, according to them, she'd been to visit me when I was first brought in, which I obviously had no recollection of. Eventually, after I kept asking, they let her visit me. She seemed uneasy. She told me she'd asked for me to be transferred to the local hospital, but that the doctors had told her I was better off here, in the private clinic. Aunt Lil was of the generation that trusted doctors one hundred per cent, so she didn't argue. And she said that Leonard himself had phoned her and reassured her I was in good hands.'

Another memory came to her. 'Leonard came to see me towards the end of my stay in the hospital.'

'What was his surname?'

'Bainbridge.'

Paul tapped the name into the search engine and found a page about Leonard Bainbridge. 'An obituary. He died two years ago. Cancer. There's a paragraph here about the CRU but it's just the usual brief history stuff. It says he left behind a wife, Jean, but had no children. So what happened when this Bainbridge guy came to see you?'

Kate felt sad for the loss of the avuncular, warm-hearted man she'd only met a handful of times, but who had made a deep impression on her. She stared at the computer screen until the words blurred together, recalling the scene when Leonard had come to visit.

12

Sixteen Years Ago

Leonard perched on a hard chair beside her bed, his smile adding warmth to the room. He was a distinguished-looking man in a tweed suit, with sharp blue eyes, a head full of white hair and a neatly trimmed white beard.

Now that he sat here beside her she could remember his visits to her parents when they lived in the big house on the South Downs, before they moved to Africa. Kate had been eight or nine. When Kate's father heard that Leonard was coming to see

84

them he became quite agitated, nipping into Lewes in the car to buy proper coffee and fresh bread. He sent Kate into the garden to choose flowers. Kate protested—she would rather see flowers in the ground than in a vase—but her father insisted. She doubted if this old bloke, this Leonard, whoever he was, would even notice, so she was surprised when the third thing he commented on, after Kate's prettiness and the well-being of her parents, was the vase of flowers sitting on the mantel and how beautiful they were.

'Though I've always thought flowers might be happier in the earth. Don't you agree, Kate?' he said.

It was as if he'd read her mind, and from that moment she found him fascinating. She was so glad that Miranda had gone to play at a friend's that day—she could do without any competition from her cute little sister. Leonard and her father went into the garden to talk, and she shadowed them, trying to eavesdrop. When her Dad turned and told her to run along, Leonard beckoned her closer and produced a chocolate bar, a Curly-Wurly, from his jacket pocket. She retreated to the house where she shared it with Charlie, their black labrador.

Lying in her bed in the clinic, she said, 'You gave me chocolate.'

'Did I?'

'Yes. I think you were trying to get rid of me.'

He laughed and patted her hand where it lay on the edge of the mattress. 'I expect I was trying to make you like me.'

'It worked. I always looked forward to your visits after that. Not because of the chocolate,' she said hurriedly. 'I was intrigued by you. You seemed like

85

the grandfather I always wanted. Kind, and wise.'

Something about the way he reacted to that made her think she'd said the wrong thing, and she blushed. He appeared troubled, but then the benign smile returned and he reached into his inner pocket and brought out a brown envelope. He handed it to her.

She studied it warily. 'What is it?'

'Your exam results.'

'Oh my God. I totally forgot about this. How could it have just slipped my mind? I feel like I'm *losing* my mind.'

He patted her hand. 'Having problems with your memory, are you? Hmm, well, you've been through a lot, Kate. I'm not surprised things are . . . hazy.'

Kate ran a finger along the edge of the envelope. 'I'm frightened.'

'Don't be. There's no need.'

'I haven't thought about Oxford or my exams for months, but when you gave me this I suddenly realised something: that I want this degree. I really need it.'

He smiled at her again. 'Open the envelope, Kate.'

Her hands shook as she slid a fingernail beneath the flap and tore open the envelope. She removed the sheet of paper that she'd imagined herself receiving so many times, back in the past, in her old life. She could hardly bear to look.

'Well?' he said. 'Are you happy?'

'A First. Bloody hell—sorry—I got a First.' She gazed in wonder at the sheet of paper.

'A Congratulatory First. Yes, I knew already. You're a brilliant young woman, Kate.'

Tears crept down her cheeks and splashed on the backs of her hands. She was laughing and crying at the same time. A First! With a distinction! She wanted to call everyone she knew to yell the news down the phone, to dance in the streets and scream 'Look what I did' to all those snobs she'd encountered at Oxford, all those snooty men who thought women couldn't be scientists, that Marie Curie had been the exception to the rule.

Leonard grinned, and forgetting herself, Kate leaned over and hugged him.

'Sorry,' she said, 'I've made your shoulder wet.'

'I assume those are tears of happiness.'

'Yes. *Yes.*' But then she thought, If only Stephen was here to share my joy, and her tears became ones of sadness. Leonard offered her a handkerchief, so she dried her eyes, and he waved at her to keep it. Sniffing and trying to compose herself, she looked at Leonard and had this overwhelming urge to ask him something—but when she opened her mouth, the question had vanished. She knew there was something she needed to ask him, not just about the fire and Stephen, or the Unit closing down, but something that had happened before, while she was staying at the Unit. If only she could drag those memories from her useless brain.

Before she could get upset about it, Leonard said, 'I have something very important to talk to you about, Kate. It makes me very proud to see that distinction in virology. And I know how proud your father would be. Viruses are one of mankind's greatest enemies, and to be involved in their study, in the fight to understand them and find ways to stop those harmful strains, well, I've always believed that this is one of the most important scientific fields. One of the most exciting too. And things have moved on so much since I was young.' He saw her attention

87

waver and said quickly, 'Don't worry, I'm not going to tell you all about what it was like when I was a lad.'

'I am interested . . .'

'It's okay. I don't want to talk about me right now. This is about you and your future. Kate, you could have a brilliant future in this battle against viruses. You could do a lot of good. An awful lot of good. The field needs people like you, with brains and vitality. And you have that something extra, don't you? A personal connection. Because of what happened to your parents. Dear Derek and Francesca.'

She waited for him to go on, wondering if perhaps he was about to shed a tear. But he quickly regained his composure.

'I do hope you won't think me presumptuous, but as soon as I heard your results, I got on the phone to an old friend of mine at Harvard University. Professor James Scott. The man's a genius, and Dean of the Immunology and Infectious Diseases faculty. I told him all about you, Kate, and he wants to meet you. He'd like to see if you'd be interested in a position as a researcher in the department.'

'Oh my God. But what about my MSc at Oxford? I'm supposed to be starting that in October.'

'Wouldn't you rather go to Harvard?'

'Yes, of course, but . . .'

'Kate, don't worry. I'll sort it all out for you. And, in fact, again, I hope you won't think I've been presumptuous, but I've already booked you onto a flight to Boston. I'm told you'll be fit enough to get out of here next week.'

He put another envelope on her bed, this one containing an air ticket.

'I don't expect it's as nice as Daddy's car. Daddy's car's really big and fast, isn't it?'

That's to make up for his small penis, she thought. 'Yes, it is.'

'Mummy, is Paul your boyfriend?'

She couldn't see herself in any mirrors, but she was certain her cheeks had turned pink. 'No, of course he isn't. He's just my friend.'

'Your new friend. Like Billy's my new friend.'

'Yes, sweetheart. Just like that.'

* * *

Her 'new friend' was waiting in the lobby. He picked up both of Kate's suitcases and strolled off with them towards his car, which was in the hotel car park. Kate noted, with another accompanying tingle, that Paul had surprisingly muscular arms. Jack trotted along behind. 'Mummy, can we stop on the highway for a KFC?'

'No.'

'Taco Bell?'

'They don't have Taco Bell in England.'

'How about a Subway?' Paul asked.

Jack screwed up his face and stuck his tongue out. 'Eww. I hate Subway.'

Paul said, 'Right, you've asked for it. We'll stop at Little Chef.'

'Alright.'

Paul and Kate exchanged a smile, and Jack looked up at them. 'Paul, my mum said you're not her boyfriend, just her friend. But she's married to my dad, so you couldn't be her boyfriend anyway, could you? Daddy wouldn't like that.'

Kate groaned. 'Ja-ack.'

She couldn't see Paul's face to ascertain whether he was amused or horrified by the idea. She knew it was stupid, but she would have been crushed if she'd seen a look of horror. And besides, Jack was dead right. Daddy wouldn't like that at all.

*   *   *

A minute after they left the car park, John Sampson drove in.

14

'How can I help you, sir?'

Sampson didn't think of his police ID as fake. It *wasn't* fake—it had been removed from the still-warm body of a detective inspector and modified later so it showed Sampson's picture. It always came in handy in situations like this. Real criminals, or people who often had dealings with the law, were usually unimpressed and uncooperative. But flash a police ID at an ordinary member of the public, and act in the right, superior way, and they would fall over themselves to help you. It was easy.

He held up the ID and said, 'Who's in charge here?'

There were two receptionists behind the desk, a brunette woman and a man who Sampson was pretty sure was homosexual. He could sense it in the same way someone with a phobia of cats could sense a feline presence. He bristled as the man leaned over and said, in a poofy voice that made Sampson grit his teeth, 'The manager's not here at the moment,

92

sir. Perhaps we can help?'

Sampson concentrated on the woman, putting a picture down on the desk in front of her. 'I believe this woman is staying with you.'

The receptionists gave each other a knowing look. Sampson said, 'Well?'

The woman said, 'She looks a lot younger in this picture, but she was staying here. She checked out this morning.'

'Was she due to check out today?'

'I'm not sure. Let me check.'

The woman knew Kate's name, even though they must have hundreds of guests come and go every day. Interesting, thought Sampson.

She brought up Kate's name on the computer screen beside her and said, 'She was supposed to be here for another week, though there's a note here to say her stay was open-ended.'

It was amazing how much confidential information people would give you if they thought you were a police official. It was the human need to gossip taken to a new level. Only fear of losing their jobs made people cautious. But if they felt they had to give the information away—or had an excuse to do so—they would squeal like piglets in a slaughterhouse.

'Why did you give each other a knowing look when I showed you her photo?'

The guy couldn't wait to tell him. 'She had a bit of an altercation last night with one of our babysitters.' He told him about the scene the previous evening.

'So, she and the child checked out this morning?'

'Yes, and the guy they were with.'

Sampson narrowed his eyes. This fucking homo was giving him the creeps. 'A guy? Can you describe him?'

'Um, he had really nice eyes. Late thirties, maybe. I wouldn't make a very good witness, would I, officer?'

The woman said, 'Are they in trouble?'

Sampson counted to three under his breath and said, 'Maybe.'

The receptionists looked at each other. This was exciting.

'Do you have CCTV here?'

The homo nodded. 'I could show you if you like.'

Sampson blanched. He nodded at the woman. 'No, you show me.'

'Okay.' She turned towards her colleague. 'Can you look after things down here, Damien?'

'I'm sure I'll manage.'

Sampson concentrated on the receptionist's butt as she led him towards the security office. She had a nice arse. Very womanly. Her hair was tied back in a short ponytail that exposed the back of her neck. A good spot to bite.

'What's your name?' he asked.

'Michelle.'

'You're being very helpful, Michelle. I won't forget you.'

She touched her hair. 'It's no problem.' She lowered her voice and cast her eyes left then right, as if checking that no-one was eavesdropping. 'To tell you the truth, I thought there was something funny about Ms Maddox, even before the scene with the babysitter.'

'Really?'

'Yes. She seemed jittery, like she was afraid of something.'

She was desperate to know why he was after Kate. She'd regret finding out, though, because then he'd have to kill her.

When he had dropped off the virus and hard disk the night before, Sampson had been given the picture of Kate. She looked a bit pale and washed-out in the photo—it didn't do her justice. Didn't show her true extraordinary beauty. The picture was sixteen years old, taken when both Kate and he had been at the CRU.

'It might take us a few days to get a more up-to-date picture,' Gaunt had said. 'Her name is Kate Maddox now.'

'I thought I'd never see her again,' said Sampson, gazing at the picture. Kate Maddox. She must be married. That thought had a strange effect on him, made him feel nauseous. It was something he hadn't felt for a very long time.

Sixteen years.

'I got tipped off that she'd entered the country. She's probably merely on holiday or visiting friends. But as a precaution I'd like you to find out what she's up to. Just in case.'

'And if she's up to something?'

'Report back to me. There's a chance we might have to do something we should have done a long time ago.'

Sampson felt himself growing hard.

Michelle knocked on the door of the hotel's security room and pushed it open. A bloke in a blue uniform sat in front of a few colour screens showing various scenes from around the hotel. The lobby, the car park, the corridors, the restaurant. He had *The Sun* spread out before him. Sampson had already checked the papers and was pleased to see the Animal Liberation Front taking the heat for Dr Twigger's death. Michelle explained to the guard

95

that the detective here needed to see CCTV footage of the lobby from this morning.

Huffing and sighing, the guard played with some buttons on the desk and they watched the silent characters in the lobby go into reverse.

'She only left half an hour ago,' Michelle said, 'so we shouldn't need to rewind far.' She scrutinised the screen carefully. After a minute or so, she said, 'There she is. Play.'

The picture was clear and of high quality. Michelle pointed as Kate walked across the lobby, dragging a pair of suitcases, a small child beside her.

'The little boy's really sweet,' said Michelle. 'Poor thing.'

Sweet? Sampson didn't agree. He had no interest in children. He'd hated them when he was a kid and his opinion hadn't changed as he'd got older. But seeing Kate had a strange effect on him. He became aware of his heartbeat, of the blood flowing through his veins. And he could taste blood in his mouth. Sweat broke out on his forehead and he started to breathe heavily.

'Are you alright?' Michelle asked, touching his arm.

He couldn't take his eyes off Kate.

'There's the guy,' Michelle said, and Sampson felt a more familiar sensation—the desire to hurt and kill—when a man, whose face Sampson recognised with shock—took the suitcases from Kate and walked off with her. They left the lobby and vanished from view.

'I need to see the car park footage,' he said.

There were numerous cameras set up around the car park, and it took a while for them to locate Kate and her companion. Finally, they got a view of them getting into a silver Peugeot, though it wasn't possible to see the registration number.

'I'm going to need these tapes,' he said. His mouth was dry and his chest felt strange. 'I also need to see her room,' he said.

'Really?' Michelle asked. 'But she vacated it hours ago.'

Sampson's stare burned into her, drawing a pink flush to the surface of her skin, creeping up from her collarbone. 'Take me there. Now.'

She led him to the lift, which they rode to the room Kate had stayed in with Jack. She tried to make small talk but he gave her a look that made her shut up. He watched her pale, slender throat bob as she swallowed. She was attracted to him; it was easy to tell. Many women found him exciting, turned on by the strength and danger that emanated from him. Almost all of them regretted it later as they nursed their injuries, or in those last seconds before death. He smiled and showed Michelle his teeth. He would love to bite that milky throat.

He was already excited by the time they entered Kate's hotel room, but seeing that it hadn't yet been cleaned made his blood pump even harder. He stood by the bed, barely hearing the click of the door behind him as Michelle closed it. He shut his eyes and inhaled deeply through his nose, the hunter scenting his prey. The room still smelled of perfume, mixed with the faint odour of sweat. He sat on the unmade bed and stroked the sheet where she had spent the night. Did she sleep naked? He pressed his nose to the sheet and took in the sweet, lingering scent of her flesh. He reached out to the pillow where he found a long, dark hair, which he pinched between his fingers, raising it to touch his lips.

'What are you doing?' Michelle asked from across the room, her voice tremulous.

He looked up. He had almost forgotten she was there. 'Come over here,' he said, patting the bed beside him.

She hesitated, then slowly walked across the room and sat next to him.

'What have you got there? A hair? Is that for checking DNA or something?'

He didn't reply. Instead, he let the strand of hair fall and reached out to Michelle, cradling the back of her head in his palm.

'You're pretty,' he said.

He watched as her pupils dilated, listened to the rhythm of her breathing change, become heavier. She peered up at him through her lashes and the bloodlust raged through him. He wanted to strip her naked, throw her down on this bed where Kate had slept, this bed that contained thousands of cells of her dead skin. He wanted to fuck Michelle right there, imagining that she was Kate. He wanted to put his hands around her throat and squeeze, to see the terror in her eyes.

She reached out her hand and put it in his lap, tentatively, then more confidently as she felt the hardness within his jeans. He didn't look at her. Instead, as she stroked his cock through the fabric— the excitement of doing this in the place where she worked evident in her touch—he pictured Kate doing this to him.

He turned towards Michelle and put his hands around her neck.

Her eyes widened with surprise.

He could do it. Would enjoy doing it. But he also knew that if he killed her here, it would cause complications. He would be on CCTV, as was his car. The police would get involved, come after him. He wasn't scared of the police but it would slow him down, interfere with the most important thing in his life right now. Finding Kate—and not just because Gaunt had instructed him to.

He removed his hands and stood up, ignoring the pain in his groin.

'What's the matter?' Michelle asked.

'I have to go.'

As he strode towards the door, leaving a confused Michelle sitting on the bed, he felt a wave of nausea come over him. Kate. It had been sixteen years since he'd seen her, but she still had the same dizzying effect on him.

He loved her.

He hated her.

He wanted her.

He wanted her dead.

15

Vernon Maddox had been in a terrible mood ever since he woke up. He wasn't sure whether the knowledge that his ex-wife and son would return from England that day was making him feel better or worse. Worse, on the whole, he decided, reversing his Buick into a very tight space in the Central Parking Garage at Logan Airport. The fact that Kate would be getting a free lift home from the airport in his car galled him no end—he'd only agreed to pick them up because he was having Jack to stay for the weekend. He'd have made her take a cab if he could, but then he would've had to pick up Jack from her house, which was even further away. He wasn't looking forward to seeing Kate's miserable face sitting in the driver's seat next to him, refusing to talk; treating him like something she'd picked up on the sole of her shoe. Maybe he should have made a sign to welcome her. 'The Bitch is Back', something like that.

He managed a tight smile at his own joke—which turned to another frown as he opened his car door, and it banged against the wing of the car next to him, leaving a small dent. He glanced around to make sure that nobody had noticed, hopped back into the driver's seat, reversed out of the space and into another one across the other side of the car park.

On the other hand, he thought, smoothing down his thinning hair and looking around for the Exit to Arrivals sign, it would be good to see his boy again. Despite everything, he loved Jack to pieces. Always had, always would. His own child; his precious son. He puffed out his narrow chest slightly with pride. It wasn't Jack's fault that Kate had turned into a paranoid bitch. No wonder Jack had been acting up a bit lately. He'd have to get Kate back to her shrink, hopefully that would sort her out. All this crud about wanting a divorce; it was ridiculous. She just didn't know what was good for her. They'd only been separated six months, and she clearly wasn't coping. Every time he crossed paths with her she seemed grey and stressed, and the lines on her face were getting deeper. She's really losing her looks, he thought, choosing not to dwell on his own burgeoning little pot belly, greying chest hair, and the gingery beard he'd grown to try and disguise his weak chin.

But I'm a decent guy, I'm prepared to do right by her. Besides, it's a nightmare finding good child-minders in this city.

Vernon took up his position next to the barrier by the sliding doors through Customs. He looked at his watch; twenty after one. The flight had landed on time; at 1.05, he'd called on his cellphone to check. So they ought to be through in another ten, maybe fifteen minutes or so, once they'd collected their bags. He wondered how long it would be before he and Kate had their first argument; they'd probably be quarrelling by the time they reached the turnpike. Maybe sooner, maybe by the time he'd turned onto I-90. It never usually took long for her to blow a gasket over something or other. Plus, she'd probably be depressed from seeing the nuts old aunt of hers.

Vernon couldn't understand the point of dragging Jack across the Atlantic to celebrate the hundred and fiftieth—or whatever—birthday of some old crust who'd probably scare the living daylights out of him with her toothless sunken face and grabbing claws. OK, so she'd been important to Kate—he understood that—but really, Jack was too young to appreciate it, and Lil was totally past it. She'd been senile for years now, living out her days in an old folks' home; incontinent, almost speechless, no marbles left whatsoever. Vernon shuddered. Just shoot me before I ever get like that, he thought to himself. Kate would probably pull the trigger, too. And she wouldn't wait till I was old, either. Ha.

Forty minutes later Vernon was still waiting. He called Kate's cellphone, but it went straight to voicemail. He exhaled with irritation. She'd obviously forgotten to switch it on again after the plane landed—typical. Then his own phone rang.

101

'Yeah—hello?'

'Hi baby boy,' cooed the voice on the other end, and Vernon's face relaxed into a smile.

'Hey, Shirl, missing me already?'

'You'd better believe it, big boy.'

Vernon blushed slightly, and ran a finger around the inside of his collar, turning away so that the large Jamaican family waiting at the barrier next to him couldn't hear the conversation.

'So when will I see you again?'

'I told you, hon, lemme sort things out this end, and clear a window for us, say, at the weekend?'

He could hear the pout in Shirley's voice.

'It's been so nice, baby, havin' you all to myself this week, is all.'

This was the reason he hadn't put up too much of a fight when Kate told him she wanted to separate—unfettered access to the voluptuous Shirley. The excitement of sneaking around had been sexy at first, but he'd quickly grown sick of musty motel rooms and all the tedious lies he'd had to tell. Shirley was a little clingy, certainly, even more so now she could smell his divorce and, God forbid, a possible impending marriage; but it had been like a breath of fresh air, being with a woman who appreciated his talents and accommodated his sexual appetites the way she did. She was so in awe of his intelligence that she would try and keep up by using lots of long words, usually in completely the wrong context. Vernon found it quite endearing, for the short-term anyway.

'Yeah, it's been good. Listen, Shirl, I gotta go. I'm picking up my boy from the airport and he'll be through any minute. I'll call you, OK?'

'OK sugar. You take care now. Kissy kissy kissy.'

'Kissy kissy kissy,' Vernon muttered back, as quietly as he possibly could. A little Jamaican boy of about seven still managed to overhear, though, and mimicked him with glee.

Vernon glared at him, putting his cellphone back in his jacket pocket, and glancing at his watch again. Where the hell were they?

A young couple pushing a trolley piled high with suitcases came through the barrier, causing the entire Jamaican clan to leap up and shout for joy, running out to greet them as if invading a soccer pitch, jumping and clapping and embracing them. Vernon could hear them talking excitedly, and the word 'London' came up several times. So they must have come off the same flight as Kate and Jack. They'd be out any minute.

*   *   *

Another thirty-five minutes later, he was still waiting. All the people who had been standing with him were long gone, and a whole new set had taken up their places at the barrier. He tried to call Kate, left a message for her. A stream of passengers in saris and turbans were now coming through, not remotely looking as if they were recently arrived from London.

Vernon tutted. He was busting for a piss, but he didn't want to leave in case he missed them. Besides, he really needed to get back to his office—he had seventeen student papers on symbolism in classic American literature to grade before the end of term next week. Keeping an eye on the sliding doors, he walked across to the Information kiosk, and waited in line there for five minutes while the man behind

103

the counter explained to an elderly Irish couple the procedure for tracking missing luggage.

'It wasn't there!' the woman, who had patchy grey hair and an anxious face, kept saying. 'All the bags were off, the belt was empty, and ours wasn't there! Has someone taken it by mistake, do you think? We had presents in there, for our grandson! What'll we do now if you can't find it?'

Her husband turned to her and put a placatory hand on her tweedy sleeve. 'Stop fretting, would you, Deirdre! It's not helping things, now is it? This gentleman will phone through to London for us, and check it got on the plane in the first place, isn't that right, sir?'

Vernon interrupted. He had a very bad feeling growing in the pit of his stomach. 'Excuse me. Did you just say you came from London, and all the bags are through?'

'Not ours,' replied the woman. 'Ours is lost, you see, and it's full of—'

'Were you on flight BA0213?'

'We were, but—'

'And there's nobody back through there still waiting for their luggage?'

'I wouldn't know about that, now,' said the man, slightly impatiently. 'But I can tell you that the luggage conveyor belt was empty, so I suppose not.'

He turned back to the man behind the counter, who was dialling numbers on a telephone.

Vernon stepped away from the kiosk, his mind racing. The flight had landed. The bags were through. Kate's phone was off. He was almost certain that he'd have seen them if they'd come through those sliding doors. Had they missed the flight? Then why hadn't she called to tell him? Surely she wasn't so dumb or thoughtless that she'd omit to do that?

He stood very still amid a sea of people weaving their way around him, motionless as they bumped into him with suitcases and trolleys, looking down at bodies of all different shapes, sizes and colours, trying to spot the woman he had once loved.

A horrible recognition swept over him; a distant memory breaking through the surface with sudden, perfect clarity. Something about Kate going over to England for Lil's ninetieth birthday had been nagging at him all week, but it wasn't until now that he realised what it was: the last time Kate had planned to go to England for one of Lil's birthdays had been five years ago, for Lil's eighty-fifth. Jack had just been a baby, coming up to his own first birthday. Kate was going to take him with her, 'so they could celebrate both birthdays together.' But at the last minute Jack had come down with a fever, and she hadn't wanted to go without him. Vernon had been secretly delighted—he'd been pissed that Kate would deny him the opportunity to be there for his own son's first birthday.

Jack's birthday was September 1st. And it was now June.

Vernon let out a noise which was a cross between a roar and a frustrated sort of yelp, causing the Irish couple with the lost luggage, as well as most of the passengers in the vicinity, to whip their heads around and stare at him.

'That goddamn *bitch!*' he yelled, kicking hard at the end leg of a row of seats, spilling the coffee of the woman sitting at the other end and causing her to jump up in alarm.

She won't get away with this, he thought, stalking back towards the car park before Security were summoned to escort him off the premises. No way is she taking my son. No way is she having him; he's mine. I'll hunt her down like a dog, and she'll be sorry she ever messed with me. She can have the fucking divorce, I'll be glad to see the back of her whining miserable back. But there is no way on God's earth that she's having my boy.

When he got to the ticket machines to pay for the several hours he'd been parked in Short Stay, he dug angrily in his pockets for change, waiting in line behind a young bespectacled man who couldn't seem to fathom how the machine worked. The man had a huge suitcase standing on its end beside him, and Vernon's rage increased as the man dithered and flapped, trying to put his ticket in the slot for banknotes. Vernon could not contain himself any longer.

'It's simple, jerkoff! Put the goddamn ticket in THERE, and the goddamn money in THERE. What's your fucking problem?'

Before the young man could reply, Vernon pushed over his suitcase, causing it to thud heavily against the ticket machine. He took out his cellphone and hit the speed-dial to call Kate. It went straight to voicemail. He strode back towards the terminal again.

He'd had an idea.

Taking a deep breath to try and calm himself down, he forced himself to walk slowly up to the British Airways Reservations desk.

'I want to buy a ticket to London. Leaving tomorrow, as early as possible.'

16

They drove in silence for a while, creeping through traffic lights and across zebra crossings towards London's western edge. These outer reaches of the city seemed so sad and run-down, the bright sunshine exposing the cracks and the filth, the boarded-up shops, black bin liners spilling their guts on every kerb. Kate couldn't help but see it as a kind of virus that had spread through the city, so that every borough looked the same: the same shops on every high street, identical gangs of teenagers in identical clothes. Actually, there was something hopeful about the kids, the way they thrived in the most barren places, their adaptability, making their own fun and enjoying life though it appeared the world hated them. Again, like viruses. And soon these parts of London would be stricken by another disease: gentrification would come and prices would soar, and that branch of Tennessee Fried Chicken would become a nice little deli, and the kids would be driven somewhere else, further marginalised but always there.

Leaving London, Kate felt like an animal that had been chased from its hole. Exposed and endangered. She turned her face from the window, looked around to make sure Jack was alright. He was fine, leaning back like a VIP in a limo, gazing imperiously at the strange streets. What was he thinking? Did he miss his dad, his friends? Or was he too excited by all this newness, this adventure? Probably a little of both. When he was older he would probably look back and wonder about this strange holiday his mum took him on as a kid.

They took the M4 for a short distance, driving past signposts that pointed to THE WEST. The words gave Kate goosebumps and she rubbed her forearms. Going west. Into the past. To a place where she was going to have to confront her memories, prise open the lid of Pandora's box. She felt fluttery panic, bird's wings in her stomach and chest. Needing distraction, she turned on the radio.

'Animal rights groups are denying responsibility for last night's shocking murder of a scientist in Oxford . . .'

Great. She switched it off. She didn't want to think about scientists being murdered—or anything to do with science or work. She missed her work, the quiet excitement of the lab, the research into the Watoto Virus that had become her obsession and her cause. She specialised in research into viruses that mainly affected Africa. There had been the research into West Nile, plus Ebola and Marburg. But her real passion was in finding a vaccine for Watoto, as if the virus had become a personal enemy, her nemesis. She dreamt of making that breakthrough and becoming, in conquering the disease, a modern day Edward Jenner, famed for developing the smallpox inoculation, or Louis Pasteur, who had developed the vaccine for rabies.

She missed the colleagues she'd left behind too. What would they think of her? No doubt, they would find what she'd done irrational and out of character. On top of that, they'd think she'd betrayed them, left them at a crucial time. Perhaps one day she'd be able to explain her reasons to them.

As they turned onto the infamous M25, they hit

108

traffic. Paul stuck his head out of the window, trying to see what was causing the hold-up. He sighed. 'Looks like an accident.'

'I'm sorry.'

'Why do you say that?'

'I've just realised that I'm dragging you away from your normal life. Your job.'

He waved her concerns away. 'Don't worry about it. I was due some leave and, anyway, we'd just finished working on a big case. You met me at a good time.'

Eager for something to take her mind off everything else, Kate asked, 'What was the case about? Can you tell me?'

'Phishing.'

'Where criminals send emails pretending to be your bank or some other big site so you'll give them your credit card or bank details?'

'That's right.'

From the backseat, Jack said, 'I'd like to go fishing and catch a fish.'

Paul said, 'Maybe I'll take you one day.'

'Cool.'

Kate frowned. 'You shouldn't make promises to kids that you don't mean to keep.'

'Who says I don't mean to keep it?'

He didn't meet her eye as he said it, but flicked a look at her in the pause that followed, and Kate suddenly became very aware of the heat inside the car. She didn't want this; didn't need it. 'How do you turn up the air-con in this car?'

Paul turned a dial on the dashboard. This was English summer all right: capricious, moody. Overcast and cool, then swinging into blazing cruelty. That made her think of Vernon, and so she prompted

Paul to tell her about the phishing case to help take her mind off her husband.

'It was a big deal. The trail led back to a crime syndicate in Russia. As it so often does. Russia, Nigeria, South Korea. Although it can be anywhere really. The most frustrating thing about computer crime is that it moves so easily across borders. The United States passed an Anti-Phishing Act last year but then they can't prosecute half of the criminals because they're in Asia or somewhere else. We work with police forces and agencies all over the world, but the only way we're ever going to win the battle is if computer users stop being so stupid and falling for these scams.'

'They keep you in work though,' smiled Kate.

'True. Although some of the cases we deal with make me wish the internet had never been invented.'

'Like what?'

'I can't really talk about it with Jack in the car. It involves kids.'

'Oh.'

'Yeah. The kind of stuff that stays with you, makes you look at the world differently. Makes you realise that there are sicknesses in society that we're a long, long way from curing.'

Another kind of virus, Kate thought, passed down through the generations. She instinctively turned to check Jack was still okay. He grinned at her, and the traffic started moving.

'So how did you get into the computer security business anyway?' Kate asked.

Paul didn't answer right away, and she thought it might be because he was concentrating on the road. Now the traffic was finally moving Kate could sense the irritation in all the metal boxes around them dissipate a little. A boxer dog watched them solemnly through the rear window of the car in front. They gradually increased their speed as the traffic spread out.

'I suppose you could say I got into it because it was already my area of expertise. And it was either cross over and go legit, or, well, go to jail.'

Kate waited for him to continue. He swung the steering wheel to the left and overtook the car with the boxer dog. He chewed his lower lip. After a minute, he said over his shoulder, 'You alright back there, Jack?'

'I just saw a man eat a booger.'

'Nice.'

They continued to chat aimlessly, Kate unwilling to press Paul on what he had inferred about the threat of prison. She was still waiting for him to tell her anything further about his past an hour and a half later, when they reached Salisbury. She filed it in her head under 'cause for concern', but didn't push it. After all, they would have plenty of time to find out more about each other. There was no rush.

17

Kate got out of the car and stretched her legs and back, squinting into the sun and wishing she had her sunglasses with her. She'd forgotten to pack them, along with her sun cream. If only the sun would go behind a cloud and the greyness would return—it was damaging her eyes and skin and playing havoc with her libido. The heat always did this to her. Like that summer at the CRU, when it was sticky and sultry and her hormones had been aflame. Like the tropical night on a budget holiday to Cuba when Jack was conceived, back in the days when she and Vernon were still sexually attracted to one another. There was no point being coy about it: hot weather made her horny. Perhaps she should do a rain dance.

Salisbury town centre was quiet, as drowsy as the wasps that circled the rubbish bins in the marketplace, drunk on Coca-Cola. Kate held Jack's hand as he eyed the wasps warily. When he was three a wasp had crawled into a can of Sprite Vernon had let him have, against her wishes—all that sugar!—and stung Jack on the tongue. Then there was the dash to the emergency room as Jack's tongue swelled up and Kate shouted at Vernon in the car as Jack screamed and Vernon shouted back and called her an 'uptight crazy Nazi health bitch.'

Not the happiest of memories. Things had changed between them so dramatically over such a short period; at a time when they ought to have been relishing every moment of Jack's babyhood, not yelling at each other. Instead, Vernon had tried to convince her that her depression at the decline of the relationship was a sign of burgeoning insanity, and that she needed intensive therapy and anti-depressants to 'cure' her.

'Where is everyone?' Paul wondered, getting out of the car and rubbing his upper arms, and then producing a pair of shades from his pocket. The shades were overly trendy and made Paul look older than he was: the opposite of their intended effect. She didn't feel that she knew him well enough yet to tell him this though. Stop trying to look like a movie star, she wanted to say. You don't need to make such an effort.

She couldn't imagine Stephen trying to be trendy. He wouldn't have known the difference between Gap and Gucci.

'Mummy, I'm thirsty.'

She ruffled Jack's hair. 'Let's go and get a drink, shall we?'

'Coca-Cola?'

'No, you can have orange juice.'

There was a newsagent across the road and as they walked towards it Jack said, 'That wasp was looking at me. It wanted to sting me.'

A couple of teens thundered past on skateboards and Jack gawped after them, the insect forgotten. Paul pointed towards a board outside the newsagent advertising the *Salisbury Journal* with the headline *Cathedral in Buddhist Row*. Another board yelled *Blues Boss Quits*.

Inside the shop, Kate took a couple of cartons of orange juice from the double-fronted fridge, a bottle of water for Paul and a copy of the *Journal* from the top of a stack of newspapers on the bottom shelf. She carried them all to the counter, where a girl leaned against the till with her index finger in her mouth. Kate thought she was trying to make herself sick, then realised she was playing with her tongue stud. The girl wiped her saliva-soaked finger on her jeans before using it to stab the price of their purchases into the till.

Back outside, Jack held his juice carton up to Paul, who helped him by stripping the cellophane from the straw and poking it through the hole in the carton. Jack sipped, then pulled a face.

'It's gross,' he said.

'What's wrong with it?'

'It tastes like crap.'

'Don't say that.' She rolled her eyes. 'A little phrase he picked up from his father.'

'I don't like English juice. I want proper juice.'

'This is proper.'

'I don't *want* it.' He threw the carton onto the floor.

Kate watched the juice dribble through the straw onto the pavement. Normally she would really tell him off, but right now she felt like she needed to hold back. He'd been so good over the last few days, acting like the model child she'd often fantasised about while she was pregnant. She'd known it wouldn't last forever, but she didn't want to be too hard on him. He deserved a break. But that didn't mean he could be allowed to get away with this behaviour or he'd get worse.

'Pick it up please, Jack,' she said in her most calm, reasonable voice.

'No. It tastes like crap.'

'Do not say that.'

'Crap. Craaaaaap. Crap crap crap.'

Paul laughed.

Kate shot him a look. 'That doesn't help.'

'Sorry.'

Kate crouched so she was on Jack's level. 'Look, I know it tastes different to what you're used to, but if you don't drink it a wasp will get it.'

'The wasps can have it.'

'Just pick it up.'

'Go on, Jack, do what your mum says,' Paul interjected.

Kate held up her hand, a sign for Paul to keep out of it. He walked a few steps away. Kate said, 'Okay, if you pick up the carton, I'll drink it and we

114

can buy you another drink. What would you like?'

'Chocolate milk.'

She sighed. 'They might not sell that.'

'But I want it.' He rubbed his eyes with the back of his hand and she realised how tired he must be.

'Okay, we'll look for a chocolate milk. If you pick up the juice.'

Finally, he did as she asked, handing her the carton. She went into the shop and, luckily, found a bottle of chocolate milk, which Jack grabbed from her hand and had running down his chin within seconds.

Kate wiped Jack's chin with a tissue while saying to Paul. 'Sorry if I snapped at you, but it's best if I deal with these things.'

'I understand. So . . . shall we go back to the car, then, and try to find the CRU?'

Kate didn't reply. She didn't need to look at any map. She remembered exactly where the Unit was. She had driven there many times. When she was living with Stephen, he would often leave her his car to use during the day, and she would drive out to the Unit to pick him up after work. She'd park in a lane down the road and sit there with the radio on, listening to Radio One—all the silly love songs whose lyrics she would eagerly embrace, waiting for the moment her heart would flutter as Stephen came over the crest of the hill towards her. Some evenings they'd drive down to the local lovers' lane and spend a while in the car before going home. Weird how she could remember some aspects of that summer in such filmic detail while the really important stuff had been . . . well, what did it feel like? Like it had been erased.

'You've gone very quiet,' Paul said. 'Everything

okay?'

'Yes.' She hoped she hadn't flushed pink. 'Everything's fine.'

They walked back to the car. Kate watched Paul, wondering what he'd meant by his comment about jail on the drive down. It worried her. She was putting a lot of trust in this man, mainly because of who he was—or rather, who his brother had been. But despite this hint that there was something unsavoury in his past, just watching him with Jack, the way he'd tried to help, even if his attempts were misguided, she was sure she was right she could put her faith in him. She hoped she was making a wise judgement.

'Do you want to drive?' Paul asked.

She hesitated. 'I don't know. I haven't driven a stick for years.'

He raised an eyebrow. 'You really have been living in the States too long.' He held out the keys. 'Go on.'

'My Daddy says my Mummy's a bad driver.'

'Does he?' said Kate. 'Right, that decides it.' She took the keys from him and opened the door on the driver's side. The car had heated up while they were in the shop so they wound all the windows down, enjoying the balmy breeze that blew through the vehicle. It was like being on holiday. She hoped Jack didn't spill chocolate milk on the backseat of Paul's car. Sod it, it was inevitable. She started the engine and the radio came on. It was the traffic bulletin: the reporter was saying there'd been a pile-up on the M3 causing long delays for drivers heading to London from the west.

'Oh great,' Kate said. She paused, then added, thinking out loud, 'Perhaps we should stay here tonight. The thought of getting stuck in that traffic in this heat is too awful to contemplate. We could find a hotel.'

Paul didn't respond straight away and Kate hurriedly said, 'God, I'm being so presumptuous, as if you've got nothing better to do. If you want to get back . . .'

'I haven't got anything better to do.'

'Really?'

'I've got my laptop and my phone, so if work needs me they can contact me. I'm owed a few days off anyway. I really need to find out what happened to Stephen, Kate.'

'Okay.'

They headed up a big hill with a wonderful view of the Cathedral behind them, filling her rear-view mirror whenever she glanced in it. Before long, they turned the corner onto the road where the CRU stood.

But it was completely gone, replaced by a housing estate—new starter homes for couples and young families. Kate pulled up to the kerb and sat silently for a few minutes, staring at the freshly-trimmed lawns and gleaming garage doors. She got out of the car and stood in the road, turning slowly in a circle. Gone.

Why had she thought the buildings would still be here? How foolish. But surely it was reasonable to think there would still be a trace of those prefab huts, the wire fence that surrounded them, all the work and research that went on.

No, it had been erased. The people who lived in these houses—like that guy over there, watering his lawn; that woman sitting reading a fat paperback in her striped chair; those kids kicking a football

117

around—all probably with no idea about what had once stood here.

She walked over to the wooden fence that marked the edge of the estate. Here was something that hadn't changed: the verdant fields and crooked mud paths where she and the other volunteers had walked, allowed to wander as long as they didn't come into contact with any outsiders. She closed her eyes, felt the sun on her face. In these fields, not so far away, she and Stephen had made love on a hot summer day like this one, beneath an oak tree, her long skirt pulled up, baked-dry grass prickling the flesh of her thighs. She had been so happy. The future was a golden place with Stephen in it.

She closed her eyes again and the images shifted.

The fire alarm screamed, smoke billowed through the corridors, Sarah held her up as they tried to find their way out of Hell . . .

She sensed Paul and Jack coming up behind her, their shoes scuffing the asphalt, and she wanted to turn to them. But she couldn't open her eyes.

Outside now, running towards the building, the firefighters carrying someone out on a stretcher. Stephen. Oh god, no, Stephen. And the doctor coming up to her and everything fading.

'Kate? Are you alright?'

The images shifted again—back to Sarah, pulling her out of bed. And further back—she and Sarah fighting. Fighting? What about?

Of course.

She opened her eyes and found Paul standing in front of her. For a moment, the walls of time flickered and Paul became Stephen: young, shy,

118

flushed from their lovemaking. But then it was Paul again.

'I've remembered what happened with Sarah,' she said. 'And I can remember her name too. Sarah Evergreen. The Green Eyed-Monster.'

18

When they'd booked into this bland, boxy, whitewashed hotel on the outskirts of Salisbury (chosen more for its relative cheapness than for any expectation of luxury), Paul had firmly informed the receptionist that they required one twin room, and one single. He'd shown them into the twin room, and announced he'd see them later for dinner downstairs. Kate liked his calm decisiveness, so different from Vernon's panicky bluster.

Later that night, Kate and Paul sat awkwardly on the edge of one of the twin beds in the bedroom. They were drinking red wine out of squat little water glasses from the en-suite bathroom, and talking softly to avoid waking Jack, who was comatose in one of the beds, snoring gently, his robot tucked under the sheet with him.

Kate had struggled with the decision to invite Paul into the room. They needed to talk, for sure, and there was no way she was going to leave Jack with another hotel babysitter—but it seemed a bit intimate, to be sitting here like this.

Still, she supposed, at least Paul hadn't even suggested the three of them all share one room.

The room was pretty small, with no sofa or desk or anywhere else to sit; and not really even enough room for one of them to sit on the floor. Paul was wearing shorts, and she a short skirt, and the hairs from his leg were tickling her own bare thigh. She'd moved slightly further away, but before long, he was somehow in close proximity to her again. She couldn't decide if he was as screamingly aware of it as she was, or even if he'd noticed at all. It was such a small thing, but one which was having the effect of making everything in her body tingle.

'It's been ages since I stayed in a room with twin beds in it,' she said, gulping wine. 'Not since the CRU, probably—although these beds are a lot bigger. I'd have got a double room for me and Jack, because he usually ends up climbing into bed with me—but he takes up all the room if it's a single bed, so then I need another bed to swap over to. We spend all night switching from bed to bed, him chasing me. Easier just to be in a double.'

She blushed. Way too much talk about climbing into beds, and chasing—even though she was referring to a six-year-old-boy.

'Did everyone share a room at CRU? Did you share with Stephen?'

'Everyone had to share, but they weren't all twin rooms. There were some "flats", as they were called: like self-contained apartments, with a sort of sitting room with a kitchenette, and two little bedrooms off it. More civilised, although the bathroom was out in the corridor. But I was in twin rooms both times I went—much bigger rooms, like bedsits. The beds were at opposite ends of the room, and the rooms had an en-suite bathroom. And no, I definitely wouldn't have been allowed to share with Stephen, even if he hadn't been staff! Strictly single-sex. We were meant to be in isolation with our room-mate.

120

Besides, nobody knew Stephen and I were a couple. He didn't often stay on site anyway, he had a rented flat in Salisbury.'

'Why?'

'Well, it was a bit dead up there. He did want some kind of life outside work, you know.'

'No, I meant, why didn't anybody know you were a couple?'

Jack snuffled and stirred in his sleep, reaching out a floppy arm to cuddle his unwieldy robot.

Kate waited until he was still again before continuing. 'I'm not sure. Stephen made a big deal about it at the time, and I never really understood why. All he'd say was that it was best if no-one knew. That was one of the other things which made me suspicious. I mean, what would it matter, as long as we stuck to the rules when we were on CRU property? But he had a real issue about it—it obviously made him anxious.

'When I confessed that I'd told Sarah about us, he was really upset. He kept saying, "This is a disaster, what if it gets out? What if the rest of the staff find out? I'll lose my job!" At first I just thought it was because he was a bit of a golden boy, and he didn't want anybody to know he'd been fraternising with the patients. It turns out there was some daft old-fashioned rule about it.'

Paul smiled. 'Old Stephen always did have jobsworth tendencies . . . So, tell me more about Sarah.'

As he spoke, he reached out a finger and softly stroked Kate's forearm. Kate froze, her eyes open wide with shock and pleasure—but Paul wasn't looking at her. He gave no sign that he was any more aware of this little movement than he'd been

121

by the fact that their legs were touching. She realised that she was more aroused than she had felt for years. This is ridiculous, she thought. I'm so sex-starved that I'll probably have an orgasm from some guy stroking my arm! She tried, and failed to remember when she'd last had sex. Probably not since Jack was out of nappies.

Paul waited for her to tell him what she'd remembered about Sarah.

She cleared her throat, willing Paul not to stop stroking her. But at the same time, she couldn't help shuddering at the memory she'd had earlier, while standing on the CRU site, of Sarah emerging with her from the building, as sooty and sick as she herself was.

'Um . . . So—Sarah. The last time I saw her was after the fire. I can't remember much about that night, except that she helped carry me out. She was ill too, so I don't know how she did it. But I do have a distinct image of her lying on the grass outside, coughing. We were all coughing, from the smoke, and the flu. I didn't see her again after that—I got taken away to this hospital. I'm sure I asked about her, but for the life of me I can't remember if I got an answer. Then I went off to the States, and didn't give her another thought, really.'

The stroking was intensifying, long slow swoops up and down her forearm. Kate broke out in goosebumps all over. She wanted to grab Paul and kiss him, but couldn't bring herself to. He wasn't even making eye contact with her; his eyes were firmly fixed on the action of his finger running up and down the skin of her arm. Surely this means he fancies me, she thought? She was so out of practice. Perhaps he was just being encouraging . . . oh don't be ridiculous, Kate, she told herself. Of course it must mean he fancies you. You don't randomly go around stroking forearms of people you don't fancy. Not like this, anyhow.

'More wine?' She jumped up abruptly, and refilled their glasses. Damn, she thought. Now he's going to think I wasn't enjoying it, or it wasn't appropriate.

But perhaps it *wasn't* appropriate. Did she really want him? Or did he just represent the closest thing to Stephen reincarnated that she was ever going to get? She sighed.

Paul looked at her then, and smiled. He patted the bed next to him. 'So her name was Sarah Evergreen. Why exactly did you call her the Green-Eyed Monster? What was she jealous of?'

She sat down again. This time, she purposefully sat a little bit closer, so their legs were touching without either of them having to move.

'She was jealous of me and Stephen. I didn't much like her, she was a stroppy cow. My sort of age, and quite pretty, with all this red hair, and I was really pleased when I first met her, because I thought she'd be fun. She was, at first, but it soon became clear that she had her eye on Stephen. She didn't realise that we were already an item, so when she started saying how fit he was, and how she'd love to be pressed against the lab benches by him—you know, that sort of thing—well, it was really difficult. I couldn't say anything, because it was a big secret that Stephen and I were together. I had to sneak out at night to meet up with him, and it really pissed me off that we couldn't be open about it—but after a while I just couldn't keep listening to Sarah going on and on about cute he was, and what she was planning to say to him to get him interested in

123

her—it was painful! And believe me, she *really* went on about it. There wasn't much else to do in there, apart from watching TV, so she'd made Stephen her little project. Eventually I decided I just had to tell her.'

'What did she say?'

Kate frowned. 'Again, I can't really remember. She wasn't happy, that's for sure. But we were both quite ill by then—it must have been a day or two before the fire. I suspect that if we'd both been feeling well, we'd have had a big row, but I think she was too out of it to do much other than moan and bitch at me.' She shuddered. 'Ugh. She was a pain in the ass. I do remember lying on my bed with a temperature, and her whining away on the other side of the room. I wanted to swat her like a mosquito. But I didn't have the energy. I felt too crap.'

'So you both had colds?'

Kate hesitated. She wished Paul would start stroking her arm again, but apart from their legs touching, he wasn't doing anything other than listening. She hoped she hadn't given out signals that she didn't want to. Although more than likely this was exactly what she'd done, since she wasn't sure that she *did* want to . . . It was all a bit weird. The last thing she'd expected to happen on arrival back in England was to meet a new man. Let alone Stephen's bloody twin brother! It was insane. She tried to concentrate on the conversation, and not on Paul's solid, sexy proximity.

'Well. I suppose at the time I assumed I had really bad flu. But now I think back to it . . . it wasn't like any flu I've ever had. I suppose it could have just been that my temperature was so high that it felt worse than it was. But the only time I've ever felt more ill was when I was a kid, with the same disease that my parents . . . well, you know . . . died of.'

She felt uncomfortable, in case Paul thought she was courting sympathy, but to her gratitude, he reacted in a completely matter-of-fact way.

'Do you think it could have been something else you had? Some other illness, I mean?'

'All I can say is that it didn't feel like flu. And certainly not like any sort of cold. But it's all such a blur, and then the fire broke out, and all I can really remember after that was what I told you before, about being in that hospital weeks later, and Leonard telling me I'd got a "Congratulatory First", as they called them at Oxford, and he'd arranged for me to go to Harvard. Anything else just comes in flashes. Or nightmares.' She paused again. 'I have a lot of nightmares. But at the time, if I was thinking rationally at all, it wasn't about the fire, or Sarah, or how ill I'd been . . . It was about Stephen. All I could think about was how I'd lost him, and how it felt as if I'd never be happy again.'

She stopped, her voice thick and choked with sudden tears. It felt insensitive for him to see her eyes so full. When she glanced at him, hoping he hadn't noticed, she saw with shock that there were tears running down his cheeks too.

'Oh god, I'm so sorry,' she said, instinctively reaching out to him and putting her arms around him. 'I only knew him for a few months—and he was your twin. It must be so much worse for you.'

He swiped his face with the back of his hand, and leaned into her embrace. 'No, I'm sorry. I'm not usually a crier, honest. In fact, I probably haven't cried since he died—apart from when Southampton

125

got relegated, of course.' He smiled ruefully, and Kate was reminded even more strongly of Stephen. He used to have that same self-deprecating humour too. And, if she remembered rightly, Stephen also used to support the Saints, Southampton's football team.

'It's not nice to see you upset about him, but it's kind of amazing to be with someone who understands the loss, and who loved him too. I know I've mentioned this before, but I can't talk to my parents about him. It's too painful for them. And Stephen and I didn't have any mutual friends, so this is the first time I've met anybody who . . . misses him like I do.'

Something in his honesty, and the catch in his voice, touched Kate deeply. Suddenly she realised that, no, this wasn't just about Stephen. She didn't just see Stephen in him, alike as they were. She was attracted to him, Paul, and the rush of adrenaline and sudden lust would have knocked her off her feet, had she been standing.

She hugged him tighter to her and, at that moment, Jack snored and rolled over so he was facing the wall. Thanks, Jack, she thought, as she gently lifted Paul's face up towards her and kissed his lips. They tasted salty with tears, and felt so soft.

He responded immediately, wrapping his arms around her waist. To her immense relief, it wasn't like kissing Stephen. And it certainly wasn't like kissing Vernon (kissing Vernon, as she recalled, had been more like being caught in the spin cycle of a washing machine). This was an entirely new and entirely lovely experience. She immediately wanted to rip off all her clothes, and jump on him. It was lucky Jack was in the next bed, otherwise she

126

probably would have done, she thought, sighing with pleasure as Paul touched her breasts with the same light finger with which he'd stroked her arm.

They didn't talk about Sarah, or the CRU, or Stephen, for the next hour and a half. The wine got finished, and Kate got stubble rash on her chin, but somehow, miraculously—particularly since they were already lying on a bed—their clothes for the most part remained in place.

'This is so wonderful,' Paul whispered at one point, their tears forgotten.

Kate nodded. 'Wonderful—but very weird.'

A thought struck her. 'I don't know much about you, apart from who your twin was. You aren't married, are you?'

He smiled and shook his head. 'Nope.'

'Divorced?'

'No.'

'Girlfriend?'

'Broke up with her six months ago. Been on my own ever since. You have nothing to worry about.'

'I'm married, though,' she said sombrely, picturing Vernon's face, twisted with rage at the realisation that she and Jack had gone. For some reason, she saw him standing in the doorway of Jack's abandoned bedroom, looking with fury at the neat Red Sox duvet cover, perhaps hurling it across the room. Perhaps sobbing, with rage and frustration. Oh god. She had a horrible feeling that the fallout from their flight hadn't even begun.

Paul merely smiled again. There was something so calming about being with him. 'Yeah, but you won't be for much longer, will you? I mean, isn't that what all this is about; you being over here?'

Kate nodded.

'Well then. What's a bit of pre-emptive infidelity between friends?' He kissed her again, and she somehow managed to forget about Vernon. For now, at least.

19

When Kate opened her eyes the next morning, her first fleeting emotion was faint disappointment that Paul wasn't in bed with her. But then, as the click and beep of Billy the robot being switched on announced the awakening of her son, she realised that that would have been impossible. Or, at least, extremely inadvisable. To her shame, she found herself wondering how on earth she was ever going to get any time alone with Paul. She dismissed the selfish thought immediately. Jack absolutely had to come first.

Although, now that she thought about it, perhaps it was time for Jack to go and spend a few days with his British cousins? Selfish reasons aside, it really couldn't be much fun for him, getting dragged around with her and Paul in their quest for answers. Her sister lived in the Cotswolds. Surely she'd be happy to have him to stay for a while? Miranda didn't even know that they were over here.

Kate decided that she would ring her today . . . and not *just* so that she could sleep with Paul, either. She probably needed to reassure Miranda that they were OK. They had never been close sisters, and Kate had held off calling her so far, knowing that this would be the first place Vernon would try to track her down. She didn't want Miranda to have to get involved. Better that she knew nothing. At least Vernon wouldn't be aware of Miranda's new address—their family had moved house a few months before.

'Hello Billy, hello Mummy, I love you both,' Jack said sleepily, stumbling out of his bed and into hers— the one he'd started out in last night. They cuddled, Kate pressing the top of Jack's head against her lips, kissing his soft hair, and Jack wrapping one of his little legs around hers. He smelled delicious.

'We love you too, Jacket,' she said, using his old nickname.

'Mum-mee, don't call me that, it's silly.'

'Alright, Potatohead.'

'That's even more silly!'

'Sorry, Mr Smellypants.'

Jack punched her in the ribs, surprisingly hard.

'Ow! That hurt!'

'Then stop calling me silly things,' he said, on the verge of sudden tears.

Kate had forgotten how sensitive he was sometimes. She supposed it was unsurprising, under the current circumstances.

'Sorry, Jack,' she said, hugging him closer. 'Hey, listen, how would you like to go and see Amelia and George?'

'Who?'

'Your cousins, you remember them? They came to Boston once. They've got blond hair and big green eyes. George is a year younger than you, and Amelia's a year older.'

'And their parents is Auntie Miranda and Uncle Pete?'

'That's right. You haven't seen them for a while.'

Miranda, Pete and the kids had flown out to visit

them in Boston about eighteen months earlier. Vernon had made the visit as uncomfortable as he could. He may as well have placed a 'Piss Off' mat on the front porch.

Jack shrugged. 'OK. I don't mind. I might let George play with Billy, but only for a few minutes.'

'Good boy. Now go and have a wee, and we'll find Paul and go for breakfast.'

*   *   *

'Today's task,' Paul said, as the two of them attacked greasy scrambled eggs and rubbery toast in the hotel dining room, 'is to track down Sarah. Can you remember where she lived?'

Kate, who was watching Jack playing with the curtain pulls—he appeared to be trying to lynch Billy—racked her brains again. She glanced up at Paul, who was chasing a clump of egg around his plate. He caught her looking, and gave her a little, but very meaningful smile, and her stomach did a small flip. She thought of the silky smoothness of his skin from the previous night, and how she couldn't wait to spend some more time kissing him.

She forced herself to concentrate and pointed towards Paul's laptop. 'You know, I'm sure she lived locally. I have this feeling that she told me she could see her house from the Unit. Can't we trace her on the net? Evergreen shouldn't be too difficult; it's not a terribly common name, is it?'

'No, but I can't get an internet connection here, so let's go and see if the receptionist's got a telephone directory, if you've finished.'

Kate took a final swig of tepid tea, and made a face. 'Yeah. It's not the best breakfast I've ever had.'

Paul smiled at her again. 'Perhaps I can take you to a hotel sometime where they do fantastic breakfasts. In the Lake District. Views to die for, and four poster beds.'

'Sounds good,' she said, trying to keep her voice level. 'I do love a good breakfast.'

* * *

There was one Evergreen listed in the Salisbury phone directory. The initials were wrong, but after all this time Sarah was probably married and living somewhere else. It was almost certainly a relative though—hopefully her parents.

'Assuming they're the right Evergreens, of course,' Paul said.

'Should we call first?' Kate asked doubtfully. 'Jack, don't do that, honey, you might get your fingers trapped.' Jack, bored, had been playing with the heavy fire door leading up to the hotel bedrooms, as Kate and Paul leafed through the directory beside the payphone in Reception.

'No. We've got plenty of time. Let's just drive over there and see if they're in. And if it's them, of course. You can just say you're an old friend of Sarah's.'

'What about Jack? Jack—stop it!'

Paul looked over at Jack, who was now kicking the door disconsolately.

'Yeah. A bit boring for him, really,' Paul said. 'I don't think he should come in with us. I'll buy a ball and take him for a kick around in their garden, if they've got one, while you're chatting.'

Kate hoped the Evergreens would be accommodating. It seemed a bit cheeky to turn up invited and then ask that Jack could go and play

131

football in their back garden. 'Or in a local park.'

'Whatever. Let's go.' Paul called to Jack: 'Come on mate, we're going to buy a football!'

*   *   *

Football duly purchased from a newsagent's near the hotel, the three of them set off in the car, heading for a village on the other side of Salisbury called Quidhampton. According to their map, the Evergreens lived on the main road through the village.

'Although I wouldn't really call this a main road,' Kate said, as Paul drove slowly down what was more like a narrow country lane.

'There! Primrose Cottage,' Paul cried, pointing at a low, Thirties-style bungalow.

'Wouldn't really call that a cottage, either,' she said, trying to swallow down the nerves in her belly at what she was about to have to do.

'Where are we going? Can we play football now?' Jack had undone his seatbelt before the car had pulled to a halt.

'Hang on, mate. We just have to go and see if these people are the mum and dad of someone your Mummy used to know, a lady called Sarah.'

'Why?'

Paul and Kate looked at one another. 'Bit tricky to explain,' said Paul. 'It's a long story.' He turned back to Kate. 'She might even still live at home. That would be handy, wouldn't it? Save a bit of time.'

'Mmm,' Kate said, not at all sure if she was ready for this. Jack opened his mouth to demand more explanations, so she added hastily: 'You're being a

132

very good boy, Jack. Promise you'll be good a little while longer, while I talk to them, OK?'

'OK. As long as I can have an ice-cream afterwards,' Jack said moodily.

*   *   *

Kate had imagined that Sarah's parents would be an elderly couple, and so when a very attractive, youthful woman in her fifties opened the door, Kate initially assumed that they had the wrong Evergreens.

'Um—hello,' she said. 'I'm really sorry to bother you. I'm looking for Sarah Evergreen's parents? I'm an old friend of hers.'

The woman was silent for a moment, and the look on her face told Kate that she hadn't come to the wrong place after all. She wondered if Sarah and her family might be estranged—Sarah had been a stroppy madam when Kate knew her.

'Yes,' she said. 'I am Sarah's mother.' She smiled then, and stuck out her hand. 'Any friends of Sarah's are welcome here. I don't recognise you, do I? Have we met before? I'm Angela.'

'Kate.' Kate shook Angela's hand, and smiled back. 'I knew Sarah from the Cold Research Unit. This is my friend Paul, and my son, Jack.'

Angela flinched at the mention of the CRU. Both Kate and Paul noticed, and Paul raised his eyebrows at Kate when Angela wasn't looking.

'Come in, come in, I'll put the kettle on. Hello, Jack, I like your robot, he's rather super, isn't he?'

'He's called Billy,' Jack said, hiding behind Kate's legs.

They processed into the small house, taking up

133

too much room in the cramped living room. There was a huge painting of Sarah, a photograph which had been rendered in oil on canvas, hanging over the fireplace, and Kate recognised her immediately.

'How is Sarah?' Kate asked, thinking how attractive she looked in that picture. 'It's been ages since I saw her. We meant to keep in touch, but . . .' Her voice petered out at Angela's expression.

'You don't know? I thought you said you were at the CRU with her?'

Kate glanced at Paul. 'I was. We were room-mates. What . . .?'

'So you were there the night of the fire?'

'Yes.' Kate had a terrible feeling in the pit of her stomach. She reached out and took hold of Paul's hand. Even Jack was quiet, sensing the atmosphere. He'd retreated to an armchair, where he was tinkering with Billy.

Angela swallowed hard, and her eyes filled with tears. 'I'm so sorry to have to tell you this. I assumed you'd already know. But Sarah—she died in the fire.'

'No she didn't!' Kate blurted, without thinking.

'Kate!' Paul squeezed her hand.

'I know this must come as a shock to you, but I'm afraid it's true. She became trapped in the burning building and . . . didn't manage to escape.'

Kate shook her head. 'No. No.'

Angela thought she was upset at the news, and ushered her over to the sofa, pressing her shoulder gently to make her sit down. 'I'm surprised you didn't read about it in the papers afterwards?'

Paul sidled over to Jack, and began chatting quietly to him about Billy's myriad functions.

'I'm not from Salisbury. Anyway, I was in hospital for some time after the fire, and then I went away

134

to the States. That's why I didn't know.'

'Were you and Sarah very good friends?'

Kate blushed. 'Um. Well. We hadn't known each other long. We had a few laughs together.' She avoided Paul's eye.

'Let me make some tea, and we can have a proper chat,' said Angela. 'Jack, would you like some juice and biscuits?'

Jack nodded. 'And please may I play soccer in your garden with Paul?'

Angela laughed, in a strained sort of way. 'Of course. I'll show you out there.'

'That's very nice of you,' said Kate, in an equally strained way. She was alarmed to find herself shaking, and wished that Paul wasn't just disappearing out into the back garden with Jack. She felt like she needed someone to hold on to. This was all too weird. Although her memory of the fire was extremely patchy, the two clearest recollections she had were, firstly, of Sarah and herself, collapsing on the grass outside; and secondly, seeing Stephen being carried out. How could they both have died in the fire? It wasn't possible. Sarah was the one who'd helped her, Kate, get out. Sarah had been coughing and spluttering as much as she had—but she'd been OK. She'd got out of the building. Kate remembered it clearly, a patch in the fog that obscured so much of her memory.

After a couple of minutes, Angela came back with a tray of tea things, and a plate of chocolate biscuits.

'I'm really sorry to turn up unannounced like this,' Kate said, declining the offer of a biscuit.

'Not at all. It's actually rather nice to have some company. And to have a child in the house again.' She spoke so wistfully.

'Was Sarah your only child?' Kate asked. 'Tell me to mind my own business if you want.'

'No, it's perfectly all right. Yes, Sarah was our one and only. Now she's gone, I won't be having any grandchildren running around the place either.'

'And your husband?' Kate ventured, feeling awful.

Angela stared at Sarah's portrait, and bit her lip. 'We divorced three years after Sarah died. It just all got to be . . . too much, in the end.'

'I'm so sorry.'

Angela nodded. 'So I live here on my own now. I'm all right, I suppose. I have some good friends, and some good memories. But nothing's turned out how I planned it. Things never do, do they?'

'I guess not,' said Kate slowly, thinking about her and Vernon. And her and Stephen. And now—her and Paul? How would that turn out?

'What do you remember about Sarah?' Angela asked.

Kate looked her squarely in the eye. 'I don't remember very much at all, about the fire—but I'm pretty sure that Sarah helped save my life. I was ill—we were both ill—we'd been given flu, or something. We both had temperatures, although I'm not sure which of us was worse. I was too unwell myself to really be aware of people around me. But she made me get out of bed when the fire alarm went off, and she helped me down the corridors. I couldn't have walked on my own, I was too weak. I remember her red hair, and her voice, urging me to hurry up. Most of all, I remember seeing her outside, on the grass, with me.'

'You can't have done,' Angela said, utterly bewildered.

'I did. I know I did.'

136

'Could she have gone back inside again, to try and save someone else?'

'She must have done, I suppose, although I don't know who she'd have gone back in for. How incredibly brave of her. *I* was in no fit state to do anything else except lie on the grass. I think someone gave me a shot of something. Did they—um—I mean, where was she eventually found?'

Angela's voice trembled. 'In her bedroom at the CRU. Apparently she had become locked in somehow, and couldn't escape.'

'That's impossible. Why would she have gone back into the bedroom, and got locked in? The fire was raging by then. Nobody could have gone back down that corridor! There was so much urgency to get us out of there; the fire was right behind us. When I think of it, it was like it was chasing us down the corridor. The smoke was everywhere . . .'

They both reached for their cups of tea, and drank in silence for a moment. Kate wished hers was a large gin and tonic. A rattling sound made her look up again, and to her horror, she saw that Angela's hand was trembling so violently that her cup shook in her saucer, and tea was slopping onto the cream carpet. Kate jumped up and gently took the cup and saucer from Angela, who was now doubled over with sobs, as if she had bad stomach ache.

'I just can't bear to think of my daughter suffering like that!'

Angela's voice was a wail, more agonised than anything Kate had ever heard. Oh God, she thought, what have we done? We shouldn't have come. Angela had seemed fine just a moment ago.

'I'm so sorry,' Kate repeated, trying to scrub at the tea stain on the floor with a napkin. She felt

137

close to tears herself. Outside, Paul and Jack were kicking the football around, oblivious.

Angela took a deep, long breath and attempted to compose herself. 'No, it's me who ought to apologise,' she said, still crying. 'You'd think it would get easier, but it doesn't. I'm the same with anyone who knew Sarah. When that man, Dr Bainbridge, came round, a few weeks after it happened, I got so distraught that I had to get a shot of tranquillisers—Sarah's dad had to call my GP. I think he really regretted setting foot in here. I had quite a go at him, you see. I just felt I had to blame somebody. I know it wasn't fair of me.'

Kate put the stained napkin back on the tea tray. 'Leonard Bainbridge came to see you? What did he say?'

'He just kept saying how sorry he was. He said that the Cold Research Unit had been set up to help people and now people were dying. He said something about it all getting out of hand. To be honest, he didn't make much sense, and I was so angry and busy yelling at him that I wasn't really listening. And then he said something that made me so mad that I threw him out. He said that I should be proud that my daughter had died doing something to help others—as if it was worth my daughter dying to stop a few people getting a sore throat and a runny nose! He said that one day he hoped I'd see that it was worth the sacrifice.'

Kate didn't know what to say. Her head was spinning too fast. Sacrifice? What on earth had Leonard been talking about? She followed Angela's gaze towards a picture of Sarah when she was a little girl, framed and fading on the mantelpiece. Like Sarah, Leonard was dead now. What secrets had he

138

taken to the grave with him? Watching a tear roll down Angela's cheek, Kate was more determined than ever to find out.

20

Sampson stood outside the hotel beside his car, smoking a cigarette. It helped him think. The trail was warm, but where did it lead? He closed his eyes and drew in a deep breath through his nose. He could smell her, sense her echo, feel the way her presence had left a mark on the air of the city. Kate.

He remembered the first time he saw her. He'd been working at the CRU then as a security guard. Not that he was known as a guard—as far as the inmates or patients, or whatever the fuck you called them, were concerned, he was the odd-job man, the mug who carried their suitcases and mended their TVs when they broke down. He painted fences and pulled up weeds. At first he'd found the work humiliating, far beneath his abilities, but after a while he relaxed and realised that it could be advantageous working undercover, pretending to be a harmless sap. He had access to the guests' bedrooms—including all those girls' rooms. He could slip in and out of shadows without being noticed, because to most of them he was invisible; just a handyman. A big nothing. Occasionally there would be more interesting stuff to do, when his paymasters sent him to do their dirty work, just like now, but most of the time he was satisfied to live this quiet, almost-Zen life.

Christ, he'd been in danger of going soft, until it

139

all kicked off.

When Kate was there.

He'd known since he was a young teenager that he was different to other boys. Everyone else—the whole fucking world—drivelled on about love and joy and happiness. He didn't get it. Every song he heard, every film he saw, the conversations he overheard—it was all love and romance and hearts and flowers. He watched the boys in his class make fools of themselves chasing after girls. It was pathetic. He didn't give a shit about girls. The nearest he got to feeling anything like happiness was when he was causing pain. Making his mother cry, beating his sister's cat's head in with a rock, fighting other boys and making *them* cry. That was joy.

Ironically, the more distant and disinterested he was, the more the girls liked him. They were all after him, to the disgust of the other boys. The prettiest, most popular girls pursued him, widened their eyes when they talked to him, licked their lips, asked him if he wanted to hang out with them. One girl even wrote him a poem, for fuck's sake, which made him physically sick. But the girls offered him their bodies too, and he liked that. He liked fucking. He liked to make girls cry while he fucked them. After a while word got around that he wasn't just a bad lad—he was really bad. They stayed away from him after that, apart from the really messed-up girls, the ones who wanted danger, the girls with problems at home, glue habits and scars on their arms. He felt nothing for them except a vague animal lust, often followed by disgust. That was it. And that was the pattern of his early life.

Then Kate turned up at the CRU. Sampson's colleague Geoffrey had picked her up and mentioned

140

to Sampson that there was a really pretty girl in room 4C. The next day, they were working in the garden when Geoffrey nudged Sampson. 'There's that lassie I told you about.' Sampson had looked up, uninterested.

It was like being kicked in the balls. He guessed he must have looked stupid in that moment, a slack-jawed moron, because Geoffrey laughed and said, 'You seem quite taken with her. I told you she was a looker.'

Sampson couldn't speak. He returned to his digging beside Geoffrey. Later, after the fire, Gaunt had been worried that Geoffrey knew too much so Sampson had disposed of the doddering old twat, burying him in the flowerbeds he loved so much.

He didn't know what it was about Kate that had this effect on him, that made him feel more at peace yet more violent than ever before, the desire to hug and the need to throttle churning around inside him. She wasn't the most beautiful girl he'd ever seen, she didn't have the best body, she didn't move in a particularly alluring way. Put her in a room with a bunch of models and she'd stand out because, well, she didn't look like a model. But she had an extraordinary effect on him.

Tormented, he'd watched her for a fortnight and then she'd gone, just like any volunteer, disappearing once their two weeks was up. He berated himself for not doing something, making an attempt to get closer to her, to overcome his paralysis in the face of the power she had over him.

And then she'd come back. Wonderful, terrible. And he realised why: she was with that doctor, Wilson, that wimpy little shit. How the fuck was she attracted to a gutless turd like him? Okay, so he was clever and handsome. He was nice. 'Nice' made Sampson's teeth hurt. 'Nice' needed to be eradicated from the face of the planet.

Sampson soon became aware that Kate was up to something. So he watched her more closely, and kept an eye on Wilson too. His job had started to bore him but now he felt renewed interest.

It all climaxed in a night of flames and smoke, violence and burning flesh. He was there when the firefighters brought Kate and the other girls out. It was madness, utter chaos, the volunteers fleeing their rooms, police and firemen arriving from Salisbury, local residents appearing to *ooh* and *aah* at the spectacle. At the same moment he saw Kate and her room-mate being brought out, his boss appeared at his side. Instructions were quickly given. To Sampson's immense disappointment, others were to deal with Kate. He was told to deal with her room-mate, however he wished.

*   *   *

Sampson found Sarah sitting on the grass, her head down, her nightdress, which was up around her knees, stained black by smoke. He said her name and she looked up at him. Her eyes were watering, her face, beneath the smudges of ash, was paper-white. She looked like she was at death's door. He felt himself grow aroused.

'I've been asked to help you,' he said. 'Come with me.'

He held out his hand and she took it. He pulled her to her feet and she stumbled. He caught her, putting his arm around her. Through the thin cotton of her nightie her skin was hot. A few feet away,

142

Kate lay on the grass, unconscious. He looked at her ruefully, then escorted Sarah away.

She kept her head down as they walked, coughing and wheezing as he led her away from the burning building towards the trees. A gate in the perimeter fence led to a copse, just a stone's throw from the building but concealed from view. Patients were allowed to go for walks beyond the grounds as long as they didn't come into contact with anyone else.

She looked up, blearily. 'Where are we going? I thought you were taking me to an ambulance.'

He didn't reply, just pulled her along. They passed through the gate and into the copse.

She began to struggle. 'I don't understand . . . Let go of me.'

He gripped her arm harder, and pinched the skin above her hip.

'*Ow*. Let go.' She coughed as she protested, and as she doubled over he pushed her to the ground and dropped to his knees beside her, glad that he had been immunised.

Sarah tried to cry out but her lungs were too weakened by the smoke and the disease that had taken root in her body. Sampson pushed her onto her back and pinned her down. It was easy. She was weak and he was strong. She thrashed her head from side to side until he slapped her face and showed her his teeth.

'Please . . .'

He cocked his head, examining her eyes. The fear fascinated him. It was pointless.

'You're going to die anyway,' he said quietly. 'There's no point fighting it.'

She started to cry. How predictable. But her weakness, her sickness, her proximity to death, it

143

excited him. He needed to be quick though. Pinning her with his forearm he unbuckled his trousers, pushed them down and pulled up her nightdress. He spat on his hand and moistened his cock. He was even more glad he'd been vaccinated.

She stopped struggling, just carried on crying.

As he approached his orgasm he held her throat in his hand and squeezed. Her neck was slender, his hand powerful. It didn't take long. As she died, at the moment he came, he looked into her eyes and saw the horror there.

It was the strongest orgasm he'd ever had.

He needed to hurry. Picking up her lifeless body he strode back through the gate and found himself at the back of the building, where flames still licked at the windows, black smoke vomiting into the night air. The firefighters were round the other side, sending jets of water arcing into the building, fighting a battle that would take them minutes more to win. Sarah had got out of the Unit once. It was unfair really. But as his dad always said, life's not fucking fair.

One of the windows at the back had blown out, and Sampson was able to step through, carrying Sarah in a fireman's lift. It was like Hell inside the building and the heat almost knocked him off his feet. They were inside a bedroom. He fought his way into the corridor and realised he was next to the room that Kate and Sarah shared. He staggered inside, dropped Sarah's body to the floor, slammed the door, locked it behind him with his master key and retraced his footsteps, fighting the urge to breathe in before he climbed back out through the window.

The moment he got outside, he collapsed.

Now, standing in the hotel car park, Sampson stepped on his cigarette and savoured the lingering memory of that night.

How much sweeter it would have been if he could have taken Kate into that wood.

He couldn't believe she was back. Now he was going to get his chance, at last. The chance to make her his. The chance to look into her eyes and see what she saw at the moment of death. They would be naked, slick with sweat, his mouth on hers, her tongue clamped between his teeth, his legs between her thighs. And the most delicious idea of all: as he fucked her he would pick up a knife and slash her throat—and then slit his own. Wouldn't that be the perfect way to go, at the zenith of experience, the apex of *feeling*. He would press his neck against hers so the blood from their jugulars flowed and mingled together, and the last thing he'd see would be her, dying too.

The fantasy excited and terrified him in equal measure. What the hell was wrong with him, imagining himself dying in the arms of some woman? It was obscene, that's what it was. Obscene and confusing. He despised the way she made him feel. He had to put an end to it, to remove this random element, this satellite that stirred the calm, dark surface of his life. He refocused on his fantasy, but this time his own throat stayed intact. Only Kate's jugular gushed. Only she died in pain.

He had to light another cigarette to calm himself, and as he struck the match he realised how stupid he'd been. How could he not have recognised the man with Kate on the CCTV film? He'd been so busy staring at Kate—but it was him. The doctor. Stephen Wilson. Except—how could it be? There was absolutely no way that could be Stephen Wilson.

What the fuck was going on?

He had to find them. And he thought he had an idea where they might be heading, where he would go if he were them. Back to where it all began. He got into his car and headed for Salisbury.

21

The St Magdalena Nursing Home made Vernon Maddox feel nauseous. Old people gave him the heebie-jeebies and he wasn't afraid to admit it. He was frightened of being like them. It only seemed like yesterday when he was young and virile with a thick thatch of auburn hair on his head and chest. Now the hair on his head was falling out and his chest hair was grey. At least Shirl still liked him. He felt a wave of sentiment, then returned to concentrating on the matter in hand. Finding his wife and son.

He'd only met Kate's Aunt Lil once before—back before she was loony tunes—and it wasn't a visit he'd ever planned to repeat. If anyone had told him that one day he'd be visiting the old bat in an old folks' home he would have told them to stop smoking crack, but here he was, clutching a droopy bunch of flowers.

He'd only just recovered from the flight. Flying scared him even more than old people, especially since 9/11. This was the first time he'd been on a

146

plane since that terrible day, even though Kate had pestered him ever since to visit the old country. She'd argued that you shouldn't give in to terrorists; that you had to live your life as normally as possible. Yeah, *right* . . . He remembered watching footage from London after the bombings, with Londoners getting back on the subway—or the tube, whatever it was called—and those ridiculous red buses the very day after the bombs went off. Brave? It was crazy, as far as he was concerned.

It hadn't been difficult at all to find the nursing home where Aunt Lil was waiting for her flight out of here. After discovering his wife's monstrous betrayal, Vernon had rushed home in a cab and scoured the house. Who would Kate visit in England? She only had two living relatives, Lil, and her mousey sister, Miranda. Although Kate had taken her address book with her she hadn't deleted the contacts on her computer, and hacking into it couldn't have been easier to guess—her password was Jack's name and birthdate. There, under L—and this pissed him off, the way she filed people by their first name instead of their surname—was the name and address of Aunt Lil's home. He moved on to M and found Miranda's address. Easy.

On his way back to the airport he had considered calling the police, getting Interpol on the case, or whoever dealt with such crimes. But how long would it take to persuade the authorities that Jack had been abducted, especially as it was by his own mother? It would be far too slow. He wanted his son back *now*. And another thing—he wanted to do it himself. He wanted to see Kate's face when he caught up with her. That would be well worth the trauma of the flight and having to spend a few nights apart from Shirl.

The nursing home was in London, so that was where he headed first, after booking into a hotel near Paddington, the first one he saw after getting off the Heathrow Express. He vaguely remembered Kate telling him some tale about how Lil had moved from Bath (pronounced with an *ah*) to London when she was in her late sixties to be near her old friends. Lil had actually grown up in London.

It was a grand Victorian detached building with ivy scaling the walls. Vernon's feet crunched on gravel as he walked up to the front door and pressed the buzzer. A woman in a crisp white uniform and a butt to die for beckoned him in, and he explained who he was and who he'd come to see, trying not to wrinkle his nose at the smell that drifted through the building, breaking through the wall of air freshener.

'Hi.' He turned on his most charming smile, the one that he liked to practise on female undergraduates. He explained who he was and who he'd come to see. 'My wife visited the other day,' he guessed. 'Kate Maddox. She would have had my son, Jack, with her.'

The nurse beamed. 'Ah, yes, the American boy. What a little angel. Such good manners.'

'Yes, he's been well disciplined.'

The nurse raised an eyebrow, then said, 'Shall I show you up to Miss Johnson's room?'

He followed the nurse up the stairs, enjoying the view of her ass in her tight uniform—Shirl's ass had passed its 'best before' date—and was shown along a corridor with a carpet the colour of a blended roast dinner. The nurse knocked on a door but didn't wait for a response. 'Lil, darling, you've got a visitor,' she said, ushering him in.

Aunt Lil was sitting in a chair by the window. When she turned her head towards him Vernon was reminded of a skeleton in a horror flick. He could almost hear the creak. Vernon clutched his head, as if proximity to such evident senility would cause him to contract it like it was an infectious disease.

'I'll leave you alone,' said the nurse, closing the door.

It was stiflingly hot in the room. Vernon could feel his shirt sticking to his back. He looked around. A stuffed rabbit lay on the bed, a sign of how Lil had returned to childhood. Jack had a stuffed rabbit that was quite similar. He'd left it behind in Boston. Vernon had felt sentimental when he saw Jack's rabbit on his bed, but was secretly pleased. He didn't believe in boys cuddling stuffed toys. He didn't want his son growing up soft. He bet that his idol, Hemingway, never owned a stuffed rabbit.

He moved as close as he dared towards the old woman. 'Hi, Lil, it's me. Vernon Maddox. Kate's husband.'

Aunt Lil looked up at him with watery eyes, half-obscured by large-framed glasses. 'Kate? Where's Kate?'

'She's not here. I'm her husband. I'm trying to find Kate and I was wondering if you might know where she is.'

Aunt Lil blinked at him. 'She's at the Unit. With Leonard. He's a lovely man, a good friend. He'll look after her.'

Vernon moved a little closer. 'At the Unit? What do you mean? What Unit?' What was she rambling on about? 'Where is the Unit, Lil?'

'Where is it? In Salisbury, of course.'

149

Salisbury? He had no idea where Salisbury was, but it wouldn't be hard to find out.

'After that, she's going back to study. She's a clever girl, you know. She's going to be a scientist, just like her father.' She paused and frowned. 'That was such a shame.'

Vernon realised that Lil was talking about the past. Or at least, this part of her conversation was set in the past. It was impossible to sort the past from the present, or even tell if she was aware of the present at all.

'Do you know where Kate is *now*? Is she at this Unit place *now*?' he said. It was possible that she could be there, if she was visiting this Leonard person.

'Pardon?'

He leaned in closer still and raised his voice. 'Where is she *now*?'

Lil studied him and then said, in a hushed, girlish voice, 'William? Is that you?'

'William?' What was she talking about now? 'No, it's Vernon. Kate's husband.'

Lil grabbed his hand. His impulse was to snatch it away, to stop her from touching him. But she held his fingers. 'I knew you'd come back, William. I knew I'd hear your voice again.'

'Listen, my name's Vernon. Who's William?'

'He was her boyfriend.'

Vernon swivelled round and saw another old lady standing in the doorway, wearing a long coat despite the blazing sunshine outside. From the look in her eye, though, this one appeared still to be *compos mentis*. She stepped into the room.

'William was an American GI who Lil was seeing during the war. Oversexed, overpaid and over here.

150

He was one of them.' She laughed. 'Awfully handsome, he was, but at the end of the War he went back to America. He promised to write but never did. Broke poor Lil's heart. She never married, you know. Nobody could live up to her William. I expect Lil heard your accent and thought you were him. Poor thing. Who are you, anyway? I'm Maud.'

Her piercing gaze was unnerving. He explained who he was and asked if she'd seen Kate or knew where she was.

'I don't know,' Maud replied. 'Lil was talking about her the other day. But I wasn't sure if she'd really been here or if she had imagined it. She doesn't make much sense these days.'

'I noticed.'

'It comes to us all, dear.'

Vernon shuddered and thought, I'll shoot myself first.

'And you probably think you'd rather shoot yourself first, but you won't.'

Vernon felt his temper heating up. What did this old crone know about him? Suddenly, he had to get out.

He pushed past Maud and ran down the stairs, not stopping to say goodbye to the nurse who had shown him to Lil's room. He caught a glimpse of his reflection in the hall mirror. His face was burning. Quick to temper, that's what his mother had said about him. It was true, but so what? He liked to think of it as passionate.

He switched on the GPS in his hire car and punched in some digits. Salisbury wasn't too far away. Then he checked how to get to Miranda's. He would try that first, and if Kate wasn't there, he would head to Salisbury and find out what this Unit

151

was and if this Leonard was still there. He vaguely remembered her wittering on about some medical trial she'd been involved in when she graduated—something to do with the common cold, but he couldn't recall any details. But he still felt hopeful, like he was getting warm. He was going to get his son back. And if Kate stood in his way, he'd really lose his temper.

22

'I don't wanna stay at Auntie Miranda's,' Jack whined, halfway along the M40.

Kate twisted round in the passenger seat to see Jack's sulky red face and downturned mouth. She and Paul had decided there was no further reason to be in Salisbury, after the visit to Sarah's mother, and were instead heading north.

'Oh Jack, you'll have such a great time. Auntie Miranda told me that you're going to go horse-riding and strawberry picking, and you can play in the sprinkler every day. Your cousins can't wait to see you.'

'Well, I can wait to see *them*,' he huffed in reply, but Kate could tell that he was slightly mollified all the same. She shot a guilty look at Paul, who was driving. Yes, it was undoubtedly far less boring for Jack to be with his cousins than trailing round the countryside with her and Paul—but she couldn't help feeling as if she was off-loading him for her own more selfish reasons . . . Paul smiled back at her, and she tried to dismiss the guilt. Miranda had moved house from the address that she'd been at

152

for years—there was little chance of Vernon finding her new address; and she'd instructed Miranda not to reply to any emails from him. Jack should be perfectly safe with her.

'Are we nearly there yet, Mummy?'

'I think we must be, honey. We have to come off this motorway at Junction Ten, and we've just passed Junction Nine.'

'Good. Because I'm bored and Billy's thirsty . . . Mummy?'

'Yes, Jack?'

'Can I call Dad?'

Kate glanced at Paul again, in panic this time. She'd been dreading this request since they arrived in England. 'Um, honey, I think Daddy's on holiday too at the moment.'

'I can call his cellphone. I know the number.'

'I know you do, which is very clever of you. But . . . I don't think his phone will work outside America. And anyway, it's only ten o'clock here, which means it's the middle of the night where Daddy is.'

'I want to leave him a message. Why didn't he take me on vacation? If he's not in America it won't be the middle of the night, will it? Where has he gone, anyway?'

Not the British Isles, please, Kate thought, although without much hope. She knew him well enough to suspect he'd jumped on the first available plane when he realised what she had done. She had texted him to say Jack was safe, and not to look for them— but it wouldn't have made any difference. Since then she had kept her phone firmly switched off and hadn't even turned it on to check her messages. Her fear that Vern would snatch Jack back again was so deep and overpowering that she couldn't even allow herself to think about it. She might lose Jack for good. Hopefully, Vern would calm down, given time, and they could sort out access then. Just not now, when it was pride and spite that would be motivating his every action.

'Oh, honey, I'm not exactly sure. And you know what? I think his cellphone is broken, because I tried to call it yesterday but it didn't even ring.' She winced at the blatant lie. 'Anyhow, look, here's the signpost for Junction Ten! We must be almost there. Let me just check the directions, so we don't get lost on the way to the house.'

*　　　*　　　*

Miranda and her husband Pete's house was a rambling, ramshackle Victorian pile on the edge of Churchill, a very picturesque Cotswolds village, with amazing views out over open countryside. Pete was a vet, and had just taken over the village practice, and Miranda was a self-confessed 'professional home-maker'. Kate noted that her sister still appeared to live in the same old green wellies and shabby cardigan she'd had for years. Nobody would ever have guessed that they were sisters. Kate's hair was chestnut brown and curly, and Miranda's light brown and straight. Miranda's eyes were brown, Kate's blue. Kate was four inches taller and two stone slimmer. Miranda had absolutely no interest in science, but knew everything about how to grow perfect tomatoes; whereas Kate couldn't even keep Busy Lizzies alive.

As they walked into the kitchen, Kate noticed Paul looking incredulously between her and her sister,

154

and she grinned. Luckily she had forewarned Miranda on the telephone that she'd be turning up with Jack, and a man who was not her husband, in tow.

'We've only been here four months. I'm so glad you managed to see it before we start renovating. It's what you Yanks call a "fixer-upper", isn't that right?' said Miranda, proudly gesturing to high-ceilinged rooms which flaked plaster as if suffering from psoriasis. 'Lord knows when we'll get around to it, with Pete working the sort of hours he is. I hope you'll be able to stay for lunch, so you get to see him too? He said he'd try and pop back after his morning surgery.'

'We'd love to—but we might have to make tracks soon. We've got a lot to do in a couple of days. Oh, and by the way, I'm not a bloody Yank!' said Kate, jokingly. She was privately wondering how on earth Miranda could bear to bring up children in a dump like this. Yes, it would be incredible when it was finished—but it was going to take years. 'The house is great, Manda. And thanks again so much for having Jack to stay. He's been so excited about seeing his cousins.'

Another lie, thought Kate. All these little tiny lies knotting together in a ball. She pictured it like a ball of rubber bands, the lies getting bigger and bigger, stretching further and further around the ball. How many more times was she going to have to lie to Jack about his dad, and why he couldn't speak to him?

'Gosh, I haven't been called Manda for years!' Miranda exclaimed, smiling. 'It's good to see you, sis. I'm sorry I haven't been better about keeping in touch.'

155

Kate felt guilty, and sad that she and her sister weren't closer. But they had always had such different personalities, and it hadn't helped that she didn't really care much for her brother-in-law Pete. And Miranda couldn't stand Vernon.

*   *   *

Later, Paul went out to play Swingball in the garden with Jack and his cousins, and Kate and Miranda were able to have a more private chat on the terrace, sipping Miranda's homemade elderflower cordial; ice-cubes in the shapes of strawberries clinking around in the tall glasses. It was a beautiful summer's morning, and the sounds of the countryside were all around—birds singing, cows mooing in a field nearby, a tractor rolling down the lane by the side of the house. For the first time, Kate envied her sister's uncomplicated family life.

'So it's all over between you and Vernon. Is it because of—?' Miranda gestured towards Paul, who was rolling around on the grass with Jack squealing and romping on top of him and the other two standing nearby looking as if they were longing to join in, but too shy to do so.

'Oh, no, definitely not! I've only just hooked up with Paul—he's the twin brother of my old boyfriend, Stephen, from ages ago, you know, the one who died . . . We literally bumped into each other in London the day after I got here. There was nobody else involved in me and Vernon splitting up—not from my side, anyway. Just Vernon, being a big fat bully. I'm sure *he* was cheating on *me*, though. And I didn't even care, things had got that bad. I just wanted out.'

156

'You could've rung me, you know, Kate. I didn't realise you were in such a state . . . So you've only known Paul for four days?'

There was an unmistakeable note of disapproval in Miranda's voice, and Kate couldn't really blame her for it. When you thought about it, it was unbelievable that she'd only known Paul for such a short time. It seemed foolhardy in the extreme that the two of them were traipsing off around the country on what was probably a wild goose chase. She opened her mouth to tell Miranda that, no, of course she'd known Paul ever since she and Stephen had been together. But then she thought—no. That's another lie. Stop worrying about what other people think of you. You don't have to defend yourself to anybody.

Fortunately, Miranda didn't wait for an answer, so Kate was spared having to tell the truth.

'Does Jack know?' Miranda asked instead.

'About me and Vernon splitting up? No. I haven't told him we aren't going back.' The reality of the situation hit Kate again, full force, and her face fell. 'Damn. I know I'm going to have to sort something out eventually; some sort of access for Vernon, but I just can't face it yet. He'd snatch him back, I know he would.'

'And that's why you brought him to England, because you think Vernon would try to get custody?'

'I know he would. He tried to take him from me before. And I know if it went to court he could make me look bad. He forced me to go to a shrink who put me on anti-depressants . . . that won't look good. And he'd tell them about all the nights I spent in the lab, being a bad mother. Plus he's a goddamn pillar of the community and I'm a resident alien.'

157

'Poor you. Poor little Jack,' said Miranda, putting her hand on top of Kate's, her eyes full of tears.

Kate got up abruptly. She desperately wanted to know what had really gone on at the CRU, but a small part of her wondered if some of that was because she needed distraction—a way of not having to think about the consequences of taking Jack away from his father.

'We'd better go, Manda. Perhaps we could stay for lunch when we come back to collect Jack again?'

'Of course. And don't worry about him—he'll be fine. Take as long as you need to. What was it you said you had to do, again? I couldn't quite understand on the phone when you were telling me.'

'It's a long story. Paul needs my help to find out the truth about what happened to his brother. There are some unanswered questions around the way he died.' She didn't know what else to say really. It was too complicated to get into.

'Crikey,' said Miranda doubtfully. 'That sounds very dramatic. You will be careful, won't you?'

'Don't worry, we'll just be making a few enquiries, and it'd be boring for Jack, that's all. We aren't going to be hunted down and assassinated by any underworld gangsters, because "we knew too much".'

Her accompanying laugh sounded forced, even to her. She had an image of Sarah, lying on the grass outside the burning CRU, no longer a survivor in her memory, but a corpse. And she thought of Stephen's letter and the weird message. Again, she had the feeling that she and Paul were moving into treacherous waters. Jack would be far better off here, even though it would hurt her to be apart from him.

'Jack!' she called, and he came running up the

158

garden towards her, panting, the colour back in his cheeks. 'Mummy's off now.' His face fell and he flung his arms around her middle, nuzzling into her stomach. 'Be a good boy for Auntie Miranda, won't you? I'll see you really soon, I promise.'

Jack's cousin George shouted from down the garden: 'Come on, Jack, we're gonna play football now, Amelia's in goal, do you want to be a winger or on defence?'

To Kate's surprise, Jack extracted himself from the hug, wiped the tears off his face, and ran off back down the garden. 'Bye Mummy, see you soon!' he shouted, windmilling his arms in the air as he galloped away from her.

23

'He's a great kid, your Jack,' Paul said later, as they stopped at a service station just south of Birmingham, for a drink and a loo break.

After leaving Miranda's, they'd driven straight on up the country towards Staffordshire, heading for the village near Stafford where Leonard Bainbridge's widow lived. Finding her address had not been difficult—the article they'd read in Starbucks, about Leonard's death, had mentioned that the couple retired to Penkridge. She was ex-directory, but Paul found her on a website that allowed users to check the electoral roll for a small fee. There was only one Bainbridge listed in Penkridge, and it was a small place, so they were fairly confident they had the correct details—even without a telephone number to be able to double-check.

'I know,' Kate replied wistfully, dunking a large cookie into a mug of coffee. 'I can't believe he was so good about me leaving him there. I thought he was going to make a massive fuss, but he didn't. I think it was far harder for me to say goodbye than it was for him!'

Paul gave her hand a squeeze, and she nearly dropped the cookie in. 'You've been really quiet since we left your sister's place. Are you worried about him?'

Kate bit her lip, and laid the soggy cookie back on the plate.

'No, not worried, not exactly. He'll have a wonderful time with his cousins, and Miranda will really look after him—it's not that. It's just . . . I suppose I feel guilty, that's all. Dragging him away from his dad, and now dumping him on my sister . . .'

'Hey, come on,' Paul said, leaning over the table and rubbing the side of her arm. 'You're a great mother, and you've done absolutely the right thing. You couldn't stay with Vernon just for Jack's sake, you know.'

'Yeah. I know all that. But still . . .'

'But nothing. And as for coming with me, well, you are doing me the most enormous favour, and I'm extremely grateful. This is really, really important to me and my family, and I couldn't do it without you. So—thank you.'

'I'm not only doing it for you,' she said.

'I know. But . . .'

He stood up and kissed her forehead, and Kate felt tears prickle. 'I'm probably just tired,' she said, managing a smile. 'We had such an early start this morning, and I don't think I'm even properly over the jetlag. This has all happened so fast. Plus, I keep

160

waiting for Vernon to somehow turn up, shouting the odds. I'm sure he won't be able to track down Miranda's new address easily—I don't think he even knows her married name—but I don't even dare switch on my mobile in case there are dozens of furious messages from him. I'll have to now, though, won't I? I told Miranda to let Jack call me whenever he wanted.'

'Well, that's easily fixed. Just call her now and give her my mobile number instead. Jack can reach you on that.'

Kate looked grateful. 'OK. Good idea. We should get to Mrs Bainbridge's by noon—time to have a chat to her, if she's in, and then go and get some lunch afterwards. Then . . . um . . . where do we go next? Will we be staying up here?'

Paul blushed, very slightly, and Kate realised his train of thought was along the same line as hers: two rooms, or one?

'I suppose it depends on what leads we get out of Mrs B, if any. And maybe we should stay for a night anyway, to give ourselves a break. We could ask Mrs B if she knows any cheap and cheerful B&Bs nearby. If the worst comes to the worst, we'll have to sleep in the car.'

'Great,' said Kate, rolling her eyes. 'You certainly know how to show a girl a good time.'

'You bet I do, honey,' Paul replied, winking at her, and Kate felt herself growing hot in all kinds of places.

'Come on,' she said briskly, 'let's hit the road.' Otherwise, she thought, I'm going to march over to the motel next door to this service station and book us into a room right now, and forget Mrs Bainbridge . . .

*   *   *

Two hours later, Kate and Paul had parked the car in the car park of a small tennis club, across the road from a pretty thatched cottage which— hopefully—belonged to Leonard's widow. On the courts next to them some elderly people were playing doubles in a fairly desultory fashion, and Kate inspected their faces carefully, in case she recognised Mrs Bainbridge. She had wracked her brains, but couldn't remember anything about her, although she'd met her once or twice as a kid.

'I wonder if she'll remember me?' she said aloud.

'I'm sure she will, if they were such good friends of your parents,' Paul replied, switching off the engine and unfastening his seatbelt.

'It's quite weird, seeing someone who knew my folks so well. I suppose it'll be for me a bit like it was for Sarah's mother when we turned up at her place. I hope she's there.'

'Only one way to find out,' said Paul, climbing out of the car. 'Let's go.'

They crossed the road and walked up to the front door; Kate nervously, Paul more assertively. He seemed full of energy, raring to go.

Kate rang the bell. 'What are we going to ask her?' she whispered. 'Where do we start?'

'Leave it to me,' said Paul confidently. 'It'll be fine.'

There was no answer. Paul pushed open the letterbox and peered inside. 'No sign of anyone in there.'

'There's a car on the drive at the side,' said Kate. 'Maybe she's in the garden.'

162

'I'll go round the back and have a look. She might not have heard the doorbell. You stay here and ring again, in case she was in the loo or something.'

Paul vanished down the path at the side of the house, past garishly flowering purple-and-pink fuchsia bushes, as Kate pressed the bell again. The house was neatly kept, with shiny brass furniture on the door, and even the glossy painted panels looking as though they were regularly wiped clean. Kate idly inspected her distorted reflection in the flap of the letterbox, wondering again if Mrs Bainbridge would recognise Kate as the skinny little girl she'd been back then. She tried to remember if Mrs Bainbridge had been around during those hazy weeks when she was in hospital after the fire. She didn't think so—although everything was such a blur from that time.

Still no answer from inside. Kate stood back and looked up at the upstairs windows, but the net curtains were white and fresh and undisturbed. What an anti-climax, if they'd come all this way and Mrs B was on holiday. Or had moved abroad . . .

Kate thought she heard raised voices coming from the back of the house. She cocked her head and listened harder. She could make out the sound of Paul's voice—not what he was saying, but the tone of it: pleading, almost outraged; and shrill, almost hysterical replies. Uh-oh, she thought. Guess he found her, then.

She was just tentatively making her way past the fuchsia bushes when Paul appeared, red in the face with anger, stalking down the path towards her.

'Come on, Kate,' he said brusquely, grabbing her hand and almost dragging her towards the gate. 'We're wasting our time here. She's nuts.'

'How the hell did you manage to upset her like

that in two minutes flat?' Kate asked, when they were back in the car. Paul laid his forehead on the steering wheel in a gesture of frustration and defeat. He shrugged.

'I can't understand it. She was at the bottom of the garden, digging a vegetable patch. I probably gave her a fright—I sort of came up behind her. I think she must be quite deaf, because I was calling her name all the way down the lawn, but she didn't respond, so I kept moving closer, until I tapped her on the shoulder . . .'

Kate groaned. 'No wonder she was scared, if you sneaked up behind her.'

'I didn't bloody sneak!' Paul retorted. 'What else was I meant to do? I tapped her on the shoulder, she jumped and held the garden fork out in front of her like she was about to impale me on it, and I tried to reassure her, but she wasn't having any of it. She's a game old bird, I'll give her that.'

'What did you say to her?'

'I just said that we were here because we wanted to talk to her about her late husband, and she went mental. I had to back away—I mean, I really thought she was going to lunge at me with the fork. "You won't get away with it!" she kept shouting. "Leave now otherwise you'll regret it!" I think she must be a bit cuckoo. I was trying to get her to listen to me tell her about you, and that she knew your parents, but by that stage she was just yelling—I don't think she even heard me. So I turned around and left.'

They looked at each other hopelessly. 'Now what?' Kate asked. 'Perhaps I ought to try.' She just about managed to refrain from saying that she ought to have been the one to try in the first place—she was sure she could have done it in a less confrontational

164

manner. 'There's no point in knocking again, she won't answer, will she? And I'm sure she'll have gone back into the house. She's not likely to have stayed out in the garden if she's all that upset. I don't want to go sneaking round the back and risk freaking her out again.'

'I was not sneaking!' Paul reiterated defensively. He looked so like Jack, when Jack was in trouble, that Kate couldn't help smiling.

'We'll just have to wait till she's calmed down. Why don't we go and have a pub lunch, and come back later?'

'OK,' Paul said. 'Sorry I messed it up. What an idiot, eh? Talk about a bull in a china shop.'

Kate hugged him, slightly self-consciously. 'Don't worry. All is not lost. Let's go and eat. There was a nice-looking pub back there on the main road.'

*   *   *

Two hours later, after ploughman's lunches containing slabs of cheese the size of small bricks, Paul and Kate walked back along the road towards Mrs Bainbridge's cottage, and Paul's car, in the tennis club car park.

'I am so full-up,' said Kate, tasting pickled onion in her mouth, and feeling her pint of lager sloshing around in her stomach as they marched along the verge.

Paul laughed, his mood restored. 'I've noticed that about you: you're either starving, or stuffed.'

'Yes, well, you'd think I'd be used to large portions, having lived in the States. But that ploughman's was enough for four grown men.'

'I like your appetite,' he replied. 'I can't stand girls

165

who constantly fuss about how many calories they're consuming. It's so unsexy.' He grinned at her, and she reached out and squeezed his hand. She felt unaccountably happy.

'Let's wait in the car for a while. We'll be able to see if she comes out, and we can nab her then. She can't shut the door in our faces if she's outside, can she? And hopefully that way it'll give her enough time to recognise me and not flip out.'

Paul squeezed Kate's hand back again, and pretended to frown. 'Wait in the car? Won't that be, like, really boring, with nothing to do?' He let go of her hand and gently caressed the back of her neck, holding the passenger door open for her as he did so.

'We could play I-Spy,' said Kate, grinning at him as she climbed in.

'Or,' Paul said, getting in the other side and leaning slowly towards her, 'perhaps we could think of something else to pass the time.'

They kissed, both of them smiling through the kiss. 'Sorry if I taste of pickled onion,' Kate mumbled, but Paul just kissed her again.

'If you do, then so do I,' he replied when they surfaced.

'That's all right then. Kiss me again?'

*　　　*　　　*

Half an hour later, they were still kissing. Paul had had to switch on the engine and lower the electric windows, since the car had become almost completely steamed up.

'We'd make rubbish private investigators, wouldn't we? Elvis himself could've been in and out of that cottage ten times, and we'd be none the wiser,' Kate said, coming up for air. She was painfully aware of how turned on she was. She was dying to touch him, but didn't dare. It had been so long since she'd kissed anyone—including Vernon—that she couldn't even remember the protocol for heavy petting. Perhaps she ought to wait till he touched her first?

'Don't worry. I've been keeping one eye open,' Paul replied.

Kate tutted. 'And there was I, thinking you only had eyes for me!'

'Isn't one eye good enough?'

'No. I'm very demanding. And sex starved.' Kate slid her hand further up Paul's thigh. It was no good. She just couldn't wait any longer, she had to feel his hardness. It felt absolutely wonderful, and they both sighed with pleasure.

'That's very impressive,' she whispered, rubbing it through his jeans.

'I don't think those two are quite so impressed,' said Paul, snatching her hand away too late, as two elderly ladies in tennis whites walked past the back of the car, looking disgusted.

'Ooops,' Kate giggled, heady with lust, and relief that he hadn't recoiled in horror at her forwardness.

'We'd better stop, otherwise I'm going to rip all your clothes off here and now, and not only will we never get to talk to Mrs B, but we'll get arrested . . .' He dropped his voice, '. . . And then I won't be able to explore your body in greater detail tonight, because we'll be in separate cells getting told off by the local constabulary.'

'Is that what you've got planned for me, then?' said Kate, feeling like a teenager again.

Paul leaned across to her, moving his own hand

up between her legs. He nodded solemnly. 'Oh yes,' he murmured, and Kate thought she might just explode with lust.

'But first,' he announced briskly. 'Business!'

Kate groaned.

'She hasn't appeared. Her car is still there. It's been—' he looked at his watch—'over three hours since I did *not* sneak up on her, so I'm sure she'll have recovered by now. Why don't you go and ring the doorbell? It's worth a try. I don't think I can sit here any longer without ravishing you.'

'You've got a point. OK. You wait here, and I'll go and see if she'll let me in.'

24

John Sampson was standing on the site of the CRU, where Kate and Paul had stood just twenty-four hours earlier, when his mobile rang. It was the phone that was only ever called by one person: Gaunt. He hesitated before answering it. He had been enjoying the sweet memories from his last night at this place.

'Yes?'

'About time. I thought you were never going to answer.'

Sampson waited for Gaunt to continue.

'Any luck tracking our quarry?'

Sampson knew that Gaunt, who spent most of his life these days in his laboratory, enjoyed the espionage, the spy thriller stuff that added a dash of colour to his days. He pretended not to, but Sampson could hear the excitement in his voice. He told Gaunt what he'd found so far.

'In other words, she's got away.'

Again, Sampson stayed silent, clenching his jaw muscles and taking slow, calming breaths.

Eventually, Gaunt said, 'You'd better get back here to the base. How long will it take you?'

'Not long.' Sampson hung up and took a last look around the housing estate. She had been here. The use of the word 'quarry' had been appropriate. He was the hound and Kate the fox; he swore he could almost smell her on the air.

*   *   *

Security at the base was strict, aimed at keeping out not just the wrong people but the organisms they carried; the bacteria, viruses and parasites that inhabited the human body. Inside the doorway, Sampson, who had been through this procedure many times, stripped, showered and washed his skin and hair—what there was of it—with an anti-bacterial solution. Next, a doctor wearing a mask checked him over, examining him and asking him questions to make sure he hadn't noticed any signs of infection recently. Had he suffered from any cold or flu-like symptoms? How about headaches, stomach pains, bowel or bladder problems, fatigue, nausea, dizziness? What about sexual partners? Had he had unprotected sex? Had he visited any of the following countries? He answered a terse no to everything; they knew he hadn't been abroad since his last visit. After the examination he put on clean underwear, a t-shirt and trousers, then slipped on a pair of soft shoes. Finally, he was allowed into the interior of the building.

Gaunt met him in the corridor. They walked past the rooms where Sampson had recently seen the Vietnamese woman and the Serbian prostitute. They weren't there anymore. The rooms were empty, scrubbed clean; all trace of their previous occupants had been eradicated.

They reached Dr Gaunt's office. He gestured for Sampson to sit down, and took a seat at the opposite side of his desk.

'I saw you looking into the empty rooms. You took a fancy to our little Serbian, didn't you?' He smiled, displaying yellow teeth. 'Nothing left of her now, I'm afraid to say. Incinerated.'

Gaunt opened a drawer and took out a gold chain with a heart-shaped locket on the end. He held it up, and it glinted as it rotated back and forth.

'Oh, except this. *This* is all that's left of her.'

Sampson recognised the locket that the Serbian prostitute had been wearing.

'Rather nice, I thought,' said the doctor. 'I removed the photo of the child that was in it.' He dropped it back into the drawer. 'It's mine now.'

Sampson concealed his contempt for Gaunt's need to keep souvenirs of the people he'd killed. 'Why did you ask me to come here?'

The smile vanished from Gaunt's face. 'I wanted to let you know that we're very close.'

'Close?'

'To finishing what we started a long time ago. Thanks to your trip to Oxford we've had a bit of a breakthrough in the lab and the final part of the puzzle has been solved.' His smile reappeared, wider and dirtier than before. 'This is very good news.'

Sampson groped for something to say, 'Congratulations.'

'Thank you. There are just a few final tests to conduct, and some other preparations, making sure everyone's in the right place and so on. But I would expect matters to be concluded during the next few days.' He leaned forward across the desk. 'Which means it's critically important that nobody and nothing gets in the way.'

'You mean Kate?'

Gaunt raised an eyebrow. 'On first-name terms, are we?'

Sampson's face remained impassive. 'I wasn't sure whether to call her Carling or Maddox.'

'Well, she's Maddox now. Although we should never have given her the chance to reach her next birthday, let alone get married and change her name. Fucking Bainbridge and his sentimentality, letting her go like that. She's a loose end.'

Sampson had an image of himself tying the loose end up. Handcuffing her, perhaps.

Gaunt went on: 'It's probably a coincidence that she's come back to England now of all times, but the fact that she's here makes me nervous. We don't know how much of her memory has come back over the years because of the way the whole thing was rushed. Bainbridge always assured me it would be okay, but I'm not so sure. Our friend at Harvard has never reported any sign that her memory has returned but we can't afford to take any chances. If she starts to remember too much and goes to the police . . .' He trailed off. 'That's why you have to find her—to make sure that those memories don't come back.'

Sampson nodded. 'I understand.'

'Perhaps I'm being paranoid.'

'I don't think so. I saw her on CCTV at the hotel

where she was staying in London. The man she is with must be Wilson's brother.'

The doctor didn't react for a moment, then blinked and said, 'What?'

'The man Kate is with looked just like Stephen Wilson.'

Gaunt looked even more concerned. He pulled his computer keyboard towards him and started tapping away, concentrating on the screen.

'What are you doing?'

'Bringing up Wilson's file.'

Stephen Wilson's details, put together from his original personnel file and stored now in a password-protected computer system, appeared on the screen and the doctor started reading through it. A few moments later Gaunt swore to himself.

'What is it?'

'I'd forgotten Paul Wilson. What the hell is Kate Maddox doing with Wilson's twin brother? She *is* up to something.'

He stood up and paced around the office. 'She must have remembered something and come here to contact Wilson's brother. She's undoubtedly told him everything.' He looked even paler than usual. 'We have to find them immediately.'

Sampson opened his mouth to speak, but before he could, the phone on the desk rang. The doctor snatched it up. 'Yes?'

Sampson watched as Gaunt's eyes widened with surprise, and then a smile appeared at the edges of his mouth. 'I'll get someone onto it straight away.'

Sampson waited.

'Well, speak of the devil and he, or she, shall appear. It seems we've found them.'

A few moments later, Sampson was on his way

172

out, Gaunt's final words ringing in his ears. *Get up there now. And tie up these loose ends before she turns into a loose cannon.*

25

Kate got out of the car, her legs so wobbly with desire that she could barely walk straight. She glanced down at herself and, sure enough, her nipples were rock hard and sticking out like light switches. Hopefully Mrs B wouldn't notice. She shook herself slightly, took a deep breath, and walked up to Mrs Bainbridge's front door again. Business first, pleasure later. The car was still parked in the drive, so hopefully she hadn't gone out anywhere.

Kate tapped, hesitantly, thinking it less intrusive than the doorbell.

'Mrs Bainbridge,' she called, loudly and clearly, through the letterbox, catching sight of a flash of white shirt retreating through a door into what looked like the kitchen. 'It's Kate Carling here, you and Leonard knew my parents, remember? Derek and Francesca Carling? We last met when I was a little girl, you came to our house on the South Downs. Are you there? I've driven up from London to see you.'

Almost immediately, Kate heard footsteps from inside, and then the sound of the door being unlocked and unbolted. Mrs Bainbridge opened the door, but kept the chain on. Her face appeared in the gap, wrinkled and pale, but with the sort of bone structure indicating a once-powerful beauty. Kate recognised her only very vaguely, although thankfully Mrs Bainbridge didn't have so much trouble with her.

'Kate Carling! I'd know that face anywhere. You hardly look different to how you were at nine years old.'

Kate smiled, relieved. Mrs Bainbridge wasn't a bit like the madwoman with the garden fork that Paul had described. 'Well, I'm not sure whether that's a compliment or not . . . How are you, Mrs Bainbridge?'

'Call me Jean, please,' Mrs Bainbridge said, unhooking the security chain and admitting Kate into the front room of the cottage. 'What may I get you? Sorry if you find me a little disorganised, I had rather a shock earlier. It's been quite a day for unexpected visitors. Anyway, would you like a drink? Tea, coffee, a cold drink? You look rather flushed.'

'Oh—er—nothing, thanks, I'm fine, really. And I'm terribly sorry, but I think the unexpected visitor you're probably referring to was Paul, my friend. He's here with me. We rang the doorbell before lunch, and when there was no answer, he came round the back to see if you were in the garden. I'm so sorry he gave you a fright.'

Jean looked horrified. 'Oh my goodness.' She sank down into a chintzy armchair, her thin fingers raking absently along the arms of it. 'Oh no.'

Kate sat down on the sofa next to her. 'It's all right, Jean, really. It's not a problem. We just feel awful, that he scared you like that.'

Jean shook her head. 'You don't understand. It *is* a problem. I had no idea he was here with you! I suppose he was trying to tell me, but I wasn't listening. I just assumed . . . He asked about Leonard and the CRU . . . If I'd known, I'd never have . . .

174

Oh no.'

'What?' Kate asked, confused. Jean seemed to be really over-reacting, over what was merely a bit of entirely understandable fear-induced rudeness.

'Never mind,' she said, composing herself and sitting more upright. 'So, my dear, it has been a very long time! What on earth brings you up here? You do know that my Leonard is no longer with us, don't you?' Her right hand flew to the third finger of her left, and twisted the large ruby ring around.

'Yes. I'm so sorry, Jean. I was very sad to learn of his death. He was so good to me.'

'He was very fond of you, Kate, and your parents. Perhaps I shouldn't say so, but you were always his favourite, because you wanted to be a scientist just like him. You had a sister, didn't you, what was her name?'

'Miranda. She never wanted to be a scientist. In fact, I think she used to keep out of your way when you came to visit, because she'd get bored with me asking Leonard questions about experiments. She preferred to stay in her room playing with her dolls.'

'And did you become a scientist in the end?' Jean was asking these questions, politely, but under the surface she still seemed very distracted and flustered. Her eyes were darting between the telephone and the front door, as if she was expecting someone to arrive or call. Paul must really have freaked her out, thought Kate, as she answered Jean's question with more than a hint of pride:

'Yes. A virologist, just like Leonard. I couldn't have done it without him, though. He organised me to go to Harvard, after the fire—you know, at the CRU.'

Jean hesitated. 'The fire. Yes. I remember.

175

Dreadful business.' She patted her beautifully-coiffed silver hair. 'Anyway, so what brings you up here? You hadn't come to see Leonard, had you?'

Kate, who had already said that she knew Leonard was dead, was beginning to wonder if Paul might be right—if Jean was perhaps not quite all there. But she looked so together: her immaculate hair, smart clothes, and tidy house. Kate had first-hand experience of senile dementia, with poor lovely old Lil, and you couldn't even begin to compare Lil and Jean. She decided that Jean must merely be a bit distracted at the unexpectedness of her visit.

'I'm sorry I didn't phone first, but I didn't have your number, just your address. No, I knew about Leonard. But you might be able to help me. I'm after some information, really—about the fire, in fact.'

Was it Kate's imagination, or did Jean's hand tremble slightly?

'The fire?'

'Yes. It's just that I seem to have an almost complete memory loss surrounding the events of that night, which is odd, considering I wasn't badly injured or anything. I was in hospital for a while afterwards, although I'm still not sure why. I'm trying to help out my friend Paul—his twin brother died that night, under slightly suspicious circumstances— and we want to find out exactly what happened. You see, his brother, Stephen, was my boyfriend at the time. Paul and I have been told different versions of the same event, and something isn't quite right.'

'Oh, my dear,' said Jean, now sounding distinctly panicky. 'Don't you perhaps think that some things are best left alone? I mean, you never know what you might uncover.'

176

Kate looked sharply at her. What was that supposed to mean? She leaned forward and stared at Jean gravely. 'So you do know something? Please tell me, Jean. I think it's important. Not just for Stephen's family, but for my room-mate, Sarah—she died that night, too. And I've got this nagging feeling that something else was going on too; that there was more than just research into the common cold going on—I think I'd discovered something at the time but I just can't seem to remember what it was.'

There was a moment's silence, broken only by the ticking of the grandfather clock in the corner. Kate realised she was holding her breath.

'I don't know, Kate,' Jean said, keeping her gaze steady. 'There were a lot of secrets. Leonard used to fret that there might be more secrets than he knew about, and it used to keep him awake at night. But he would never tell me. He always said it was better for me not to know what his fears were. And I think it might be better for you not to know, too.'

Kate shook her head. 'Now I *really* want to know,' she said simply. 'Please.'

Jean stood up, her legs still long and enviably slim in smart navy trousers. She walked over to a polished walnut writing desk in an alcove under the stairs of the cottage, fished around in a small china dish to retrieve a key, and unlocked the desk. Folding the slanted front of it down to reveal a series of small drawers, she brought out an A4 brown envelope from the largest of them.

'Honestly, Kate, I really don't know anything. I don't have any of Leonard's research papers or documents apart from what's in here. It was just a few loose sheets that I found under our bed after he died. He must have been looking over them one

177

night before he went to sleep. I don't know why I kept them, it's all classified material so I should have sent them back to the lab. They're mostly just numbers and formulas, as far as I can tell. Some sort of case studies perhaps? I kept them because I saw your name on one of the sheets. You have them—but I don't know if they will be of any use.'

'Thank you,' said Kate, mystified, opening the envelope. Inside were five or six sheets of printed reports. 'It's probably just my medical records from when I was a volunteer there.'

'Kate, dear, while you look at those, would you excuse me for a moment? I have a rather important telephone call to make upstairs.'

'Of course,' said Kate, engrossed in studying the sheets, trying to find her name.

Jean vanished upstairs, and it occurred to Kate that it was odd that she couldn't wait until Kate had left to make the call. What could be so urgent, and private? She heard a door close, and stood up to investigate. There was a phone downstairs, but she felt it would be too sneaky to attempt to listen in on another extension. Besides, Jean might hear the click as Kate picked up.

Kate put the envelope back in her shoulder bag, and moved silently towards the stairs. She couldn't hear Jean's voice, so she started climbing the staircase. She could pretend to be in search of the bathroom—and did, in fact, need it.

When she reached the landing, she saw the bathroom ahead. To her right was a closed door. Feeling awful, and horrified at her lack of respect for Jean's privacy, she gently pressed her ear against the door. She could easily hear Jean's voice now— she obviously had only just been connected.

178

'Hello. It's Jean Bainbridge again . . . No, I must speak to him . . . When? Well, you must get a message to him . . . It was a misunderstanding. There is nothing to worry about, he was a friend of a friend, I just panicked when he . . . What? Oh my word. No, I'm sure that's not right, they aren't—no, please don't.' She was becoming more agitated. 'Leonard wouldn't want this. You must get hold of him and stop him! Hello? *Hello*?'

Kate shot into the bathroom, although her need for a pee had been forgotten. She flushed the toilet, pretended to wash her hands, and waited till she heard the bedroom door slowly open again. Kate timed it so she emerged at the same moment as Jean.

'Sorry, hope you don't mind, but I was dying for the—Jean? What's the matter?'

Jean's face was ashen, and her eyes full of tears. She reached out and clutched Kate's sleeve, an expression of abject panic on her face. 'You must leave, now. You and your friend. Immediately!'

'Why? What's happened? What's going on?'

'Oh Kate,' Jean said, her voice trembling. 'I've done something very silly . . .'

26

Kate jogged across the road to the tennis club car park where Paul was standing beside the car, fiddling with his mobile phone. His face lit up with delight when he saw Kate, but when he saw her expression his smile vanished.

'What is it?'

'We've got to get out of here. Now.'

'Why? What's going on?'

Kate felt like the old woman who'd swallowed a fly . . . and a spider and the rest of the menagerie: panic wriggled inside her. Why did Paul insist on knowing what was going on before he would do as she asked? It was such a typical male trait. She just wanted them out of here, this second.

'Get in the car and I'll tell you later.'

Still, he hesitated.

'Come *on*.'

'All right. But I wish you'd tell me.' He got into the driver's seat and Kate jumped in beside him. She dropped the envelope Mrs Bainbridge had given her on the back seat.

'It's Mrs B,' she said. 'When you scared her earlier, she called someone, and they're on their way now.'

His eyes widened. 'What, the police?'

'No—I wish it was. Listen, Mrs B was given a number to call if anyone ever turned up and started asking questions about Leonard. That's what she did earlier, after you went into her garden.'

'What? Who did she call?'

'I don't know exactly. But she almost shoved me out the door and told me I had to make myself scarce. She said I was in danger if I didn't get away.'

Paul had inserted the key into the ignition, ready to start the engine, but now he removed his hand from it. 'But these people might be able to give us the answers we're looking for. We should stay and wait for them.'

He pushed open the door and got out.

'No! Paul, don't.'

She muttered a curse, then chased Paul as he marched across the main road towards Mrs

180

Bainbridge's house. She could see why he was reluctant to run away, but he hadn't witnessed how palpable and contagious Mrs Bainbridge's fear had been. There was so much Kate and Paul didn't know, and whoever was on their way, they didn't sound like people willing to sit down and provide them with answers over a nice cup of tea.

Paul had almost reached the house, Kate a few steps behind, when a black Audi pulled up. At the same time, Mrs Bainbridge came out of her front door and made 'go away' gestures to Paul, her face pale with fright.

The Audi stopped a few metres from Mrs Bainbridge's house and a man got out.

Kate felt her knees buckle and she almost fell. He was older and was wearing sunglasses, and she hadn't thought about him for sixteen years. She flashed on an image of him in the garden at the CRU, turning to watch her as she walked past.

Sampson. That was his name. Stephen had warned her to stay away from him, that there was something predatory about him. She didn't need to be persuaded: he gave her the creeps. His chiselled good looks were cold and evil.

'Kate,' he said, unsmiling but intense. 'Good to see you again.'

'Sampson.'

Paul looked at both of them and took a step forward, saying, 'Listen, Mr Sampson, or is that your first name? I wonder if . . .'

Sampson pulled out a gun and pointed it at Paul's chest.

Paul immediately put his hands up at shoulder height, the blood draining from his face. Sampson took a step towards him, the gun held steady. Kate

181

watched Sampson's finger tense against the trigger. She shouted, 'Paul!' and then somebody screamed, and the bang was quieter than she'd always imagined a gunshot to be. She realised she had closed her eyes, and when she opened them she expected to see Paul's body sprawled on the asphalt. But Paul was still standing. So was Sampson. The body on the ground was small, and old.

With surprising agility for an elderly woman, Jean Bainbridge had run in front of Paul, just as Sampson squeezed the trigger, blocking the bullet with her body. She had saved Paul's life.

Kate felt a pain go through her like she'd been shot herself. At the same moment, Paul launched himself at Sampson.

Paul was lucky: Sampson was momentarily off balance. Paul struck him in the stomach and Sampson gasped, swinging up the gun to hit Paul around the head, but Paul lifted his arm and blocked the blow. The gun fell from Sampson's grasp and Kate stepped forward and kicked it away. It span across the road and under a parked car.

Sampson moved towards the gun, and Paul shouted, 'Run!'

They sprinted towards the tennis club, Paul ahead again, looking back over his shoulder to make sure Kate was with him, reaching back so she could grab his hand. He could see that Sampson was on his belly, trying to extract his gun from under the parked car. Paul yanked open the door of his own car— thank God they hadn't locked it—and leaned over and shoved open the passenger door. A second later he started the car and they skidded out of the car park.

There was Sampson, on his feet now, gun in hand.

182

Paul drove straight at him. Sampson fired but the bullet bounced off the bodywork, and then he had to jump backwards onto the pavement to stop Paul from knocking him over. Paul swerved around Mrs Bainbridge's body and watched the mirror anxiously, as Sampson ran towards his Audi and climbed in, giving Paul and Kate just a few seconds' lead before he managed to accelerate after them.

'Fuck, he's coming. Which way shall I go?' There was no response. 'Kate?'

She turned to him, her eyes wide with shock. 'He killed Mrs Bainbridge.'

Paul reached and touched Kate's arm. She was trembling. Or was that him? 'Who the hell is this guy?'

'He was at the CRU.'

Very quickly, they left the village behind, the streets of Penkridge giving way to countryside. They passed a nature reserve sign and Kate wondered frantically if they were doing the right thing, leaving the safety-in-numbers of civilisation behind. It was too late to turn back now though. Paul swung the car left. The road was clear ahead, but that would help Sampson catch them as much as it would help them get away. Sampson's Audi was much faster than Paul's seen-better-days Peugeot 205. They would need to outmanoeuvre him. But Paul, who didn't know these roads, had no advantage. His hands, sweaty with stress, slipped on the wheel as he spun it and turned right onto another quiet country road, putting his foot down. Kate watched the speedometer rise until they were doing eighty.

The Audi was still close behind them.

'Have you got your seatbelt on?'

'Yes, of course. Paul, we have to . . .'

183

'Hold on tight.'

Kate looked up and saw what Paul had spotted a moment before: an enormous, bright green four-wheel-drive tractor trundling around the bend ahead. Paul floored the accelerator, moved to the wrong side of the road—the right—and headed straight towards it. Kate gasped and closed her eyes.

It all happened in a couple of seconds. Paul drove straight at the tractor, waving his arms at the driver, motioning for him to change lanes. Behind him, Sampson was still on the left, a second behind them, obscured behind the tinted glass of his car windscreen.

Kate pushed herself back in her seat and whispered a rapid prayer.

The tractor driver pulled on the steering wheel of his huge, unwieldy vehicle, heaving it onto the left side of the road. Paul spun the wheel again, tyres squealing, swinging to the right and shooting past the tractor—which was now directly in Sampson's path. As they cleared the tractor, they both heard another screech of brakes, the angry stabbing of a car horn.

'We're still alive,' Kate said quietly.

Paul twisted his head and took a glance backwards. 'No sign of him, not yet. But he won't be held up for long.' They drove around the next bend, moving steadily upwards until they came over the crest of a hill. Farmland stretched to either side of them, sheep grazing in silence behind low stone walls. Some poor creature lay in the road, its fur matted with blood: roadkill.

'Do you have any idea where we are?' Paul asked, as they continued at high speed along the empty road. 'Apart from the middle of nowhere.'

Kate snapped out of her trance. 'I think this is

Cannock Chase.'

'How far till the next town?'

'I don't know. I think if we keep heading north we'll reach Stafford, I saw a signpost back there.'

She looked out the back window and saw the black Audi appear over the crest of a shallow hill and start closing on them.

'He's catching us. Paul, he's catching . . .'

'I know, I know. I'm going as fast as I can. The road atlas should be on the back seat. Can you try to find out how far it is till Stafford?'

Kate retrieved it and started flicking blindly through the pages trying to find the road they were on. She couldn't even find the right page. Why the hell didn't Paul have Sat Nav in this cruddy old banger?

Calm down, she told herself. She used a technique that she had learned when Jack was a baby, screaming in the night, when nothing would make him stop crying and she felt as if she would explode from the stress. She started to recite the periodic table under her breath: H—hydrogen; Li—lithium; Be—beryllium . . . She knew people would think this technique weird, but it worked for her—immediately, she felt soothed by the effort of concentrating, her brain working again in the way it should, and she was able to check the map at the front and quickly turn to the correct page in the atlas.

Kate found Penkridge, where they'd seen Mrs Bainbridge die, and traced their route with her finger.

'I should have bought a decent car, one with GPS,' Paul muttered. Kate bit her tongue to prevent herself from saying anything, then pointed at the wiggling line indicating the road they were travelling along.

185

'We're heading into the forest. I reckon Stafford is about fifteen minutes away.'

As she spoke, a wall of trees appeared ahead of them. Moments later they were speeding through the forest, pine and lark and birch trees lining the narrow road.

'Oh shit,' said Paul.

'What?'

He nodded at the rear-view mirror. Sampson's black Audi was behind them again, its reflection growing larger by the second.

'If Stafford is still fifteen minutes away, we can't outrun him. He's much faster than us. Maybe we should stop, confront him?'

'No. He'll kill us.'

At that moment, just as Sampson was gaining on them, a stag appeared from between the trees and ran into the road. Paul swerved, Kate yelled out, and for a moment they left the smooth surface of the road, the car vibrating violently as Paul wrestled with the steering wheel. Somehow, they didn't hit a tree and made it back onto the road, Paul panting with the effort of saving their lives.

Behind them, Sampson was less lucky: he too spun the wheel to avoid the stag, and found himself completely off the road, his car lurching to a halt an inch away from a pine tree. As the stag trotted away into the trees, oblivious to Sampson's murderous glare, he reversed back onto the road, giving Kate and Paul more precious seconds with which to gain a lead over their pursuer.

Paul laughed wildly. 'A tractor and a fucking stag. If I was religious I'd think someone was looking after us. What next?'

They headed deeper into the forest and Paul

continued to drive as fast as he could on this bumpy road. The forest began to thin—and just as it did, the black Audi reappeared in the rear-view mirror.

Kate grabbed his arm. 'What are we going to do?'

'Hold tight again.'

As they emerged from the forest, Paul spotted a turning to the right, a crooked wooden signpost pointing towards what was probably a tiny hamlet with more deer than people, but they had no choice. They had to find help.

They swung into the lane and found themselves driving down a curving, narrow lane, overhung with trees. They crossed a bridge over a gurgling stream, the suspension shaking as they hit a bump in the road. Kate had had dreams like this—nightmares in which she was being chased, and her pursuer was close behind, gaining by the second, the panic growing ever more intense. In those dreams she was always saved when she woke up.

She fished her mobile phone out of her bag.

'What are you doing?'

'Calling 911—I mean, 999.'

He reached out and snatched the phone from her.

'What are *you* doing?'

'I don't want you to call the police.'

'Why the hell not? We're being chased by a guy who just murdered someone. If I call the police they might be able to get someone out here. Someone to stop Sampson.'

He took the next bend at high speed. They swayed in their seats. 'No. I'm sorry—I'll explain later.'

'No.' She tried to grab the phone and he snatched it away, throwing it out of the window.

She gawped at him. 'What the hell did you do that for?'

187

'I'll tell you later.'

She shrank away from him. 'Who are you?'

'What? You know who I am.'

Kate pressed herself against the door. 'I don't understand why you just . . .'

Bang.

Kate jumped in her seat. 'What was that? Did we hit something?'

'Fuck's sake. He's shooting at us.'

Another *bang.*

'And you wouldn't let me call the police?' Kate started to cry. 'He's going to kill us. Oh, Jack . . . I'll never see Jack again.'

Paul grasped her hand. She tried to pull it away but he held firm, steering the car with one hand. 'Kate, listen. You have to stay calm. I'm going to get us out of this. And then I'll explain about the police. I promise. Just trust me. Okay?'

She blinked. 'Okay.'

'Good. Now, see that house in the distance? The big white one? That's where we're going.'

It looked like the kind of house the lord of the manor would live in. Huge, picturesque and surrounded by rolling fields. A hill rose up behind it, with a few other small stone buildings dotted around. The narrow lane they were driving down widened out as they reached the hamlet of Little Marrow, and another thin road led towards the large house. Paul turned into it and carried on at top speed. A pair of horses watched them over a fence. A second later, the Audi turned onto the road behind them. This was what it felt like to be hunted.

'Keep your head down,' Paul instructed.

They swerved left onto a road marked 'Private— Keep Out' and found themselves at the end of a

188

long driveway, the start of which was marked by a gate that stood open. They drove up it, and the house loomed into view.

Gravel crunched beneath their tyres as they approached the house—more of a mansion—and saw a group of five men and a woman, all in their fifties and sixties, dressed in Barbour jackets and wellies.

All the men were carrying shotguns. It was a shooting party, heading into the countryside to shoot pheasants or rabbits. A couple of English pointers ran around their heels. All of them, people and dogs, stared at the Peugeot as it came to a halt, and Kate and Paul jumped out of the car.

The dogs came barrelling towards them. Kate held her breath, but the dogs just sniffed at her, then Paul. The woman in the Barbour squinted at them.

'Can I help you?' Her voice was so upper-crust it was almost regal. Then, to the dogs: 'Plum, Pudding, get back here.'

One of the shotgun-wielding men stepped forward. Kate had lived in America, supposedly a country populated by NRA-approved trigger-happy killers, if you believed the English media, and had never seen a gun, not once. Now, in England, she had seen enough in one day to last a lifetime.

'What's going on?' the man asked in a voice that matched the woman's.

Paul said, 'I'm really sorry to intrude on you but we need your help. We've . . . run out of petrol.'

The man looked over Paul's shoulder. 'And what about him? Has he run out too?'

They looked back. Sampson's black Audi waited menacingly at the end of the drive.

27

The man who had spoken to Paul, clearly the lord of this manor, took a few steps towards Sampson's car.

Sampson weighed up his odds. Five men with shotguns, and they looked like they knew how to use them. They'd probably been killing things since they were at boarding school. He put his foot on the accelerator and drove on. Kate and Wilson had got away, for now. It was time to put some more distance between him and the scene of the widow's death, anyway. Stupid old bitch. Still, she'd be with her husband soon. Not in Heaven or Hell—Sampson didn't believe in all that shit—just mouldering in the grave.

He headed back towards the forest. There was something he needed to pick up before he left the scene completely—he'd seen the phone bounce to the ground from the window of the Peugeot as he came around a bend. The sudden movement near the hedgerow had caught his eye, even at speed.

*   *   *

As the sound of the Audi's engine faded into the distance, Kate and Paul exchanged a look of relief, and Kate put her hand on her chest. It felt as if her heart was about to burst out. She turned, as the woman in the Barbour said, 'Who was that?'

Kate didn't reply immediately.

'A friend of yours?' pressed the woman, licking her lips as if the taste of intrigue was a rare treat.

The first man turned to his four friends. 'Why don't you chaps get on and I'll catch you up in a little while?'

The men nodded and strolled off with their shotguns, one of the dogs scampering behind them. As she and Paul followed the woman and, presumably, her husband into the house, Kate silently hoped that they would have a fruitless day's hunting. Then she thought again about Jean Bainbridge lying in the road, gunned down. She took a deep breath, fighting the urge to throw up.

'You look like you could do with a cup of tea. I'll put the kettle on,' said the husband.

The kindness of strangers, thought Kate. They were led into a vast sitting room, where they sat down on plump sofas with a view of the garden. The remaining dog sat down by the French windows, looking longingly towards the hunters walking away towards the woods. Kate could hardly speak; not until the tea had been placed in front of her. She could have expected a bone china cup in a saucer, but it came in a mug with a chip in the rim.

'Thank you.' Kate sipped the tea. Sometimes, in Boston, she felt like she was turning into an American, but the reinvigorating effect of the tea persuaded her that she was still English through and through. 'Mrs . . .'

'Mrs Braxton. But call me Penny. This is Andrew.' She nodded towards her husband, who smiled at Kate. He had a pleasantly craggy face and exuded an air of old money. But he was passive, cast into shadow by the fierce brightness of his wife's personality. Penny clearly wore the jodhpurs in this relationship. Kate suspected that Andrew probably ranked somewhere below the dog in the domestic

191

pecking order.

'I'm Kate, and this is Paul.'

Introductions over, Penny put her tea on a coaster on a small occasional table. 'So why was that chap in the black car chasing you?'

Paul said, 'We don't know. Just some random nut.'

Kate stared at him but he ignored her and continued, 'We made the mistake of overtaking him up on the main road—next thing, he was right on our tail, horn blaring, trying to barge into our car. We couldn't shake him off. If I'd been on my own I might have pulled over, had it out man to man, but I had to think about Kate here.'

'I see,' said Penny, looking over at Kate, who was trying to rearrange her face from a look of incredulity. What the hell was Paul playing at? Why was he lying? She still couldn't believe that he hadn't let her call the police. And that he'd thrown her mobile out of the window.

'There are a lot of lunatics about on the roads these days,' Andrew said. 'Only the other day . . .'

'Yes darling,' Penny dismissed him and turned back to Paul. 'Do you want to call the police?'

'Yes,' said Kate pointedly to Paul. 'Do we?'

'What's the point? It was just road rage. He'll be long gone by now. And he didn't actually do anything they could prosecute him for. It's not as if we've got any evidence either.' He avoided Kate's gaze. 'We don't even know who he was.'

'Didn't you get his licence plate number?'

'No . . . Look, I really don't think there's any point calling the police.'

Penny looked at him long and hard. She obviously knew he wasn't telling the whole truth. But he returned her stare without flinching.

'Well, it's your decision,' she said after a while.

'That's right.'

Kate could feel her heart jumping beneath her blouse. The pointer padded over to where she sat and stuck his wet nose into the palm of her hand. Suddenly, a wave of tiredness washed over her. She knew that, in times of extreme stress, the human brain sometimes takes the option of shutting itself down to avoid trauma. Mrs Bainbridge; seeing Sampson again; the pursuit, the confusion over Paul's strange behaviour. She wanted to sit here and stroke the ridiculously-named dog and not have to think about any of it.

But that wasn't an option. Oh, how she missed the cool atmosphere of the lab, where all made sense; where everything could be measured and weighed and analysed. Where, if things didn't go as they should, there was always an explanation.

'We ought to get going,' Paul said.

'But what if this road-rager is still out there?' Penny asked.

Andrew said, 'I could take the Land Rover out and check if the coast is clear.'

He moved to the door.

'Be careful, darling,' Penny said, with a tremor of genuine concern in her voice.

*　　　*　　　*

Andrew returned fifteen minutes later—fifteen minutes during which Penny paced the sitting room with the dog at her heels, her nervousness a reproach to Kate, to not make snap judgements about other people's relationships. Or her own relationships, for that matter, she thought. She was desperate to get Paul on his own to find out why the hell he'd been acting so weirdly.

'No sign of the bugger, so I think it should be safe for you to leave,' said Andrew, throwing his Barbour down on an armchair.

Paul stood up immediately. 'Excellent. Let's go, Kate.'

As Kate rose to her feet, Andrew added, 'Big story on the local radio news. Some elderly woman has been found shot outside her house.'

'*Shot?*' Penny exclaimed.

'Yes, in Penkridge.'

'Good heavens, that's where I play boules! How could something like that happen in a sweet little place like Penkridge?'

Kate tried to remain calm, but she couldn't shake the image of Mrs Bainbridge crumpling in front of her hollyhocks and lavender. She had taken a bullet meant for Paul, and Paul was now standing here, staring intently into the garden, grim-faced.

'*You* didn't come through Penkridge, did you?' Penny asked.

'No. No, we didn't,' said Paul.

'We should go,' Kate said, her voice trembling. 'Can I just use your toilet first?'

'Of course.'

When Kate emerged from the loo, Penny and Andrew were deep in conversation, holding hands. She was sure she heard Penny call Andrew 'poppet'.

Penny said, 'Your friend has gone out to his car already.'

'Oh. Okay. Well, thank you both so much.'

'Think nothing of it.'

*　　　*　　　*

After the young couple had driven away, Andrew turned to Penny. 'What did you make of that?'

'I didn't believe a word they said.'

'No. I certainly didn't believe all this stuff about road rage. I didn't believe that Paul chap when he said they hadn't been through Penkridge either.'

He saw his wife's face light up with an expression of thrilled horror. 'Good heavens. You don't think they might have had something to do with the old woman's death, do you?'

Andrew strode towards the phone. 'I made a note of their registration number when I went out. I'm going to call the police.'

After dialling the Stafford police and explaining about the strange couple that had visited them, Andrew went outside, keen to join the rest of his hunting party. He looked around for his shotgun.

'Penny, darling,' he called, 'have you seen my gun?'

She emerged from the house. 'No—where did you put it?'

'I left it right here, propped against the wall. I . . . oh, blast.'

They both looked towards the road.

'I'd better call the police again,' Andrew said.

*   *   *

At Kate's insistence, she and Paul had backtracked a little way to try to find Kate's phone but there was no sign of it. Paul used his own phone to call Kate's number, but nothing rang, even though they walked back and forth along the road close to the spot where Kate was sure Paul had thrown it, nervously half-expecting Sampson to jump out at them from

195

behind a tree. While they were searching, Paul asked Kate about Sampson, and she explained about the creepy odd-job man at the CRU who never seemed comfortable in the role.

After ten minutes' fruitless searching, Kate was forced, reluctantly and with bad grace, to accept the fact that her phone was gone. She felt annoyed with Paul, both about the phone, and about his odd behaviour. They drove in silence to the outskirts of Stafford, glancing behind them in the car's mirrors all the way, and as they passed a row of shops and a pub, Kate said, 'Pull over. We need to talk.'

Paul pulled up outside the pub, The Red Lion.

Kate took a deep breath. 'Why did you lie to them, Paul?'

He reached for her hand, and she flinched away. 'Kate . . .'

'No. Don't touch me. Not until you've explained yourself. Why did you tell them you didn't know who was chasing us? Why did you lie about Penkridge? And why wouldn't you let me call the police?'

He pinched the bridge of his nose and stared at the dashboard for a long time. He thought about the shotgun in the boot of the car, wondered if his impulsive move to take it had been a mistake that would destroy Kate's trust in him even further. Finally, he turned to look at her. 'Okay. I'm going to tell you the truth now. I'm sorry I didn't before, but when you hear it, you'll understand why. But first I need a drink—and so will you.'

28

They pushed open the saloon door of the pub, which was empty apart from a few young blokes in football shirts, and a couple of old men restlessly toying with their cigarette packets at the bar, looking as if they couldn't wait to get outside to smoke the next one. A middle-aged barmaid leaned on the bar and showed off a crêpey tanned cleavage as she pulled Paul's pint.

They sat opposite one another at a wobbly table next to the cigarette machine. Kate, who had been calling Miranda whilst Paul was at the bar, put down Paul's mobile and took a huge gulp of her vodka tonic.

'How is he?'

'He's fine. It took Miranda a while to drag him away from the PlayStation to talk to me. He seems to be having a great time. Not missing his mum as much as she misses him.'

She watched Paul sip his bitter, and sensed that he was struggling with the urge to down the whole pint in one.

'Go on then,' Kate said. 'Tell me why you threw my mobile out of the window rather than letting me call the police.'

It was a few moments before Paul could summon up the courage to speak.

'Don't you ever wonder why you never knew Stephen had a twin brother? Because I bet he never mentioned me, did he?'

Kate shook her head. She had often wondered.

'I'll tell you why he didn't talk about me when you

were both at the CRU.'

She waited.

'Because I was in prison. That's where I was when he sent me that letter.'

Kate pushed herself back in her seat, almost toppling over backwards. 'Prison? What . . . what for?'

Paul leaned forward and tried to touch her knee but she pulled away. 'I didn't murder anyone, if that's what you're thinking. I'm not a rapist or a mugger.'

'What then?'

'Hacking.'

'Computer crime?' She relaxed a little. She was still shocked, but there was something about computer crime that didn't seem as harmful as other crimes. As long as you weren't selling child pornography or creating viruses that destroyed people's computers or stole their personal details . . . although, she thought, perhaps that was exactly what he *had* done.

'What did you do?'

'I robbed a bank.'

'Oh.' She refused his outstretched hand.

'I was twenty. Stephen was already working at the CRU. I was living in a bedsit in London and had an incredibly dull job, working in the IT department of a sixth-form college in Southwark. But during the evenings I had a whole different identity. I was a hacker called Shadowfax—I know, it's embarrassing, but I was a *Lord of the Rings* fan. I was obsessed with the challenge of getting into places where I wasn't supposed to go. There was a small group of us—we used to chat on Usenet, which was a kind of precursor to the internet. There was a guy called

Dark Fox—I know, I know—who was renowned as the top hacker in the UK. Actually, he was a cracker, which is what the true hackers, who weren't criminals, call people who use their hacking skills maliciously.'

'And you weren't a cracker?'

'No. Just a hacker.'

They both laughed at the ridiculousness of what they were saying. But then Kate stopped laughing. 'Except you robbed a bank.'

Paul sighed. 'It was a dare, another challenge. Dark Fox had been boasting about how he'd got into Midland Bank's system and wiped out his overdraft. Everyone was hugely impressed by this. It took an enormous amount of skill to get into a bank's system. Except I wasn't that impressed. Why just wipe out your overdraft? Why not make yourself rich?'

'Because if your bank balance suddenly shoots up, the bank might notice?'

'Yes. Well, of course, I thought of that, so I came up with a scheme. I would invent a new identity, a fake account under a made-up name. I used the hints and information that Dark Fox had revealed and used my own skills—and I was bloody good—to get into the bank's system, set up this bogus account and credit it with £10,000. Not an enormous amount, but I thought I'd start low.'

'And I expect £10,000 was a lot to you back then.'

'Yeah. It's a lot *now*.'

'Let me get you another pint,' Kate said, noticing the forlorn way he was staring at the now-empty glass. She returned a minute later with refills of their drinks.

'Thanks. Okay, so, the first part of the plan worked. I got in, set up the account, credited ten grand. The

199

next bit was the genius bit, I thought. I got the system to send me a cash card along with a pin number assigned to this bogus account. I set up a PO Box and collected the card from there, strolled down to the local Midland and took out my first grand.' He grinned. 'It was so exciting. I could hardly believe it had worked. That evening I went online and started telling all my hacker buddies about what I'd done. Suddenly I was their hero. Even Dark Fox said he was impressed.'

'But you got caught.'

'Yeah.'

'What happened?'

'It turned out Dark Fox was an undercover cop. It must have been one of the first cases of computer entrapment. They traced me to the PO Box and that was it. I was arrested and charged for theft. Sent to prison for five years, though I was out in three.'

Kate took Paul's hand again. He hadn't hurt anyone. The money was a drop in the ocean of the bank's vast profits—it wasn't like he'd taken it from some little old lady's account.

'I still don't get it, though,' she said. 'You were convicted of a computer crime. You did your time, as they say. Why did that stop you from wanting to call the police about Mrs Bainbridge?'

'I haven't finished yet. It gets . . . a lot worse. I feel scared to tell you, Kate. I'm worried that it will make you hate me.'

'I need to know, Paul.'

'I don't know . . .'

She stood up. 'If you don't tell me I'm going to walk up to the bar, ask to use their phone, and call the police right now. I mean it.'

The men at the bar were watching Kate, their

200

hands momentarily stilling their cigarette packets as they witnessed the rising tension. Paul gestured for her to sit. 'Okay, I'll tell you.'

He hesitated. 'They put me in a cell with a bloke called Tony Plumber. He was a bit older than me and a lot harder. This was his second time inside.'

'What was he in for?'

'Tony was a traditionalist. He'd robbed a bank the old fashioned way, with a stocking on his head, and a sawn-off shotgun. He thought it was hilarious that he'd been stuck in a cell with some nancy who'd tried to rob a bank with a computer. "What you should have done," he said, "was take the computer into the bank and whack the cashier over the head with it. You want to try robbing the proper way."'

It was then that Kate realised where this story was going. 'Oh, Paul . . . You didn't.'

He nodded, shamefaced. 'I was angry. With the system, the world. I felt like I hadn't done anything that bad, not compared to someone like Tony, who walked into a bank with a gun and terrified a load of people—yet he'd got the same sentence as me. Also, I was furious about the entrapment. And then the final straw—I heard about Stephen's death . . . I was fucking furious with the whole world. Bitter. And Tony could sense that. He said that when he got out he was planning another job, one that was foolproof, and that if I wanted I could be part of it. He liked me, he said. He wanted to show me how to rob a bank the proper way.

'He got out a couple of months before me, and when I was released, he was waiting for me. To be honest, I'd had second thoughts since he'd left, without having him there winding me up every day, but then I went through all the predictable shit that so many ex-cons go through: my old friends had all moved on and I couldn't get another job, especially in IT, not with my record. My family were in trauma after Stephen's death and that, added to their shame over what I'd done, meant they didn't want to know me. The girl I'd been seeing when I went inside had stopped visiting almost immediately. I was alone. Apart from my old cellmate, Tony Plumber.'

Paul ploughed on. 'I had a habit of falling in with bad influences, didn't I? First my old school mates, then Tony. He took me under his wing. Me and him, we were going to be rich, he said. One job, then off to the Costa del Sol.' He laughed. 'It all seems so clichéd, but that was the world Tony existed in. And I went for it.

'There were the two of us plus a driver, some bloke called Colin. Tony told me to meet him at his garage one Thursday morning. We were going to hit the NatWest in Bromley. It was raining, I remember. When I turned up, Tony handed me a pistol. I think it was then it struck me, that this was actually real. I tried to back out, but Tony got angry and told me that it was too late. He pointed his gun at me. I was shitting myself. We drove to the bank—I felt so sick, Kate. My legs were wobbling when we got out of the car. Tony hissed at me that I'd better pull myself together because we were going in *now*.'

Paul's face had gone white.

'We pulled stockings over our heads and ran into the bank, me a couple of paces behind him. It was nearly empty—just three people in the queue and two cashiers, a bald bloke and a young girl. It's as clear now as if it had happened yesterday. Tony started shouting, pulled out his gun and the customers automatically hit the deck. Tony pointed his gun at

202

the female cashier and was screaming at her to put the money in bags. I was pointing my gun at the other cashier, though my hand was shaking so much I nearly dropped it several times. I could see cameras filming us, and I was so desperate to get out of there. But Tony was getting angrier and angrier. The cashier was being too slow. She was stuffing the money into a bag and then she dropped it on the floor. When she bent down to pick it up, Tony started screaming, *You bitch. You fucking bitch*. She just pressed the panic button. I could see his finger tensing on the trigger. He was going to shoot her.'

He looked into Kate's eyes. 'So I shot him.'

'You . . .?'

'I shot him. In the side, here.' He touched his right side, just beneath his ribcage. 'It was a fluke shot—I was lucky I didn't shoot the cashier by mistake. He fell on the floor, thrashing about in his own blood. The rest of it is a blur. I dropped my own gun and waited for the police to arrive.'

'Oh Paul. What happened?'

'Tony survived, though he lost a lot of blood. And I was sent back to jail, although my sentence was a lot shorter than it would have been because my barrister successfully argued that I was an innocent who had acted to save the life of the cashier, blah blah. Tony testified against me but that actually helped because he was so awful, and the jury really took against him. Plus the cashier that I'd saved spoke up for me. It was quite big news at the time, though you would have missed it because you were in America.'

He told her the rest of the story, about how after this spell in prison he was head-hunted by a computer security firm who had realised that taking on

203

ex-hackers was a sensible move, even ones who had dallied with armed robbery. Paul's brilliance with computers, along with his insight into the way criminal minds worked, made him a perfect employee. And he wasn't angry any more, he said. He was reformed and grateful for the chance to start again.

'But I have a record with guns. There were no witnesses to Mrs Bainbridge's shooting, so what do you think the police would think when they checked my background? They'd assume that I did it.'

'No, because I'd tell them it was Sampson. I'm a witness.'

'It wouldn't be that simple, Kate. We'd both be arrested, probably. And what would you tell them about Sampson? That he was the odd-job man at some place you stayed at sixteen years ago who always seemed a bit creepy and that we're investigating my brother's death because we think there was something suspicious going on there, but you've lost huge chunks of your memory? Sounds really plausible, doesn't it? And are you going to tell them that you're on the run from your husband with your little boy, who you probably shouldn't have brought out of the States?'

'What? How did you . . .?'

'Come off it, Kate. I'm not stupid. For one thing, I overheard a lot of what you told Miranda, and the rest I figured out. You've just confirmed it. What do you think will happen to Jack if we go to the police? At the very least they'll tell your husband where Jack is. Also, there's the risk that if we get derailed now we'll never find out what happened to Stephen.'

'But what about Mrs Bainbridge? She was murdered; we saw him kill her. And she saved your life, Paul. Like you saved that cashier's.'

'I know. Don't you think I feel sick when I think about it? But telling the police about Sampson isn't going to bring her back. We need to find more evidence about what was going on at the CRU, including more about who Sampson is and where we can find him. *Then* we can go to the police. But if we go now, we'll risk screwing up everything.'

Kate didn't know what to do. Her instincts screamed for her to call the police right now, but what if Paul was right? Vernon would be over on the next flight—if he wasn't already here—and she'd lose Jack. Paul would be arrested and most likely charged, and she might be seen as an accessory if they really believed Paul was the killer.

In her head, she could see Stephen. He was telling her to trust Paul, to go along with it.

She studied Paul's worried, earnest expression. Looked at the lips she'd kissed earlier that day. He had made mistakes in the past, there was no doubt about that. But it was a long time ago, and he'd saved a woman's life.

It was crazy, but she felt closer to this man, whom she'd only known for a few days, than she ever had done to her husband.

'Okay,' she said, making up her mind and praying she wasn't going to regret it. 'What next?'

'We should think about finding somewhere to stay.' He lifted his empty pint glass, the insides streaked with foam. 'Somewhere nearby because now we've both drunk too much to drive with a clear head.'

'Okay.' She looked up at him. 'We'll get a room.'

'*A* room?'

Kate became suddenly aware of the ache that had been growing unnoticed inside her. She didn't reply to Paul's question, but didn't break eye contact either. When he reached across the table, touching the side of her face, running his fingers along her jawbone, she felt the urge to drag him from the table into the toilets and order him to take her, right there and then, and the image made her bite her lip. She could wait. But not for much longer. She felt close to him . . . but she wanted to get a lot closer.

*   *   *

Paul went to the bar to ask if the barmaid could recommend a nearby hotel or bed and breakfast. Beneath the roar of adrenaline that rushed through his veins was a whisper of anxiety: the shotgun in the boot. What was Kate going to say if she found out, especially after he'd just told her about his past? His only defence would be the truth: that despite his past experiences with guns, the promise he'd made to himself years ago to never use one again, when he saw the shotgun he knew it was an opportunity that had to be grasped. He had watched that maniac Sampson shoot an old woman, with a bullet intended for him. He needed the shotgun to protect himself and Kate, a woman with whom, he realised, he was falling in love.

And who knew? If revenge needed to be taken for what happened to Stephen, at least he now had the means with which to take it.

29

Sampson held Kate's discarded phone in his palm, stroking the screen with his thumb. He navigated to the phone's photo album and flicked through the pictures. Most of them were of the brat, but among them was a photo of Kate, slightly blurry, probably taken by the kid. She was smiling and leaning forward towards the lens, revealing the shadow of her cleavage. He stared at the photo for ten seconds, running his tongue over his dry lips, then put it into his pocket.

The stillness around him was absolute, the dark spaces between the trees seemed to beckon to him. When all this was over, he decided, he was going to go fishing. Head up to somewhere remote, like the Highlands of Scotland, and camp out beside a loch. He had done it before, spending whole days watching the still, flat surface of the water, waiting for the fish to fall into his trap; then the one-sided fight. There was something elementally satisfying in watching the fish flap and gasp for breath on the shore, before finally lying still.

The most content he'd ever been was when he lived at the CRU, close to nature—even if many of the things going on in that place were far from natural. After the fire had destroyed it, he'd felt an unfamiliar emotion: an ache of regret. It soon faded, though, replaced by the familiar flatness of his emotional landscape.

Today there was a weird feeling beneath his skin, a crawling unease. He had done his job badly—but there was more to it than that. He'd felt it for several days, since he'd heard that she was back in the country, and seen her dash across a CCTV screen.

When he had aimed at Wilson, he'd hesitated a moment too long. Not because he'd had second thoughts about killing him. Oh no. It was because he'd wanted to savour it, like a wine enthusiast taking a moment after opening a vintage bottle. And by screwing up in this way—which was so unlike him; usually, he was like a machine, a *Terminator*—he'd given the old lady time to get in his way. He had done something he should never have done—let emotion influence his actions.

As soon as he got back in the car, his thoughts were interrupted by the rude chirrup of a mobile. He first glanced at Kate's phone, but the ringing was coming from one of his other mobiles.

He picked up, to hear Gaunt's familiar voice. 'What the hell happened today? I'm getting reports that Jean Bainbridge is dead. Please don't tell me that was anything to do with you.'

Sampson explained what had happened.

The doctor exhaled. 'You fucked up.'

Sampson clenched his teeth until his jaw muscles trembled.

'You'd better get out of the area, quickly.'

'What the fuck do you think I'm doing?'

Gaunt's voice dropped from cold to Arctic. 'Don't use that tone with me. Remember who you're talking to.'

Sampson drew in a deep breath and held it, fighting the urge to tell the doctor what he thought of him, allowing himself a satisfying fantasy in which he snapped Gaunt's scrawny neck: grip and twist, and let go. The image calmed him.

'Call me when you're somewhere safe and we'll

talk,' the doctor said. 'In the great scheme of things, the old woman's death isn't important. I just don't want anything to get in our way at this critical moment.'

'I know that.'

'Good. Don't forget it. I still need you to deal with Maddox and Wilson.'

Sampson drove on, north out of the forest towards Stoke-on-Trent, and on into Hanley, the city's central shopping area. He parked outside a supermarket, went in and bought some sandwiches and cigarettes, then retreated to the haven of his car.

He ate the sandwiches and picked up Kate's phone. It was a clamshell phone; he flicked it open and the screen sprang to life. She hadn't personalised it with a photo or stupid piece of wallpaper. He liked that, because he despised childishness. He bet she wouldn't have a musical ringtone either. Sampson had been forced to endure a train journey a year ago and by the end of the journey had heard every piece of shit in the Top Forty. There was this fuckwitted teenage boy sitting near him, one of only a few passengers in the carriage, who spent the entire journey fiddling with his phone, making it bleep and chirrup, ringing his mates and talking bollocks from beneath his hoodie. Sampson had leaned over and asked him to switch it off, to be quiet, and the boy had told him to fuck off.

A few minutes later the boy had got up to visit the toilet. Sampson followed him. First, he smashed the boy's phone, then made him eat it, piece by piece, stuffing the plastic shards into his mouth and telling him to chew. The boy cried, snot poured from his nose, he wet his pants. Sampson pulled off the

209

boy's belt, wrapped it around his throat and tied him to the light fitting, getting off at the next station and walking calmly away. Boy hangs himself in train toilet. What a tragedy.

No, Kate wouldn't have an irritating musical ringtone.

He flicked through the phone's menu and discovered how to listen to Kate's voicemail.

You have five new messages.

The first one was from an American man:

'Kate? It's me. Where the hell are you? I've been stood here like an idiot waiting for you and Jack and every other goddamn person has gotten off your flight, so what's going on? If you're held up, call me. Or maybe you're trying to piss me off.'

Second message: *'You bitch. You're still in the UK, aren't you. With my son. You think you can get away with it, huh? Huh? I'm coming to get you. I want my son back.'*

In the third message, the man sounded a little more controlled.

'Kate. I'm in England. Listen, I just want to talk to you, okay? We can sort things out, amicably. I know things have been difficult recently but surely this . . . what you've done is a little drastic, wouldn't you say? Call me, please. I want to talk to you.'

In the fourth message, the anger was back. Sampson had to hold the phone away from his ear as the caller sprayed distorted threats about what he was going to do to her when he caught up with her.

'. . . and once I've got him back I'll do everything I can to make sure you never see Jack again.'

So, Sampson thought, this was the father of Kate's boy, the boy he had seen on the hotel's CCTV. And

210

it was also pretty clear that Kate had snatched the boy. Naughty naughty. He admired her spirit as much as he hated hearing this Yank scream threats at her. What a loser. Just accept it, he thought. She's better than you. And why make so much fuss over a kid, anyway? He ought to be pleased that Kate had taken the brat off his hands.

But where was the kid now? He definitely hadn't been with Kate and Wilson when he had shot the old bat. He'd had a niggling feeling that something was missing at the time, and now he realised what it was.

Fifth message: *'Hi sis, it's me. I guess you must have your phone switched off. Are you and Paul taking advantage of the fact that I've taken Jack off your hands, eh? Lucky you. Anyway, I was only ringing to find out how everything's going. I'm curious . . . Jack's fine, having great fun—they're all on the PlayStation at the moment. He said to tell you that Billy is missing you. Um . . . that's it. Bye.'*

Sampson felt a little thrill run through him. The kid was with Kate's sister. He switched the phone into camera mode and flicked through the photos as he pondered what to do next. They were all of Jack, smiling at the camera, playing in the snow, sleeping, waving against the London backdrop.

Cute. Very cute.

After checking the caller logs, he programmed Miranda's number into his own phone, then called the number.

A kid answered. A little girl. Excellent, thought Sampson.

'Hello,' he said. 'I'm calling from Toys R Us.'

'Toys R Us? Really?'

'Yes. You've won a special prize and I need to

know your address to be able to send it to you.'

The child said, 'What is it?'

'It's a big teddy bear. A giant teddy bear.'

'What colour?'

Bloody hell. 'What colour would you like?'

'Pink?'

'Okay. Pink it is. Now, just tell me where you live. What town do you live in?'

'We live in Churchill.'

Where the hell was that? It would be easy enough to find out.

'What street, sweetheart? You do know your address, don't you?'

'Yes, I do. It's the Old Rectory, Mill Lane, Churchill. Mummy made me remember it.'

'Good for Mummy.'

He heard a woman call out, 'Amelia? Who are you talking to? Are you on the phone?'

Sampson ended the call.

Good little Amelia. He was half-tempted to go and find a pink teddy bear to take to her as a reward for being so helpful. He wouldn't, of course. But he would be visiting her house soon.

Like any good fisherman knows, if you want to catch that big fish, you need the right bait.

30

'They've got rooms here, upstairs,' said Paul, returning from the bar and waving a key on a large plastic fob, trying unsuccessfully to keep a smile off his face at the thought of an available double bed so close above their heads to where they were sitting.

'Oh. Good!' Kate said brightly. Paul couldn't tell if she was excited or petrified.

'Shall we?' Paul held out his arm for her.

'Let's,' she agreed. 'But I need to get my bag out of the boot first. Can you give me the car keys?'

Paul felt the blood drain from his face, and Kate frowned. 'What's the matter—you haven't lost them, have you?'

'Er . . . no, I don't think so,' he stuttered, making a big show of patting down his jeans pockets. 'No . . . here they are. I tell you what, could you get us a couple of drinks to take upstairs? I'll get your bag for you. Meet you back here in a minute—I'll have a large brandy, if that's OK.'

He was gone before Kate had a chance to object; bolting out into the car park. He had to lean against the back wall of the pub for a moment, breathing heavily at the thought of Kate discovering the shotgun, so soon after she'd decided to trust him after all.

He retrieved Kate's overnight bag, and then did some discreet rearranging of the boot's contents, so that the shotgun was now hidden underneath a plastic groundsheet he kept in there, pushed right to the back, and covered up by a pair of wellington boots and a tennis racket in its case. It wasn't ideal to have it so inaccessible, he thought—but he couldn't take the risk that she might discover it, and panic completely.

'Thank you,' Kate said when he got back. She handed him a glass of amber liquid. 'I'm not sure whether you were being super-chivalrous by getting my bag for me, or super-unchivalrous, by making me buy the drinks!'

He managed a smile. 'Oh, chivalrous, definitely.

213

You never know who might be hanging around pub car parks at night.'

'No,' Kate said, serious again. 'I guess you don't.'

They both paused, thinking of the terrifying events of the day. 'Come on, Paul, let's go and lock ourselves out of harm's way for the night, shall we?'

'I can't think of anything I'd rather do,' Paul said fervently.

*   *   *

Their room was cramped and smelled slightly of stale cigarettes, but it seemed clean enough. It was dominated by a large bed with a white candlewick bedspread, crammed around which were a small wardrobe, a wall-mounted television, and two bedside tables. The sound of the jukebox floated up through the floor. Kate switched on the light long enough to put their drinks down and their bags on the carpet, and then switched it straight off again, so the only light came through a gap in the curtains from a streetlight outside.

'Come here,' Paul said, more bravely than he felt, taking Kate into his arms as soon as he had locked the door behind them. They kissed, and immediately toppled on to the bed.

'Ah, that's better,' Paul murmured, as they allowed their clothed bodies to fit together from top to toe. He rolled on top of her, breaking away from their kiss to lean across her, take a swig of the brandy on the bedside table, and offer her the glass too. When he kissed her again, he tasted the sweet fire of the alcohol on both their tongues. He thought he had never wanted anybody quite as much.

'Are you OK?' he asked, a few moments later,

214

when Kate still hadn't said anything. She was kissing him back with what he thought was enthusiasm, but it was dark in the room, and he suddenly worried that perhaps he'd moved too fast for her.

To his relief, she laughed. 'I'm fine,' she said. 'I'm absolutely fine. Let's have a shower. All that fear got me quite sweaty.'

'Great idea.'

She pushed him off her, and rolled herself off the bed and into the bathroom. A moment later he heard the sound of water splattering into the bath tub, and the ripping sound of a shower curtain being pulled along a rail. He wondered if she meant for him to come in with her, or if she wanted them to shower separately. It would be awful if he barged in there unwelcome. He dithered, stalling for time by taking off his shoes, socks, and belt, and then she reappeared. In the dim light he saw that she was stripping off her top, and then her bra. Her breasts were beautiful, and he groaned with lust.

'Can I come into the shower with you?' he asked, grabbing her again, unable to stop himself cupping her breasts and rubbing his face in them.

'Of course,' she said, giggling. 'I need someone to wash my back for me, and you'll have to do.'

'Oh, you've definitely picked the right man for the job,' he murmured, helping her out of her jeans and underwear until she stood before him naked. 'Washing backs is my speciality and your body is gorgeous.'

'Well, thank you. Come on then, get your kit off so I can see yours too.'

Paul liked this assertive, overtly sexy version of Kate. He felt he was getting a glimpse of a side of her that she'd kept hidden from him until now, and it was a huge turn-on. He slipped his hand up the inside of her thigh, and stroked her between her legs. She moaned, and then giggled again.

'Stop it, otherwise we'll never make it into the shower.'

Two minutes later they were both jostling for position, under a frankly very feeble stream of water. In order to even get both their bodies wet enough to wash, a great deal of touching was required.

'Budge up, my back's getting cold,' Paul pretended to grumble, pushing himself up against her.

'I'll warm you up,' she said seductively, hauling him to her by clasping his buttocks, and then putting one of her feet up on the side of the bath, so it just seemed completely natural for Paul to slide himself inside of her. They both gasped with pleasure, which soon changed to shock, as the shower suddenly turned icy. Paul leaned forward and turned off the taps, without breaking his stride.

'Oh god, this is wonderful,' Kate said, as his thrusts increased in urgency. Paul was alarmed to see tears rolling down her cheeks, although she hadn't made a sound.

'Kate, what's wrong? Am I hurting you?

She sniffed and laughed and slapped him on the arm. 'Don't flatter yourself! No, you aren't hurting me. It's just so . . . lovely. It's been so long since I . . . I never thought . . .' She dissolved into sobs. Paul pulled out of her.

'Come on,' he said, gently putting a towel around her shaking shoulders. 'Let's go and get into bed. It'll be more comfortable.'

He led her out of the bathroom, and the cool air hit their damp skins, making them shiver. The sheets were even colder, but as Paul started to make love

216

to her again, they forgot about everything except the sensations going on between them. Even the terrors of Sampson shooting Mrs Bainbridge, and then trying to kill them—it all receded, temporarily, and Kate and Paul gratefully embraced the reprieve.

31

Kate slipped out of bed into a patch of sunlight. Blue sky was visible through a gap in the curtains, a gentle draft buffing away the scent of last night. Paul was still sleeping, his broad naked shoulder visible above the quilt. She reached down to stroke his face but, not wanting to wake him, thought better of it, and padded to the bathroom instead.

After dressing, she scooped up Paul's keys from the corner table and crept out of the room, closing the door quietly behind her.

The brightness of the morning hurt her eyes, but it felt like a kiss on her skin. She stretched; yawning, smiling. She felt fifteen years younger, a girl of twenty, a girl in love, just waking up to the beauty of the world. All the aches in her body were pleasant ones. His touch reverberated on her lips, her belly and thighs. She was sore between her legs—the kind of soreness that can only be soothed by more sex. She stood still, the pub behind her, and drew in a deep breath

When had she last felt this way? Oh, she knew very well: that summer sixteen years ago with Stephen. It had never been the same with Vernon. Their relationship was more like a science project; no, a business transaction. Each had something the other wanted. She was lonely, her soul bruised by what had happened in England, and she didn't want intensity, just companionship. Someone to talk to, to go out with. Someone to make her feel safe at night when she woke up shivering, fleeing the fires that roared through her dreams. Vernon wanted somebody to help his career, and Kate, the beautiful and friendly English scientist so respected around the university, was perfect. She was sure he had loved her too, for a time, especially when she became pregnant with the son he so wanted. But Vernon had never taken her breath away. He had never made her feel like running naked down the street, singing.

She headed towards Paul's car, jangling the keys and humming an old song that she hadn't heard for years. What was it? Some song that she and Stephen had danced to in his flat. The Cure, that was it. It was called 'Just Like Heaven', and the lyrics came back to her: a song about a girl who loved a boy too much; a boy who lost the girl because he couldn't give her everything she wanted. She had deliberately avoided music from that period for years, because she hadn't been able to bear the reminder of what she had lost. Now, though, the tune made her feel happy again, and it was all because of last night. When she pressed her body against Paul's she didn't feel his brother. When she closed her eyes, she hadn't seen Stephen. It had all been brand new. She had been afraid that making love with Paul would be like making love to a ghost. In fact, it had been more like an exorcism.

Besides, she thought with a little smile, ghosts aren't warm. Ghosts don't leave you feeling tender and sated. Ghosts don't have eyes and hands that pin you to the bed. Ghosts don't make you climax like the world is folding in on itself.

Unlocking the car door, she leaned over to the back seat and picked up the envelope that Mrs Bainbridge had given her.

Kate used to think that Stephen had been stolen from her by fate, by God or destiny or bad luck. Now, she was sure the thieves had human hands. Sampson, of course. He must have had something to do with it. But who else? And why? She carried the envelope back to the room hoping its contents held some answers; at the same time dreading what she might find.

*   *   *

Paul was sitting up in bed when she got back.

'Were you dreaming about being dragged through a hedge backwards?' she laughed, going over and smoothing down his hair and kissing his stubbly face.

'Eh? I thought you'd done a runner.'

'Hoped?'

'Don't be silly. I was actually hoping that you might come back to bed.'

The quilt had fallen to reveal his naked torso. She almost licked her lips. She wanted to lick *his* lips. But that would have to wait for a while. She sat down on the bed and held up the documents.

'I need to take a look at these—you know, the papers Mrs Bainbridge gave me.'

Paul flung aside the quilt and got up, giving Kate a full view of his body. A few seconds ago, this might have been enough for her to say the documents could wait; but by now she had started reading.

Subject: Fem 634

Personal details
Sex: F
Ethnicity: White European

Kate gasped when she saw her birthdate on the next line. She was reading about herself. She tried to read on but her eyes skidded across the text, and she had to take a moment to steady herself and concentrate.

Medical history: contracted Watoto Virus, aged 12. (Note: Parents, known to CRU director Bainbridge, were killed by the virus.) No other history of serious illnesses. Subject is physically fit.

Mental health: subject suffered withdrawal following parents' deaths, but no known recent history of psychiatric problems.

Subject admitted to psych unit following fire at CRU on Aug 27th for quarantine and reconditioning.

Kate, who had started reading the report out loud to Paul, paused. Her voice wobbled. 'Reconditioning?'

Their eyes met. Paul's were round with concern, and he gripped her free hand as she read on.

Quarantine successful. Subject is free of virus. (See separate report on the investigation into errors made.)

Subject has knowledge of microbiology and virology, and had embarked on relationship with Dr S Wilson of CRU. CRU security believed subject had become high-risk individual, and interview following fire confirmed this. Therefore reconditioning necessary to allow subject's release into society, at request of Unit director.

We embarked upon course of treatment known as the Pimenov Technique. Subject responded well to drugs and hypnosis.

For your reference, the Pimenov Technique is based on

Kate turned to the next page. The sentence never finished.

'I don't believe it. There's a sheet missing.'

Instead, the next sheet started with the end of a separate, chilling sentence:

recommend subject for disposal.

Awaiting clearance from Unit director.

ENDS

Kate dropped the papers onto the bed and clutched her face. Paul picked up the papers and quickly read through them.

'Recommended for disposal.'

He put his arm around her shoulders. 'You're shivering.'

'Disposal.'

He held her, stroking her hair until the shivering

221

subsided. Then she pulled away from him and said, 'What the hell is the Pimenov Technique?'

'Kate, there's another sheet you haven't read yet.'

She hoped it might be the missing sheet from the report, but it was a letter, addressed to Leonard.

> *Dear Leonard*
>
> *I must stress again that I am not at all happy with your decision to allow Kate Carling to leave the Unit when we are not yet 100% sure that her treatment has been fully successful. I appreciate that you have an emotional attachment to the young woman and I do not wish to accuse you of being unprofessional; however, I wish to remind you again that sacrifices sometimes have to be made for the common good.*
>
> *Having said that, I understand that you have arranged for her to take a place at Harvard. I am happy that she will be leaving the United Kingdom, and it is fair to say that I hope she does not return. This is nothing personal: simply that if reconditioning has not been wholly successful— and I am not convinced that it has—then it is best that she stays far from the places and people who might cause her memories to resurface. I seek permission to monitor Ms Carling on return visits to this country. I trust that your contact at Harvard will be keeping an eye on her there.*
>
> *Yours*
> *Clive*

Kate got to her feet and made a few lurching steps towards the bathroom. Paul sprang after her; she toppled and he caught her.

'I think I'm going to be sick.'

'Come and sit down.'

'No, I really am going to be sick.'

She broke away from him and completed her staggering journey to the bathroom. Crouching over the toilet, she vomited. Last night's dinner and drinks. She spat and flushed the toilet, falling back onto the floor, her hair in her face, her mouth sour. Paul, who had been hanging behind her in the doorway, came tentatively into the room and crouched beside her. He stroked her hair gently and she grabbed him, burying her face against his shoulder.

'What did they do to me?' she whispered.

'I don't know . . .'

She pushed him to arm's length, her face contorted with anger. 'What did they fucking do to me? Those bastards. Leonard. He was like an uncle to me. A kindly uncle.'

'It seems to me that Leonard was trying to protect you.'

'But he was involved in it all.' She clutched her head as if trying to dig out the memories that refused to be found. 'And I don't even know what *it* was. Because I was reconditioned.'

'Let's find out what the Pimenov Technique is.'

'How are we going to do that?'

Paul got up and went back into the bedroom, reappearing a moment later with his laptop. 'I checked earlier. Someone around here has wireless internet and hasn't password-protected it.'

'Give it to me.'

'Kate, maybe you should try to calm down a little.'

'Don't order me around! Who do you think you are, my husband?'

'Kate . . .'

'Just give me the laptop.' She opened it up, but paused before she started typing. She looked up and caught a glimpse of herself in the mirror on the wall. She was a mess, her hair wild, lips wet, and eyes bloodshot. She said, 'I'm sorry, Paul. This is just such a shock.'

'I understand.'

He got down on the floor and sat next to her, both of them leaning back against the bath.

'I must stink,' she said.

He kissed her cheek. 'Hmm, more of a pong, actually.'

'Hey!'

'Do you want me to do the honours?' He gestured towards the laptop and she handed it over. He Googled 'pimenov technique' but there were no useful results, just a load of pages with the Russian surname Pimenov. Nothing about memory or 'reconditioning'.

'Let me try Pimenov on its own,' Paul suggested.

But that was fruitless too. Pimenov appeared to be the name of a contemporary Russian football player, and there were pages of results about matches he'd played in. Useless.

Kate said, 'Try it with different words, like memory, or, I don't know, reconditioning.'

'Good idea.'

He typed all three words in for good measure. The first few results were rubbish, but Kate pointed at the screen: 'What's that?'

The link was to a site called *www.allinthemind. com*. Paul clicked the link, and they waited. 'Come on,' Paul urged, watching the blue bar creep to the right. Finally the page appeared.

'It's a forum,' Paul said. 'A messageboard where

people chat about issues they're interested in.'

'I know what a forum is.'

'Sorry.'

But Kate was already scanning the page for the mention of Pimenov. Paul hit CTRL-F to bring up a box so he could search the page for the word. He searched up, then down. It wasn't there.

'This happens sometimes. The search engine finds a page but then the page disappears before they realise it's gone. That's because search engines can't crawl every site constantly.'

They went back to the search engine results page. There were two lines of text that must have been pulled from the original page on allinthemind.com.

. . . like the CIA, the KGB developed reconditioning techniques. There are reports that Pimenov, a Russian scientist . . .

. . . using a combination of LSD and hypnosis to erase the memory of undesirables, though the methods were said to be . . .

Paul took Kate's hand. 'It's all there,' he said. 'In your head. They can't have completely erased your memories. We know that because they didn't want you to come back to the UK. And that's why Sampson is after you—to stop you remembering whatever it is they tried to make you forget.'

'About what happened to Stephen and Sarah.'

'I know what we need to do,' Paul said. 'But you might not like it.'

32

Vernon rang the doorbell of Miranda's house and took a step back, looking up at the bay windows with their Laura Ashley curtains. Miranda had always been a bit twee, he'd thought—not that he'd met her many times. She lacked Kate's spunk, her vivacity, although he had always suspected that his sister-in-law had the hots for him. The times they'd met, she'd looked at him in a certain way, from under her lashes. Shame she was so wussy. It would be quite deliciously thrilling, having Kate's sister; a great way of getting one over on his wife.

Thinking about siblings, his thought trail led on to Jack and his regret that the poor little guy didn't have any brothers or sisters. Vernon had wanted another child—a girl, preferably—but Kate had turned frigid on him while she was pregnant with Jack and had never thawed. She had always been an ice princess. She had the lowest sex drive of any woman he'd ever been with. Coaxing her legs open was like trying to persuade a cat to go walkies. He pitied whichever man she moved onto, assuming she didn't spend the rest of her life locked up in a lab studying creatures you couldn't even see. He could foresee her future: she'd end up with some other boring asshole in a white coat, pouring all their passion into their research, winning some dull award and having a disease named after them.

He was lucky the marriage hadn't dragged on any longer. It was far better to extricate himself now, while he was still young enough to enjoy life. And he was going to have his son by his side while he

226

did so. Well, perhaps not exactly by his side—he didn't want his style cramped too much. He had plans to send Jack to boarding school once he got him back to the States. Somewhere his mother wouldn't be able to poison his mind and make him soft.

Vernon heard footsteps coming towards the door inside the house, causing his heartbeat to speed up. It was possible that Kate was here, and with her, Jack. At the very least, Miranda would be sure to know where they were.

The door opened and a portly middle-aged man said, 'Can I help you?'

Vernon looked past him. No sign of Jack. He fixed the man with his most authoritative Harvard lecturer's stare. 'Is Miranda here?'

The man appeared confused for a moment, then his face cleared. 'You mean Miranda Hetherington? I'm afraid she doesn't live here any more. She and her family moved away about a month ago.'

Vernon processed this information. 'That's a real pity. I'm an old college friend visiting from America. I guess I've had a wasted journey.' He shook his head disappointedly and exhaled a long, tragic sigh.

'Oh, don't worry,' smiled the man. 'I've got her new address. I'll just fetch it for you.'

Vernon grinned. 'Would you? That would be marvellous.'

*　　　*　　　*

On the way to Kate's sister's house, Sampson found himself driving past a large out-of-town shopping estate, a Toys R Us standing out among the DIY superstores and carpet warehouses. On impulse, he pulled in and minutes later was walking the aisles of robots and plush monsters, videogames and karaoke machines, looking for a pink teddy bear. He hadn't intended to do this, and he wasn't doing it because he found it amusing—he had no sense of humour—or for sentimental reasons. He just thought the bear might be useful.

He remembered little Amelia's happy voice on the phone. He had never killed a child. He'd never had call to, or been instructed to do so. He wondered what it would be like: if it would feel any different to killing an adult. When he had taken his first life, it had excited him, thrilled him, and he had spent the years since hoping in vain to replicate that thrill. That first murder had been when he was eighteen. A girl called Kelly who had spat in his face when he raped her on their first date. He put his strong hands around her throat and pressed his thumbs into her windpipe. The disbelief and terror in her eyes turned him on. When she went limp and stopped breathing he was still inside her. It was a beautiful moment. Come to think of it, she looked a little like Kate had when she was around that age, at the CRU. Not as stunning as Kate, but there had definitely been a similarity.

Since Kelly, no murder had given him that charge of excitement. Perhaps killing a child would do it.

Killing Kate's child. Now *that* would be something.

He could picture Kate's face as she watched her son die at his hands. Hear her screams. She would be in thrall to his power. Her pain would be like a star bursting. Immense, intense. Afterwards, she wouldn't struggle or fight any more. She would be dead inside. And she would be his.

At the checkout, he paid for the teddy bear. The

insipid smile on its face made him sick. But the young woman behind the counter smiled at him like he was a kindly father or uncle. He looked around the store. There were children everywhere, little girls and boys of every size and colour. Perhaps he should take one, see what happened. Practice. But as the cashier slipped the bear into a carrier bag he decided not to waste his time. He had to get on.

In the car, he consulted his map and headed south—towards Kate's sister. Towards Kate's son.

*   *   *

Miranda peered out of the window and wished it would stop raining so the children could go and play outside. The boys were in George's room, playing video games, watched by Amelia. Every now and then she heard Amelia squeal, 'Let me have a go.' The PlayStation was an even better childminder than the TV, though Miranda felt horrible for letting them play on it for so long, especially Jack, who had never been allowed to play video games before. Miranda had this nagging voice in the back of her head telling her she should be encouraging them to create their own entertainment with pens and coloured card. But that would be deemed 'boring'.

She checked her watch. Five thirty. Was it too early for a glass of wine? She had a really nice bottle of Merlot on top of the fridge. She could already taste it, the fruitiness on her tongue, the smoothing of her nerves. But she would wait half an hour. Then pour herself a really big glass. If she timed it right, she might be in a good mood when Pete got home from work. Assuming he came home at the usual time and didn't stay behind for a drink as he'd often been doing recently. There was a new woman working at the veterinary surgery, some skinny young creature called Jennifer, who Pete talked about a lot, as if he couldn't help but mention her at every opportunity. Miranda didn't think anything would come of it. It was probably just one of those little workplace crushes that time would dampen and kill. The thing was, she found she didn't really care as much as she should. She wondered abstractly what it would be like if Pete left her, bringing up the children on her own. It wouldn't be too bad. At least it would be a change.

Damn rain, she thought, making her feel melancholy and discontented. It was always the same when it rained in summer. She went into the kitchen—refusing to look in the direction of the Merlot—and opened the cupboard doors, trying to decide what to give the children for their tea. Kate was bringing up Jack as a vegetarian, which was annoying, but he certainly looked well on it. He was a lovely little boy. Mercifully unlike his father.

It had been lovely to see Kate, of course, but Miranda couldn't help but feel envious of her sister. She had always envied her—her career, living in America, her brains and looks—and now, more than ever, she wished that her life was as exciting as Kate's. Okay, perhaps leaving your husband, fleeing halfway across the world and going on some bizarre hunt with the brother of an ex-love could be better described as traumatic, or at least stressful . . . but it wasn't domesticity. It wasn't being stuck at home longing for a glass of wine while your husband flirted with his junior—his *young*—colleagues.

Maybe she should have that glass of wine now. It

was *nearly* six. And it wasn't as if it would do any harm. Just a small glass, sipped slowly. Then she'd make tea. She took the bottle down from the fridge and uncorked it. She filled the glass up rather higher than she'd intended—how clumsy—but she really shouldn't waste it. She took a big, warming gulp. Then another.

That was better.

She sat at the kitchen table and ran a finger around the rim of the glass. She heard a shout from upstairs, and her first instinct was to leap up and make sure everything was okay. But then she heard laughter and relaxed. The children were merely enjoying their game. George and Amelia seemed to like having their cousin over from the States. The first thing George wanted to know when they met was whether he'd ever seen a gun; Amelia wanted to know if he'd been to Disneyland.

The telephone rang. She jumped up, thinking it might be Kate. 'Hello?'

'Hello darling.' It was Pete. 'I'm sorry, sweetheart, but I'm going to be late home. We've had a hell of a day—it's been like a whole series of *All Creatures Great and Small* rolled into one.' He chuckled. This was an old joke of his. 'Anyway, I had to rush up to the Grange to see one of old Mountford's favourite horses, which I managed to save, and now Mountford wants to take me and the whole surgery out for a drink to say thanks. You know how hard it is to say no to him.'

Miranda wanted to ask if Jennifer would be there—in her mind's eye, the veterinary nurse had long, dark, lustrous hair and a cleavage that men daydreamed about diving into it—but just said, 'Fine.'

231

Would she ever feel brave enough to leave Pete in the same way Kate had left Vernon? Well, she knew she would never run away. That was far too dramatic. Though if she were married to the dreaded Vernon perhaps she would run away. She could never understand what Kate saw in him. Okay, so he was very clever, academically, but there was something about him that gave her the creeps. He was the kind of man who fancied himself a ladies' man but came across more as a knicker-sniffer. A man who stared at the breasts of flat-chested women, as if willing them to grow boobs for him to leer at. Yuk.

Pete wasn't like that. Except with Jennifer perhaps. Did their fingers touch when she passed Pete the worming tablets? Had their eyes ever met over a sick hamster? Did she wear a tight white uniform that stretched perfectly across her pert bottom? There was another cry from above, then a thump, shaking her from her green-eyed reverie. She stood up, noticing as she did that the wine glass was empty, just a smear of red at the bottom like a bloodstain, and she felt a little woozy and unsteady on her feet. She stood at the bottom of the stairs and called up. 'Is everyone alright up there?'

Before any of the children replied, the doorbell rang.

*　　　*　　　*

Vernon took the wrong exit—nine instead of ten—and spent the next fifteen minutes cursing the British motorway system before getting back on track. He'd just been to what had to be the worst 'restaurant' in the known world, something called

232

a Little Chef. It made Taco Bell seem like *cordon bleu*. Most Americans would be shocked if they saw the real Britain and realised it wasn't all castles and stately homes. It was just like America, all endless roads and wretched fast food joints, but with worse customer service and more sex on TV. The bad teeth clichés were true though. What if Jack had to grow up here? He'd end up looking like a Brit, teeth like yellowing tombstones, with a drink habit and an addiction to soccer. The rain clichés were true, too. It was raining now, and this was supposed to be summer.

Most of his fellow Americans would love this village, though. Churchill. Good British name, too. The village was—what was the expression?— chocolate-box pretty. Quaint as hell.

He smiled to himself. He felt certain that Kate and Jack were going to be at Miranda's. There'd be a scene, no doubt. But he relished the thought of the confrontation, Kate trying to justify what she'd done. Just watch her try to take the moral high ground, he thought.

He found the address the man at Miranda and Pete's old house had given him, and parked outside. The wipers squeaked back and forth across the windscreen before halting. Vernon got out of the car, rehearsing what he was going to say, and rang the doorbell.

*   *   *

The SPEED KILLS sign almost made Sampson smile. He screeched round the corner by the church, roaring on past the neat low Cotswolds stone balustrade edging the churchyard. The pink

233

teddy bear on the back seat toppled over. A cat was crossing the road up ahead, trying to escape the rain, and Sampson put his foot on the accelerator, but the animal darted to safety with a split second to spare.

He felt good. More alive than he could ever remember. It must be the proximity of Kate's blood, he thought.

He found the street he was looking for and pulled to a halt a few doors away. He stood in the rain for a few seconds, enjoying its feel on his face. He held the pink teddy under his jacket. Then he walked up to the door and pressed the bell.

*   *   *

Miranda opened the door.

The man standing before her had damp hair and a strange smile on his face, the look of a man who is about to get what he wants.

'Hello Miranda,' he said. Before she could reply, he darted past her into the hallway.

'Hey,' she said. 'What are you . . .?'

He cocked his head, listening, and looked up the stairs. Then he turned back to face her. She folded her arms protectively across her chest.

'Where is she?' he demanded.

'Who?'

'Who do you think? Kate. Is she here?'

Miranda shook her head. 'No . . . no, she's not. Is she—is she in England?'

He gave her an incredulous glare. 'I take it from the smell on your breath that that was a drunken question. I'm sure you know I'm not stupid, Miranda.'

'Oh yes, I know that very well, Vernon.'

'So don't treat me like . . .'

There was a cry from upstairs. A squeal of laughter followed by a happy outburst from Amelia. 'Well done, Jack. You beat him.'

Vernon dodged past Miranda and ran up the stairs. 'Jack? Jack?'

Miranda listened in horror from her position frozen at the bottom of the stairs as Jack came running out of the bedroom, short of breath, gasping, 'Daddy?'

'Jackie.' Vernon swept him up into an embrace as George and Amelia poked their heads out of the bedroom and gawped. 'I'm here to rescue you.'

Jack said, 'Like Superman?'

'Yes, son. Just like Superman. Where's your mother?'

'She's gone on an adventure with Paul.'

'What? Who's Paul?'

'Mummy's new friend.'

'Her boyfriend,' giggled George, who immediately pulled his head out of sight.

Vernon stomped down the stairs, still holding Jack in his arms. He pushed past Miranda then swung round to face her. 'What's all this about Kate and some guy called Paul? Where are they?'

Miranda shook her head. 'I can't tell you.'

Vernon felt the blood in his veins heat up. This stupid drunk slut. How the hell could Kate have left their son with this unfit mother? Because Kate was an unfit mother herself—that was the truth. He was going to take Jack so far away from here, and make sure that Kate never got her hands on him again. She'd blown it. Jack would be a million times better off without her.

'It doesn't matter anyway. Come on, Jack. Let's

235

get out of this place.'

Jack's little blue wheely suitcase was standing by the front door, still packed but with the zip open, presumably where his pyjamas and toothbrush had been removed at bedtime the night before. Vernon could see a corner of the boy's passport sticking out of the front pocket, where Kate always kept it. He zipped the case and picked it up.

Miranda stepped in Vernon's path as he led Jack towards the door. Blinded by a flash of anger, Vernon pushed her aside, using Jack's case as a shield. She banged her hip on the side table and fell to the floor, staring up with shock. Vernon pointed a finger at her. 'Don't try to get in my way.'

Upset by the violence, Jack started crying and squirming, and Vernon had to struggle to hold on to his hand. 'Come on, Jackie. We're going on an airplane. Soon you'll be home and you'll see Tyler and all your other friends again. You'll like that, won't you?'

Jack shook his head, his face red, tears rolling down his cheeks. 'I want to stay here with George. I want Mummy.'

'Shush. Come on, stop wriggling.'

But Jack wouldn't stop. As Vernon opened the front door, hefting Jack up into his arms, the boy screamed, 'Billy. I want Billy.'

Vernon clenched his teeth, trying to bite back the intense irritation that crawled up his spine, trying to ignore the veins pulsing in his temple. 'Who the hell is Billy?'

'My robot.' He stretched out his hands towards the open door of the living room, where Billy had been left on the sofa.

Vernon ignored his pleas. He carried the bawling

236

Jack out to the car, wrestled him onto the back seat, threw in his case after him, and locked the doors, ignoring the persistent pleas for Billy the robot. What was it? Some present that Kate's new boyfriend had bought Jack as a bribe? Well, fuck it. Jack would soon forget all about Billy and Paul and his mother.

Miranda stood in the doorway and watched them drive off, Jack pressing his tear-soaked face to the window.

Miranda shut the door and ran to the phone, dialling Kate's number. It went straight to voicemail.

She sat down on the bottom step, her head in her hands. George went back into his bedroom to obliterate memories of what had just happened by playing videogames, while Amelia crept down the stairs and sat next to her mum, leaning against her, whispering, 'I don't like Uncle Vernon.'

'Neither do I, sweetheart,' Miranda said.

The doorbell rang again. Miranda sighed.

'It's okay, Mummy,' Amelia said. 'I'll get it.'

33

The hypnotherapist was called Doreen, which Kate thought seemed incongruous. She had half-expected a caricature of a stage hypnotist, called something like Wanda, who, in her mind, would be a cross between a fairground fortune teller, with a fringed headscarf and too much eyeliner; or else a male showman, cummerbunded and pomaded, waving his hands around and saying 'You are feeling sleepy, look into my eyes, look into my eyes.'

Paul had looked on Yell.com for hypnotherapists

in the Richmond area, near his flat, and Doreen was the first one who had come up with an available appointment. Kate hoped it wasn't because Doreen was a charlatan and hence had no clients. But she had a respectable-looking website, and numerous glowing testimonials from satisfied customers, whom she had mostly helped with problems like quitting smoking, or confidence boosting. There weren't, however, any testimonials of people whose memory Doreen had helped restore after having been reconditioned by rogue scientists using the Pimenov Technique . . . but that would probably have been too much to hope for.

Now, Kate stood nervously with Paul outside Doreen's house, a tiny modern terrace backing onto a busy dual carriageway in Twickenham.

When Doreen opened her glass front door and greeted them, Kate wanted to laugh at how normal she looked. She was a grey-haired, friendly-faced lady in her mid-fifties, a little stout around the middle, wearing a nondescript blouse, glasses on the end of her nose, and a pleated woollen skirt.

'Come in, come in,' she said, ushering them through a narrow hallway and into a small living room too cluttered with furniture: a large velour three-piece suite fought for supremacy with an over-large dining table and eight chairs. In combination with a swirly carpet, the overall effect was somewhat claustrophobic.

'Do you live around here?' Doreen asked, pointing Kate towards the armchair, and gesturing for Paul to take a seat at the dining table. She herself settled on the sofa, with her back to Paul.

'I don't,' said Kate. 'I'm just staying in the area with my—um—with Paul here.' She found she

238

couldn't quite bring herself to say 'my boyfriend', and hoped Paul wouldn't think it was because she didn't want to think of him that way. The truth, she realised with a shock, was that she did. She blushed.

'You didn't mention on the telephone what it was you wanted to see me about. How can I help you?'

Kate glanced at Paul. 'It's . . . kind of complex,' she began. 'I mean—it's possibly not something you'll have come across before. I'm not sure that you even will be able to help me.'

'Go on,' Doreen said.

'Well. We've got reason to believe that—oh, it sounds mad—but we think . . .'

She stopped. Suddenly the whole idea seemed preposterous. 'Paul, could I talk to you a minute outside?'

Doreen raised her eyebrows. 'I assure you, Kate, anything which takes place inside these four walls will remain confidential, if that's what you're worried about.'

You might not be so sure about that when you have Sampson pointing a gun at your head, demanding you tell him what you know, thought Kate, shuddering.

'I'd still like a quick word first, if that's OK,' she said.

Paul stood up. 'Could we go out into your back garden? Sorry about this. But like Kate said, it's rather complicated.'

He sounded casual, but Kate could tell by the set of his shoulders that he was frustrated with her. She followed him out onto a tiny patio that comprised Doreen's garden. There was barely room to stand out there—pots of different shapes and sizes crowded round the edges, overflowing with rampant foliage

239

and elaborately flowering shrubs. It was as cluttered as Doreen's living room. Through the fence next door, they could hear the sound of a couple bickering over some domestic issue. A plane flew overhead, on its way in to land at Heathrow, drowning out the neighbours' voices.

'What's the matter?' Paul asked, under cover of the aeroplane noise. 'I thought we'd agreed what you were going to say?'

'I can't,' Kate said, flapping her hands agitatedly. 'She'll either think I'm insane, or she'll call the police, and if that happens, Sampson will definitely kill us before the truth gets out. How is she ever going to believe that I've been "reconditioned"? It sounds like some crappy B movie!'

'It's not her job to believe you or not believe you, it's her job to hypnotise you to see what you remember. Don't tell her about the reconditioning, or even about the CRU. Just tell her you've got a memory blackout about the events of that summer. It's perfectly understandable—you blocked it out because of the trauma of the fire and Stephen's death.'

It sounded more logical when Paul put it that way.

'OK,' Kate conceded, more quietly now that the plane had passed. 'Sorry. I just panicked. I guess I'm nervous about the whole thing anyway; about what might come up.'

'Don't worry,' Paul said, squeezing her hand. 'I'll be right here. And I think you're fantastic to do it.'

She smiled at him, and kissed him lightly on the lips. 'Thanks. Sorry, again, for going all wobbly on you.'

*   *   *

Doreen didn't appear to be perturbed by Kate's eventual explanation, once they were all reinstalled in their positions in the living room. She nodded gravely, as Kate spoke of Stephen's death in the fire, and how she, Kate, had barely any recollection of what happened in the weeks before or after. That she felt it would benefit her to remember, so that she could finally move on, now that she and Paul were an item. She talked merely of 'the place' they had both been staying during that week in summer, making it sound more like a hotel than a scientific research centre, and of how, although very ill, she had escaped with some friends down a corridor as the smoke closed in on them. How she was sure she'd seen Stephen being brought out afterwards, but then been told he had died inside the building, and that this information had confused and haunted her. That she had been in hospital for some time afterwards, with no further memories of that night.

Paul nodded encouragingly at her from his seat at the table, and Doreen made a few discreet notes on a pad of paper on her lap.

'I see,' Doreen said. 'I am sorry to hear your story, it must have been extremely painful for you, to have blocked it all out for so long.'

'So, do you think you can help me?'

'I'm sure I can, now that you've decided you want to uncover this hidden information. Your brain has been shielding certain things from you, and I will just try to allow you access to them. It's not complicated really. You just need to relax, and focus on the words I say. Your brain will do the rest. Are you comfortable? Shall we begin? I'm going to record this, so you can listen to it afterwards. Right.

241

Here we go, then. Close your eyes please.'

Kate obliged, closing her eyes and rolling her shoulders to try and release the tension in her back. She heard the click of a dictaphone being turned on. Then Doreen's voice, lower in pitch than her conversation had been, slow and soothing and soporific. *This will never work*, was Kate's last conscious thought. *I'll be asleep in minutes, especially after everything Paul and I got up to last night . . .*

*   *   *

Some time later—Kate had no idea how much—she opened her eyes, expecting to find herself curled up in the enormous king-sized bed she'd shared with Vern in the house in Boston. She felt warm and drowsy and utterly relaxed, like the best lie-in in the world. A split second afterwards, her eyes relayed the information to her brain that in fact she wasn't in any bed, but in a strange house surrounded by too much cheap furniture, and Paul was staring at her with concern and what looked like shock.

He walked over to the armchair where she was sitting, and, squeezing himself in next to her, tentatively embraced her.

'Oh God, Kate,' he muttered into her hair. 'You were right. There was something going on. We can find out now. Thank you so much, you're so brave, you've always been so brave . . .'

Kate blinked and pushed him away slightly. 'What happened? What did I say?'

Paul hugged her again. 'It's all been recorded. We can listen to it later.' He stood up, extracted a crumpled wad of notes from his jeans pocket, and handed it to Doreen.

242

'Forty-five pounds, isn't it?'

'Thank you. Do you need a receipt?' Doreen asked politely, putting the money into the drawer of a small desk next to the sofa.

Paul shook his head, smiling. 'I don't think I'll be able to write this one off against tax.'

'I'll just quickly burn you a CD of it,' Doreen said, plugging the Dictaphone into a laptop on the dining table, then inserting a blank disk. 'I hope you find it useful, Kate. I must say . . . I'm surprised at what came up. It—well—it wasn't the sort of thing I'd assumed it would be. But it must have been important for you. And I'm quite sure that it will help you in coming to terms with your loss. If you need any more sessions to go into it in even more depth, do telephone me for an appointment, won't you?'

'Thank you,' Kate said, somewhat bemused. She felt completely woolly-legged, and mellow, as if she'd either smoked a large joint or had a very good massage; but this was gradually being superseded by a sharply growing desire to find out what she had said. 'Um . . . is it normal, that I can't remember what I said? Or does it mean that I'm, like, still blocking it out?'

Doreen looked over her glasses at her. 'No, whatever came out while you were under means that you aren't blocking it. However, it's fairly unusual for you not to recall anything you said. Unusual, but not unheard of . . . You don't remember anything at all?'

Kate thought hard. 'Well . . . at one point I thought I was dreaming, about . . . about a forest, lying down in dark trees, and overhearing something . . .'

'Yes,' Doreen said. 'You talked about that. Two men, conversing. Shortly before the fire.' She looked

243

oddly at them both, as if she knew there was more to it than they'd divulged.

Kate glanced at Paul in near-panic. What had she said? Who were the two men?

'I'll play you the CD as soon as we get home,' said Paul, exaggeratedly looking at his watch. 'We must be off, actually, if we're to avoid the rush hour. Thank you so much, Doreen, for seeing Kate at such short notice. I'm sure she will find that really helpful.'

Vernon had a habit of talking about Kate to other people as if she wasn't there, and Kate reflected woozily on how much it had wound her up. But, somehow, now that Paul had done the same, she felt merely protected. She liked it. She slipped her hand into his and smiled at both him and Doreen.

'Thank you,' she said to Doreen. 'I do feel better, weirdly, even though I don't yet know why. It was . . . very relaxing.'

Doreen ejected the CD, put it into a paper cover and handed it to Paul. She showed them both to the door, and they walked back to Paul's car in silence, Paul clutching the disk. He unlocked the doors, and they climbed in, and stared wordlessly at one another.

'What did I say?' demanded Kate, 'tell me!'

'Listen for yourself,' Paul replied, slotting the CD into the car stereo. 'But it was very, very interesting . . .'

34

Dazed by Vernon's visit, Miranda was unable to shift herself from her position on the bottom stair. She watched Amelia skip up to the front door in response to the chime of the doorbell, her emotions tumbling over one another like socks in a dryer. Guilt, because she had allowed Vernon to take Jack. Resentment, because Kate was too busy having a good time with her new boyfriend to answer her phone. Anger, because Pete was boozing with his pretty colleague and hadn't been here to protect her and Jack. And beneath all that, the craving for another glass of wine. No, sod that. She wanted the whole damn bottle.

Amelia opened the door and Miranda heard a man say, 'Hello. You must be Amelia.'

The next thing Miranda knew, Amelia had rushed happily inside clutching a pink teddybear. 'Look, Mummy, look.' Behind her stood a handsome man. But although he was handsome, he wasn't attractive. It was his eyes, she decided, as she pushed herself to her feet and realised that she ought to be very scared.

'Where's the boy?' the man asked in a low, even voice.

Amelia had already run up the stairs to show the teddy to her brother—not that he would be interested in such a girly toy. Miranda felt sober now. All her maternal sensors were buzzing, screaming red alert. This man was far more dangerous than Vernon. Her voice shook as she replied, 'Get out or I'll call the police.'

The man took a step closer. She noticed how big his muscles were beneath his shirt. How strong his hands looked, spiderwebbed with thick veins.

'I want Kate's son.'

'He's not here.'

Sampson lifted his chin and directed his gaze up the stairs, moving towards Miranda. She pulled herself up to her full height—all five foot three of her—and tried to turn herself into a human barrier.

Sampson grabbed her by the neck and flung her aside. She flew into the wall, smacking her head on the frame of the living room door. She fell to her knees but, driven by fear for her children, was on her feet again within seconds, chasing Sampson up the stairs. She tried to grab the back of his shirt to pull him back, but it was like trying to hold onto a train.

He walked straight into George's room, staring down at George, who looked up from his PlayStation with confusion. In the game, he was playing a killer cyborg, and when he saw the stranger enter his bedroom it was as if the video game character had become real flesh and metal. Amelia grinned gappily at the nice man who had given her the teddy bear. But then she saw her Mummy's face as she tried to get around the man, and she started to cry, the bear instantly forgotten.

'Where's Jack?' Sampson said.

Miranda scooted round him and grabbed George and Amelia, protecting them with her body, pushing them into the corner and standing in front of them.

'I told you, he's not here.'

Sampson stared at her, reading her face. Then he reached past her and grasped Amelia by the arm, pulling her past her sobbing mother as if she were

246

as light as a feather. Amelia punched him with her little fists but the blows were like puffs of air. He held her facing outwards, so Miranda could see her terrified face, and said, 'Where is he?'

Miranda reached out for Amelia and Sampson swatted her away.

Calmly, as if bored by the whole situation, he said, 'If you don't answer my questions I'll kill your daughter.'

Miranda tried to console her child, 'It's okay Milly, just keep quiet and everything will be fine. It's okay, darling.' She wished she believed her own words. She felt like she was about to start hyperventilating. She always told the children, when they woke up in the night, that there was no such thing as monsters. Now, she realised, that was a lie.

Sampson said, 'Where is Jack?'

Struggling to keep control of her breathing, Miranda replied, 'His father took him.'

'When?'

'About five minutes before you got here.'

'Where is he going?'

'I don't know.'

Sampson turned Amelia to face her and put his hand around the little girl's throat.

Miranda gasped, reached out, pulled her hands back. 'They're going to the airport. He's going to take Jack back to Boston. Please, let her go. You're terrifying her.'

Sampson ignored her plea. 'What kind of car is he driving?'

Miranda shook her head. 'I don't know. It was grey, I think. I didn't notice.'

George spoke up, in a subdued voice. 'It was a silver car. The one with the sticking out bum. It's called a Megan, like a girl in my class is called Megan.'

Sampson turned his attention to the boy. On the screen behind him, soldiers were crouching with huge guns amidst a firestorm of smoke and bullets. 'A Megane?'

'A Megan. I saw it out the window.'

Sampson nodded. He paused for just a moment, then put Amelia down. She ran into her mother's arms and Miranda squeezed her more tightly than ever before. Surely this bastard would go now, leave them alone. Then she could call the police, get them to protect Jack. But it was almost as if Sampson read her mind.

'Your son is going to have to come with me.'

'No!'

'Yes.'

Miranda started to cry again. This was too much. Why couldn't George just have kept quiet? Even in this crisis, he couldn't help showing off. She tried to plead with Sampson: 'I promise I won't call the police. You can take my mobile, disconnect the phone. Tie us up. I won't call the police.'

'I don't believe you. And I need him to help me find the other boy.'

Miranda started to cry harder. Where was Pete? Why the hell wasn't he home? What had she done, to invite this monster into her and her children's lives?

'Come here.' He beckoned to George, who reluctantly stepped forward. 'What's your name?'

'George.'

He turned to Miranda. 'If George behaves, he'll be safe. As soon as I find Jack, I'll let him go. He'll call you to let you know where he is. But if you call

248

the police or try to follow me, I'll kill him. Then I'll come back here and kill your whole family. Understand?'

Miranda nodded tearfully.

Sampson crouched down and put out his hand. Miranda flinched, and then realised that he was giving her something.

'This is Kate's mobile phone. When she comes here, give the phone back to her and tell her I will call her. Tell her that if she calls the police or involves anyone else, I will kill whichever child I have with me: George or Jack.'

He stood up and looked down at them. 'Remember—call the police and pay the price.'

Miranda nodded again.

'George. Come with me.'

Sampson walked out of the room and George followed him, looking back once at his mother and sister, who held on to each other, unable to speak.

At the bottom of the stairs, George darted into the front room and grabbed the white robot. 'Jack will want this.'

'Right. Just get a move on.'

*   *   *

'Get in the passenger seat.' Sampson climbed in and locked the doors. He didn't want the boy trying to escape. He stuck the robot on the backseat. He'd been successful with the teddy bear so thought he might be able to do the same with this toy. Before setting off he lit a cigarette. The boy coughed as smoke filled the car but Sampson ignored him.

The village disappeared in the rear-view mirror as they made their way towards the motorway, Sampson

249

driving fast, but slowing down for speed cameras. It was a simple rule: don't break minor laws; don't draw attention to yourself. He existed in the shadows, the underground tunnels, co-existing with normal society like a city fox or rat. When he killed or hurt people, nobody knew he was there so nobody looked for him. It was a trick he learned long ago. Keep moving, keep changing, live on the outside, but don't stick out.

He looked at the boy, who sat rigid, staring straight ahead.

'Do you remember the registration of the car?'

George hesitated. 'I think it was a Y reg.'

Sampson nodded, pleased. He wasn't surprised the boy had noticed the registration. When he was George's age he had played a game when travelling with his parents. While his parents sniped and bickered in the front seats, he would note the registrations of passing cars, assigning an imaginary fate to their passengers depending on their registration. C meant they would be crushed. B meant they'd burn. P—paralysed. H—heads chopped off. It was a fun game.

Sampson chucked his cigarette out of the window and followed the signs south, heading towards Heathrow. Sticking in the outside lane, he put his foot down. There were no speed cameras on this stretch of road, and Sampson eased up to eighty, then ninety. The Audi was smooth, but he noticed George grip the sides of his seat. The kid was brave, Sampson realised. Most kids would have blubbed by now. Sampson admired the fact that George hadn't kicked up a fuss about being brought on this impromptu roadtrip. It didn't mean he liked the boy or felt any sentiment towards him. But if George had snivelled or wept it would have been deeply fucking irritating. As long as the boy doesn't piss me off and his mother doesn't disobey me, I'll let him live, he decided.

'Tell me about Kate,' Sampson said.

George looked at him. 'P-pardon?'

'I want you to tell me about Kate.'

'Auntie Kate?'

'Auntie Kate.'

George was quiet and Sampson began to get annoyed. Perhaps he would have to strangle the brat. But then George started to talk, as if he was reciting something he'd written for school. 'Auntie Kate lives in America. She is my mum's sister. She is quite old. She has a son called Jack. Her hair is dark brown. She is . . .'

'Stop. For fuck's sake.'

George clamped his mouth shut, staring straight ahead through the windscreen. He made a quiet whimpering sound.

Sampson said, 'That doesn't tell me anything. I want to hear what she's like.'

Another drawn-out silence while George thought hard. 'Don't you know her?'

'Of course I know her. I just . . .' Sampson trailed off. What exactly did he want? It made absolutely zero sense, but he wanted to talk about Kate. To hear someone else talk about her. Even if it was only this kid.

'What's your earliest memory of her?' he asked.

George said, 'I don't remember.'

'Think. Remember.'

Shaken by Sampson's menacing tone, George blurted, 'I was really little and she came over from America and brought us some sweets, M and Ms I

251

think, and I ate too many and was sick.'

'What else?'

'I remember her and my dad talking about boring science stuff, but Auntie Kate made science sound interesting. Even though it's not.'

'And?'

'I don't know.'

'What does she smell like?'

'What?'

'You heard me. Tell me what she smells like.'

'I don't know.'

Sampson glared at him.

'Like perfume?'

Sampson shook his head. 'No. She smells like—like water. Like a clean, pure lake. Pure, yes.'

'Water.'

'Except she's not pure.' That was right. Kate was tainted. She had fucked Wilson. And now Wilson's brother. And in between—well, who knew how many men she'd been with? But one of them was this Yank husband, Vernon, and she'd spawned his child. Sampson's eyes were clouded by visions of Kate naked, having sex, riding some undistinguished male torso. Her eyes were screwed up tight and her skin gleamed with sweat and . . .

'Are you alright?' George asked.

'What?'

'Nothing.' He paused. 'You made a funny sound.'

Sampson glanced at the boy, aware that he was grinding his teeth. He exhaled through his nose and grabbed another cigarette. He wanted to talk about Kate more, but he despised himself for it. Weakness, weakness. He had to concentrate, do his job, stop thinking about Kate.

'Do you love my Auntie Kate?'

'*What?*'

Sampson snarled it, his voice cracking. George went rigid, flinching and waiting for the hit. But it didn't come. Instead Sampson thumped the steering wheel with the flat of his hand. What the fuck was the kid talking about? The idea that he was in love with Kate was beyond idiotic.

'Shut up and keep your eyes on the road,' he growled to himself then, addressing George, 'You know what we're looking for you, don't you?'

Quietly, George said, 'Yes.' He sounded very close to tears. His lower lip trembled and he sniffed.

'Tell me.'

'A s-silver Megan. Y reg.'

'Now shut the fuck up unless you see it.'

They continued to speed down the outside lane, both of them concentrating on the cars they passed. They overtook three Meganes, including a silver one, but it contained a single occupant, a woman. Heathrow was sixty miles away. Worst case scenario, they would catch Vernon and Jack there. It would be a pain, having to do it in such a public space, but not impossible. He had done such things before, a silent assassin, a pickpocket of lives, a body thief who vanished into the shade leaving madness and bewilderment in the light.

Ten miles down the road, Sampson glanced over and saw that there were tears leaking from the corner of George's eyes, and he was leaning forward in a strange manner.

'What is it?' he snapped.

George just shook his head.

'*Tell* me.'

George squeaked, 'I need to go to the toilet.'

'Are you going to piss yourself if we don't stop?'

George nodded and Sampson sighed. He didn't want the boy leaking all over his leather seats. For fuck's sake. Looking up, he saw a sign for a turn-off to a service station, and without having time to work out whether he could afford the delay, he followed the signs, screeching into the car park and pulling up beside the building which contained several fast food joints, a shop for essential driving supplies like boiled sweets and porn mags, and the public toilets.

Sampson pulled into a parking bay.

'Right. Come with me.'

He strode into the building and towards the toilets, George trotting along beside him. This was risky. George could start screaming about being kidnapped at any second. Why hadn't he just stopped in a lay-by and let the kid piss behind a bush? It was all that stuff about Kate—about loving Kate. It had muddled him, interfered with his decision-making. This was not good. From the look on George's face, though, he was too frightened to do anything stupid. He'd been trained to do what adults told him. Sampson said, 'Be quick.'

He waited by the hand drier while George used the low urinal at the end of the row. Sampson tapped his foot, his face down so he didn't catch anyone's eye. The boy was taking forever. What the hell was his problem?

Finally, George finished, zipped up and plodded mournfully to the sink to wash his hands. 'Come on,' Sampson snapped, and George followed him out.

As they walked past McDonald's, George, who was feeling hungry despite the twist of dread in his stomach, looked through the window. Sampson, who was watching him, saw his eyes widen.

'What is it?'

George averted his eyes and shook his head. 'Nothing.'

But he was clearly lying. 'Tell me or . . .' Sampson drew his index finger across his throat and George gulped.

He pointed through the window towards the queue. A bearded man stood with a small boy. The boy who Sampson recognised from the photos on Kate's phone, didn't look very happy, and the man appeared deeply irritated. 'That's them. That's Jack and Uncle Vernon.'

Sampson stared at them. So this was the man Kate had married; the man who had impregnated her. And there was their spawn, in the flesh, with a protruding lower lip, waiting in line for a Happy Meal.

'Follow me,' Sampson said, striding off towards the exit and out into the car park. After a lull, the rain had started up again, but Sampson didn't feel it. 'Help me find their car.'

He lifted George up and, hoisting him on to his shoulders—something George's dad hadn't done for years—jogged up and down the rows of cars until George pointed and said, 'There.' A silver Megane was positioned at the end of the row. Sampson's brief elation at the discovery was tempered by the ludicrousness of having a small child's legs around his neck. He was sorely tempted to chuck George into a nearby hedge.

Instead, he jogged back to the Audi, opened the doors and swung the kid down onto the back seat.

'When I give you the signal, I want you to hold up the robot. Okay?'

George hesitated.

'*Okay?* If you don't do it, I'll hurt you.'

The boy pressed together his lips and nodded mutely.

Sampson waited until Vernon and Jack emerged from the building. They were carrying their food, but Jack still didn't seem particularly cheerful. Sampson started the engine and drove along just ahead of them, circling the car park until he reached the spot where Vernon's rental car was parked. He waited until Vernon was looking at the car, put his foot on the accelerator and drove into the back of the Megane, smashing the rear left light.

He watched as Vernon gave a shout and broke into a run.

Sampson got out of the car just as Vernon arrived. Jack lagged behind.

'What in hell are you doing, asshole?' said Vernon incredulously.

Sampson said, 'I'm sorry. It was an accident.'

'Jesus,' Vernon exclaimed, putting his hands on his head. 'I'm going to have to explain this to the rental company.'

'Your rear light is smashed,' Sampson said. 'Sorry about that.'

He didn't sound sorry.

*   *   *

Vernon bent down to check it just as Jack arrived. Sampson gestured at George who held Billy the robot up to the window. Jack saw, and gawped at the sight of his cousin and his beloved toy. At that moment, Sampson put his foot on Vernon's back and pushed. Vernon sprawled on the wet asphalt, his burger and fries scattering before him, and in

256

one swift motion Sampson swung open the door of his car, swept Jack off his feet and placed him inside, slamming the door.

'What the . . .?' Vernon tried to get to his feet but Sampson stamped on the hand he was using to push himself up. Vernon cried out and fell back, rolling over and clutching his hand.

Sampson threw himself into his driver's seat and told George to get out. George didn't hesitate—he flung open the door and jumped out, shutting Jack in behind him. Jack stared at George, at Sampson, at his Daddy who was by now on his feet, trying to pull open the door, which Sampson had locked. George was crying and shouting, 'I'm sorry, I'm sorry.' Jack hugged Billy while Sampson put his foot on the pedal and screeched away, leaving Vernon gesticulating after him in the rear-view mirror, his face red, his eyes clouded with anger and terror and bewilderment.

'Who are you?' Jack asked in a high-pitched terrified voice.

'My name's Mr Sampson. I'm a friend of your Mummy's.'

35

They sat in the car, outside a petrol station near Doreen's house, and listened to the CD. Paul found himself getting drowsy just hearing Doreen's voice again, clear and low, as she conducted the relaxation that had put Kate into her trance.

'Perhaps we ought to fast-forward this bit, otherwise we might both end up in a trance every time we listen to it, and then you'll never know what you said,' he quipped. He knew he sounded half-hearted, though, as if he were forcing himself to make a joke when he didn't feel at all like it.

'You'll have to tell me yourself, then,' Kate said, clearly too tense to acknowledge the joke. 'Although I don't think there's any chance of that, not the way I'm feeling now. I'm too desperate to know. Shhh, listen, she's got to the counting backwards bit.'

'I'm going to count backwards from five, and click my fingers when I get to one. When I click my fingers, you will be back on the day of the fire. Five . . . four . . . three . . . two . . . one . . . and you're back there. Look around you. What do you see?'

They heard Kate's voice on the recording, slow but distinct:

'I'm walking towards the field at the back of the centre . . . it's so hot. I want to lie down because I feel ill . . . everything's aching . . . but I don't want to go to my room because Sarah's in there, and we'd had a row . . . I can see Stephen through the window in the lab; he's working today, so I won't be able to talk to him till later. He's moving around among the benches, frowning at test tubes. I love to watch him when he can't see me. I love the way he walks, and the way his back muscles move under the white coat, when he stretches up to open a cupboard . . . I could watch him all day . . . He's so gorgeous. I'm going to marry him some day . . .'

Kate glanced across at Paul, wincing. 'Sorry. It's weird. I've got a vague memory of some of the things I said, in a sketchy sort of dreamlike way—but I don't remember saying that.'

Paul made a dismissive gesture. 'It's fine,' he said tersely. Then, less tersely, he said, 'No, it's really fine. Just feels a bit weird to be jealous of my dead twin, that's all . . . Anyway, shhh, it gets way more interesting in a minute.'

'But you're feeling ill?'

'Yes. I feel terrible. My head's throbbing. I shouldn't be surprised that I'm getting a cold, but I'm still pissed off about it. I was lucky last time I was here, because I didn't get one then. It's totally unreasonable but I feel like you do when you get ill on holiday, sort of outraged. If I'm ill I won't be able to enjoy seeing Stephen so much. I decide to go for a little walk, to try and clear my head. If I'm about to be ill it might be my last chance for some fresh air for a few days.'

'Where are you now?'

'I'm still looking through the lab window but without Stephen noticing . . . I didn't want him to catch me spying on him, but then he looks up and sees me . . . I pretend I'm just passing, on my way to the woods. I wave at him, and he waves slowly back, his eyes all wide as he gets distracted from his task. He smiles at me, but suddenly the smile goes, and he snaps his attention away from me and on to the man who's just walked into the lab.'

'Who is this man?'

'I don't know. He's in a lab coat too. He's thin and bony and bald and it's silly but he's so creepy-looking that I think, "Oh look, it's Doctor Death". That's what he looks like. It must be Stephen's boss, the director of the centre. Dr Gaunt—that's what his real name is. Stephen doesn't like him, he said before that he thinks he's a cold bastard. I remember he laughed at the pun: a cold bastard. Stephen turns his back on me when the man's talking to him, so I wander off across the field. I think if I go into the woods it might be a bit cooler.'

'Then what happens? Is there a fire yet?'

'A fire? No. No fire. It's just hot because it's summer and I think I've got a temperature as well . . . I want to lie down.'

'So what do you do?'

'I walk into the woods. It isn't so hot there. The trees are all shady and old, and it's dark and quiet. I feel like I can breathe better in there. The ground is mossy, and I think: perfect. I decide to have a nap because I'm so tired . . . I lie down under a tree, between two big roots, and it's lovely and soft. I'm asleep really quickly . . .'

'Do you sleep for long?'

'I don't know. But I'm woken up too soon. Something wakes me up.'

'What wakes you up, Kate?'

'Voices. Voices wake me up; men's voices talking.'

'Can you see these men?'

'No. They're on the other side of the tree from me. I sit up and look around. They're standing a few feet away from me with their backs to me, but it's so quiet in there that I can hear every word they're saying. One of them is Doctor Death, I mean, Gaunt, without his lab coat, and the other one is a fat man in a suit, with a German accent. He's a visiting scientist.'

'What are they saying?'

In the car, Kate and Paul were both leaning forwards in their seats, gripping hands. Paul of course had heard it before, but he was as agog as Kate, perhaps waiting for her reaction to what was coming next. Kate remembered that she had talked about falling asleep under the tree, but she genuinely had no idea what the conversation she'd overheard was about. She thought briefly of Doreen, and wondered if she was surprised at all this talk of labs and scientists—they hadn't mentioned that the place was a research laboratory.

'*They're laughing,*' Kate said on the disk, slowly and clearly. '*The German one goes "We're ahead of you on this one." Doctor Gaunt says, "Ah, but you've lost five already." I'm confused. I can't think what they're talking about. Maybe the football. Then the German says, "You're being far too timid in your experimentation—you'll never catch us up, with your insistence on these ridiculous ethics." Now I know they aren't talking about football . . .*'

Kate squeezed Paul's hand involuntarily, with shock. 'Oh shit,' she said.

'Wait,' Paul replied, 'it gets worse.'

'*Do they say anything else?*' Doreen's voice betrayed no surprise at the unexpected turn of recollection. She retained the same calm, soothing monotone.

'*Yes. Doctor Gaunt says, "If it were down to me . . . We're completely handicapped by Bainbridge—he's becoming a liability. He's even got old family friends staying here now, though she won't be here much longer. What we've just discovered is going to blow you out of the water, my friend . . . But it's difficult—funds are tight, you know how it is . . . Mangold has been more than generous, but he's starting to demand results . . . Imagine, if the press knew what was going on here, they'd close us down and we'd all be in jail. If they think what Porton Down does is controversial, God knows what they'd make of this!"*'

'*What do you do next?*'

'*I huddle up behind the tree with my arms wrapped around my knees. I try to make myself as small as possible because I suddenly just know that I will be in big big trouble if they see me here . . . I can't let them see me . . . I'm really scared now, especially because*

261

they mentioned me. I keep thinking about Stephen and wondering if he knows about any of this stuff. I'm going to have to ask him—but what if he does, and he's been hiding it from me? It sounds bad. They aren't talking about the common cold, that's for sure.'

'Do you ask Stephen about it?'

On the recording, Kate had started to cry. *'No. Because I never saw him again. He died before I could talk to him. The scientists eventually left the woods and I waited a bit longer and then went back to my room. I felt even more ill by then anyway. I went to bed. Sarah was there, but I was too sick to talk to her so I didn't even care. I just ignored her. The next thing I remember was being woken up by someone screaming, and Sarah pulling me to get up.'*

'Tell me about the fire, Kate . . .'

'It was like the world was on fire . . .'

Kate clicked off the car stereo, her fingers shaking so much she could barely turn the knob. 'I can't listen to any more, not at the moment. It's too much.'

'So you really don't remember saying any of that when you were in the trance?' Paul caressed her tense hand.

'Well. Like I said—sort of. But not in so much detail. And not what Dr Death and his friend were talking about . . . But it makes sense, in a way. It makes sense now why Sampson's after us. He works for Dr Death. He doesn't know how much I know, and he's freaking out. Oh God, Stephen, they'll kill us both—'

Kate didn't even notice her mistake, until Paul removed his hand from hers.

'I'm Paul, Kate. Not Stephen.'

262

Kate slapped her head, mortified. 'Oh Paul, of course I didn't get you mixed up! I'm so sorry, it only slipped out because I'd been thinking so much about him, and talking about him so much on the CD . . . Forgive me, please? It doesn't mean anything. It's you I want, really.'

Paul stared out of the window. He knew she was right, that it was an understandable slip of the tongue under the circumstances, and yet he couldn't prevent himself saying the one thing which had been preying on his mind for some time: 'So, what if Stephen were here? Would it *still* be me that you wanted?'

There was a brief silence. Kate leaned over to him, hugging him sideways on. But she couldn't look at him.

'Paul . . . how can I answer that? Surely it doesn't matter now? What's important is *you* and me. And figuring out how we get out of this without getting seriously hurt, or killed. I don't think this is the time to worry about our relationship. But, for what it's worth, I'm so glad you're here. And I really, really want us to be together. I don't want anyone else.'

Paul leaned down and kissed the top of her head. 'I know. I'm sorry. It all feels so overwhelming at the moment, that's all. I know I'm not helping matters by saying things like that.'

'It's OK.'

They hugged again and Paul closed his eyes. Kate was warm; she felt so right in his arms. He had never been the hearts and flowers type; never been a romantic who believed that certain people were meant to be together. An ex-girlfriend had, at first, tried to persuade him that fate had introduced them, that they were two halves of a whole, twin souls who would be forever entwined. Then she cheated on

263

him and left him. Since then, he hadn't gone looking for love, and he certainly didn't believe in destiny. But meeting Kate . . . well, it did feel like that. He couldn't imagine life without her now.

'You're still trembling,' he said.

Her voice was quiet when she replied, speaking close to his ear. 'I can see him, Paul. Dr Gaunt. His face. And I feel like he's watching me.' She squeezed him tighter. 'He's still out there somewhere. I know it, and it terrifies me.'

*   *   *

Kate went into the petrol station to buy a bottle of water, leaving Paul in the car. He thought about when she had called him Stephen. It had hurt, made jealousy flare up inside. But he believed her when she said she wanted him. He also knew that if he thought about it too much, it would drive him insane.

Wanting to fill the silence, he turned on the engine and switched on the radio.

'Police investigating the murder of pensioner Jean Bainbridge are looking to question a man and a woman who were last seen in Cannock Chase. They are known to be armed, having stolen a gun, and may be dangerous. The man is described as . . .'

Paul switched off the radio just before Kate got back to the car. There was no point giving her even more to worry about.

264

Dr Clive Gaunt punched the code number into the panel and waited for the door to slide open. As he stepped inside he felt that familiar tingle, the thrill he got from his toes to the few hairs remaining on his scalp. It happened whenever he entered this cool, brightly-lit room. Only he and one other were allowed in here. This was his space, where his life's work resided, where his most treasured possessions dwelled in suspended animation, waiting to be brought to life.

He walked around, running a gloved finger over the dull metal surfaces of the freezer units, surrounded by state of the art lab equipment. He didn't need to label the units; he knew by memory what was in each one. When he closed his eyes he could see inside—no, more than that. In his mind's eye he could picture the viruses as magnified by an electron microscope. So beautiful. For example, the human papillamovirus, like a bright cluster of sea anemones swimming in a warm sea. Or the herpes viruses, each like some exotic flower, their capsids blooming in vivid colour. HIV was another favourite, bringing to mind an alien species from the dark edges of the universe.

His father had collected fine wines, and when Clive was a boy, Gaunt senior would very occasionally allow him to accompany him into the wine cellar. He wasn't allowed to speak during these worshipful visits, which usually happened on a Sunday, when Father would return from church (or rather, his post-church visit to the pub). 'Come with me,' he'd say, and he would lead Clive down the stairs and switch on the low-hanging light. The bottles, shining darkly in the dimness, were racked from floor to ceiling. His father would trace their labels with his finger, pick them up and cradle them, murmur sweet nothings before replacing them. On very special occasions, a bottle would be taken upstairs, opened, sniffed, savoured, sipped. And Clive would sometimes be allowed a small glass, given a clip round the ear if he didn't pull an adequately appreciative face as he tasted it.

When his father died, he sold off the entire collection and had the cellar of their huge country house converted. He wondered what Father would say if he'd known what the great fortune he had left his only child would be used for; or if he'd known that one day his house would be the headquarters of the British cell of a worldwide network of very special scientific researchers; that what was once his wine cellar would house what was arguably the world's finest collection of viruses, rivalled only by those of Ryu Koizumi in Japan and Charles Mangold in Utah. Though Koizumi was merely a rich collector—he didn't do anything with his viruses—and Mangold had become a recluse since the demise of his business. Years before, when his father was still alive and Gaunt was not so wealthy, Mangold—who had run a pharma company in Utah—had been a useful ally, secretly funding much of the research that went on behind the scenes at the CRU.

Gaunt sat down in a chair that allowed him full view of his collection, and rubbed his aching knees. He was an old man now, a long way past his physical prime. Over the last few years he had developed a sense of time running out, his brain getting slower,

266

his memory less reliable, his bones stiffer. After years of slow, painstaking research, this sense of life's hourglass running empty had spurred him on, made him work harder and faster. Now, at seventy-eight years old, he was exhausted. But—thank science!—he was almost there now. He could see the finishing line. Could taste victory.

He sometimes dreamt of writing an autobiography to tell the full story of his life and work. How the chattering classes would gasp. It was a shame that the world would die without hearing the truth.

After the frustrations of his early life as a scientist, when he worked for the Ministry of Defence, the Cold Research Unit, where he had led the lab team, had allowed him to do what he loved most: experimenting with viruses new and old. Under cover of the official research into the common cold—tedious snot-studying work which he left mostly to the junior virologists—Gaunt had pursued his true passion, work that had begun in that glorious post-war period before being stamped on by meddling politicians.

His international contacts, made during those MoD days, had given Gaunt both the impetus and the means to pursue his virological passions. Although his chief private benefactor, dear old Mangold, would have had a fit if he'd known that Gaunt in fact had two paymasters. If Gaunt ever revealed the truth about the involvement of the British Government in his activities, it would have given conspiracy theorists multiple orgasms and caused an international scandal.

But those days were long behind him. He'd had no contact with the secret services or the MoD for years, and he had fallen out with Mangold. For a decade and a half, since the fire that destroyed the CRU, he had been on his own, living off the money his father—who had conveniently died shortly before the destruction of the CRU—had begrudgingly left him. He had built his own lab, filling it with state of the art equipment. And this freedom, far from the prying eyes of do-gooders like Leonard Bainbridge, had allowed Gaunt to make great strides. Sometimes he even amazed himself with his own genius.

He stood up and strolled proudly around the chamber. In these cabinets, below the ground in an English country house, were some of the most dangerous and hazardous organisms on earth. Here was stored the variola virus, which caused smallpox, last seen rampaging through Somalia in 1977. After the initial symptoms—vomiting, fever, delirium—it turned the body into a patchwork of lesions before it destroyed the immune system. Officially, smallpox only existed in two facilities in the world, in Georgia and Siberia, but Gaunt had managed to acquire some from a terrorist group in the Middle East.

Here too were Ebola and Marburg, and a range of VHFs, viral haemorrhagic fevers, like Lassa Fever and Rift Valley Fever from Africa and Machupo from South America. Another favourite was SARS, a coronavirus, the same kind of virus as that which caused the common cold. SARS, of course, came from Asia. This was a truly cosmopolitan collection.

In the corner of the room, to which he made his way now, were the jewels in his crown. The influenza viruses. The 1957 vintage Asian Flu, H2N2. From 1968, here was H3N2, or Hong Kong Flu. There was the lesser-known H9N2 flu, plus H7N7, which hit Holland in 2003, leading to the slaughter of 30 million chickens.

And here was one of the most interesting and exciting viruses, which had cost him many favours and a small fortune to acquire: H1N1, aka the Great Influenza, aka the Spanish Flu, which devastated populations in 1918, killing somewhere between 20 and 40 million people. H1N1 turned people blue as their lungs became clogged and their blood was deprived of oxygen. Their lungs filled with fluid and they suffocated, drowned from the inside. H1N1 made the medieval Black Death look like, well, the common cold. Dr Gaunt stroked the surface of the unit that stored it, wondering what the Americans who had recreated it through reverse engineering just a few years ago would think, if they had known that Gaunt would be able to copy their experiments and create his own stocks of the virus.

Finally, Dr Gaunt stopped in front of the furthest cabinet, the one with its own double combination lock, secured by a code only he and his little helper knew. Inside was Avian Flu, H5N1, plus the virus they had acquired from the young Vietnamese woman. Here too were the goodies that Sampson, who was on his way now, had taken from the lab in Oxford.

And on the top shelf, like a bottle of 1787 Château Lafite—the most expensive wine in the world, the one his father would have killed to own—was the virus that made him want to bow down before it like a serf. The culmination of his, and numerous others', life's work. For thirty years he had been moving towards this moment. There had been disasters along the way. Setbacks and many unfortunate but necessary deaths. Many of his closest colleagues and friends had died. He had sacrificed everything—family, mainstream scientific acceptance, wealth—for this. But now he knew that at last, with just one more test to complete and one more obstacle to remove, it was nearly time to unpop the cork.

Here she waited: the Pandora Virus.

Gaunt and his underground team had been working on it for years. In fact, research stretched back to the days of the CRU, when Gaunt had first started to experiment with flu strains. It had become his obsession. Now, after many years of sculpting this work of beautiful art, the final piece of the puzzle was in place, the breakthrough coming after Sampson liberated the AG-769 virus from Dr Twigger's lab. AG-769 performed a clever trick, the protein in which the virus was wrapped effectively turning off the immune response of the host's cells. Gaunt was able to emulate this effect in Pandora, massively increasing the fatality rate. Now she was complete. She was perfect.

And when she made herself known, the world of science—no, the entire world—would gasp in awe.

Just before they drew their last breath.

37

MI6 officer Jason Harley had been working towards this moment for a long time, the culmination of Operation Castle, the first substantial war crimes case he'd been involved with, a case that had led from Serbia back to London, via a human trafficking investigation.

It was 2.30 am, English summer rain gleaming on

black asphalt in this Tottenham back street, the windscreen wipers of his car pausing, then sweeping, their ponderous rhythm at odds with his own thumping pulse. Inside the ordinary-looking terraced house, with its peeling bay window frames and crumbling brickwork, women from Eastern Europe were kept prisoner and forced to work as prostitutes. Most of them were from Serbia, from dirt-poor families, coming to England in search of a dream but finding a nightmare.

'They're going in,' said Simon Donahoe, the SOCA agent Harley was working alongside, nodding towards the van, out of which poured half a dozen police officers. They watched them ascend the steps, bang on the door, then batter it down. Lights flicked on in neighbouring houses.

Harley waited. They heard shouts from within, a woman's scream. Mercifully, no gunfire. It was over quickly. Within minutes, a police officer approached their car and nodded at them.

'Let's go meet our Serbian friends,' Harley said.

*　　*　　*

Harley walked around the house, peering into rooms in which emaciated, dark-eyed women sat on beds on which they had been raped many times by many men. He had no idea what would be going through their heads. Would they feel relieved, rescued? He didn't see much hope in the eyes of these women. Most of them appeared to be so strung out on drugs they barely knew what was happening. The house stank of stale cigarettes and semen, mould and some vile cooking smell.

'How many?' Harley asked.

271

'Five,' Donahoe replied.

'Hmm. Less than we thought.'

'Fewer,' Donahoe said.

'What?'

'It's fewer than we thought. Not less.'

Harley rolled his eyes. Donahoe could be a dick sometimes. But the cross-agency cooperation had been mostly smooth. Donahoe, like many of his colleagues from the Serious Organised Crime Agency, shared Harley's burning need to do the right thing, to make Britain a better place. Sometimes their older colleagues laughed at their youthful fervour. 'Post 9-11 idealism', they called it. Harley didn't care. For him, the service was not a career, it was a calling.

The men who ran the operation—a trio of Serbians with wiry muscles and shaven heads—had been rounded up and handcuffed to chairs in the kitchen, where police guarded them. Harley stepped into the room. Two of the men kept their eyes downcast but one, the biggest, a man who Harley knew to be called Dragan Popovic, looked up at him and smirked. Harley's fists itched. He knew what this man was responsible for, the pain and suffering he had caused. He was scum. When he was dead, the planet would be a fractionally better place.

It was the pursuit of Dragan Popovic that had led him here. Operation Castle had been a nightmare from start to finish. MI6 were not supposed to be involved in tackling organised crime—that responsibility lay with SOCA—but the Security Service had become involved in this operation as Dragan Popovic and his gang were wanted on suspicion of war crimes carried out during the Kosovan conflict of the late 90s. For over a decade,

272

Popovic and his sidekicks had scorched a trail of misery and death that made Harley yearn for a return to anti-terrorist ops.

*   *   *

Popovic surprised Harley by speaking. 'Can I have a cigarette?' he asked in a polite voice.

Harley clenched and unclenched his fists. They could take this man into a room, administer a beating. Resisting arrest. No one would care. A part of him wanted to do it, that base part that thirsted for vengeance on behalf of the women this man had brutalised.

He was composing a suitable reply in his head when Donahoe came into the room, looking pale.

'What is it?' Harley asked.

'There's a kid. A young girl, about six years old. Yvonne is with her now.' Yvonne was one of the SOCA officers who had taken part in the operation.

'Oh my god.'

He turned back to Popovic, who was still smiling. Harley felt anger course through his veins. Maybe he should shoot him now. One bullet, in the head. Instead, he followed Donahoe out of the room, down the hallway and into the dim room where a small girl with black hair was sitting on a bed with one of the prostitutes, the female officer standing over them. She looked as sick as Harley felt.

The prostitute who was sitting on the bed, an ash-blonde with a dark bruise on her cheekbone, was murmuring to the girl in Serbian. She noticed Harley standing in the doorway.

'I hope you kill them,' she said. 'The men.'

Harley entered the room. 'They'll be dealt with,'

273

he said.

The woman's eyes were almost black. 'Put into one of your cushy English prisons?' she spat.

The use of British slang surprised Harley. 'What's your name?' he asked.

'Monica.'

'And is this your daughter?'

She shook her head. She still had her arms around the girl. 'No, not mine. This is Tatjana. Her mother was here but . . .' She looked at the child. 'Maybe we can talk outside?'

'Of course.'

Harley and Donahoe took Monica into another room, Yvonne staying behind with the girl.

'The little girl,' Harley said. 'Has she been . . . Do they make her work?'

'Not yet. Not like the rest of us,' she replied, and Harley felt his body flood with relief. 'But they make her clean, change beds.'

'My god, it's fucking Victorian,' Donahoe said.

Harley asked, 'What about her mother? Where is she?'

Monica's face darkened. 'He took her away. The doctor.'

'What doctor?'

'I call him Doctor Mengele. You know, like the Nazi. An old man. Sometimes he comes here, he comes, walks, he looks at the girls, chooses one. And then he takes her away. Most recently, he took Slavna, Tatjana's mother.'

'What for?'

She shrugged. 'Some of the girls, they like to think . . . positive. They say he is a rich old man, taking the girls to live with him, to live a good life. When he comes, they smile at him, try to be nice. But I

274

think,' she sniffed, 'he smells bad. Like death. One month ago, he took my friend, and now I look after her little girl.'

'Do you know this man's name?' Harley asked.

'No. But Dragan, he will know. Maybe you can beat it out of him. Maybe I could watch.'

Harley thanked her for her help and took her back into the other room. He looked at the little girl, sitting on the bed, shivering despite the warmth in the room, her eyes wide with fear. What had she seen in her short life? And who was this 'doctor', who had taken her mother?

He stood up straight. He had thought that tonight Operation Castle would be over. But it wasn't. There were more women to find, if they were still alive. For this little girl's sake, for justice, he was going to find this old man, whoever and wherever he was.

38

If I pause now, Kate thought, if I try to absorb everything, it will overwhelm me.

The sky shifted overhead, clouds that had obscured the sun parted to let the late afternoon rays through. Her stomach was knotted, her head throbbed. And her heart—well, it was beating a new rhythm. She looked up and saw Paul watching her, and they exchanged a smile. His was laced with concern. But there was more than that. The look he gave her was the same one Stephen used to give her. It told her that he loved her, and it made her catch her breath.

But she missed Jack. All of a sudden, she had an urge to hear his sweet voice, a voice that sometimes

275

whined and demanded, but that never failed to make her feel happy when she thought of it—even if occasionally his intonation was horribly reminiscent of Vernon's.

'Can I use your mobile to call Jack?'

'Of course.' He passed it over and she rang Miranda's number.

When Miranda answered the phone she was crying. 'You have to come. Now.' Kate tried to get more information out of her but that was all her sister would say. The line went dead, leaving Miranda's sob echoing in her ear.

Paul came over and put his hands on her upper arms. 'What is it?'

Kate broke away and ran towards the car. Every other feeling was swept away by the terror—the overwhelming fear that something had happened to her child.

*   *   *

By the time they got to Churchill the sun had gone down. Paul drove while Kate stared out of the window at the stretching shadows, vivid horrors parading through her imagination. She tried to call Miranda again, to drag sense out of her, but Miranda wouldn't answer the phone. Paul kept asking her if she was okay, which got really irritating after a while, until she snapped at him and he apologised and she felt guilty. But the guilt didn't last long, because the fear was too strong, and any guilt she did feel was directed towards herself. Why had she left Jack? How could she have been so selfish?

'We don't know that anything has happened to

276

him,' Paul said, though he sounded far from confident.

'What else could it be?'

'I don't know. Let's just wait until we get there.'

They pulled up outside Miranda's house. Kate half-expected to see police cars, ambulances, Miranda standing hollow-eyed on the pavement, draped in a blanket with a policewoman beside her. But the house was dark and silent. There was no-one around.

The front door was ajar. Kate pushed it open. 'Miranda?'

There was no reply.

They looked in the living room, which was empty and dark. Kate called again, 'Miranda? Jack?' and Paul joined in.

Then they heard a little girl call, 'Auntie Kate?'

They ran up the stairs, taking two steps at a time.

Miranda and Amelia were sitting in the darkness in one of the bedrooms, huddled together on the floor, Miranda's arm thrown around her daughter. Kate flicked on the light and Amelia buried her face against her mum's belly. Kate quickly realised this was George's room, though there was no sign of George.

'Where's Jack?'

Miranda shook her head and started crying. 'I'm so sorry.'

Kate knelt down, reached over Amelia and grabbed her sister by the shoulders, shaking her. 'Where is he?'

When Miranda answered her breath smelled sour, like someone who'd gone to bed without cleaning their teeth after a drinking session. 'Vernon took him.'

'*What?*'

'He just turned up and . . . and I couldn't stop him. He was too strong. He pushed me over.'

'Shit. What time was this?'

'I don't know. Just before six.'

Kate stood up, her hands in her hair. 'He'll be at Heathrow by now; he might even be on a plane back to Boston. Oh . . .' She turned back to her sister. 'Where's Pete? Couldn't he have stopped Vernon?'

'He went for a drink after work. He'll still be in a pub somewhere, I don't know which one. His phone's switched off.'

Kate was beginning to realise that, as bad as it was that Vernon had turned up and taken Jack, there was something even worse going on here. Something really wrong. 'And George?'

Miranda burst into tears again. Kate wanted to scream with frustration. Then Amelia said, 'After Uncle Vernon went off with Jack, the bad man came.'

Kate stared at her.

'He came and took George. They were going to look for Jack. He made Mummy tell him that Jack was going to get an aeroplane. He said . . . he said . . . he'd kill me if Mummy didn't tell him . . .' Amelia's lip trembled and she stared wide-eyed back at Kate.

Paul stepped forward. 'What did this bad man look like, sweetheart?'

Amelia pressed her face against her mother's breasts. 'Like a monster.'

Miranda managed to speak. 'He left your phone. Look.' She pointed, and Kate saw the astonishing sight of her lost phone lying on the carpet.

And at that exact moment, it rang.

Kate stared at it, frozen. Paul picked it up and

278

was about to answer it when Miranda shrieked, 'No! Kate has to answer.'

Kate took the phone and pressed the green button. She whispered, 'Hello?'

'Hello Kate. Want to say hello to your son?'

Amelia was right—he was a monster. But in the real world, monsters didn't have fangs and horns and scales. Some of them, the kind Kate encountered in her work every day, were invisible to the eye. And some monsters were invisible because they seemed so ordinary. Everyday people, with ordinary faces and voices and flesh and blood. The thing that made them different was inside them, in their hearts and their screwed-up minds.

When Sampson spoke, Kate had the sensation of being stroked by cold fingers. She could hear the darkness inside him. All this time she'd been so terrified of Vernon getting Jack, and now someone far, far worse had him. At least Vernon wouldn't ever put his son's life in danger—but that was exactly what she herself had done. Oh God. She couldn't believe this was happening to her.

She couldn't speak for a few moments.

'I'm going to call the police.'

'No, Kate. Do that and I'll kill him.'

'No! Please don't hurt him. If you do anything to him . . .' She trailed off. What was the point of making threats? 'Let me speak to him.'

'Mummy?' Jack's small voice penetrated her head, and she didn't realise she was crying until she felt the warm tears drop from her chin. Paul stood beside her, rocking from foot to foot, his face dark, pained by his inability to make everything right.

'Jack,' she said, 'Jack, sweetheart, it's me, Mummy. Are you all right?'

279

'The man said you were coming to find me.'

'I am, darling. I'll be there as soon as I can. Where are you?'

'I don't know. I don't like it.'

'Oh, Jack, I'm so sorry. I promise . . .'

'Save it.' Sampson was back on the line.

'You bastard! Why the hell are you doing this? I don't know what you want from me.' Except that you want me dead, she thought.

'Haven't you worked it out yet? It's all in your head.' He paused and Kate could hear somebody else in the background, a man's voice. She strained to make out what he was saying. What Sampson had said confirmed her fears: that they were after her because of what she had found out sixteen years ago. But they didn't know she had been to see a hypnotherapist, and they didn't know she couldn't remember everything. She realised, though, that she was a loose end that needed to be cut away.

For a horrible moment she thought the line had gone dead and that the thread between her and Jack had been broken. 'Hello? Hello?'

'If you want your son back, you and Wilson have to come to us now. Don't tell the police or the kid will die. Don't try to be clever. Just get here if you want to see him alive again.'

'But where are you?'

'I can't tell you that.'

'Then how the hell am I supposed to come to you?' she shouted into the phone.

He didn't reply instantly and her heart bungee-jumped into her stomach.

'Go to the village of Blackmarsh in West Sussex. Be there by one am. Then wait for more instructions.'

'By one am? How long does it take to get there?'

280

But he had hung up.

Paul gently turned her to face him, and cupped her face in his palms to force her to look him in the eyes, but she shrugged him off.

'We haven't got time, we've got to get to Blackmarsh, it's a village in East Sussex, by one o'clock in the morning, oh God, Jack; they're going to hurt him, oh God . . .'

Paul held her. 'Kate, calm down. Shhh. Come on.'

The tears burst and she pressed her face against his shoulder and let it all out. Jack, oh, Jack, and it was all her fault, if she hadn't come to England, if she hadn't been so stupid and selfish, and then leaving him here with Miranda while she swanned off so she could shag her new man. The guilt hit her so hard it nearly knocked her off her feet.

Paul waited for her to stop crying, holding her close and kissing her hair, shushing her and whispering that it would be okay. But she struggled free again.

'We have to get going. We have to get to Jack. And to George.'

Miranda was still sitting in the corner, ashen-faced, cuddling Amelia. 'I'm so sorry,' she whispered, 'I think, if that man has Jack, then George must be with Vernon. He said he was going to trade them . . .' She tailed off, at the expression on Kate's face.

Kate could see the hope and relief flickering across her sister's features and, although it was irrational, she felt even more angry with Miranda.

'We have to go, Paul,' she said curtly.

'Okay, but first . . .'

'We have to go, now!'

'Kate, listen. We need to work out *where* we're going. Okay? What was the village called again?

281

Blackmarsh?'

She nodded mutely.

'I've never heard of it.' He turned to Miranda. 'Do you have GPS in your car?'

'No, sorry.'

'Damn, nor do I. I've got a maps App on my iPhone—I'll look it up on there but the 3G isn't always reliable.'

Paul started jabbing at the screen of his iPhone, but it seemed to Kate to take an eternity before he found directions to Blackmarsh. She paced the room, feeling sick to her stomach.

'Okay,' he said eventually. 'It's just under a hundred and thirty miles, and if we follow this route it should take two hours fifty-five minutes, unless there's bad traffic.'

'What time is it now?'

Paul checked his watch. 'Nine forty-five.'

'Oh shit. We'll never make it.'

'Yes, we will. We've got three and a quarter hours, and the roads should be quiet now.'

'But what if we get held up? There might be roadworks somewhere. Or an accident. Oh . . . Jack.'

Paul took her chin and made her look directly at him. 'We will make it, Kate. I promise you. Let's leave now.'

There was a heavy rap on the front door: Paul turned to Miranda. 'Will that be your husband?'

Miranda's eyes were wide with fear. 'No. He's got a key. And he'll be in the pub till closing time. He always is when he's with *her*.'

Paul didn't have the time or the inclination to ask who *she* was. He quickly scanned the room and saw a cricket bat propped in the corner. He crept back down the stairs and pulled open the front door,

282

swinging the cricket bat, ready to strike if necessary.

A man with a gingery beard and a long brown coat stood in front of him; a shaken, pissed-off man. A small boy pushed past Paul's legs and ran into the house.

'Is my wife here?' said Vernon.

39

'Kate.'

'Vernon.'

He opened his mouth to speak but Kate just walked past him, still gripping her mobile phone like it was her only connection to Jack. A few days ago this would have been her worst fear: coming face to face with Vernon, the confrontation she had dreaded since she fled America. But now her ex-husband's presence was little more than an irritation, an inconvenience.

'So . . .' Vernon began, following her as she went into the kitchen and ran water into a glass. They could hear the sound of relieved sobs coming from upstairs, as George was reunited with his mother and sister.

She turned. 'I don't have time for any of your shit, Vernon. We have to get going now.'

'Because, if what George tells me is true, you let our son fall into the hands of some psychopath.'

'Actually, I think it was you who allowed the psychopath to get him.'

'If you hadn't brought our son to England in the first place, he'd still be safe in Boston, where he belongs.'

'He belongs with me.'

'Yeah, well, great job, keeping him so close. Didn't you dump him here with your sister so you could spend some sack time with lover boy here?' He jerked his thumb at Paul, who had entered the room.

'At least I didn't have a lover while we were still together.'

'Oh yeah? I'm supposed to believe that?'

'It's true. And I left Jack with Miranda because I thought he'd be safe here.'

'Hah! Safe? I'll tell you . . .'

Paul stepped in between them. 'Please, both of you, stop it.'

Vernon's face was turning purple. 'Don't you tell me what to do. You have no right. I can talk to my wife anyway I like.'

'Ex-wife,' Kate interjected.

'We're not divorced yet.'

'Please,' Paul said, raising his voice. 'Stop. We have to get going. If we're going to make it to Blackmarsh by one, we should leave now.'

Kate turned angrily on Vernon. 'See, you're holding us up. Come on, Paul.' She headed out of the room, Paul behind her.

Vernon followed. 'I'm coming too.'

Kate put her hands on her hips. 'What? No way.'

'He's my son too. I want to help.'

'You'll only hinder.'

'Kate, I'm coming.'

'If you think I want to share a car with you, then you've got . . .'

'I think we should let him come,' Paul said. 'He might be able to help.'

'At last,' said Vernon, 'somebody who talks sense.'

Kate couldn't believe her ears. But they had

284

already wasted far too much time arguing.

'Okay, whatever. Let's go. I assume you've got a rental car, Vernon. Does it have Sat Nav?'

Vernon nodded.

'Right, we'll take yours then, it'll probably be faster than Paul's. Let Paul drive, though, Vernon—he knows the UK roads far better.'

The men did as they were told, though Vernon handed the keys to Paul with undisguised reluctance.

'I'll get our things out of the Peugeot, just in case,' said Paul. 'We don't know how long we're going to be away.'

Kate got into the passenger seat of Vernon's car and punched the word Blackmarsh into the Sat Nav, not wanting to have to rely on Paul's iPhone. But she struggled with the unfamiliar instructions being issued by the car's computer screen, and misspelled the location several times. The letters skidded about on the screen in a jumble; she pinched the bridge of her nose and told herself to focus. This usually worked, in the lab when she'd been working all night, always on the verge of a breakthrough, or fighting a deadline, and she'd stare at her papers and the numbers and characters would dance and sway. But now, nothing would calm her: her heart was moving too fast, her brain felt like it was dividing, splintering into pieces, thoughts like flies buzzing around a light bulb.

She handed Paul's iPhone to Vernon on the back seat. 'You hold onto that,' she ordered, 'that Maps app lets you know if there are any accidents or traffic jams on our route.'

'I don't have my reading glasses.'

'For pity's sake . . .'

Paul slammed the boot closed, and the car rocked.

'It's okay,' he said, climbing into the driver's seat. 'The Sat Nav will let us know about any hold-ups too, I'm sure.'

He started the engine and was just executing a three point turn outside the house when they saw Miranda's husband Pete return, visibly tipsy after his night at the pub. Before he'd even got his key in the door, Miranda had flung it open and was berating him like a fishwife for not having been there to protect her and the children.

'That poor bastard's in for a shock,' Paul commented as they drove away.

They were soon on the A44, heading south towards Oxford. The road was reasonably quiet, which was the first bit of good news of the evening. Kate was still terrified that they might get held up by an accident and, reclaiming Paul's phone from Vernon, obsessively checked the roads on the Maps app to make sure they were clear. She believed Sampson when he gave her a deadline. Not just because she couldn't afford to risk it, but because he was too cold, too robotic, to be bluffing or to be malleable in any way. Trying to persuade him would be like trying to negotiate with a computer.

Vernon leaned over between the front seats. 'Does somebody intend to tell me what in hell is going on? Who is this guy who's taken our son? And why haven't we phoned the police?'

'If we call the police,' Kate said, 'they will kill Jack.'

Vernon didn't say anything for a moment. 'Kill him? My Jack . . . My boy. But *who*? Who are they, Kate? What have you done to get involved with these people?'

'It's a long story.'

'I got nothing better to do back here.'

'And we don't know half of it yet.'

'I don't care. Just tell me what you do know.'

'Okay. The guy—the man who took Jack—is called Sampson. He used to work at the CRU . . .'

'The what?'

'The Cold Research Unit.'

'That place where they were hunting in vain for a cure for the cold? You stayed there when you were a student, right?'

'Yes.'

'And had a nice vacation, as you told me.'

Kate glanced at Paul. There was another feeling crawling beneath her skin, beneath the terror and panic over what was going to happen to Jack: this awkwardness caused by the fact that she was in a car with Vernon and her new . . . well, what was he? Lover? Boyfriend? It was too weird. 'There's stuff I haven't told you about.'

Vernon snorted. 'Why doesn't that surprise me?'

'No—it's stuff that I didn't tell you about because I couldn't remember it. It seems . . . apparently, I had my memory wiped.'

'You're kidding me.'

'Do you want me to tell you about this or not? If you do, stop interrupting. Okay? We discovered that there was something going on at the CRU. I went to see a hypnotherapist. That was after Mrs Bainbridge was shot.'

Vernon's voice rose by about an octave: '*Who?* I think you'd better explain from the beginning.'

So Kate did, telling him everything they'd discovered so far; the gaps they'd filled in. She told him about going to the CRU and meeting Stephen. About how she went back for a second stay. She recounted the

287

night of the fire, when she had been sick, and Stephen and her room-mate Sarah had died, and — how she, Kate, had woken up in a strange hospital.

Then Paul took over, telling Vernon about how he had received a letter from his brother shortly before the fire, a letter that made it clear that Stephen also knew that everything was not what it seemed.

'So we went to see Mrs Bainbridge—Jean—the widow of Leonard, the man who ran the centre, my old family friend, and while we were there Sampson turned up and shot her. Before she died, though, Jean had given Kate some papers that described a procedure that had been done on her—Kate—while she'd been in hospital, altering her memory. Then we made an appointment with a hypnotherapist, who uncovered all these suppressed memories. And then Sampson came after Jack.'

There was silence in the car, just the sound of traffic rushing past on the other side of the road. Finally, Vernon said, 'So what do you think was going on at the CRU? And why is this happening now? I mean, it was over fifteen years ago, wasn't it?'

Kate thought back to what she'd learned from the hypnotherapy session. The conversation between Dr Gaunt and the fat German had chilled her, even though she hadn't understood what they were talking about and didn't know what had happened next. But she must have gone looking for answers, her curiosity piqued. That was what she did: looked for answers. A curious cat. And others might have been killed because of her: Sarah, possibly. Stephen —probably.

'I don't understand how they knew to come looking

288

for me; how they knew I was back in the country,' Kate said. 'It's as if they've been watching me. It gives me the creeps.'

Vernon leaned forward again. 'What, you think these people have been keeping tabs on you all this time?'

'Presumably. Maybe it was Professor Scott at Harvard, the one who got me the job. He was a colleague of Gaunt's. Perhaps he was in on this too—there was something about him I found a bit creepy, and he was always asking me odd sort of questions, now that I think about it . . . Shit. What if he's had someone spying on me for years?' She couldn't resist a dig: 'That means they've probably got some nice footage of you sneaking the lovely Shirl in and out of the house.'

'What? I never . . .'

'We're nearly in Oxford,' Paul said, in an attempt to get them to stop arguing.

'Oxford,' sighed Kate, picturing herself in her gown celebrating the end of her University exams. 'The last time my life was normal.' Then something came to her. 'Paul, do you remember on the news the other day there was that story about a scientist being murdered in his lab here? I can't remember his name but they definitely said he was a specialist in viruses.'

'You think Sampson could have had something to do with it?'

'It's possible, isn't it?'

Vernon leaned forward between their seats. 'Hey, can we just stay focused on finding my son please?'

Kate leant her head against the window and stared out at the lights of the motorway, the passing cars, the illuminated signs above. They entered Oxford, driving around the ring road, still heading south.

Paul was very quiet, and Kate assumed it was because he was concentrating on the road, but then he blurted: 'I have a gun.'

Kate's hand flew to her mouth. 'What?'

'In the boot—there's a gun. A shotgun. I took it from Andrew and Penny's house in Cannock Chase. Then I moved it from the Peugeot into this car. I thought we might need it.'

'Paul . . . How could you? With your past and everything—I thought you would do anything to avoid guns.'

But Vernon said, 'No, this is good news.'

'Do you know how to use a gun?' Paul demanded.

'Uh-huh. I hunt. Not as often as I used to—Kate was always giving me grief about it—but I'm a damn good shot.'

This was true. Kate and Vernon had argued about the tradition being passed on to Jack. Kate abhorred the thought of it, of her son killing a helpless animal; Vernon insisted the blood rite would make him a man.

'You're not suggesting that we stage some kind of shoot-out with Sampson, are you? You're insane. Sampson is almost certainly better with a gun than either of you, and if Jack's going to be there I don't want guns going off, bullets going astray. Look what happened to Mrs Bainbridge. I really can't believe you would consider it.' At the same time she said all this, she pictured herself blowing a hole in Sampson's chest.

'I'm just saying it's an option,' Paul said.

'I think we should do it,' said Vernon. 'He won't be expecting us to have a gun. No-one in this stupid country has guns, normally, do they? Let's take him unawares.'

290

Kate slapped the dashboard. 'No! It's too dangerous. We have to do what they say. All I want is for Jack to be safe—and he won't be safe if you two have a bloody shotgun pointed in his direction.'

Paul and Vernon exchanged a look, the kind that passes between men when they want to say the word 'women'.

'Okay,' Paul said. 'You're right, I suppose. We'll just leave it in there.'

But somehow Kate didn't believe a word.

They drove on in silence for another five miles or so. 'We're going to need petrol soon,' Paul said.

'You're joking.'

'Kate, don't panic. There are services ahead. It will only take a couple of minutes to stop and fill up. We're making good time.'

'If you're sure.'

'Yes.'

A few miles later they saw a sign for services and Paul pulled off the motorway, Kate drumming her hands on her knees with impatience as they waited for a pump to become vacant. Vernon got out of the car and paced around for a few minutes, going into the shop while Paul filled the tank.

As Paul went off to pay for the petrol, Kate had a sudden impulse. She grabbed Vernon's ridiculous full-length brown waxed mackintosh from the back seat (he thought, erroneously, that the deep pockets and plaid lining made him look like an English country gent) and put it on. Jumping out of the car, she ran around to the back, checked that neither of the men were looking at her out of the petrol station shop window, opened the boot and saw the double-barrelled shotgun lying there on top of Jack's little wheely suitcase. She shuddered at the sight of it.

291

She'd never touched one before, but she forced herself to pick it up and slip it under the long coat, tucking it into her side. There was no way she was going to risk any of their lives—and particularly not Jack's—by either Vernon or Paul trying to act the gun-toting hero.

She wrapped the coat around her body and, head down, marched into the garage. Vernon was looking at the display of chocolate, and Paul was at the till paying for the petrol.

Vernon looked up. 'Why are you wearing my coat?'

'Cold,' she said. 'I think it's shock, and nerves. Dodgy tummy. Just going to the loo, I'll try not to be long.'

Ignoring his disdainful expression, she dashed into the single toilet cubicle, thankfully unoccupied. She bolted the door, then took out the shotgun and examined it. She'd seen Vernon do it a number of times: there was a latch somewhere near the hinged bit in the middle, wasn't there, that cracked the thing in half to expose the chamber of bullets? She found a metal spur near the chamber and pushed her thumb on it, trying hard to avoid going anywhere near the trigger. After a bit of fiddling around with it, to her great relief, the spur gave way, the gun broke open, and she saw the little stubby bullets in the chamber. She emptied them into the palm of her hand and dropped them into the swingbin for the sanitary towels. But what the hell was she going to do with the gun itself? Someone knocked on the door, and she jumped out of her skin.

'Just a minute!' she called, trying to keep the panic out of her voice.

'Kate? Are you OK in there? Vernon said you were feeling ill.'

292

'I'm all right,' she shouted back, looking wildly around the small tiled room. There was nowhere to conceal a gun. She couldn't leave it in there in case the garage staff found it and alerted the police before they could get to Jack. 'Just been sick.'

'Oh baby. Poor you! But we have to get going.'

'I'm coming. You go on out to the car, I'll be right out.'

'I'll bring the car up to the door,' he said, and she heard his footsteps fade away. She clicked the empty shotgun back together, took off Vernon's coat and hid the weapon in its copious folds, clutching the whole thing to her chest. Before exiting the toilet, she checked her reflection to make sure the end of the shotgun wasn't sticking out under the coat. She looked a state, she realised—her face was ashen, her long hair a massive dark tangle, and her lips bloodless. She took a deep breath to try and compose herself, and unlocked the door.

When she came out of the garage, Paul had the car waiting and the passenger door open for her. 'One sec,' she said, heading round the back and opening the boot again. She shoved coat and gun inside, shaking the gun free so it—she hoped—looked as though it had been there all along.

'What the hell are you *doing?*' Vernon yelled at her.

'Just, um, checking in case there's a road map we can use. In case our phones lose signal . . .'

'This car has Sat Nav! You programmed it! What the hell? Come on!'

'In case the Sat Nav malfunctions, or we lose signal on our phones,' she said lamely, sliding into the passenger seat and putting on her seatbelt as Paul pulled away as fast as he could. 'There isn't a map, anyway. I put your coat in there—I've warmed up again now.'

'God, Kate, you're insane, you know that?'

Kate bit her lip and folded her hands in her lap. Then she jerked up her head. She spoke calmly but forcefully: 'Vernon, dammit, I will *not* be talked to like that, not by you or anyone else. Our son is in danger, and we have to get to him as quickly and safely—and accurately—as possible. It's an incredibly stressful situation, but does not give you the right to speak to me in that abusive manner. Don't ever use that tone with me again. Understand?'

'For fuck's sake, quit lecturing me. Like you pointed out earlier, you're not my wife anymore.'

'I never lecturered you, or nagged you. I was always a good, dutiful wife, putting up with your indiscretions, entertaining all those boring professors and deans you were desperate to impress. I worked all day and came home and cooked your dinner and washed your underwear. I put up with your moods when the books you wrote failed to get published. I put up with your tempers and your outbursts. I taught you how to use your damn mobile phones and got music onto your iPod for you. I gave you twelve years of my life. And I *never* lectured you.'

Vernon shook his head. 'You never used to be like this. You've changed, Kate.'

She didn't look round at him. Paul glanced across at her and smiled: the kind of small smile that said, 'I know I shouldn't be feeling any happiness right now but I can't help it'. And she felt a little jolt of love. She could still feel Paul's imprint on her, from when they had last made love.

'You're right, Vernon,' she said. 'I have changed.'

Kate leaned across and kissed Paul's hand, not

294

caring about the sensation of Vernon's eyes burning into them.

They drove back onto the motorway. The minutes passed: Kate watched them on the dashboard display, watched the speedometer, obsessed over the mileage on the signs they passed. London 50 miles, 40 miles, 30 miles. They left the M40 and hit the M25. Still no sign of accidents or hold-ups. Paul put the radio on to check the travel news and everything seemed unnervingly normal.

This is all a dream, thought Kate. But when I wake up, where am I going to be? In Boston, still married to Vernon, with him grumbling in his sleep beside me? Or in a London hotel, sweating with the anxiety of being caught?

Or even back in the flat she shared with Stephen all those years ago? She'd wake to find he was watching her as she slumbered, as he sometimes had, and he'd kiss her before she had a chance to say, 'I had the strangest dream.'

40

They rolled into the small Sussex village of Blackmarsh with half an hour to spare, passing through silent country lanes, the headlights illuminating the trees that lined the road, eerie in the darkness. Not really knowing where to stop, Paul followed a gentle hill up to what appeared to be the main street. They parked outside a church with a graveyard stretching downhill beyond its uneven stone walls. There was no-one around, no lights in any windows. The village could be deserted apart from them, and when Kate spoke she found herself whispering.

'So what do you think we do now?'

'Wait for the call,' Paul replied.

All three of them stared at the phone on the dashboard. Kate picked it up and pressed a button, waking it up and making the screen shine. Paul reached across and rubbed Kate's shoulder, which made her start and pull away.

'Sorry. I'm so on edge.'

'I'm getting the gun,' said Vernon, climbing out of the car and opening the boot. Kate held her breath—would he notice? She was beginning to regret her rash decision to remove the bullets—what if it gave the men a false sense of confidence, believing they were armed, when in fact they weren't? Should she confess, before they got to Sampson? She didn't know what to do.

'Why don't we call this asshole ourselves?' Vernon suggested. He appeared not to have noticed that the gun wasn't loaded.

Kate didn't bother turning to look at him. 'Because he told us not to.' She almost added, 'Stupid', but she was sick of squabbling with Vernon. He really wasn't worth it. Not any more. He'd never been worth it—it was just that she'd taken a long time to realise it. It saddened her to think of all those wasted years, young years, when she could have been free, or with someone who would make her happy. Jack was the only good thing that had come from their marriage.

Jack. A wave of nausea and exhaustion swept over her as she pushed the door open, suddenly ready to be really sick, wondering faintly if it was sinful to throw up in the grounds of a church. As she did so,

296

the mobile rang, its jaunty tune ridiculously inappropriate.

Paul went to pick it up but she shoved his hand away, grabbed the phone and swallowing down her nausea, said, 'Yes? We're here. Where is he?'

'I knew you wouldn't let the boy down.' Sampson's voice was, as ever, cold and flat.

'His name's Jack, you bastard.'

'There's no need to be like that, Kate. This is a simple transaction. You give us what we want and we'll give you what you want.'

'But I don't even know what you want!' Kate felt like banging the phone against her forehead. Or better still, smashing it against Sampson's skull. She realised with a stark clarity that she would kill him if it would save Jack. Hatred boiled through her veins, giving her a false sense of power because ultimately she knew that she was completely weak and helpless—this was so out of her control. All she could do was to follow his instructions. 'Who's in the car with you?' Sampson asked.

'Just . . .'

'Don't lie, Kate. That would be your worst mistake.'

'I'm with Paul. And Vernon.'

'Your boyfriend and your ex-husband. You're very popular. Doesn't this Wilson care that you fucked his brother?'

Kate held her breath.

'Stephen Wilson was weak, when it came to the crunch. I expect his brother is no better. An old woman saved his life last time. He wouldn't be so lucky again . . .

'Here are your instructions. Drive out of Blackmarsh towards Crawley. You'll pass a garage, then go straight across the roundabout. After that, you'll see a pub standing on its own to the left, with a car park behind it. Go into that car park.'

'Are you there now? With Jack?'

But he had already cut her off.

Kate relayed the instructions to Paul and Vernon. 'He said something about Stephen, too. It sounded like he knew what had happened. Like he was there.'

Paul's knuckles paled as he gripped the steering wheel and accelerated out of the village.

'What did Stephen's letter say again?'

Paul recited it from memory, where it had been seared for years: 'Tell her she was right. And tell her to forgive me.'

'Stephen must have known what was going on.'

'And Sampson found out that he knew.'

'But we still don't know what he wanted me to forgive him for.' A sickening thought crept into her head. 'Oh Paul, you don't think he was involved in some way, do you?'

They drove on for a couple of miles, the tension in the car palpable.

'I think this must be it,' she said, as they went over the roundabout that corresponded with Sampson's directions. A minute later, they spotted the pub, and its car park.

They pulled in, slowly, all three of them rigid with fear. Kate glanced at her shaking hands. But she felt one hundred per cent focused and alert. She felt like this was a moment she had been heading towards for a long time. She was here to reclaim her baby.

There was a single car parked in the car park: Kate recognised the menacing silhouette of Sampson's Audi, but with only moonlight to see by, it was too dark to make out much inside, though she was sure she could see the shape of a boy in the back seat. Her heart pounded. She watched the door of the Audi open, and the orange glow of a cigarette tip that sent out a shower of quickly-dying sparks as Sampson flicked it away. There was no time to tell Vernon that the gun was empty.

Sampson stopped in front of his car and called out. 'Get out. All of you.'

Kate hissed at Vernon: 'Don't do anything stupid. Okay?'

'Okay, okay, I hear you.'

'We're going to do whatever he says,' she whispered in Paul's ear.

*   *   *

The three of them pushed open their doors and got out. Kate and Paul walked slowly towards Sampson, their bodies close but not touching. It was silent in the car park and, over the sound of her heart thudding in her chest, Kate could hear grasshoppers chirruping in the grass beyond.

Sampson lit up another cigarette, the flame of his lighter casting a flickering shadow on his face. In his other hand he held a gun, which he casually lifted and pointed towards them. There was a small sound behind Kate, and Sampson heard it too. He swung the pistol towards Vernon, who had tried to lift the shotgun. 'Drop it now, asshole, or you're a dead man.'

'Do it, Vernon, please,' said Kate in a strangled voice. She clutched Paul's hand tightly, hardly able to bring herself to turn round to see what was going on.

Vernon dropped the shotgun on the ground and

299

began to cry as Sampson walked up to him and put his pistol against his ear. Sampson held it there for many long seconds, letting Vernon shake and whimper, before spinning it around and cracking the barrel of it hard against Vernon's temple. Vernon screamed and rolled over, curling himself into a foetal position on the tarmac, clutching his head.

'The only reason you're still alive, you worthless piece of trash,' said Sampson conversationally, picking up the shotgun, 'is because someone needs to give your kid a lift home. And the kid's mother is required elsewhere. So, this is what's going to happen next: I'm going to let the boy out of the car. You,'—he pointed the pistol in Kate's direction—'and Wilson are going to get into the car in his place, and we're going to leave.'

'No way,' said Paul.

'This is not a negotiation,' Sampson said, his voice low. 'You do what I say.'

'Yes,' said Kate. 'We'll do it.'

'Kate . . .' Paul protested, but she shook her head.

'Jack can go with Vernon. He'll be safe then. That's what matters.'

'But he'll kill us.'

There were tears in her eyes. To Paul she said, 'Maybe one day you'll be a parent, and then you'll understand.'

'Actually, it's extremely unlikely you ever will be a parent, Wilson, but you should still do as I say,' Sampson said, almost conversationally, now aiming the gun at Paul's chest.

Throwing down his cigarette, Sampson took a few backward steps to the car and opened the back door. Jack jumped out and ran straight into Kate's arms.

She lifted him up, hugging him tighter than she'd ever hugged him before. He smelled so good, felt so warm in her arms, and she cried against his soft hair as he said, 'Mummy, that man was smoking. And he hurt Daddy.'

'Daddy's OK, sweetheart, look. He's fine, see, just a bump on the head. You're going to go with him.'

Jack tried to wriggle away. 'Where are you going?'

'I'm just going for a drive.'

'With that man? I hate him! Him and the doctor.'

'What doctor?'

Sampson spoke up. 'That's enough. Put him down and come with me. Now.'

'Mummy!' Jack tried to cling to her, but she had to push him away, every instinct making her want to hold on to him, feeling his distress bore into her.

He started to cry, sniffing back tears and making that awful, keening noise he made when he was really upset. Or maybe she was making the noise. She couldn't tell. But this was the only way. He would be all right with Vernon. This was, in fact, better than she had expected. She had thought Sampson would try to kill them all, but she didn't try to understand what was going on. There would be time for that, she hoped.

Or she might be dead in a minute. This might be the last time she ever saw her son.

Putting Jack down and walking away from him was the hardest thing she had ever had to do.

She got into Sampson's car, in the back seat, and Paul got in beside her. Sampson climbed into the driver's seat, put the shotgun in the footwell and sped away, leaving Jack behind. In the rear-view mirror, Kate saw her son standing in the car park, sobbing, clutching onto the kneeling Vernon. He

301

was safe. That was all that mattered.

'Where are we going?' she asked, in the calmest voice she could manage.

But Sampson didn't reply. He just watched her in the mirror, until she had to look away. Paul tried to take her hand, but she didn't want him to touch her. Not right now. At this moment, she felt like she didn't ever want anyone to touch her again.

Ten minutes later, after driving down a long, dark lane, they pulled up outside a large white house.

This is where it ends, Kate thought.

41

It was 1.25 am, according to the clock on the dashboard. Kate remembered nights, before Jack was born, when she could often still be found at her lab bench at this time, and on into the morning, until she would look up from her work and see the sun rising outside, the sky a delicate pink and the city quiet beyond the sheltered realm of the university. That world, and the dawn, seemed a very long way away now.

Sampson switched off the engine and turned to look at her and Paul. He seemed tense, and at first Kate wondered why his mood had changed since the start of the journey. Then it struck her that this was more than odd: it was the first time she'd ever noticed him display any hint of emotion.

She ached inside for Jack; prayed that he was okay, that Vernon would be taking care of him. Where would Vernon go? Surely he would wait to see what happened and wouldn't whisk Jack straight back to

America. Maybe he would head back to Miranda's. Or maybe he would go to the police now that Jack was safe. She wished she'd had a chance to talk to him after Sampson had said Jack could go with him. Her phone was in her pocket, and she itched to send Vernon a text. But could she do it without being seen? Maybe once they were inside.

'Come with me,' Sampson said, taking the empty shotgun with him. Kate was suddenly very glad indeed that she had removed the bullets.

He led them across the courtyard, gravel crunching beneath their feet, to the front door of a large, shabby Georgian house. It had been a handsome house once, but now the paintwork was flaking from the window frames and sills, and a thick layer of dust dulled the gloss paint of the front door. Ivy crept up the walls, and dead leaves and sweet wrappers had piled up in the corners of the porch. There were no other buildings in sight, except for a few abandoned farm buildings just visible on the horizon. They were alone.

Sampson pressed a button and spoke into the intercom, too quietly for Kate to hear. Paul caught her eye and they looked at one another, the tension taut between them.

The door was opened by a uniformed young man with a shaved head, who nodded at Sampson before retreating into the shadows. They found themselves in the entry hall to a traditional English upper-class home: dark wood and dusty chandeliers, paintings of men with gundogs lining the walls. The place smelt musty, like a museum that rarely opened its doors.

'Follow me,' Sampson instructed, and they followed him down the hall, the bald security guard taking

303

up the rear.

Sampson stopped in front of a metal door, incongruous in its traditional surroundings. The guard stepped in front of him and took out a mobile phone, murmuring a few words into it. Almost immediately, the door opened and Sampson nodded for them to follow.

The first things Kate noticed were the drop in temperature and the bright lights. They were standing in a small, bare room with metal surfaces and the hum of an air conditioner. It was like a shift in a dream, when you suddenly find yourself in a new landscape with no connection to where you were before. Sampson shut the door behind them, leaving the guard on the outside, and another door opened at the other end of the room. An Asian man entered, wearing a white lab coat.

He began to ask them questions—Had they been abroad recently?, Had they suffered from any viruses?—but Sampson told him to shut up.

'These are Gaunt's special guests,' he said.

The Asian man raised an eyebrow. 'I see.'

'Where is he?'

'He's in his office. I think he's waiting for you.'

The man stared disconcertingly at Kate, as if she were a fascinating specimen he'd heard a lot about.

'Follow me.'

He opened the door to reveal a stairway leading downwards, into what must be the cellar of the house. It was almost too surreal to be frightening, thought Kate—almost, but not quite. Yet at the same time, she felt an involuntary twinge of excitement: she was surely so close to the truth now. She caught Paul's hand and gave it a squeeze. She could tell he was trying to be courageous, but that, underneath, he was as nervous as she was.

At the bottom of the stairs, they found themselves in a long, brightly-lit corridor, as spotlessly clean as the upstairs part of the house had been grimy. They followed Sampson. There were several rooms to the left and right, with windows revealing empty bunks that had been stripped of bedding. There was something intensely creepy about the empty rooms. They reminded Kate of the rooms where mental patients are kept. Except it was as if all the patients had died. Or maybe these were simply the rooms where the inhabitants of this strange place slept when they were working overnight.

Sampson knocked on a door at the end of the corridor.

42

Harley watched Dragan Popovic through the one-way glass that turned the interrogation room into a kind of TV show. Dragan was sitting upright, a smile playing at the edge of his lips, the smile that made Harley want to punch him.

He entered the interrogation room and sat down opposite Popovic, who still wore that damned smirk. This was to be a private conversation. No tapes, no witnesses.

'I want to know about the doctor,' Harley said. 'The women you held prisoner called him Doctor Mengele.'

'Can I have a cigarette now?' Popovic asked. His English was perfect, his accent light.

'This is a non-smoking building,' Harley responded.

'But, Mr Harley, I find it difficult to think without nicotine.'

Harley leaned forward across the desk, looking directly into the Serbian's eyes. 'You do understand what's going to happen to you, don't you? You are going to be extradited to the Hague to face charges for war crimes. It would definitely be a good idea for you to start thinking. Without nicotine.'

Popovic leaned back and tilted his head to one side. 'If I give this information to you, you can help me?'

Harley didn't blink. 'I will do everything I can.'

'Why do you want to know about the doctor?'

'Don't treat me like a prick, Dragan. We know at least one of the women you brought into the UK was taken away by this doctor character. There's a little girl wondering what's happened to her mother. I want to know who he is, and what happened to Slavna.'

Popovic laughed. 'Emotions, Mr Harley. Surely these are not helpful in your line of work?'

Like a cobra striking, Harley shot out his arm and grabbed Popovic by the collar, pulling him across the desk until their faces were inches apart. 'Stop fucking with me, Dragan. Tell me about the doctor.'

He let the Serb go and waited. Eventually, Popovic nodded. 'OK, OK. But I don't want to go to the Hague. We can strike a deal, yes? I serve my time in England, in an English prison. Slavna was not the only woman the doctor took from us. Over the last two years there were five women. I can tell you what I know—but only if we can make a deal. Yes?'

Harley hesitated. 'Yes, we can make a deal.'

'That's . . . marvellous.' He smiled. 'So—the

306

doctor. I don't know his name. We just called him doctor.'

'Why did you call him that?'

Popovic looked at Harley as if he was stupid. 'Because he is a doctor. He asked questions like a doctor, examined the girls before he accepted them, made sure they were healthy. One time, when one of the men was sick with a cold, the doctor talked to him, told him what it was, what medicine he should take.

'And every few months he would call me, ask for a girl. We would negotiate a price and then we would make the exchange. He paid very good money.'

'What did he want the women for?'

Popovic shrugged. 'I never asked. Maybe to clean his house?'

'You're trying my patience again. I need more information. Did he collect the women?'

'No. I delivered them.'

Harley felt a bubble of excitement rise in his stomach. At last, he was getting somewhere. 'And I do hope you're not about to tell me you can't remember where it was.'

'No, Mr Harley, I remember. I can give you the address. And then you will help me? I can spend my days in an English prison?'

'That's right,' Harley lied.

*   *   *

Two hours later, Harley stood in the office of his superior, Sir Terence Brann, conveying the information Popovic had handed over. He didn't tell Sir Terence that Popovic believed he was no longer going to be extradited.

307

'We checked the address Popovic gave us, and this name came up. We have a classified file on him.'

He handed a piece of paper to Sir Terence.

The older man's white eyebrows arched.

'You know of him?' Harley asked.

Sir Terence stroked his chin. 'Yes . . . Although I haven't heard or seen that name for a long time. Since the nineties. What *is* he up to?'

Harley explained what he wanted to do. That he needed a team, would require back-up. His superior listened carefully and, at the end, nodded.

'That's all fine,' he said. 'I confess, I was about to pull you off this operation, hand it over to SOCA, let them deal with it. Human trafficking is not our business. But if Gaunt is involved, I want you to carry on, just until we can find out what he's been up to.'

He studied the piece of paper again and smiled to himself. 'So . . . Gaunt. I think it's time you were brought in from the cold.' He chuckled. 'If you'll excuse the pun.'

43

The door was opened by a thin man with a grin that revealed yellow teeth. When he spoke, a blast of halitosis almost made Kate retch. Or perhaps it wasn't just the smell—it was the memory. Kate knew him. He was the man she had seen in the woods; and the doctor who had given her the injection after the fire. Other memories swam back. He had been there in the hospital when she was recovering. Dr Gaunt. Dr Death.

He licked his dry lips with the tip of his tongue.

'Ms Carling,' he said. 'How delightful to see you again. Or should I call you Dr Maddox?

He turned to Paul. 'You look so much like your brother. Well . . . how your brother *used* to look.'

He laughed and Paul lunged at him, but Sampson was too quick, grabbing Paul and pushing him into the office.

'Maybe I should kill Wilson now,' Sampson stated coldly.

Dr Gaunt thought about it. 'Perhaps . . . oh, not just yet. There'll be plenty of time for that later. Did everything go smoothly with the child?'

'Yes. His father has him.'

'Wonderful.' Gaunt rubbed his papery palms together. He took a seat behind his desk and picked up a locket which he played with as he spoke. 'It really is charming to see you again, Kate. Last time I saw you, you were excited about your new life in America. And it seems you did very well out there. I checked up on your progress every now and then, asked my contact out there to keep an eye out for you. You owe me one, for helping set all that up for you.' He sighed. 'And then you had to spoil everything by deciding to come back to England.'

Kate felt sick. Had her whole life been engineered by these people? 'I don't owe you a thing.'

'Oh, you do. Actually, you owe Leonard Bainbridge most of all. He had this horrible sentimental streak. Though, to be fair, there was some pragmatism in his decision to help get you into Harvard to continue your studies. He thought—and I agreed—that you might be useful to us one day. I suppose you could say that day has now come . . .'

'What are you talking about?'

309

He smiled what he clearly thought was an enigmatic smile.

Paul spoke up: 'You wiped her memory.'

Gaunt looked mildly surprised. 'You know about that.'

'Yes,' said Kate. 'You used something called the Pimenov Technique on me.'

'Been doing some investigating, have we? You're right. Except we never finished the job properly.'

All the way through this conversation, Kate was aware of Sampson watching her intently, staring at her in a way that made goose pimples rise on her flesh. She half-turned to look at him and was shocked to see an expression she recognised: lust. He was thinking about having sex with her. The thought made every part of her cry out in horror. Is that why they had brought her here, so Sampson could rape her and kill her? For the first time since entering Gaunt's office, she was terrified.

But she managed to speak. 'Is that what you're going to do now—finish the job? Wipe my memory properly?'

Gaunt smiled. 'There's no need.' He leaned back in his chair. 'Things have been set in motion tonight; things that are impossible to stop.'

'What are you talking about?'

'I wonder . . . when you had your little boy—Jack, isn't it?—I wonder if you imagined a great future for him. A scientist like you, perhaps. I expect his father imagined him as a famous baseball player. Successful, anyway. A star.'

He laced his long bony fingers together, like a man who has just enjoyed a satisfying meal.

'Jack is going to be famous, that's for certain. The little boy who changed the world.'

And Kate realised, with a jolt of horror that brought tears to her eyes and bile flooding into her mouth, what Gaunt was talking about.

'You've given Jack a virus.' She had to grab the back of a chair to stop herself from fainting.

Gaunt waved a hand dismissively. 'Not just any virus. This is the *crème de la crème* of viruses. The Pandora Virus. The culmination of many years of work. I've been working towards this for more than twenty years.' A vein twitched in his forehead and his eyes glistened with excitement.

He touched a key on his computer keyboard and the PC sprang to life. On the screen was a computer representation of the virus, rotating slowly in 3D. Kate couldn't help but be interested. She leaned forward for a better look. Like Gaunt, Kate found viruses awe-inspiring and fascinating; unlike him, though, she didn't see them as beautiful. They were the enemy, and she had spent her entire life not only studying but fighting them; viruses like the one which had killed her parents. Sometimes, as she pored over test-tubes, she felt it was a very personal crusade.

'Perfect, isn't it?' said Dr Gaunt.

'It's an influenza virus.' Kate knew this instantly.

'How can you tell?' asked Paul.

'See that?' Kate pointed dully at the virus coating; its furry spikes of haemaglutinin. 'Those are the proteins—they're called H. And those things, on the edge of the virus, they're the enzymes neuraminidase—N. Each type of flu virus has its own combination of H and N. Hence Swine Flu being H1N1, and Avian Flu was H5N1, and so on.' *Jack, oh Jack*, she thought.

'Yes, essentially this is a flu virus,' said Dr Gaunt.

'But it's been engineered to be unlike any other flu virus. It's brand new, so that nobody in the world has any resistance to it. And it's incredibly strong. It rushes through the body like a tidal wave, causing intense headaches, coughing fits, hallucinations, all the usual nasty flu symptoms, multiplied by ten, plus bleeding from the eyes, ears and skin. The way it kills is that it floods the lungs and causes cyanosis, your blood starved of oxygen which makes you turn blue. Basically, you drown in your own fluids.'

He spoke as if he were describing an interesting natural phenomenon like the mating habits of some exotic species. 'The Spanish Flu—another H1N1 virus, as we now know—that swept through the world after the First World War killed one in twenty of the people who caught it. That was impressive enough. Pandora will kill eighteen out of twenty. Conservatively speaking.'

'And you have just infected my son, my Jack . . .' Kate's throat felt so tight that she could barely get the words out. She thought she was going to vomit as the enormity of it all continued to sweep over her.

Gaunt gazed dispassionately at Kate, as if she hadn't even spoken: 'One of the most remarkable things about this virus, a little characteristic that we borrowed from some Asian friends of ours, is that it has a safe period of fifteen hours before it becomes contagious. That allows us to move carriers where we want them without endangering ourselves. We know that your ex-husband is planning to take Jack out of the country because he headed straight towards the airport after he took the boy from your sister's place. Fortunately, that time Sampson was able to intercept them. This time, we don't want to

312

stop him.'

'When did you give it to Jack?' Kate's voice trembled.

Gaunt checked his watch. 'Eleven hours ago.'

'Is . . . is there an antidote?'

Gaunt smiled. 'Oh yes. We developed that in tandem. Although to be certain it will work, you have to be given the anti-virus during the safe period. But there's no point in holding out any hope for Jack. It's too late for him, and for your ex-husband. They're both going to die. Jack is only one child. He's not important in the great scheme of . . .'

Kate snatched up the gold chain that Gaunt had been playing with and leapt onto the desk, skidding across it on her knees and crashing into Gaunt. They fell to the floor and as he tried to right himself, she wrapped the chain around his neck, noticing it held a locket which she tightened her fist around to get better purchase, and pulled it tight, praying the metal wouldn't snap.

'Tell me where the antidote is.'

Gaunt gasped. 'Sampson . . .!'

Paul tried to block Sampson, but Sampson aimed a low punch at his solar plexus, making Paul bend double, then brushed him aside. He grabbed the desk and shoved it back, throwing it halfway across the room as if it were made of plywood, not oak. Kate pulled more tightly on the chain, wanting to choke the life out of this monster, this sick little man who went against everything she believed in, who had described Jack, her precious Jack, as *only one child*. If Gaunt was telling the truth, and if she couldn't get the antidote and get out of here within the next three and a half hours, Gaunt had murdered her son. She pulled even tighter, making him croak.

She felt strong hands on her wrists. Sampson squeezed, and the pain made her loosen her grip on the chain. Gaunt slumped forward, rubbing his throat and wheezing. Sampson wrapped his right arm around her, pinning her arms at her sides.

Gaunt climbed to his feet. 'Put them in a cell. Separate cells.' He pointed a shaking hand at Kate. 'You'll be seeing your son very soon, Kate. I'll let you hold his body.'

44

Kate sat on the bare bunk in one of the empty rooms she had seen on her way in, and tried to control her thoughts, to stop them rushing in every direction. Her wrists still throbbed from where Sampson had squeezed them, but that was the least of her concerns. She checked her watch every ten seconds; every moment stabbing her. *Jack, oh my baby.* She had to get out of here; had to get the antidote. Suddenly, she remembered her phone, and making sure no one was looking through the window, pulled it out of her pocket. How lax of them not to take it. But she soon realised why they hadn't bothered: there was no signal in these cellar depths. 'No network coverage.'

She wanted to lie down on the bunk, to sleep and wake to find it was all a nightmare. But at the same time she was abuzz with energy—she banged on the door with the flats of her hands and cried out. Her voice echoed around the tiny room.

There were still so many questions that she didn't know the answers to. *Why* was Gaunt doing this?

What did he hope to gain from unleashing a fatal virus? He didn't seem to be doing it for political or ideological reasons—he didn't come across as a religious fanatic. Was he doing it for money, and if so, how did he plan to cash in? Did he have some grudge against the world, nursed since he was a child? Or was he merely mad? Could it really be that simple?

Other questions swirled: Why had Sampson brought her and Paul here rather than kill them in the car park? And she still didn't know what had happened sixteen years before at the CRU. What exactly had she discovered before they wiped her memory, and how was it connected to the deaths of Stephen and Sarah? What had Stephen been trying to say in that letter?

So many questions—but she would gladly go without answering any of them if she could save Jack.

That was the only thing that mattered now. She would do anything.

Before she had a chance to contemplate what 'anything' might be, the door opened and Gaunt came into the room, followed closely by Sampson.

She stood up, but Gaunt gestured for her to sit back down on the bunk and, hesitantly, she acquiesced. He sat down beside her, just a few inches separating them, his proximity making her itch.

'So,' he said. 'Are you ready to apologise?'

She couldn't believe her ears. 'You want *me* to say I'm sorry? You're . . .'

'What? Are you going to accuse me of being mad again?' His voice was soft, like a comforting doctor by the bedside of a cancer patient. 'I'm sane, Kate. I'm a rational man. Like you, my life has been

315

dedicated to science, to the pursuit of truth.'

'You're nothing like me. Nothing at all. You want to kill people; I want to save them.'

She nodded towards Sampson, lurking by the door, staring at her with his blank eyes. 'You don't just want to kill people—you send this robot out to do it. I watched him kill Leonard Bainbridge's wife. Your former colleague's widow! How can you condone that?'

'That was unfortunate. She got in the way.'

She leant forward, even though he repelled her. 'Please, I'm begging you. Don't let my son, my Jack, die. You could save him, show mercy. Surely that would be the rational thing to do.'

He raised a thin eyebrow, scratched it, and contemplated what she had said. 'Mercy, rational? Do you really think so? Surely mercy is an emotional response, far removed from rationality.'

Sensing that he might waste more precious moments pondering this question, Kate repeated, 'Just save him. Please.'

Gaunt looked up at Sampson. 'She's begging, Sampson. So unoriginal. I'm beginning to lose my respect.' He turned back to Kate. 'Things could have been different. We could have worked together. Me, you . . .' He smiled to himself before continuing.

'I've watched you over the years Kate—seen the papers you've published and had an old friend keep an eye on you, let us know if you left the country. Professor Scott. He speaks very highly of you.'

'Oh my god,' Kate said. 'Professor Scott?' Her mentor at Harvard. A man she had trusted.

'Yes. And I've been highly impressed too. You understand viruses, you know how they work, how they think. Yes, yes, I know viruses don't actually think, but you know how they operate. You respect them, don't you?'

He was right. She nodded. But she wanted him to hurry. Time had accelerated, like one of those speeded-up films in which flowers bloom and clouds race across the sky.

'You remind me of Leonard in many ways. A good scientist, but limited in ambition. Held back by morality; irrationality; emotion. You remind me of your father, too.'

'You knew my dad?' As soon as she'd said it, she wished she hadn't spoken. It was just more time, wasted. *Jack!* she screamed inside her head, barely listening to Gaunt's response.

'Briefly, in the seventies. Leonard introduced us. We had a very interesting chat about ethics and science. He felt that science should never be divorced from morality, that scientists have a duty to think about what's right in everything they do. We had a big argument about nuclear arms. Were the scientists who first discovered how to harness the power of nuclear fission wrong to take their discoveries further? He thought so. I argued he was being ridiculous.'

In the corner, Sampson stood impassively, though Kate sensed tension beneath his rock-like blankness.

'My argument is that scientists have a duty to follow their discoveries wherever they can. The pursuit of knowledge, of discovering something new, that's the key. So you get all these fools bleating on about stem cell research and genetics and fertility treatment, artificial intelligence, cloning and so on. Should these things be banned? Are they morally wrong? Where is science leading us? Yawn, yawn. I say, if humans can do it, they should. It's what

317

we're for. To shape the world as we can.'

Kate listened, still willing him to get to the point but not daring to interrupt. *Shut up, shut up, shut up,* she chanted silently.

Gaunt went on: 'Which leads us to my research. When the Cold Research Unit was set up, the aim was simple: to find a cure for the common cold. If they'd ever succeeded, it would have upset a lot of people—think of the companies who make billions peddling cold remedies. But when I went to work there, twenty-five years ago, nearly thirty years after they'd started, they were still no closer to finding the answer. It seemed obvious to me that they were never going to get anywhere. It was such a cosy place, though, with its government funding and volunteers. The scientists who worked there acted like they had colds themselves, half the time; bunged up, stuffy people.'

He licked his lips. 'But it was the perfect place to work on what I was really interested in. During the Second World War, the Nazis and the Japanese did a great deal of exciting work with viruses and bacteria. The Americans did a few deals after the war to get their hands on this knowledge. A number of eminent Nazi and Japanese scientists bought their freedom, and lives, by working with the Americans. The British government too. I should explain that in the fifties and through the sixties I worked for the MoD. I spent time in Germany, Russia, China. I met these great scientists. I documented their findings. And I met a lot of people who thought like me: who appreciated the beauty of a great disease, of fine research that discovered how these viruses and bacteria could be harnessed and used to . . .'

'Kill people.'

'Not just that, but yes, warfare was part of it. A lot of it, though, was the intellectual challenge. When a new strain of flu or a brand new virus appears, it's exciting. Working out exactly what the effects of these viruses are and how they work—well, I don't have to tell you how thrilling it is. I became part of a network of microbiologists around the world whose passion was viruses. Some men collect butterflies, others study the stars. We loved viruses.'

He raised his head. The look in his eyes chilled her. If the eyes were the windows onto the soul, then she was looking at a place in which the warm emotions had died: kindness, compassion, empathy, replaced by cold logic and cruelty. He was worse than Sampson. Gaunt was like a virus himself— doing what he did because he could; infecting others; destroying without thought or pause. Being this close to him made her feel physically sick.

'So yes, the CRU provided the perfect environment. The perfect cover, if you like. While Leonard ran the administrative side,' he spat out the words with distaste, 'I ran the labs. I recruited like-minded people: young men who were tired of the restraints put on them by ethics, rules and regulations. In my lab, the world was their oyster. We wanted to be the best in the world.'

'You talk about science like it's a competition,' Kate said.

'And you think it isn't? How disingenuous of you. Of course, it's a competition. A delicious intellectual game. There were people like us around the world, little cells of scientists taking part in a secret competition to create the best viruses and diseases. We had access to the findings of all those wartime scientists, those brilliant men who could do whatever

319

they wanted. All those prisoners to experiment on without anyone to stop them. Beautiful. We worked in government-funded labs, under the noses of the authorities. In America, South Africa, China and Japan. Russia and West Germany. Some of the world's most impressive viruses were created in these labs. Like HIV. We were enormously jealous of that one.'

He sighed. 'After the CRU shut down, we moved here. Since then, a number of amazing viruses have come from our rivals in Asia. SARS for example.' He sighed. 'For a long time, our cell, the British cell, has been seen by the others as a very poor show. A sickly cousin. We haven't done anything to impress them for years. I must confess that we didn't do anything truly groundbreaking at the CRU— bloody Leonard holding me back. But it's been better since we got out of there. Less need to sneak around. Nobody to answer to. And less chance of being caught by volunteers snooping.'

He looked at Kate when he said this. 'Plus we have one or two geniuses working for us here, and the advances in technology over the last decade have made things immeasurably easier. And now our masterpiece is ready—the one that will blow AIDS and SARS and all those others out of the water. We won't be the poor relations any more. We will have won. We have engineered the most awe-inspiring virus the world has ever seen, and scientists around the globe will bow down before us. Before me. I'll be a hero.'

Kate gawped at him, his words sinking through her fog of terror. 'So is that what all this is about? Winning some *competition?* You're prepared to kill millions of people to make yourself look good in the eyes of your equally-warped peers? I don't believe it.'

Gaunt shook his head as if what she had said made him very sad. 'Oh Kate, I thought you would understand. You're a scientist. You know how thrilling it is to have your words published, to be known and respected by those you look up to. Don't try to tell me you don't.'

'But science should be used for good. This is just insane.'

'Oh, we're going round in circles now. I'm bored. I used to fantasise that perhaps you could have worked well here. I had plans to bring you here, but Leonard insisted on sending you to America where you'd be safe. There was little I could do. He didn't even know this place existed; it was all too complicated so I let you go. We didn't need you in the end.'

A vision of Jack's sweet face filled her head. Where would he and Vernon be now? She wanted Gaunt to shut up, to tell her why he had brought her here, but he kept going.

'You nearly uncovered us, you know, back at the CRU. I had always told Leonard that I didn't want scientists or science students coming to the centre but then he stupidly let you come.'

'Did Leonard know everything that was happening at the centre?'

'Most of it. Of course. But he thought we were doing it for the good of the country. He was a deeply patriotic man. And he had his orders.'

Kate blinked. 'I don't understand.'

'It doesn't matter. As I was saying, you almost discovered what was going on. Stephen, who I hasten to add, wasn't one of my hires—he was brought in by Leonard to look after the volunteers and do the menial common cold testing work, even though his abilities were far beyond that—well, he gave you a tour of the lab, remember? This was after you had overhead me and a visiting German colleague talking in the woods. We found out about that when you were in hospital and we got everything out of you. You were curious, you had suspicions that something was "not quite right". When you looked around the lab you found papers that described a virus we were working on at the time. You tried to persuade Stephen that something was amiss, as it was no ordinary cold virus, but he refused to believe you. He loved the CRU. He trusted Leonard and he couldn't entertain any notion that things were . . . corrupt.'

As Gaunt spoke, Kate had flashes of memory. She remembered touring the lab. An argument with Stephen. Her storming out of his flat. Persuading him to let her go back to the CRU for a second stay.

That fatal error.

The barriers that Gaunt and his cronies had built around her memory when she was in the hospital came crashing down and the sights and sounds and smells—the happiness and pain—rushed over her, filled her, nearly knocked her over and out in a flash of kaleidoscopic light. Stephen's skin pale in the light from his bedroom window; the artificial glow of the laboratory, the smell of summer grass outside the centre; fighting with Sarah who was in love with Stephen and jealous of his and Kate's relationship; the terror of the fire, smoke pouring through the corridors . . .

'Sampson, who I had employed at the centre as security, overheard you and Stephen talking one

322

afternoon. You were trying to persuade Stephen that he needed to let you back into the lab so you could get a better look around. Sampson immediately told me. I decided that we needed to silence you. You were too dangerous.'

'The virus we were working on at the time was a variation on Watoto. It wasn't particularly sophisticated or ready. But it was fatal. When you thought you were being given a cold, you were actually being given this virus. You had to go; you'd been snooping around too much. What we didn't know until afterwards—a stupid clerical error on our part, omitting to check your medical forms—was that you had already had Watoto when you were a child, and had survived it. So your body was resistant to it. Yes, you got ill, but you weren't going to die.

'Stephen didn't know what disease we'd given you. After seeing how ill you were he got scared and decided to do some investigating of his own. He went into the lab at night, the night of the fire, checked your records and discovered what we had done to you. Imagine his horror when he discovered that his girlfriend had not only been right about the place he worked, the place he loved, but that she had been given a fatal virus. He went mad . . . Sampson—do you wish to continue?'

Sampson was like a computer booting up after a long sleep. 'I was doing my rounds, when I saw Wilson in the lab. He had taken the antidote for Watoto from the freezer. He was going to take that to you. But first, he tried to burn down the lab. He had a bunsen burner and was going round setting fire to the paperwork. He spilled some chemicals onto the floor and threw some burning papers onto it. That's when I arrived. We fought. He was weak,

323

but angry and desperate. I overpowered him but it was too late to stop the fire. It was out of control.'

Kate couldn't believe it. Stephen had started the fire.

'And you got out and left him there to die?' she croaked.

'I have something to show you. Sampson, fetch Dr Maddox's boyfriend. We don't want him to miss out on the fun, do we?'

45

'I want Mummy,' Jack wailed, incoherent with grief and confusion, drumming his feet against the dashboard of Paul's car.

'Stop it, Jack,' snapped Vernon, more harshly than he'd intended. Jack desisted, but his sobs were so wretched that Vern pulled over to the side of the deserted lane, struggling to change down the gears because his head was throbbing so badly.

They were a few miles outside of Blackmarsh, but Vernon had not the faintest idea where; nor what to do next. The one positive thing about this situation was that he had Jack—and, equally importantly—he had Jack's passport, safe in Jack's case. He had a car to get him to the airport, and he was free to leave the country if he chose.

Well—almost free. What the hell was he going to do about Kate? She was a pain in the ass, and his life would be a lot easier if she weren't around—Vernon guessed that Sampson wasn't taking her and Wilson for a walk in the park—but she was Jack's mother.

He looked over at his inconsolable son, and ruffled the boy's hair with a heavy hand.

'Come on, buddy,' he said, in what he hoped was a placatory tone. 'I'm sure Mommy will be just fine. She's got Paul looking after her—although I bet that she's the one who'll end up looking after Paul, ha!'

His weak joke did nothing to quell the flood of hysteria. Sighing heavily, Vernon unclipped his seatbelt and leaned over to hug Jack.

'I need your help, bud,' he said, trying a different tack. 'I think that nasty man Sampson took Mommy to the place where he took you. I need you to be a really brave boy and tell me whatever you can remember about that place. Can you do that?'

In his father's arms, Jack began to calm down. 'Are you going to call 911, Daddy?' he asked.

'Well, I would—but my cell phone battery is dead, and I don't have a car adaptor to charge it up. So we need to look out for a red telephone box, if there are any left these days. Or maybe some kind person might loan us their cell phone. Shall we see if we can see anyone who looks friendly?'

Vernon felt his son's nod. 'Good boy. You're my great little helper, aren't you? Now, what was this place like?'

'It was a big house with no other houses next to it,' Jack whispered tremulously. 'It had a downstairs bit what didn't have any windows, like in Scooby Doo.'

Vern frowned, trying to second-guess his son's thought processes. 'You mean like a basement?'

The nod came again. 'Yeah. It was kind of like a hospital down there, and a regular house upstairs. I think the downstairs bit is a secret, like a prison.'

'How come it was like a hospital?'

Jack shrugged, sniffing mightily. 'There was beds in some of the rooms, and I had to go and talk to a lady in one of the rooms, and she was sick in bed. Her door was locked, 'cos I think she was a bad ghost what would've run away if the door wasn't locked. But she was pretty sick. I don't think they needed to lock the door.'

'You had to visit with this sick lady?' Vernon felt cold fingers of dread clutch at his heart.

'Yeah. She was sad. I wish I'd had Billy with me to cheer her up. Maybe she wanted her mommy too.' Jack's voice started to fade and Vernon hugged him closer.

Holy shit, he thought, what the hell was going on in that place? His mind raced through the possibilities: was it the same Cold Research place that Kate had been to? No—that burned down, she said. Anyway he had a feeling that place had been somewhere near Stonehenge.

'Daddy, I'm tired.'

'I bet you are, son. It's way past your bedtime. Why don't you hop in back and take a nap? I'll drive us right to the airport, and then we'll jump on a plane, and guess what? By tomorrow you'll be home. Maybe you can even go and see your pal Tyler, if he's free.'

Even as he said it, Vernon felt guilty. Because they couldn't really go home, could they? If Kate managed to escape from Sampson, she'd have the police onto them in no time. If they made it back to Boston, they'd probably have to stay at Shirley's—not the most kid-friendly of apartments—till he could rent someplace for him and Jack . . . Man, this was horrendously complicated.

Vernon helped the now-quiet Jack into the back

326

seat. The poor kid was all cried out. In shock, probably, he thought, as he covered him tenderly with his jacket.

'Will Mommy be back when I wake up?' Jack asked sleepily.

'I bet she will be, don't you worry, son,' lied Vernon, gunning the engine and roaring away down the dark quiet country lane.

*   *   *

By the time he eventually found his way to the motorway that led to the airport, Vernon had made up his mind. I'm outta here, he thought. I've done my bit. Now all I got to do is get my boy home again.

He would call the police once he was safely on the plane and no-one could stop him from taking Jack out of the UK. Then, a matter of hours later, they would be far away from Kate and the chaos she surrounded herself with. If he was honest with himself, he had always found her straight-laced and kind of boring. And now she was involved with rogue scientists and their henchmen and who knew what else. If only she'd been so interesting when they were together he might never have needed to go to Shirl to get his kicks. Not that there was any going back. He had surprised himself that he'd felt no jealousy when he'd met Paul. He actually liked the guy. Good luck to him. As long as he didn't plan on playing step-Daddy to Jack.

He glanced over his shoulder at his sleeping son on the back seat.

Why had they made Jack visit 'a sick lady'? What the hell were the people who had snatched his son up to?

Jack's just fine, Vernon thought, trying to convince himself. He just needs to be taken out of this screwed up country and away from its wacko populace. If he gets a cold, or whatever the hell this is all about, he'd get Shirley to take Jack down to the Medical Centre in Boston tomorrow afternoon once they were home. One more day wouldn't make any difference, would it?

46

Gaunt led Kate back out into the harshly-lit corridor, gripping her wrist hard, breathing his foul halitosis into her hair and face.

Sampson unlocked the door of the room across the corridor, and dragged out a protesting Paul, bending his arm up behind his back to incapacitate him. 'Move it, Wilson, you've got a meeting to go to.'

Paul glanced at Kate, glad she seemed to be unharmed, apart from the fear etched on her face.

The awkward procession halted outside another heavy door, this one with a glass porthole cut into it. Gaunt poked several of the keys on an alpha-numeric keypad beside the door. A light turned from red to green, and he pushed the door which opened into a large subterranean laboratory, illuminated by long strip lights.

As they shuffled inside, Paul glanced again at Kate's face. Her eyes were glassy with stress. She looked like she wouldn't mind right now if someone put a gun to her head, just so she wouldn't have to worry any more. He knew that the only thing keeping her going, stopping her from curling up into a ball, was the hope that burned inside her, the hope that she would somehow be able to save her son.

'I love you,' he mouthed, but Kate was in no fit state to respond, or even acknowledge the declaration. She felt as if she was inside the sort of bad dream which just goes on and on, silently unfolding and transmuting from one nightmare scenario to another.

A very thin, hunched, bald old man in a white coat was seated at the far end of the room, his back to them, tapping away on a keyboard.

'Who's this?' Kate said in a tired voice. 'Another member of the Gaunt family?'

At the sound of Kate's voice, the old man on the computer turned his head slowly, like a tortoise.

Gaunt laughed. 'Oh no. He's not a member of *my* family.'

Looking thoroughly pleased with himself, Gaunt gestured to the thin bald man, who was now advancing towards them, an expression of fear and confusion on his deathly white face.

Sampson closed the lab door behind them, released Paul, and leaned back against the wall, his arms folded, as if he was waiting for a show to begin.

It was Paul who realised first.

'Holy shit,' he muttered, grabbing on to the edge of a workbench for support. 'Holy—fucking—shit. No . . .'

Something in the tone of his voice snapped Kate back to reality, back to an acceptance of the full, terrible reality of the situation.

She looked at the ghostly man still advancing like a zombie, and half-gasped, half-sobbed: '*Stephen*?'

It was undoubtedly her former lover. He looked like he'd spent the last decade and a half in the grave, and that Gaunt, like some real-life necromancer, had brought him back from the dead, built his very own Frankenstein's monster. But it was definitely him.

Stephen had been alive all these years.

He was motionless, gripping the nearest bench with weak fingers. Kate looked at Paul, who was staring at his brother, a cocktail of emotions on his face: shock, pity, horror. It was impossible to believe they were twins. Stephen appeared twice as old as Paul. He had burn marks down one side of his face and on his hands, long-healed scars from the night of the fire.

Without thinking, she stepped towards Stephen, her arms outstretched, wanting to hold him, to fling her arms around him just as she'd fantasised about doing so many times, in dreams and daydreams, all those times she had found herself caught in a reverie in which Stephen was alive. But in all those dreams, he hadn't looked like this. He'd been the same beautiful young man she'd known that summer sixteen years ago. She tried to hug him and he made a squeaking noise and cowered away.

'Stephen,' she said, in the voice she used when Jack was upset, 'It's me, Kate. Don't you remember?'

He wouldn't look at her. Couldn't look at her. He kept his eyes fixed on the laboratory floor.

Paul stepped forward. 'What about me, Stephen? Do you remember me? It's Paul. Remember, Stevie? Remember me?'

Stephen looked up, his eyes bloodshot and watery. Kate wanted to know what he was thinking: what was going on inside that head? His eyes spoke of terrible confusion, of pain and incomprehension. But there was something else there, when he looked at Paul. A sign of the old Stephen. Maybe in Paul he could see the man he should have been. Maybe it gave him strength.

But when Paul moved towards him and tried to touch him, he backed away like a dog that has spent its whole life being beaten. Tears filled Paul's eyes. 'Oh Stevie,' he said quietly. 'What have they done to you?'

Kate turned to Gaunt, who couldn't stop grinning.

'Such a beautiful reunion,' Gaunt sneered. 'Brothers and lovers brought together again.'

'You bastard,' Kate said.

Gaunt raised his hands. 'Now, now. I thought you'd be pleased. Here I am, making your wishes come true, and you're so ungrateful.' He shook his head in a fake demonstration of disappointment. 'You thought Stephen had died in the fire. And he very nearly did die. When the firefighters brought him out of the building, he was burned and unconscious from inhaling so much smoke. But he was still alive.'

Kate remembered it so clearly: seeing them carry Stephen out of the CRU. She had rushed to reach him but Gaunt had stopped her. That was when he had injected her and knocked her out. And when she woke up they told her Stephen was dead.

'We rushed him to hospital. I mean, you really ought to be grateful because we actually did save his life.'

'Which hospital?' Kate asked. 'The same place as me?'

'That's right.'

'You mean, all the time I was there, Stephen was there too?'

'Just down the hall.'

'But why?' Paul asked. His eyes had been fixed on

331

his brother, but now he stared at Gaunt. 'Why did you pretend he was dead?'

'Isn't it obvious? I knew I'd need help to continue my work, and I saw the ideal opportunity. We had funding at first from an old friend, Charles Margold in Utah, who had also helped fund research at the CRU. That was very useful, but I needed help in the lab here. Stephen was bright, a good scientist. Frankly, his talents were wasted at the CRU. I knew that because of his . . . ethics, he wouldn't willingly join me. So I made everyone believe he had perished in the fire. I sent Sampson out to find a homeless person, who he set on fire, and presented that body as Stephen's.'

'There's somebody else in Stephen's grave? Some other poor soul you murdered?'

'Yes, some unfortunate soul Sampson found wandering the streets at night.'

Kate shook her head. 'My God.'

'And you brought him here?' Paul said. 'Kept him prisoner, like a slave.'

Gaunt shrugged. 'Well, not a slave exactly.' He paused. 'Oh, okay, yes. Like a slave. But he enjoys his work here. Don't you, Stephen?'

Stephen didn't react, just continued staring blankly into space.

Gaunt raised his voice. 'Don't you?' he said harshly.

Stephen flinched and nodded. 'I like it.' His voice was sandpaper rough, weakened by years of little use. But underneath, Kate recognised the soft, gentle voice of her old lover. Her first lover.

'Has he ever been allowed out? Has he—has he seen the sun? Been allowed any sort of life at all?' She hated talking about him as if he wasn't there, but she knew that if she asked Stephen directly he wouldn't be able to answer.

Gaunt didn't smile. 'His life is down here.'

Kate heard someone sniff, and turned to see that Paul was crying, tears rolling down his cheeks as he stared at his twin. 'You bastard,' he said to Gaunt. 'You fucking inhumane bastard.'

For a moment, Kate thought Paul was going to try to attack Gaunt again. Sampson sensed it too, and stepped in front of his boss, a human shield. Not that she would describe Sampson as 'human'. But Paul didn't move towards Gaunt—instead, he grabbed hold of Stephen and although his twin tried to shrink away again, he held on to him, forcing him into an embrace.

'I'm so sorry.' Paul's voice was muffled, his face pressed against Stephen's shoulder. 'I should have been a better brother to you. I should have . . .' He couldn't get the words out. 'But we're going to get you out of here, and things will be different. We'll make you better.'

'Ah, it's so touching,' Gaunt sneered. 'But you really shouldn't feel pity for your brother. He's done great work. If it wasn't for his brilliance—brilliance that lay untapped until I helped him discover it—the Pandora Virus would still be a dream. Stephen Wilson has an important role in history. When the world—'

Kate gritted her teeth and prepared to listen to Gaunt launch into another of his megalomaniacal speeches. But he was drowned out, as a siren suddenly started to scream, the noise piercing through everything, and bouncing off the white walls and low ceilings of the room that had been Stephen's entire world for so many years.

333

47

The wail of the siren threw Kate back in time to the night of the fire. She remembered it all so clearly now—how desperate she had been, even in her fever, to find Stephen. That time, she had been tricked into believing he had perished in the flames. But now he was here, and though he might be a sick shadow of the man she had loved all those years ago, she still wanted to save him.

Except there was no fire this time, and she wished there was. A fire to destroy this place, to cleanse the earth of the viruses that were stored here, to wipe Gaunt and Sampson and all their evil from the planet. To set her free to find Jack.

Gaunt turned to Sampson, and for the first time since she had met him he appeared worried. 'Go and find out what's going on,' he commanded.

Sampson went to push the door open, then stopped. 'I need the card.'

Gaunt had designed the system to make it as difficult as possible to get in and out of the lab because he didn't want anyone else getting in, and he didn't want Stephen getting out. His prisoner wasn't allowed to roam the building at will. Like a caged pet, he could only come out when his master allowed him. So to get into the room you had to know the code on the keypad; and to get out you either had to get someone else to punch in the code, or use the card that Gaunt always carried with him.

Gaunt handed Sampson the keycard. Sampson pushed it into the slot beside the door, turning the LED light from red to green, and left the lab. Kate

334

watched him through the glass, walking calmly towards the stairway that led back up to the house.

That was when they heard the first bangs, like firecrackers above the shriek of the siren. Gunshots.

Paul said, 'Sounds like you've got visitors.'

Outside the room, the Asian scientist they had encountered on their way into the cellar appeared and exchanged a few words with Sampson. He looked terrified.

'What the hell's going on?' Gaunt said. He walked over to the door and pushed it, then swore. Of course, he couldn't get out because Sampson had taken the keycard with him.

Stephen cowered in the corner, behind the lab bench. Kate went to comfort him, to put her arms around him, but he backed away. Feeling unable to grab him in the way Paul had, she let her arms fall limply by her sides.

'Stephen, it's okay. It's not a fire. And we're going to get you out of here.'

Gaunt sneered. 'Don't give him false hope.' But his eyes betrayed him. He was scared.

Sampson came jogging towards the room and let himself back in, using the code that Gaunt had entrusted him with earlier that day, just in case he needed it.

'Utada's just told me the police are here.'

'What?' Gaunt's face lost whatever colour it had previously had.

'It's all over, Gaunt,' said Paul with relish. 'You'd better let us go.'

'Shut up.' He pinched the bridge of his nose. 'It doesn't matter anyway. Pandora is already out there. Your son is doing my work now.'

All the hope that had filled Kate in the previous

335

minutes left her like air whooshing out of a balloon. Gaunt was right: even if the police came down here now and killed Gaunt and all his cronies, Jack still carried a time bomb inside him, and she didn't know where the antidote was.

She felt Stephen staring at her, but when she turned to look at him he cast his eyes downwards, staring into his own private void.

Sampson let himself out of the lab again and ran up the corridor, pulling out his pistol on the way. He disappeared up the stairs and they heard more gunshots. Kate clasped her hands together and prayed beneath her breath for him to be on the receiving end of a fatal bullet.

*   *   *

Sampson took the stairs two at a time, two heartbeats to every step, gripping the handle of his pistol, his finger ready on the trigger. His head was filled with a rushing, pounding roar that dulled the screech of the siren.

This was what it felt like to be alive.

All his life, he'd felt nothing for anyone. Not for his mother or his father. Not for any of the other kids at school (apart from a low-level contempt); not for the people he'd tortured or murdered or maimed. He felt nothing at all for Gaunt, but did what he told him to do because he paid him and because, well, because he enjoyed the power over other, weaker, people. He had been working for Gaunt for so long now. Though he had a feeling it would end tonight.

During this long night, something weird had happened to him. If he stopped to think about it,

336

he might have realised that it had been coming for a while. Since Kate had returned to England. Because it was all about her.

It was Kate who made him feel alive.

In the car earlier, driving her and Wilson to this place, alien thoughts had crept into his head. He had imagined himself pushing Wilson out of the car, leaving him behind, and ignoring Gaunt's instructions, driving on with Kate; just driving, the two of them heading into the darkness. Together. She would sit beside him in the passenger seat. She would put her hand on his thigh. And she would smile at him, the smile making him feel . . . good.

Downstairs in the lab, he had felt it too. He couldn't keep his eyes off her. The scent of her fear intoxicated him. He wanted to lie down with her on the hard floor and feel the heat of her body against his. He wanted to hear her say his name. No—*sigh* his name. Gaunt and the Wilson twins would fade away, evaporating into nothingness, and it would just be him and Kate. For one insane moment he had even imagined himself rescuing her son, because he knew it would make her happy. In the moments after he emerged from this reverie, he felt sick. What was wrong with him?

He reached the top of the stairs and paused, panting. He felt unfit, the effects of many cigarettes burning in his lungs. But even that felt good, sharpened his senses. Beyond the door he could hear shouting, more gunshots. The shotgun he'd taken from the snivelling American was leaning against the doorframe, so he grabbed it as back-up.

He pushed open the door and threw himself through it, immediately going into a crouching

337

position behind a leather sofa. Behind him, cowering in the corner, was Utada. Beside the doorway ahead of him, one of the security guards was pressed against the wall, his gun arm raised. The police were surrounding the building, one of them speaking through a megaphone, appealing for them to come outside.

The security guard looked at Sampson, his eyes wild with panic, seeking instructions. Sampson gestured for him to go out and fight, and as the security guard stepped into the doorway he was felled by a police marksman's bullet.

Sampson scuttled over to the door, snatching a look outside. at the same time picking up the gun from the dead guard, juggling it with the shotgun and his other pistol. Three further guards lay dead in the hallway between this room and the front door, through which Sampson could see the police advancing.

I'm the only armed one left, he thought, and along with the adrenaline rush came another new feeling: fear. He was outnumbered, outgunned. There was no way he could win. He thought about Kate downstairs. If he died now, he would never see her again.

Why did the realisation make him go cold inside?

A black-clad police gunman appeared in the doorway and, instinctively, Sampson raised his pistol and fired. The policeman dropped to the ground and Sampson heard yells from outside. Bullets crashed into the walls around him.

He could stay here, hold the police up. Try to protect Gaunt for longer. He might take out one or two more policemen. It would give more time for the boy to spread the virus.

But he didn't care about that. He never had.

He crawled back across the floor to the stairway, pausing to throw the gun he had taken from the dead guard to the cowering scientist, Utada. This wasn't an act of kindness. He knew that if the police saw the scientist with a gun they would shoot him too.

Sampson also knew what he wanted. He was going to take Kate with him. All the way to Hell.

*   *   *

Downstairs in the lab, Gaunt was pressed against the glass, desperate to know what was going on.

Behind him, Paul said, 'You're not so brave without your bodyguard, are you, Gaunt?'

'Shut up.' He tried to sound in command but his voice cracked.

Paul walked up to him and grabbed him by the throat, pushing him up against the glass. 'I really, really feel like killing you, Gaunt. For what you've done to Stephen. For giving Jack the virus. I should kill you right now.' He squeezed, pressing his hand hard against Gaunt's windpipe. Gaunt made a pathetic, strangled noise.

'Where's the anti-virus?' Kate demanded, standing at Paul's shoulder.

Gaunt tried to shake his head.

'The Pandora anti-virus. Where is it?'

Paul loosened his grip on Gaunt's throat so he could speak. 'I'll never tell you.'

Kate said, 'It has to be here, in one of these freezer units. We'll find it. We might have to search through every one, but . . .' she knew this would be a difficult task, but she didn't want Gaunt to think his life was valuable to them.

'I don't care if you kill me,' Gaunt said. 'I'm not going to tell you.' But Kate saw his eyes widen with horror, and she turned to see what he was looking at.

Stephen had opened one of the freezer units. A cloud of cold steam wafted out as he slid open a drawer. He had pulled on a pair of gloves, and he took out several vials and held them out on his palm towards Kate. A look passed between them, and for a tiny moment, that old connection sprang back into life. Kate felt as if her heart would burst with sorrow and gratitude.

She smiled at him, while Gaunt made a gasping noise behind them.

'It doesn't matter,' he said. 'It's too late.'

'Definitely too late for you,' Paul said, increasing the pressure on Gaunt's throat. 'Tell us how to get out of this lab.'

'There is no way out without the card.'

'There must be. You built this place. You must know.'

'There isn't any way out!'

'It doesn't matter anyway,' Kate said. 'The police will be down here in a . . .'

Her words were cut short by the sight of Sampson appearing at the end of the hallway and running towards the lab.

Sampson, whose hands were full of guns, tucked the shotgun under his arm while keeping hold of the pistol in his right hand. With his left hand he punched in the code on the keypad and pulled open the door, keeping it propped open with his foot. In one swift motion, Paul shoved Gaunt further back into the room, grabbed Kate's hand and charged at

340

Sampson in the doorway, barging past him. The shotgun clattered to the floor.

Paul and Kate stumbled into the hallway, knocking Sampson to one side, and the lab door swung shut, leaving Gaunt and Stephen inside.

Gaunt banged on the glass but nobody took any notice of him. Paul aimed a punch at Sampson, but the larger man blocked it and threw a punch back. Paul ducked, then kicked out, connecting with Sampson's right hand. The pistol went spinning across the floor and beneath a desk.

'You fucker,' Sampson cursed. He looked around and saw the shotgun lying by the door, then crouched down and got hold of it by the barrel-end, rising and swinging it at Paul as he tried to grab him. The gun's handle connected with Paul's face, cracking his nose and sending him crashing to the floor, clutching his face, blood pouring into his palms.

'Run,' he said to Kate through the blood. She had been frozen to the spot as she watched the brief fight, but now she obeyed, sprinting up the corridor towards the doorway, knowing that the police, and safety, were upstairs.

Sampson raised the shotgun and aimed it at the back of Kate's head.

*   *   *

In the lab, Gaunt continued to thump the glass, screaming for Sampson to let him out. He was so busy demanding his release that he didn't notice Stephen opening the doors of the storage freezers behind him. Methodically, Stephen pulled opened drawers and took out vial after vial, collecting them together on the bench.

341

The finest pieces in Gaunt's virus collection lay side by side. Marburg. Spanish Flu. SARS. Avian Flu. Watoto. Pandora.

And another virus, one that Stephen had worked on a couple of years before. It was code-named Piranha and was a kind of super-charged Ebola that was absorbed by the skin, attacking the body at breathtaking speed, melting the insides within minutes, causing haemorrhaging from every internal organ and an agonising death. Gaunt had abandoned research on Piranha because it kept killing lab assistants. It was simply too dangerous to work with, and would have been impossible to spread effectively into the world.

Stephen picked up the test tube containing Piranha and walked calmly across the lab, tapping Gaunt on the shoulder.

Gaunt turned around and Stephen smashed the vial in his face.

*　　　*　　　*

In the second before she reached the door at the bottom of the stairs, Kate looked over her shoulder. Sampson was pointing a shotgun at her. His face was contorted with pain, and even in that moment she registered the strangeness of seeing emotion on Sampson's face.

She threw herself at the door, fully expecting that at any moment she would feel the hot burn of the bullet. She would never see Jack again, never be able to save him.

But for some reason, Sampson hesitated, his face still etched with pain, allowing her an extra second in which she crashed through the door into the stairway, almost hyperventilating, and ran up the stairs two at a time, stopping short when she heard a gasp above her.

Utada was standing at the top of the stairs, a gun loosely held in his hand. He was shaking, looking at the door, then at her. She stopped. From the other side of the door she could hear the police ordering Utada to let them through.

The scientist was drenched with sweat and looked like he would collapse at any second.

'Give me the gun,' Kate said firmly, holding out her hand as she reached Utada. He hesitated, not knowing what to do. The police were banging on the door. Utada slumped, releasing the gun, and Kate scooped it up, just as Sampson appeared below her.

He raised his gun. Kate raised hers. Her hands shook; she had never used a gun before. Sampson slowly ascended the stairs. He stopped a few steps below her. Kate was still trembling, trying to aim, tears of terror filling her eyes. The gun was wavering all over the place. She couldn't do it. This was it. It was all over.

Then Kate realised the gun he was holding was the shotgun from which she'd removed all the bullets. And behind Sampson, creeping silently along the corridor, was a police marksman. Sampson hadn't seen him—all his attention was focused on Kate. She still had a chance.

'Please don't shoot me,' she whispered. 'Please.'

*   *   *

Sampson sneered. Behind him, the policeman crept closer, assessing the situation.

343

'I've wanted to do this for a long time,' Sampson said. Was she imagining it, or was his voice cracking with emotion? 'Ever since I met you.'

'I hate you,' Kate said, watching the marksman raise his gun and point it at Sampson's back. 'You're pathetic. Gaunt's little puppy. You're not a real man.'

'You bitch,' said Sampson, and she saw his finger tighten on the trigger.

Click.

'What the fuck?'

Kate nodded to the policeman, which made the bewildered Sampson turn his head, and she threw herself onto her belly, her own gun clattering down the stairs behind her. The last thing she saw before she blacked out was Sampson futilely taking aim at the police gunmen, followed by a burst of gunfire that blew Sampson down the stairs and splattered his life blood up the walls behind him.

48

Jason Harley realised that he was going to have to physically prise Paul away from the locked door of the laboratory, where he had been repeatedly beating his fists against its thick steel surface.

'Stephen! Stevie!' Paul cried, over and over again, tears flooding down his face. He was clearly either totally unconcerned for his own safety, or oblivious to the frenzied gun battles which had just taken place on the stairs not twenty feet away.

'Stevie, mate, come on, open up! We can fix it, we'll get you out of here, it's not too late!'

Harley had heard Paul's shouts from the top of the stairs; heard the raw emotion in his cracked voice; knew that Paul realised the impossibility of what he was saying.

He risked a glimpse through the porthole window of the lab door, and looked hastily away again, sickened to his stomach at the carnage inside: the two still-writhing bodies on the floor, thick black blood spread in a sea around them, obscuring what was left of their features.

Harley hadn't expected Operation Castle to end like this. Not in a locked laboratory with two bodies inside it, including the body of one of the men they'd come to arrest. What the hell had happened here?

'We've got to help him!' Paul sobbed. 'He's my twin . . . he's been locked in here for fifteen years . . . I had one chance to get him, and I fucked it up! Now I've lost him all over again . . .'

One of the armed police officers approached Harley and spoke softly to him. Then his colleague from SOCA, Simon Donahoe, came jogging down the stairs, panic evident on his face.

'Have you got any idea what's been going on here?' Harley asked.

Donahoe nodded. 'I've just been talking to Kate Maddox. You're not going to like this. We need to get out of here. And keep that lab sealed.'

'Why, what's the story? We come here thinking we're going to find a bunch of prostitutes and instead it's like the frigging *Andromeda Strain*.'

Donahoe looked blankly at Harley then moved over to Paul, taking him by the arm. 'Sir. We need to get you out of here now.' He turned back to Harley. 'I'll explain everything when we get upstairs.' Paul leaned his forehead on the cool steel door,

345

exhausted. He suddenly straightened up. 'Kate—where's Kate?'

Donahoe put a hand on Paul's shoulder. 'She's fine, sir. She's upstairs in the car. We need you to come with us back to London so we can . . .'

Paul interrupted. 'No! I'm coming with Kate.'

Harley sighed. 'I'm sorry, pal, but I don't think you're in any fit state—'

Paul grabbed him, wild-eyed and tear-stained. 'I'm *fine*. She needs me—I'll be strong for her, I promise. I've let Stephen down, I'm not going to do the same to Kate. Come on, let's go—time's running out. We've got to get to Jack.'

Harley shook his head, suddenly feeling very tired, and wondering what kind of situation they were dealing with here. And whether heads—namely his—were going to roll.

But his sympathies were directed towards Paul when he saw the expression of grief on his face. That was his brother in there? Poor sod, he thought, as they made their way gingerly up the stairs, stepping over the bullet-ridden bodies of Sampson, Utada, two policemen, and the security guards.

*   *   *

Kate was sitting with a female MI6 officer called Susan French in the back of a squad car, rocking back and forth, pulling at her own hair. When she saw Paul and the two other officers emerge from the house, she flung herself out of the car and into Paul's arms.

'Paul, oh God, Paul, are you OK? Thank God you're safe! Did you get Stephen? It was all such chaos, I . . .' She tailed off, at the sight of Paul's

346

face.

For a moment Harley thought that Paul was about to break down again, and he sighed, with mingled pity and irritation. His patience had just snapped. He wanted to know what was going on. Now.

'Talk to me,' he said to Donahoe.

But Kate interrupted. 'We have to get to Jack.' Her voice was high-pitched with hysteria.

'Who's Jack? And why is he so important?'

'Jack's her son,' said Donahoe. 'Six years old. We need to get to him because he's got a virus. Safe period of fifteen hours—but he's had it for twelve . . . We've got approximately three hours to find him, otherwise all hell's gonna break loose.'

He told Harley what Kate had already told him, in a barely-coherent babble, when they'd pulled her out of the building. Donahoe and French had also since quizzed Kate and she'd managed to explain about how Sampson had snatched Jack, and then handed him back in Blackmarsh, complete with deadly cargo.

Harley swore.

'Apparently it makes Swine Flu and SARS look like a mild dose of hay fever.'

'Wait a minute,' said Paul. 'Isn't that why you're here? Because of the Pandora Virus?'

'No, we're here because . . .' Harley hesitated, unsure of how much to tell them. 'Did you see any young women down there?'

'Young women? What are you talking about?'

Donahoe spoke up. 'We came here looking for victims of human trafficking. Young women. This guy Gaunt had them brought here for . . . god knows.'

'Experiments. That must be what they used the

347

rooms for, the ones with the bunks,' Paul said, almost to himself.

Kate half-screamed. 'What about Jack?'

'Okay, miss,' said Harley in his practised soothing voice. 'Calm down.'

'No, I won't calm down! My son has a virus that will not only kill him if we don't get to him but start a chain reaction that could wipe out half the world. Especially if my idiot husband takes him on a plane to Boston.' She had a sudden clear image of Jack at the departure gate, contagious after the safe period had run out, inadvertently passing the virus to passers-by of every nationality. And all those people would get on their separate planes and head off around the world, taking Pandora home.

'Relax, Miss Maddox,' Donahoe began.

'Doctor Maddox,' she said automatically.

'Sorry. Doctor Maddox. As soon as you told me about this before we put out an APW on Mr Maddox and your son. We're watching all the approaches to the airports. We know where they're going. We'll apprehend them.'

'What's the latest?' Donahoe asked Susan French, who had just been talking into a mobile.

'Nothing. No Vernon or Jack Maddox booked on any flight out of any airport, nor have they turned up at any port, or Eurostar. No sign of anyone meeting their description. They've vanished.'

Harley groaned. 'Fuck. And we've got—how long, exactly?'

French looked at her watch. 'The little boy's safe period will expire in . . . two hours and forty-five minutes.'

Kate wailed out loud; half-wail, half-scream. '*Do something! We have to find him!*'

'Right,' Harley said, taking charge. His mind whirred. 'They're clearly not trying to leave the country. Therefore they can't be more than a couple of hundred miles away, at most. Does Maddox have any friends he might have taken refuge with?'

Kate shook her head. 'He doesn't know anyone in England, to my knowledge, apart from my sister, and I doubt he'd have gone back there.'

'No, he hasn't—we've already checked that. Your sister is still giving her statement at Oxford police station. Can you think of anywhere at all he might have taken Jack to? A particular hotel? A B&B you once stayed at?'

Clutching at straws here, Harley, he thought to himself.

Kate ran a trembling hand through her hair. 'No . . . well, if he's in a hotel, it wouldn't be an expensive one. Vernon's so tight. They're probably sleeping in the car somewhere. I hope they're sleeping . . . I'd say he's most likely to have taken Jack back to London. He doesn't even know that Jack's in danger, does he; so his main objective would be to get him home. If he hasn't tried to get a flight tonight, I bet he will in the morning. Most likely from Heathrow— that's the airport he's familiar with, and he's a creature of habit.'

Donahoe said, 'Forces out across the country will be looking for the car within the next half an hour. All ports and airports will be closed in case they try to access them. If he's in the car, we'll find him. We're also trying to trace him via his mobile, even though it appears to be switched off.'

'We will find him, Kate, don't panic, we will,' said Harley, with more confidence than he felt. 'The antidote. Do we need to bring along a doctor, to

349

administer it?'

'No,' Kate said, 'I can do it. Jack's phobic about injections. He'd go mad if anyone else tried to.'

Harley winced, thinking of the global consequences of one little boy refusing an injection. But how could they inject him when they didn't know where he was? 'Where's the antidote now?'

'It's here,' said Kate, reaching into her pocket. Her expression changed. She checked her other pocket. Then frantically checked the first one again.

'Kate, what is it?' Paul asked urgently.

'I haven't got it. It's not here.' She had gone white.

'Are you sure?'

'Yes. Oh . . .' She pulled the lining of her pockets inside out. Her mobile clattered to the floor.

The vial that Stephen had given her was missing.

49

Kate and Paul ran back inside the building before any of the officers could stop them.

'I must . . . I must have dropped it when you pulled me out of the lab. Or when Sampson chased me up the stairs.'

They arrived at the door that led down into the cellar but an armed police guard blocked their way.

'We need to go downstairs,' Kate said. 'Let us through.'

The officer shook his head.

Harley and Donahoe were close behind them. 'Let them through,' Harley ordered.

The guard stepped aside and the four of them descended the stairs, treading carefully and scanning the steps in case the fragile glass vial was there. What if it was smashed? Would there be more in the lab? Kate felt a wave of sickness flood through her. How could she have been so careless? What if they found Jack but couldn't find the antidote? It would be as if she had murdered Jack herself, through her own incompetence.

Sampson's body, along with Utada's, had been removed from the stairs. When Kate saw the empty blood-soaked space where his body had lain, her first thought was that he'd risen like some horror movie anti-hero and that he'd be waiting for her downstairs. She hoped he had suffered when the bullets ripped into him.

She would never forget the look on his face when he had pointed the gun at her and squeezed the trigger. The naked hatred, mixed with something else. Lust. Naked desire. That look would haunt her.

The vial was nowhere to be seen on the stairwell, or in the corridor downstairs.

Kate approached the lab but Harley caught her arm. 'I don't think you should look inside there, Miss . . . Doctor Maddox.'

She shook him off. 'I need to find that vial. I'm the one who lost it—I need to find it.'

Another armed guard stood in front of the lab. Kate thought he looked a bit green. When she looked through the window she realised why, and she almost wished she'd heeded Harley's advice.

Gaunt and Stephen looked as if they'd melted from the inside; blood pooled around them. If she didn't already know it was them, she wouldn't have recognised them. Bile rose in Kate's throat and she put her hand over her mouth, using all her willpower to stop herself from throwing up. She had to stay focused. She had to find that anti-virus.

Paul, who looked as sick as she felt, pressed his face against the window.

'I can see it,' he said.

Kate joined him and peered through the porthole. 'Where?'

But she didn't need him to show her. She saw it straight away, lying on the floor a few feet away from Stephen's body.

'It must have fallen loose when you pulled me out of the lab,' Kate said.

Without thinking, Paul tugged at the lab's door handle, but of course the door didn't budge.

Harley grabbed his arm. 'What the hell are you doing? Do you want to end up like the poor bastards in that room? Do you want us all to end up like that?'

Paul turned angrily to the officer. 'One of those "poor bastards" is my brother. But anyway, the door won't open.'

'Oh no . . .' The relief Kate had felt at spotting the anti-viral agent drained away. It was locked in the lab.

'You didn't see the code that Gaunt used to get into the room, did you?' Paul asked, examining the keypad beside the door. Letters and numbers—a full QWERTY keyboard. That was unusual. Most security locks like this used numbers only.

Kate shook her head. 'No.'

Paul started to tap at the keypad, trying a few common passwords: HELLO, PASSWORD, the user's name. But they only used letters; the password was bound to use a combination of letters and numbers.

Harley grabbed him again. 'Mr Wilson, will you

please stop trying to open the door. We need to seal this area. We can't allow whatever killed your brother to get out of that lab.'

'But if we don't get that antidote out of there, Jack is going to spread the Pandora virus around the world.'

The two men turned to look into the lab at the same time, rendered silent by the problem.

Without warning, Kate ran off up the corridor.

Harley called out to her, but she didn't reply. She threw open the door to Gaunt's office and went inside, looking around, the gold locket on the desk catching her eye momentarily. She pulled open cupboard doors and drawers. But the thing she was looking for wasn't there.

She exited the room and went back to Paul and Harley.

'I was sure he'd have one, but apparently not . . . We need a biosafety suit. Full body, gloves, mask, everything. There must be one in here somewhere.'

Harley looked at French and Donahoe, who had joined them in the corridor. French nodded. 'We'll find one.' She walked briskly away, pulling out her mobile as she went up the stairs.

'So . . . if we get a biohazard suit, we still need to get into the room.' Harley inspected the door and keypad. 'We need to get one of our computer guys down here.'

'How long would that take?' Kate asked.

'I don't know. An hour for them to get here, then I don't know how long to get through this door . . .'

Kate pulled at the roots of her hair. 'We're going to run out of time. Oh, *Jack*!'

'I can do it,' Paul said.

Harley looked at him sceptically. 'You should leave

this to the experts.'

'I *am* an expert,' Paul asserted. 'This is what I do. We have two options. We either find a way to disable the system, or we find Gaunt's password.' He inspected the keypad again. It was fused into the wall, with no wires in sight. He walked the length of the corridor, then went upstairs, leaving Kate and Harley wondering what his plan was.

When he returned, he said, 'There's no sign of a control panel anywhere up there.'

He went into Gaunt's office and looked around, echoing Kate's movements of a few minutes ago. 'Or here, so it must all be controlled by Gaunt's computer.'

The hard drive of the computer, which was a Mac, several years old, was under the desk. Paul stooped to turn it on, then waited for it to boot up, pressing a button on the monitor at the same time. Kate paced around impatiently, while Harley picked up the gold locket, and turned it over in his hand.

'The computer's password protected,' Paul said, as a screen appeared asking him to log on.

'Of course,' said Kate, who couldn't keep still.

'But that's no problem. I can easily reset it. I just need the installation disks.'

'Just!'

Paul and Kate opened all the desk drawers and rifled through. Kate looked at Paul, impressed by the way he had taken calm control, trying to absorb some of his calmness. She was just about managing to suppress her panic.

'Found it!' Paul exclaimed triumphantly, holding a small pack of CD-ROMs aloft. 'It was at the bottom of this drawer. Most people keep the installation disks near their computer. You set up

354

the computer then chuck the disks in a nearby drawer.'

He bent down, switched off the Mac then inserted a CD in the drive. Moments later he turned on the computer again, holding down the C key on the keyboard as he did so.

'They make it easy because so many people forget their password and can't use their own computer any more,' Paul said.

A box appeared on the screen prompting him to change the user admin password. Kate watched him type in the word 'brother' to set a new password— 'it's the first thing that came into my head,' he said— and a minute later they were in.

Using the mouse, Paul navigated his way around the system, looking, he said, for the program that controlled the security lock on the door. It didn't take long. He double-clicked to open the program, then scoured the help menu, looking for a way to over-ride the system or disable it.

Kate watched in agony as Paul tapped away, opening the terminal and filling the black window on the screen with what looked to Kate like gibberish.

'That might work,' he said, leaning back. 'Go and try it. Don't try to open the door, just tell me if the light on the lock has turned green.'

Kate ran out of the room, returning swiftly with a look of frustration on her face. 'It's still red.'

'Shit.' He tapped his fingers on the desk. 'I'm impressed. This is a really secure system.'

'Never mind his impressive bloody system. What are we going to do?' Kate said, the pitch of her voice rising.

'We're going to have to find the password. It's stored on here, but it's hidden—look.'

He tapped away on the keyboard again and brought up a box that said 'Password'. But the password was just four black dots.

'So it's just four letters or numbers. What do we know about Gaunt? What kind of word would he choose? Or maybe it's a date.'

Kate and Paul stared at each other, then rushed back to the lab door.

'Try the year the CRU closed,' Kate suggested. But it didn't work.

Kate's hand hovered helplessly over the keypad. 'It could be anything.'

'And if you try too many times it might lock up completely.'

Kate couldn't hold back any longer. She started to cry. 'My little boy is going to die. Why did I have to bring him to England? It's all my fault.'

Harley appeared behind them. 'Listen, we'll get into that room even if we have to blow the doors off. We'll get industrial cutting equipment down here. Don't worry.'

'But we're running out of time!' Kate sobbed.

'I've had an idea,' Paul said, jogging back to the office and throwing himself down in the desk chair. He typed in more apparent gibberish and then said, 'Yes.'

'What?' asked Kate, appearing behind him.

'Remember I told you that people often forget their password? Well, it's like when you register for online banking or something—they give you a password hint. It's buried pretty deep but there's a file on here containing a hint.'

'What is it?'

Paul tapped in a few more commands and a picture appeared on the screen.

A picture of a virus.

'Weird hint,' Harley said, peering over their shoulders.

'No, said Kate. 'It makes perfect sense. Most people wouldn't know what they were looking at—or if they did know it was a virus, they wouldn't be able to read it. It's the kind of thing that would amuse Gaunt, too.'

'But you can read it?' said Paul.

'Of course,' replied Kate. She pointed at the screen, 'Three proteins. H3. And two enzymes. N2. H3N2. It's the name of a really nasty virus. And it's the password. H3N2.'

At that moment, French appeared, carrying what looked like an astronaut's suit. The biosafety suit. 'Here it is,' she said. 'I found it in one of the other labs.'

'Let me go in,' said Kate, taking the suit from her. 'I'm used to wearing these things.'

'Be careful,' said Paul.

'Don't worry, it's fine.' She kissed him. 'We make a good team, Paul. Now all we have to do is find Jack.'

'Any news on Dr Maddox's son and husband?' Harley asked.

French frowned. 'No. But everyone right up to the PM has been informed of the danger. The army have been mobilised. Everybody is out looking for them. *Everybody.*'

50

In a small, stuffy room in a two-star hotel on the perimeter road of Heathrow Airport, Vernon Maddox surveyed with displeasure the mustard-coloured walls and grimy cream bedspread. Red lights, flashing around the edges of the blinds at the window, caught his attention, and he walked over and peered out.

'What in hell's going on out there?' he wondered aloud.

Despite the fact that it was four in the morning, the road was full of armoured vehicles. Police and army in flak jackets were jumping out of cars and vans, and the crackle of walky-talkies punctuated the still pre-dawn air.

'Jeez,' said Vernon. 'Look, Jack—soldiers!'

Jack didn't respond. He was sitting on the double bed, his thin knees drawn up to his chest and his eyes heavy with bewilderment and lack of sleep.

'Soldiers, Jack!' insisted Vern, with more enthusiasm than he felt.

'Don't care about soldiers. I want Mummy,' came the response.

Vernon exhaled gustily. 'We've been through this, Jack. You can't talk to Mommy right now, it's the middle of the night.'

'She told me I could call her anytime,' said Jack, too worn out even to sound petulant.

'Come on, son, let's get some sleep. I'll just turn on the TV here, see if it says anything about what-all's going on outside.'

The hotel room television, however, did not run

to cable 24-hour news channels, and all that Vernon found, when he flicked through the stations, was some men playing poker; a chat show discussing exploding breast implants; and a late-night music show featuring footage of a band he didn't recognise on stage at some open-air festival. Vernon picked up the phone by the bedside and dialled zero, watched listlessly by Jack.

'Hello? This is room 242. What's going on there? Some kind of bomb scare or something? . . . Huh . . . Right . . . OK. For how long? Oh. Yeah. Goodnight.'

He looked at his son, who was fiddling with Billy's on-off switch. 'Crap. It's some kind of security alert, they didn't know what. All flights grounded till at least mid-morning. Oh well, nothing we can do about it, is there, pal? Let's get a few hours' sleep, and we can get something figured out in the morning. Get into bed there, Jack. I'm just gonna use the bathroom, then I'm joining you.'

Before disappearing into the bathroom, Vernon turned up the music on the television. Some guy with long hair was singing about how someone had come along on a glorious day. Even in front of his son, Vernon was squeamish about the sounds of bodily functions being overheard through thin walls, and his gut had been playing him up all day.

Jack gazed at the band on TV. Then he stretched out a small hand to the telephone and dialled zero, just as he'd seen his father do. The receiver was still warm and smelled of his dad.

A lady answered.

'Hello,' said Jack. 'I want to speak to my Mummy please.'

The night receptionist, a young, artificially-enhanced Irish woman called Sheila, had been watching with interest the chat show about the exploding breast implants until the kerfuffle outside distracted her. She was new in the job, and when she heard Jack's request, was unsure what the rules were regarding the assistance of small children to make phone calls. She had noticed Jack when they checked in, though, and thought how sweet he was, clutching his robot, and how exhausted he looked.

'It's direct dial, sweetheart,' she said, hoping that Al Qaeda weren't about to launch a suicide attack on the airport. There had been some staying at the hotel last night who looked like Muslims. Foreigners, anyway. Maybe she should tell the police. 'I think you'd better ask your Daddy to do it for you.'

'He's in the bathroom. He takes ages, and I have to talk to her now.'

Sheila heard the tremor in the boy's voice. Jesus, Mary and Joseph, she thought, I hope that man hasn't abducted him. Surely there was no harm in helping the boy speak to his mammy?

'Do you know the number, darling? I can help you ring it, shall I?'

Jack solemnly recited a long telephone number. 'That's the country code as well,' he said, with a hint of pride. 'Mummy made me learn it.'

'Good for your mammy,' said Sheila, baulking slightly when she realised it was an international mobile number. Would she get into trouble for this?

'I want my Mummy,' came a plaintive little voice on the line, and Sheila sighed. She'd just have to risk his father's wrath—not that she'd get it directly,

360

though—she was to go home at six thirty when her shift ended. If she was still alive then. She crossed herself discreetly.

'OK, darling, it's ringing for you now,' Sheila said, putting him through.

She looked nervously out of the hotel's front doors. Perhaps she ought to have taken that job in Tesco's after all. The pay had been much worse, but at least the hours were reasonable, and there wouldn't have been armed soldiers parading up and down outside, in the middle of the night . . .

*   *   *

Kate's mobile rang as she sat close to Paul in the back of the unmarked car, speeding towards London with less than ninety minutes left of Jack's safe period. The anti-virus was safely in the possession of Susan French. The screen flashed up 'private call', as she pulled it out of her jacket pocket, held her breath, and pressed 'answer'.

'Mummy?'

'It's him!' she said to French and Harley. French immediately took out her own mobile and made a quick call.

Kate held back her tears, trying to sound as natural as possible while Jack whined about how he wanted to see her and how Daddy was in the bathroom doing a smelly poo and Billy was bored.

'I'm coming to find you, Jack,' she said.

'What about that scary man?'

She hesitated. Should she tell him Sampson was dead? 'The police got him, sweetheart. He can't get you. Where are you, Jack?'

'I'm in a hotel. There are soldiers outside. Oh,

361

Daddy just flushed the toilet. I'd better go. See you soon, Mummy.'

Jack hung up.

Kate looked expectantly at French, who nodded. 'Traced him,' she said.

* * *

Less than half an hour later, Kate, Paul, and officers Harley, French and Donahoe were in a police helicopter, swinging towards Heathrow Airport, the only object flying in the entire airspace of the British Isles.

* * *

Twenty minutes after that, Sheila the receptionist was chatting to Ernesto, the night security guard, speculating about the nature of the terrorist threat outside their hotel—and, by the looks of it, the whole airport.

She was re-attaching one of her stick-on fingernails when the front doors of the hotel burst open and a team of armed police charged in, followed by a young woman with wild dark hair, flanked by three young men and a woman in an expensive suit.

'Vernon Maddox,' barked one of the men. 'What room's he in? Him and his son. Quick!'

Sheila dropped her false fingernails.

'Two . . . four . . . two,' she stammered, her mouth hanging open as she watched them running full-pelt up the stairs towards the second floor.

Odd, she thought. The woman appeared to be carrying a *syringe*.

Harley knocked on the hotel room door. The moment Vernon opened it, one of the armed policemen grabbed him and pulled him out into the corridor.

'What the hell? Kate? What's going . . .?'

'Shut up Vernon,' Kate said, pushing past him into the room.

As Vernon was escorted out of the building, shouting about his human rights and how the US Ambassador was gonna hear about this, Kate approached her son. Jack was sitting on the bed, looking up at her and all the strangers with wide eyes. Billy was cradled in his lap.

Kate hugged him tight, and kissed his scalp. The Pandora Virus was inside him, not contagious yet, but there were only minutes remaining before it became so. And surely the safe period couldn't be predicted to the exact minute. He might even be contagious already. Kate knew that she, Vernon and everyone else in this room were in danger; they would all have to be treated and quarantined.

'Mummy, I was scared,' Jack said. 'And I'm so tired.'

'There's nothing to be afraid of any more,' she soothed. But as she said this she was aware of the syringe in her hand. And as if Jack could read her thoughts, he turned his head and saw it. He immediately pulled away.

'Mummy, why have I got to have a shot?'

She tried to pull him closer. 'Jack, I'm so sorry, but you need it.'

'No!' he screamed, wriggling and pulling away. She held on to him as he struggled. She had already

363

prepared the syringe just before entering the building.

'Do you need a hand?' asked Paul, who was standing in the doorway.

'No. He won't let anyone else near him when he's in this state.'

Paul hesitated. She could tell he really wanted to help, to do something, but this was down to her.

'Jack, if you let me give you the injection I'll take you to McDonald's.'

'I don't wanna go to McDonald's.'

'I'll buy you another robot to be friends with Billy.'

'I don't want another robot.'

'I'll get you anything you want.'

'Will you and Daddy be married together again?'

She flinched. 'I can't promise that, Jack. But we'll both always love you, you know that.'

'I don't want you to love me.'

She laughed. 'I'll give you a big, wet kiss.'

'Yuk!'

She stroked his hair. 'I want you to be really brave now, Jack. Like a big boy.'

'But injections hurt.'

She wasn't going to lie to him. 'Only for a second. And it will be a bit sore afterwards. But remember when you got stung by that wasp? It won't hurt as much as that.'

'It will.'

'No, it won't. I promise.'

He shook his head and closed his eyes, and as he did she grabbed him and pulled him over her lap, pulling down his trousers and pants. He screamed, but she had to do it. He might hate her for a while but he'd recover. She just prayed the anti-virus would work. As Jack tried to punch her, she sunk the needle into the soft flesh of his bottom, and the volume of his scream intensified, then she let him scamper away, pulling up his pants, tears streaming down his red face. He clutched Billy the robot while she carefully put the syringe aside and took her son in her arms, cuddling him until he stopped struggling.

Now all she could do was wait, and pray it had worked.

Epilogue

Jason Harley and his superior, Sir Terence Brann, sat in the parlour of what had once been Dr Gaunt's home. In the cellar below them, scientists in biohazard suits were clearing up, removing and cataloguing the many vials of viruses and bacteria that made up Gaunt's collection.

'Quite a treasure trove,' the older man said, with a smile.

Harley nodded. 'Not including the Pandora and Piranha viruses, there are enough diseases down there to wipe out entire countries.' He took out a cigarette. He'd been meaning to quit but his motivation had taken a nose-dive this week.

'The entire world, I'd say.'

'What's going to happen now?' Harley asked. 'I imagine it's all going to be taken somewhere and destroyed.'

The older man laughed. 'Destroyed? Well, that would be the official story—if there was an official story.' He gestured for Harley to pass him a cigarette and lit up.

'Shame about Clive Gaunt,' he said. 'He was a brilliant man. Very good at chess, as I recall. Such a pity how it turned out.'

Harley tried not to show his shock. He was ambitious and wanted to go far in the Service. He wanted this man to be impressed by him. But he couldn't help but say, 'But he was a murderer. A human trafficker. And I haven't even mentioned the viruses. Surely he was never on our side?'

Sir Terence smiled at Harley's naivety. 'On our

side. Hmm. I don't think Gaunt was really ever on anyone's side except his own, but he was useful to us for a time. When the CRU was set up, intentions were good, and the original aim was genuinely to find a cure for the cold. But then came the Biological Weapons Convention, which banned the development of germ warfare. It was decided, however, that the Convention was rather too inconvenient. So Gaunt was installed at the CRU and given the funding to work on his little side projects. We didn't want the UK to fall behind, you see. We were rather suspicious that the Russians saw the Convention as something akin to toilet paper, and I won't even mention what the Americans thought of it. Anyway, we also placed Leonard Bainbridge at the Unit to keep an eye on Gaunt, make sure he didn't bring back bubonic plague or give the volunteers at the Unit smallpox.' He chuckled. 'Gaunt was given the go-ahead to hire his own staff, including this unpleasant Sampson fellow.'

'I'm . . . shocked,' said Harley.

Sir Terence sighed. 'The whole thing was a waste of time, anyway. Gaunt never produced anything of any use to us. He couldn't even find a cure for the bloody common cold. Looks like he achieved a lot more once he was no longer in our employ. We should have kept closer tabs on him but, you can imagine, personnel changes, priorities shift . . . Gaunt was out of sight and out of mind.

'Like I said, shame. He could have done a lot of good, working for us.'

Harley tried to suppress a shudder at the thought of working alongside Gaunt.

The older man stood up and gestured for Harley to follow him.

'Do you think Dr Maddox and Wilson will stay quiet about what they've seen?'

Harley thought about it. 'I'd say so. I got the impression they wanted to put it behind them.'

'Hmm. Well, just in case, I want you to arrange ongoing surveillance of both of them. It's best to keep an eye on them. Ask the Americans to do the same with Vernon Maddox too.'

He turned and put his hand on Harley's shoulder. 'You did a good job here, Harley—even if it was partly by accident. You'll go far.'

'Thank you, sir.' He swallowed, his throat and mouth dry.

'You alright, Harley? You look a touch pale.'

'I'm fine, sir.'

'Good, good. Perhaps you need a holiday. Look at that,' he said, nodding towards the astonishing blue sky. 'It's a beautiful day. You should get some sun. Or perhaps we can find you an assignment somewhere hot, hmm?'

'Thank you, sir.'

The older man walked away, and Harley went back into the house. The thing was, he didn't feel at all well, all of a sudden. He felt cold, despite the heat of the day. His throat was sore. He glanced over at the door that led down towards the cellar, where all those terrifying microscopic diseases were kept. What if . . .? No, he shook the thought away. He was just being paranoid.

He could do with a holiday though. Somewhere a long way from here. He'd go online later, see if he could get a cheap flight somewhere. America maybe. Or Asia.

He sat down, fishing in his pocket for a tissue.

He'd sort out the surveillance of Maddox and

Wilson when he got back from his holiday. When he felt better.

* * *

The cremation took place on a Wednesday, the hottest day of the year; one of the hottest days ever recorded in England, in fact. Kate and Paul sat in the front row, holding hands as the coffin slid behind the purple curtain. There were only four people there: Kate and Paul, and Paul's parents, who were still in a state of shock. Paul's mum, Eileen, was clearly on medication. Before the service, Paul's dad, Michael, had stood outside in the full glare of the sun smoking cigarette after cigarette, occasionally patting his bald head with a handkerchief. He'd started smoking again despite quitting—for the second time—ten years before.

Not many people have to bury their son twice.

'I hope Jack's okay,' Kate fretted, half to herself. She had felt constantly on edge since the events of the previous week.

'He'll be fine.'

'I just keep thinking about what happened last time I left him with Miranda.'

'Kate, nothing's going to happen to him now. Sampson and Gaunt are dead and Vernon's back in Boston.'

'I know . . . It just makes me twitchy being apart from Jack at the moment, even for one day.' She paused, shading her eyes with the hand that wasn't holding Paul's. 'I'm going to have to get used to it though when he starts his new school. Next month! I hope he's not going to be too traumatised, he's been so clingy . . .'

370

Paul hugged her. 'Kate, please try to stop worrying, OK?'

They fell into contemplative silence. Kate wondered if she'd ever be able to stop worrying again; at least where Jack was concerned.

*   *   *

After giving him his injection, Kate had been forced to endure hours of further torment, waiting to see if the anti-virus had worked. She, Jack, Paul and Vernon were taken into quarantine, to a place very much like the hospital where Leonard and Dr Gaunt had kept her after the fire. This time, though, she wasn't disorientated and drugged. Instead, a frightening clarity kept her awake, as she waited and waited. Jack had been quite happy: he was put in a little room next to Kate's with a TV and a PlayStation and loads of toys, and was given as much chocolate milk as he could drink. Even Vernon stopped complaining after a short spell of threatening to call his lawyer, the US Ambassador, CNN and the President of the United States.

Finally, after a few days, they were given the all clear and released in time for Stephen's funeral. Before being let go, they were all made to sign the Official Secrets Act.

'What's the alternative?' Paul had asked. 'The Pimenov Technique?'

Susan French, the officer who had asked them to sign the forms, seemed surprised he had heard of it.

'You understand,' she said, 'that everything that happened at that lab needs to remain a secret. It's for the public good. Do you think we want to cause

371

a nationwide panic, paranoia that there are . . . mad scientists in our own midst waiting to kill us all with deadly viruses?'

'Maybe it's better for people to be vigilant,' Paul argued.

French shook her head, her sleek blonde hair shining in the artificial light. 'No. Gaunt was a one-off.'

Vernon had stayed in the UK for another day; a day during which he and Kate sat down and tried to work out what was going to happen.

'I'm not going back to the States,' Kate said firmly.

'I figured that.'

'And I want Jack to stay here with me, start school, make new friends. I might look for a place near Miranda so he can be near his cousins.'

'Well, if you're taking him away from me, you'd better not be after alimony too, because you won't get it,' Vernon said with bad grace.

Kate had half-smiled at the predictability of this comment. 'I'd appreciate a contribution, but it would be for Jack, not me. I'm going to get another job. I'm going to start contacting universities next week.'

Vernon snorted. 'Hasn't all this put you off wanting to be near viruses?'

'It's what I do, Vernon. What I'm good at. In fact, knowing there are people like Gaunt out there—and despite what French said, we can't be sure he's a one-off—I feel even more driven now.'

'Fighting the good fight, huh?'

'Somebody's got to do it.'

Vernon was quiet for a while. 'I'm gonna miss Jack,' he said. 'Not you, but I'll miss my boy.'

'Boston's not that far away. I'll bring him over once or twice a year, and you can visit here, if you can stand to come to England again.'

'If my son's going to have a goddamn Brit accent, I'd better learn to like it.'

And that was it. The first time Kate and Vernon had sat down and talked to one another like adults since . . . well, she honestly couldn't remember the last time. She felt sad, and a little guilty. She knew Jack would miss his dad. But it was the only way. And it would work out. That's what Aunt Lil always used to say. 'Things always work out, Kate. People say God moves in mysterious ways, and I really believe that.'

Privately, though, Kate wondered if it wasn't just *life*. She couldn't be sure if God had anything to do with it.

*　　　*　　　*

'You all right?' Kate asked Paul after the service, as they stood outside the crematorium waiting for Paul's parents to finish talking to the minister.

'I'm okay. I think.' He nodded, as if trying to convince himself. 'Yeah, I'm fine.' He hesitated. 'One thing that's been worrying me—was is it, you know, *safe* for them to have cremated him? Handled the body? It doesn't spread the viruses, does it?'

Kate put her arm around him and massaged the back of his neck with her fingers. 'No. It's a bit of a myth that dead bodies pose a serious health hazard, even in epidemics. They'll have been very careful with him, of course, and if he was on a pyre in a field in India it might be different—but no, we don't need to worry. Not about that, anyway.'

They both looked up at the long chimney of the crematorium. 'Apart from that, how are you feeling?'

she pressed, anxious at how quiet he'd been since the service.

He leaned into her, and sighed heavily. 'I think I probably feel exactly the same as you. I feel cheated, because I found him and then lost him again. But I'm glad that we've given him a proper funeral. I suppose I also feel that the real Stephen died a long time ago. That wasn't the real Stephen working in that lab. He wasn't the brother I remembered. Or the man you loved.'

Kate nodded.

'I did love him very much, once,' she said. 'But you know I love you now.'

He kissed her cheek lightly and then they embraced, holding each other and not needing to say anything more. She meant it when she told Paul she loved him, but she wondered if it was going to work out between them. How would they fare in the real world, away from hunts and shootings and car chases and all the terror and excitement that had ignited their relationship? And she wondered if Stephen would always cast a shadow over them. She couldn't help but think that Paul would always fear that she loved him because he reminded her of his brother, her first love. And maybe he wanted to be with her because she was a link to his twin.

She didn't know how things were going to work out with her and Paul. All they could do was try.

Right now, though, she couldn't bear the thought of being without him.

Paul went up and spoke to his parents, hugging his mum and squeezing his dad's shoulder. Then he and Kate headed for the carpark, to make their way back to his flat.

It was like a furnace inside the car—Kate almost

said this aloud, then stopped herself, thinking of Stephen's coffin sliding through those curtains. Paul switched on the aircon and started the engine.

Driving out of the crematorium, Kate felt a tickle in her nose. Hayfever, or something worse? For a second, panic flared inside her. It was the Pandora Virus; the safe, incubation period had been longer than Gaunt had claimed. Or the virus had mutated . . . She caught her breath—then told herself not to be ridiculous. She was fine. It was a cold, that was all. Just a common cold.

Acknowledgements

We would like to say thank you to: Jennifer Baugh for the brilliant original cover; Sam Copeland and Kate Bradley for making it all happen; and to that wonderful community of 'indie' writers who have been so supportive, including Mark Williams, Lexi Revellian, Dan Holloway, Cheryl Shireman, J Carson Black, HP Mallory, Sibel Hodge, Scott Nicholson and Stephen Leather.

Also, huge thanks to Lorna Fergusson, John Harding, Debbie Blackburn, Glenn McCreedy, Edward Baran, Stephanie Zia and Alison Baverstock for all your help and kind words, to everyone at studentbeans.com, and to Dr Jennifer Rohn of Lablit.com for help with the 'science bits'.

Last but not least, love and thanks to Sara and Nick, and to our families, for all the support and belief and for listening to us go on and on about our books.

The setting of this novel was inspired by the Common Cold Unit, the history of which can be read about in the fascinating *Cold Wars* by David Tyrrell and Michael Fielder. The authors also found the following books useful when researching this novel: *Plague Wars* by Tom Mangold and Jeff Goldberg; *Bird Flu* by John Farndon; and *Viruses* by Dorothy Crawford. And who could forget that essential bedside companion, the *Communicable Disease Control Handbook*.